Finding Ruby Draker

3rd Edition

A DRAKER SERIES THRILLER

MARIANNE SCOTT

crowecreations.ca
Ottawa Canada

Finding Ruby Draker © 2016 by Marianne Scott

1st Edition FriesenPress January 2016
2nd Edition FriesenPress April 2022
3rd Edition Crowe Creations June 2023

Edited by Jenna Kalinsky
Designed by Crowe Creations
Text set in Times New Roman; headings set in Beatnik SF

Cover photo needpix.com
Cover design © 2023 by Crowe Creations

Crowe Creations
ISBN: 978-1-998831-13-5

This book is dedicated to the memory of my wonderful husband. I love you and hold you in my heart forever.

You never know what life is going to throw at you.

Who knows what life is come to, one knows.

One

IT ALL ENDED WITH A FIRE that took away my parents, my little brother, and everything I was or ever knew. That part of me is gone, but now and then I'm haunted by brief incomplete memories that fade away as quickly as they appeared.

The day was otherwise unexceptional except for the fact that I was very happy knowing that I was going to have my last final exam *ever* that morning. My internship would start in the fall and I was looking forward to this next phase of my life.

Earlier that morning, I did some times tables with my brother before he went off to school, then cleaned my room, promised my mom I'd pick up her stuff at Rite Aid, and started out toward the city. I had Pink blasting on the car radio and I was amped and ready to conquer Soc. Neuroscience at 11 a.m. Wouldn't you know it, when I got to the room and saw that they'd switched the time to 2 p.m. due to "last minute problems with the lighting" according to the sign posted on the door, I just kept cool. I went and got my mom's things and made it back with lots of time to double-check my notes.

Finally, when my exam was done, I burst from the building onto Broadway into the warm spring air. It had gone well; I was sure I'd aced it. I could have cared less if there was traffic, or if Brittany still hadn't called about shopping tomorrow, or if the stoned weirdo weaving through the lanes of cars, dancing with his eyes closed to the honking horns, was holding things up. I was going to celebrate with my family. Mom had made reservations at some expensive restaurant where she usually took her important clients and we were going to blow the budget. They were so proud of me and so was little Johnny.

I opened the car windows on the bridge and let my hair fly. Getting out of the city felt like taking off a thick wool sweater. I daydreamed so much I didn't notice much more of the drive home at all except that my stomach was grumbling, and the light, the way the sun was slatting orange over the rooftops and pinging off windows.

But when I turned onto my street, I had to slam on the brakes to avoid hitting an ambulance that had parked in the middle of the road. The whole street was lined with police cars, fire trucks, and people, just everywhere, like ants. My window was still down and that's when the heat blasted in.

There was no place to put my car so I just got out. Snakes of hose lay over the asphalt. The smoke was so thick it choked my nose, neighbors and people I didn't know all jabbering in high-pitched voices, which clashed with the urgent shouts of the firefighters. I pushed to the front where the heat was fierce, wondering whose house it was, fighting off a niggling worry in my stomach.

When I got to the front of the crowd just before the yellow-taped barrier, my throat closed up. My house. It was my house. I blinked a few times. I forgot about the police and the people and ducked below the tape. My family was in there, they were supposed to be home. I heard my voice as if I were someone else screaming their names, "Mom, Dad, Johnny," over and over again struggling against the mass of people and emergency workers who were preventing me from reaching the inferno.

Then, somehow, I was on the other side, walking toward my home as if everything were normal except that even in the heat coming from the flames, my legs felt like ice. When I got so close I could feel the light hairs on my forearm start to crinkle, wondering in a daze what I'd do once I got there, a tall, dark-haired man wearing black sunglasses and a charcoal suit approached me, flashing a gold badge.

"Kathleen Jones?" he said, taking my arm. "You'll have to come with us down to the station."

He was accompanied by another man, bald, but of similar height and dress standing just behind him. He and his companion grabbed my arms and moved us in the opposite direction from the scene.

This was wrong. I knew instantly they weren't police.

They forced me toward a black unmarked car that was parked behind the fire trucks. I screamed and flailed, but their grip was too tight. Why didn't anyone notice? I saw another burly man in jeans looking curiously in my direction, but he didn't make a move to help. I tried screaming again, but they shoved me into the back seat, flipped a U-turn, and sped off, tires screeching.

I don't know what happened next, maybe I passed out, maybe I was drugged, I don't know, but the last thing I saw before the room glazed over and went dark were three bright white lights focusing on me from the ceiling of an operating room.

***

When I awoke, I could hear people moving around me, but I kept my eyes squeezed shut. For a minute or two I listened to what was going on around me, but then I just had to see what was happening. I cracked open my eyes, but my vision was blurry, and I couldn't make out much of anything except shapes and colors. All the people who floated in and out of this quiet place were dressed in white. A man with dark hair stood from his chair in the corner and leaned over. I knew right away it was him, from the fire. He tapped the IV pole to my side while a nurse covered me with another blanket and adjusted the pillow under my head. In a few seconds, the white fog went black and I passed out again.

I have no idea how long I was like this; it could have been a day, a week, a month.

When I woke up again, my face was tightly bandaged and again everyone around was fuzzy and white. The bandage felt like a strait-jacket, and my hand flew to it to pull it off. Someone saw I was conscious and came over to scoot me into a sitting position in some kind of high-backed chair and rested my head on a cushion. Why was every-thing so white? My heart was like a rock, heavy in my chest. I didn't feel anything, no pain, no fear, just like I'd been emptied out. I didn't even know if I was breathing. I couldn't move or talk or see much. My eyes and lips seared against the air.

The dark-haired man entered the room, whistling. He greeted every-one cordially, sat down in the chair beside mine and took up my hand in his while he stroked my shoulder with his other. Up close I could see he was around my dad's age. His hair was silver at the temples and he had olive skin and a very nice watch. My skin shivered and I tried to pull away, but he squeezed harder.

He spoke to the doctor gently and reassuringly. "What's your opin-ion, Dr. Brooke," he asked, "is my daughter ready? Can the dressings come off?"

My whole body had seized up under his touch. I tried to pull my hand away, but he had an iron grip. Who was this man? Why did he care about me? I wasn't anybody. My heart was panicking. I wanted to shout that he was lying, that something very scary and wrong was happening, but I was immobilized. But then I felt the cool slip of scissors against my cheek as someone, a nurse probably, began to remove the bandages around my head. The hard white gauze fell to my shoulder and my whole face felt new and stung in the cool antiseptic air.

Another man, the doctor, bent down to examine me. "Very nice! Everything looks excellent. Reinhardt, I think you'll be pleased with the cosmetic result." He gently lifted my chin and peered critically at my face. He leaned over to a desk and grasped a handled mirror. He held it up so I could see my face.

I gasped. It was swollen and bruised but not a face I recognized. I couldn't stop staring, mute, even as I began to tremble.

Reinhardt. A German name, but he sounded American. He leaned down to me and murmured, "That's good news, isn't it? We'll be able to fly home in a few days, Ruby. Everything is going to be fine."

Hot icy fear started pooling up around my chest and began to rise into my throat. I couldn't breathe. It seemed everyone in this room was in on his plot.

Why were they calling me Ruby and where was my face?

I ached for my parents and wished they would burst into the room, fairy-tale style, and tell me it was all a dream. My eyes throbbed painfully at the thought of them. I knew they were dead. No one had told me, but I wasn't stupid. This was actually happening, and I was going to have to rescue myself from this impostor named Ruby. *I'm Kathleen… I'm Kathleen,* I repeated in my head. My voice was still my own at least. No one was going to rob me of the only thing it seemed I had left.

***

I counted the next days by the rise and fall of sunlight and darkness that moved across the window of my room. The fuzzy sounds and images from the days before were clear now, the eeriness of it all lifted like a veil. I tried to figure out where I was: the bed had rails and could be raised and lowered with controls like they'd have in a hospital, but in the corner was an elegant white leather chair and footstool with a floral throw over it. A narrow antique table topped with an arrangement of cheerful yellow tulips stood against the lavender walls, which were hung with watercolors. I'd never been in the hospital, but I'd seen enough TV shows to know this was a far cry from New York Pres.

Soon came a morning, at least I thought it was morning, when I realized I was alone in the room and felt OK, not well, but not dizzy or sick. I also then realized that not only was I alone, but I was not chained to the bed, and the door was ajar.

Slowly, I tried to sit up. The change in position made my head spin. I grabbed the cold metal bars of the bed. My ears started to buzz and I thought I might pass out, but I held on tight, hoping it would pass and I could get out of here, wherever I was. The light-headedness finally subsided, but I was wet with sweat and shivering.

Taking some deep breaths, I tried to figure out how to lower the bed rails, but my hands were shaking too hard.

Suddenly, the door to my room burst open and two nurses in crisp white uniforms rushed to my bedside.

"I see you're awake, Ms. Draker," the brunette nurse said. Her voice was friendly, soft, dripping with concern. She lowered the metal rail with long, slender fingers and grabbed my arm while she steadied my back and bent down close to talk to me. "You're not ready to do that on your own, dear," she said softly. "You should have used your call button. Why are you trying to get out of bed by yourself?"

When I started to speak, my voice betrayed me. "Where am I? Why am I here?" I blurted out. "I don't know what's happening to me. Who are you people?"

The two nurses glanced at each other in alarm. My voice was high pitched and sounded hysterical.

The blonde nurse went to a chart on a clipboard at the bottom of my bed.

I bit the inside of my cheek, wishing I'd kept my mouth shut. They probably had orders to sedate me if I seemed like I was getting out of control. That was the last thing I needed if I was ever going to make sense of what was happening.

"Sorry," I said, trying to laugh. "I don't know where that came from. Would you help me to the bathroom? I have to pee like crazy."

"Well, that would make me cranky as well," the blonde nurse said. She chuckled as she slid her hand under my arm and the two of them helped me to my feet and led me to the bathroom, slowly lowering me to the toilet seat.

I was glad I'd used this as an excuse because I hadn't realized how much I needed to go. When I was done, I felt a lot better, and I smiled at the nurses as winningly as I could without stretching my face too hard. I was going to have to remember to keep my panic in check.

"I think I can manage to walk on my own," I said as I got up from the toilet. "Will you let me try, please?"

"OK, but just take it slowly," Nurse Brunette said. "We'll stay with you until you're ready to go back to bed."

When I got up, I tried to hold the sides of my hospital gown shut so my butt wouldn't show.

The nurses hovered as I made my way to the sink. My legs felt like custard and my hands trembled terribly, but I managed to turn on the water and wash my hands. When I was reaching for a paper towel, I caught my face in the mirror and reared back. It was less swollen and bruised than the last time I saw it but nonetheless it was still someone else staring back at me. Nausea rose into my throat but I fought it. I lifted my head again and studied myself for a while. The face was actually quite attractive. It might even be beautiful once it healed and had some makeup on. I stared at myself, at this face that was completely unfamiliar, wishing for it to give me some answers. But it just stared back at me, with eyes that at least I still recognized as mine. I felt grief and relief wash through me.

"Don't worry, dear," the brunette nurse offered. "You're healing extremely well. You'll be ready to go home by tomorrow. Your father will be here shortly and fill you in on your travel details. He's such a nice man."

I shuddered. I wanted my father, my real father who, if he were here, would put this situation right and roll a few heads besides, but she meant the man that Dr. Brooke had called Reinhardt. She said he was a nice man, but I didn't think anything about him was nice. Nice men don't drag you off to a place where they surgically change your face and call you by another name. The nurse had called me Ms. Draker. Who the hell was that? He seemed to have everyone in this place convinced that he was my father. Why did no one see or understand that there was more going on? His syrupy tone might have made it seem like he was a good guy, but to me, he was just creepy and dangerous.

Now it seemed that he had plans to take me somewhere else. But where? Nothing made sense. He had made the hospital believe that I was Ruby Draker and I could tell if I tried to tell them otherwise they'd only drug me again. At the moment I was powerless, weak from surgery and drugged to stay docile. I was incapable of escaping this predicament.

The nurses helped me back to my hospital bed.

I closed my eyes and soon drifted off.

Two

ARCING IN THE FIRE WERE DARK, menacing figures, their bodies reflecting off what looked like hundreds of shards of mirror, every single shard the size of a person but suspended in darkness, obscuring the floors and walls, each one showing another angle of their faces. I was searching for something in the glass. The more I searched, the more bizarre the faces became.

Someone called to me, "Ruby, it's time for us to go." I let myself gently pass from dream into consciousness but paused before fully waking to look around my dreamscape in the darkened chamber of mirrors. The distorted faces in the jagged splinters of mirror looked as well.

We saw no one but someone called to us again. "Ruby, it's not safe for us here anymore," the person with the soft voice said. The dream slowly faded and my room came back into focus. Reinhardt was standing there, staring at me. I pulled away from him so far that my pillow slid off the bed. He was fumbling with the controls on my bed trying to get the side rails to lower. He seemed to be in a hurry, his forehead and brow wrinkled up, and even though he moderated his voice to continue to sound gentle and soft, he seemed worried, anxious in a way I hadn't seen him before. Something was wrong. My heart began to race.

He looked up. His eyes were tense but almost seemed kind. "Ruby." He said the name purposefully. "We have to go immediately. Rose will help you get dressed." He glanced at the other person in the room, the brunette nurse from earlier. I'd thought she was neutral, a real nurse, but now it looked like she was working with this guy who kept claiming to be my father.

She moved quickly toward me with her eyes on the door, flicked her long hair back and began unpacking clothes from a small black travel bag on the side table. She came over and laid the clothes at the end of the bed then quickly helped me to get up. She held onto me as my feet found the floor.

"I know you're still unsteady," she said, "but I'll help you get dressed. Don't worry. Everything will be fine, but I need you to recognize that we don't have much time."

While she spoke, Reinhardt moved to the door. He opened it a crack and kept his eye on the dimly lit hall.

Though the curtains were drawn, I could make out the pale light of dusk, lamps sporadically lighting rooms in the low buildings and apartments nearby. They'd made me sleep during the day so we could leave under the cover of night. I wished I knew where we were.

Even though all was quiet, I figured someone had to still be on staff. I thought about yelling for help until Reinhardt, his eye still at the door, quietly pulled a gun from his coat pocket.

I shrank back down and let Nurse Brunette-Rose dress me. She brusquely undid my gown and let it slide to the floor, leaving me standing shivering and naked, grabbed a chair and sat me in it. Within seconds, she had dressed me in dark pants, a dark, long-sleeved shirt, running shoes, and a hooded jacket. Reinhardt kept his back to me during this, which was at least a small, kind gesture.

She stood me up and gave me a quick once-over. "That will have to do," she said.

She turned to Reinhardt and whispered, "She's dressed. Let's go."

Reinhardt hustled over to the window, moved the curtain only slightly and looked out at the street. "Robert is parked in the alley," Reinhardt said, nodding. "We'll leave by the side door."

Just then, the door opened and the blonde nurse barged into the room. Reinhardt and Rose froze and exchanged shocked looks as the nurse glared at them. I let out my breath that I hadn't realized I'd been holding. She would save me. She would see what they were doing.

"What on earth is going on here?" she clucked as she came to my side, nudging me to get me back into bed. "It's way past visiting hours, and… Wait a second now, why are you dressed?" she scolded me. "You're not discharged until tomorrow morning."

She started to move her ample bottom past Rose to help me up when Rose pulled a plastic baggie from her pocket, grabbed a white cloth from it and let the bag fall to the floor as she grabbed the nurse in a bear hug from behind and pressed the cloth to her nose. Reinhardt rushed to help hold down the struggling nurse.

They held her, like a reverse rescue, until she went limp and collapsed into their arms. Reinhardt propped the slumped nurse onto the bed, and Rose grabbed my crumpled hospital gown from the floor and draped it over her. Wordlessly, they lifted her legs and arranged the motionless woman onto her side with her head facing away from the door so it looked as though I were still in bed sleeping. Rose tucked her in before they both paused and turned to look at me. They were both breathing heavily from the exertion and their eyes were wide.

"If you want to stay alive," Reinhardt said, his voice hoarse, "I suggest you stay quiet and cooperate."

He pulled out his pistol again and went to the door. I bit my tongue against screaming. Rose started getting ready and put on a dark jacket.

"It's clear," he whispered. "Go, now." He jerked his head toward the door.

Rose put her hood up, grabbed the travel bag in one arm and wrapped her other arm securely around my waist to steady me. I was shaking and could barely walk as if my legs were not mine and refused to listen.

Once she steered me into the hallway, I lamely imagined wrenching free and running for it, but I barely made it out the door before stumbling over my own feet. Reinhardt reached out and grabbed me on my other side with his free arm, his gun securely in his other hand. Between the two of them, I was trapped. I could smell the metal of his gun.

"Help me," I whispered. I began to cry. My voice was whispery, the rustle of a tissue. No one came. Tears started down my cheeks.

Reinhardt gripped me so tight his fingers dug into my ribs. He leaned in. "You have to trust me," he hissed as they strode us as a single unit down the hall. "I know what this looks like, but I'm trying to help you. Now cooperate or Rose will have to drug you again."

We arrived at the elevator located in an alcove at the end of the hall. The whole floor was dimly lit for night, and no one was around, the nursing station empty.

The elevator arrived and as Rose and Reinhardt ushered us in, I saw out of the corner of my eye two darkly dressed men run into a room— my room—holding guns. They wore brimmed hats. Maybe police? I wondered whether they would see us before the elevator doors closed, but I wasn't completely sure I wanted them to.

As the doors were closing, I heard a series of low thuds. Were they gunshots? I'd never heard them in real life. If they were, then they'd just shot the blonde nurse in my bed.

The elevator chimed and the doors shut. I could hear heartbeats, but I didn't know whose they were. It made me dizzy to look up, but I had to see. Both Rose and Reinhardt were sweating and watching the floor numbers illuminate as we descended.

When we arrived at the lobby, they barely waited for the doors to open enough before rushing us out and through the marble-floored lobby and then a metal side door that led to a dark alley filled with garbage bins and discarded boxes. They turned a corner where two buildings squeezed the alleyway even more. A black car, its engine heaving, was waiting with its lights on. Reinhardt threw open the back door and shoved me in.

"Robert, I think they're right behind us," he said.

"I know. I saw them enter the clinic," said Robert, his face stony.

Behind me, Rose hoisted me over so she could get in after me. Reinhardt climbed into the passenger front seat and before his door was closed, the car roared away into the night.

***

For the next several blocks, Rose and Reinhardt checked nervously out the side and back windows. Our car sped past the dark exteriors of multi-storied buildings and shops barricaded with metal bars and gates. Robert and Reinhardt kept their guns just below the window and eyed every passing car warily. Between the lights, the buildings, and the crumbling disrepair of the streets, I knew, with some relief, we were still in New York.

"Nothing yet," muttered Reinhardt, "but I'm sure they'll be along soon."

Robert smiled, his lips a thin line. "I've got a plan to throw them off track long enough for us to take the back route to the Westchester Airport. The plane is fueled and cleared for takeoff as soon as we arrive," he said.

Rose's words came back into my mind, *You'll be ready to fly home tomorrow.* Where was that, I wondered. But, I let myself feel heartened, an airport was good: lots of officials and security. Maybe someone would spot me; maybe I was considered missing, though as soon as that thought came, I chastised myself. No one would have reported it. Everyone who would have was dead.

I pinched my thigh, hard. No one was going to save me. If this man had enough power to surgically change my face, he would also easily be able to get me a passport or other important documents. I wished they would at least say where we were going.

"I have another car waiting at our hotel where we'll make the switch. Our decoys will lead them to LaGuardia," Robert said. "Westchester is only thirty-two minutes away in the other direction. We'll be in the air before anyone realizes what's happened."

"What about the flight plan?" Reinhardt questioned. "How will we keep them from tracking our destination?"

"Our charter is scheduled into St. John's. Another Challenger with our flight number will land there. Côte d'Azur Airport will pick us up on flight number RD 354. A computer glitch will make it disappear off the flight records soon after we land. It'll be like we never existed." Robert laughed. I was surprised, he had the whitest teeth I'd ever seen.

Our sedan swerved wildly as Robert maneuvered the car over the curved streets. The violent jostling and swaying turned my stomach into a knot. I bent over feeling dizzy and nauseous. "I'm going to be sick," I said, my tongue thick in my mouth.

Rose pulled out a white plastic box from the pocket behind the passenger seat and popped two white tablets from a blister pack. "Here," she said. "These will settle your stomach."

She forced the pills between my teeth, pulled me back to a sitting position and poured bottled water into my mouth to wash them down. The liquid dribbled down my chin and neck. I tried not to swallow, but Rose had poured enough water into my mouth to cause an automatic reflex. I coughed and sputtered, much of it going down the wrong way.

The sedan pulled up to a covered carport in front of a large hotel. Reinhardt's gun was glinting in his lap, and Robert's was nestled in the holster under his left arm, so I sat still and waited to see what they would do. Running away was a dream at this point; whatever was in those pills was making me feel woozy on top of still being light-headed and sick.

Tears started to stream down my cheeks, and then I began to silently sob. It made my face hurt to cry, or not my face, whoever's face it was, but I couldn't stop it. My body was on its own now, and it was going to happen with or without my permission.

But then Robert stopped, shut off the engine and Reinhardt got out and pulled me from the car. He wordlessly handed me a handkerchief, and I accepted it without looking at him to blow my new nose. Once I was cleaned up, I looked out into the heavy warm night. I figured it was either very late or this was a terrible motel because ours was the only car there. But then from a shadowy corner of the carport, four people approached. They looked eerily like us.

No one said a word. They made brief eye contact and nodded at each other before they stepped into our sedan in the same seating pattern we had used and drove off, I assumed, to LaGuardia where no doubt they would be questioned and maybe arrested. I wasn't sure whether I wished I were with those guys or the ones I was with. I had no idea who the good or bad ones were.

Robert and Reinhardt had an iron hold of me now and started to run. Their grip was so severe, my feet barely touched the sidewalk. We dashed a short distance down the street to where a silver SUV was parked. Robert pulled a fob out of his pocket and opened the doors. I felt like I was under water. Reinhardt handed me fully off to Rose who basically put me into the car, limb by limb, then fastened my seat belt for me. I lamely tried to lift my arms, but they just hung there. Once more, Robert hopped into the driver's seat and Reinhardt into the front passenger seat.

We drove away, but this time it was in the opposite direction of the black sedan. As we pulled away from the street parking spot, another dark sedan sped past us after our decoy car, which already had a sizeable head start on the highway to LaGuardia.

Reinhardt smiled. My head felt like it was a brick. A ton of bricks. I laid it back against the seat.

The night countryside raced by in a blur as I fell in and out of sleep.

At some point, we slowed down, which woke me. We were in a dark field or empty parking lot with a row of lights. An airstrip, I thought. I felt a terrible anxious tingle in my stomach. I was about to be abducted out of the United States. And then what? How would I get home? My stomach plunged. I couldn't begin to understand why this was happening to me. I was boring, a completely normal, boring person. This had to be a mistake. But whatever their reasons, they made sure I didn't have a home anymore. And if I did get away, how would I explain my face to anyone who knew me? I knew the danger of throwing up was over, but I wanted to vomit anyway, just to purge the thoughts racing through me that were frightening beyond what I could handle. I was shaking now, uncontrollably, my teeth clacking loudly against each other.

We drove past a large, illuminated sign: Westchester Airport. Robert raced across the parking lot and stopped near the entrance. Rose and Reinhardt helped me out of the SUV and the second all of our feet were on the asphalt, Robert reached back, slammed our doors, and took off without a word. Reinhardt and Rose didn't turn around to say goodbye either but moved to the glass doors. The terminal was empty, which was good because I was suddenly embarrassed about looking drunk. I couldn't walk straight and my head was lolling around.

They steered us to the New York Private Charter Service check-in counter. I squinted at the wall clock: 1:45 a.m. No wonder the airport was empty. The petite man with a severe comb-over behind the counter was looking anxiously at his watch, and when we showed up, he seemed to relax.

"Good evening, Mr. Draker," he said and began ticking away on his computer.

Reinhardt opened three burgundy passports and laid the stack on the counter, and the man began to go through them, looking up at each person as he checked us in. When he got to me, he raised an eyebrow then wrinkled his forehead in disgust. He smiled tersely at Reinhardt and nodded toward me.

Reinhardt smiled a charming smile with all his teeth showing. "Oh, we'll put an espresso in her and she'll be fine," he chuckled.

The man shrugged and continued to click on the keyboard. I wondered why he seemed to be the only person in the whole airport still working. "Everything looks in order, sir," he said. "The plane is ready and loading from Gate B."

"Thank you for your patience," Reinhardt said, smiling even more graciously. "Your charter service is always so efficient and accommodating. Please give my best to Maurice."

While the men were acting as if everything were as normal as Sunday brunch, I wanted to scream. I was wracking my brain trying to remember which countries had burgundy passports. What picture would he have used? Why didn't the guy see that mine was a fake?

A heavy glass door a short distance from the check-in counter opened out onto the tarmac at Gate B where a mid-sized aircraft waited. The stairs were down and someone in an airline uniform was standing beside them waiting for us. I'd never been on a private plane before. These criminals sure liked to travel in style.

Rose took up my waist again, but I tried to shake her off. I wanted to walk on my own. She let me but kept very close. When we got to the stairs, the pilot took Rose's travel bag and we boarded immediately.

"Good evening, sir, ladies," the pilot said. "I'll notify the flight tower that we're ready for takeoff. The weather is favorable and it should be smooth to Malta where we'll refuel."

"I trust that you have dinner for us on board? We haven't eaten yet this evening," Reinhardt asked.

The pilot looked taken aback. "But, of course, sir, all your needs have been looked after. Soon after takeoff, our co-pilot will provide you with an aperitif before your meal."

I made it slowly up the stairs with some gentle prodding from Rose and used the leather seats to steady myself as I waited for my heart to slow. Looking around, I didn't think I'd ever seen so much cream color in one place: the seats, maybe only seven or eight of them, the walls, the plush carpeting. I plunked down in one of the seats by a big window and looked out at the darkness.

Rose fastened my belt for me before she and Reinhardt took their seats.

Within what felt like seconds, the door was closed, the plane started to move toward the runway, and then we were in the air.

I sat in a stupor in my luxurious seat feeling adrift and utterly alone and frightened. I used to complain that my life was uneventful, but it had actually been wonderful, the kind of life people always realized was perfect when it was too late. I had everything I wanted, great parents, my adorable, annoying, beautiful little brother, close friends, a nice house, everything. I thought about the fist fight I almost got into with Larissa Evans in high school when she and a bunch of her jerk friends made a comic book about my parents doing disgusting things to each other because they'd had my brother so late, and now I even wished I could see her smug face.

A lump formed painfully in my throat and my eyes became wet as I let myself then think about how I was about to graduate and start my internship at the psych clinic that Dad had helped me get with one of his million connections—it seemed he "knew a guy" for just about every-thing; about Johnny, who worshiped the ground I walked on, and how I was going to take him to his first Mets game. And now my family was dead, some crazy people had kidnapped me, had me surgically altered, were calling themselves "my family" and me "Ruby" of all the ugly old-lady names in the world, and I was drooling on some strange clothes on a private plane headed for Côte d'Azur and didn't even have a clue what day it was, let alone what was happening to me or why.

I stared at Reinhardt and Rose, fear welling up in my stomach and inching its way to my throat. Reinhardt's gun was in a holster on his belt. Rose was tall and willowy, but she was extremely strong, beautiful—although not very nice—and almost seemed to enjoy sticking syringes into my arms. I wished I could think of this as a movie, but it was completely real.

The hum of the engines and the gentle sway of the plane made me so drowsy. I fought to stay awake, but my eyes kept falling closed. I felt myself drift into a fraught, upsetting sleep.

***

I was in the deepest, darkest sleep of my life, surrounded by a pillow of the blackest darkness I'd ever known, when there was a huge bump and a crash of some plates or glass. I shrieked and jumped. We were still flying; Rose and Reinhardt looked comfortable and relaxed, the tension gone from their bodies and faces even though we were going through a pocket of turbulence.

Rose looked at me and smiled. "Is anyone else ready for dinner? I'll tell Lisette we're ready." She got up from her seat and walked carefully to the front of the plane.

Reinhardt leaned forward. "How are you doing, Ruby?" He paused, not to wait for me to speak, but to look me over. "I know you're confused by what's going on, but I assure you, you're safe now. We'll protect you." There it was again, that syrupy soft voice he kept using when he talked to me. As if it alone would somehow placate me, make me forget everything that had happened.

"Protect me from what?" My throat was dry and my voice scratchy and cracked. Apart from plugging me full of sedatives, they might have been treating me kindly, but I didn't trust him one bit.

"You should try to have some dinner. It's been a while since you've eaten," Reinhardt said.

I turned my head away from him. Even the mention of food made my stomach churn.

"It won't benefit you to be stubborn, Ruby. At least have something to drink," Rose said, returning with bottles of water. "We don't want you to get dehydrated. That will make you feel worse." Rose held out a small bottle of Volvic.

I cracked the top and sipped it slowly while Reinhardt prepared the couch with a pillow and blanket. I watched him tuck in the corners like a doting father would. When I'd downed a few sips, they helped me up from my seat over to the couch, making sure that my head comfortably rested on the pillow, and tucked the blanket around me. The last thing I felt was him gently stroking my shoulder as if he were soothing a child who'd had a bad dream, before I slipped into another fitful nap.

As I drifted in and out of sleep, I caught snatches of their conversation. Now and then I became aware of the smell of food and the tinkle of flatware on china, but I kept my eyes shut.

"I wonder what Rosalind will think of her," Rose whispered.

"I'm sure we're all going to be very fond of our Ruby," Reinhardt added. He sounded sad. "But it's going to take some time before she learns to trust us. We'll have to be patient." He sighed. "I'm sure you remember how it was for us. It's been a long time since we've been in her shoes."

"She'll come around. She has to if she wants to survive," Rose said. "You all did."

Three

WHEN I AWOKE, my head was pounding, the heavy drone of engines buzzing in my brain. I cracked open my eyes hoping that somehow I'd had a terrible nightmare and that I'd be back in my room, my Klimt poster staring at me from the opposite wall, Mom downstairs making French toast, Dad on the phone with his office and Johnny tapping out rhythms on my door so I'd let him in to play on my bed.

Instead, Rose and Reinhardt were calmly sitting in their seats, whispering to each other, looking down occasionally to tick away on their phones.

My head was blasting but my vision was clear and everything was in focus. I blinked a few times. Reinhardt glanced at me, and my breathing started to quicken again. Without the drugs keeping me calm, panic was starting to fill every cell of my being. I had an overwhelming urge to run. I needed to get out of here.

Reinhardt looked up and frowned. "What is it, Ruby?" He glanced at Rose who looked down at her purse.

"No, don't you reach for your stupid pills. And stop calling me that. My name is Kathleen!" I felt like my head was no longer attached to my body. It was so light, I couldn't feel it. "Who are you people? What do you want with me? Where are you taking me? Why are you doing this?"

I got up from the couch. I didn't care that we were on an airplane. I didn't care about anything. I wanted out.

"Ruby," Reinhardt said. "You have to calm down." He stood up and motioned to me waving his hands, palms downward, for me to quiet myself. I glared at him. What was he, a conductor? "Everything is going to be all right. We're not going to hurt you," he said.

I realized by the way I was backing away from him that I was penetratingly afraid of him. When he approached me to try to restrain me, I flailed against him, doing everything I could to fight him off. I hadn't eaten in who knew how long, I was so tired. I didn't have a chance.

In seconds, he had me in a tight hold.

"Let me go," I pleaded.

"Shhhh," Reinhardt whispered. "We won't let anything happen to you."

I cried out. A sharp pain pierced my arm. I didn't have to look to know that Rose, who was backing away with a hypodermic needle in her perfectly manicured fingers, was to blame. In seconds, my head started to spin. I sank into Reinhardt's tight grip.

"Ruby, we're not going to hurt you," Reinhardt said again. "But you have to stay calm and composed."

"This particular sedative will keep her calm but awake," Rose said. "We still have to get her through immigration, but quickly. Reinhardt, can you arrange that?"

I glared at her; the bitch seemed to really get off on her power as a walking pharmacy.

Another person appeared. "Is everything OK, sir?" The co-pilot.

I looked down and hoped he would help me. Please, please, I thought.

"I'm afraid my daughter isn't well," Reinhardt said. "Can you radio the airport and get us priority clearance through immigration? My wife is waiting for us with medical help."

"Of course, sir," the co-pilot offered. "I'll make sure you're accommodated. We'll be landing in half an hour." He returned to the cockpit without further questions.

In my head, I was whispering, come back, come back, but my lips couldn't form the words. My throat was closing up. A sob burst out of my mouth.

Reinhardt brought us back to the couch and sat us down. He loosened his hold on me as he rocked me back and forth, but still kept his arms around me. "Shhhh. Don't fight this. You're safe now and you'll understand what's going on soon enough."

"Ruby, I'm sorry that I had to drug you again," Rose said. "It's for you own good."

She sat at my other side and put her arm around my shoulders, now and then gently stroking my back. Fresh thick tears welled up in my eyes. Their hands were all over me. "It's all going to make sense. Just hang in there."

I was definitely hanging. Whatever she injected me with this time left me completely limp. When I couldn't sit up anymore, Rose said, "Let's get her buckled into a seat. We'll be landing soon."

Reinhardt helped Rose lift me to my feet. They hefted me over to one of the seats and buckled me securely in place. I wanted to keep crying, but I'd grown too numb. The tears just pooled up and fell down my face.

A voice came through the on-board intercom. "Mr. Draker, we'll be landing in twenty minutes. Immigration will meet you on board. "They've been advised about your daughter's condition. They've also notified your wife who is waiting with special land transportation to a medical facility. The ambulance will be waiting on the tarmac."

Ambulance? I tried to work my fingers over to the seat belt, but they wouldn't cooperate. They were going to put me in another hospital bed. Maybe they'd restrain me this time. I tried to practice making meaningful glances with my eyes. Maybe they'd see I'd been drugged. If anyone were to notice that sort of thing, I imagined, or at least I hoped, it'd be someone in the medical profession.

I watched out of the plane's window as buildings, roads, and vegetation grew larger with our decent. A bump, a few screeches from the plane's tires, and we were on the ground, the landing throwing me forward in my seat. The plane taxied to a place a sizeable distance away from the terminal. I sank back into my seat and waited.

Why France, I wondered. I'd only ever seen photos of Nice when it was bright and sunny, people walking around in expensive summer resort wear and huge floppy hats, but today it was gray and raining and looked ugly and sodden.

The plane maneuvered into its spot and came to a full stop.

The co-pilot stepped out of the cockpit and opened the door hatch.

Shortly after, two stern-looking uniformed officials entered the cabin. They looked around and stopped at me, then turned to give Reinhardt a strict and lingering look.

Reinhardt greeted them in what sounded like perfect French, our passports in his hand.

I wanted to signal that this wasn't what it seemed somehow, but I lost my nerve.

"*Bonjour M. Draker, si je comprends bien, il y a une urgence sanitaire,*" the agent said.

"*Oui. Ma fille a besoin de soins médicaux,*" said Reinhardt.

"*Je vois l'ambulance est en attente pour elle. Votre passeport s'il vous plait,*" the other agent replied.

A few questions and answers later, and the customs officers stamped our passports and left.

Reinhardt and Rose watched them carefully as they walked away from the plane and back into the terminal.

Shortly after they left, a petite woman with fine, delicate features entered the cabin. She could have been my mother's age, but she was strikingly beautiful with porcelain skin, white-blond hair in a chic bob and sharp, blue eyes. She couldn't have been much more than five feet tall yet she carried herself as if she were someone of importance. In a way, her confidence seemed almost a front given how fine-featured her small pointed face was, like a china doll's. I could tell already her face was going to be deceiving.

"Hello, darling," she said to Reinhardt. "I see you've brought our daughter home."

She looked over at me slumped down in my seat and frowned at Reinhardt. "She looks like an underfed chicken." A wrinkle formed between her shapely brows.

"Rosalind," Reinhardt smiled brightly as he embraced her and kissed her tenderly. "I've missed you. I'm afraid our Ruby…" He paused and looked at me, my belt still fastened, as I slumped in the seat, "… is under the weather."

"I can see that." Rosalind gave him another disapproving look before coming over to where I was seated. She crouched down to evaluate me. "No worries, darling," she said. Her black leather pants and jacket, like mine, creaked when she bent down. I wondered why we needed to be dressed the same. This was getting stranger by the minute.

I tried not to wince when she kissed me on the cheek and brushed away a wayward strand of hair that had fallen over my face. My hair. For some reason, they hadn't changed it.

"We'll have you feeling better and up on your feet in no time. Let's get you into the ambulance."

Again, Reinhardt and Rose hoisted me to my feet and guided me down the plane's slippery narrow steps. It was humid and warm, the rain coming in bursts. A short distance ahead was an ambulance. When we got to it, they opened the back doors and an attendant in a white uniform with nice biceps and a pleasant smile pulled me up as if I didn't weigh more than a bag of laundry and lay me onto the stretcher.

Rosalind stepped up inside and took a seat on the bench seat beside him. She signaled to Reinhardt to close the door. The loud thud of the closing doors momentarily startled me, reminding me of the thuds I heard coming from my hospital room. I felt suddenly very cold. The engine engaged, the ambulance rocked, and we began to drive.

She pointed to the attendant. "This is Rowan, and I'm Rosalind, otherwise known as your mother," she said with a cautious smile. She paused to watch my eyes. "Rowan is… Well, let's just say he's like an uncle. He's part of our family. Just rest quietly. We'll be home in forty minutes."

"No… hospital?" I asked. They were all nuts, but I'd sooner endure whatever they were in a house than be drugged and tied up alone in a hospital.

"Oh, God, no," Rosalind laughed. "I hate those places. Anyway, all you need is to sleep off those nasty drugs Rose keeps pumping into you. When you're sober again, you can meet the rest of your new family." She looked like she would've kept talking but stopped herself and smiled.

"Rest of our family," I said flatly. She seemed like she was a sympathetic person, but still, I wished she'd stop with all that talk about family. It was unnerving.

"Yes, your brothers are anxious to meet you," Rosalind said, that smile still on her face. She winked a second time, but this time it was directed at Rowan.

I had the uncomfortable impression that I was mistaken; she wasn't actually nice, she was teasing me and having fun doing it. I tightened my mouth, which pulled on the still-tender skin on my face.

She looked at me again and softened her expression. Taking up my hand in both of hers, she laughed out loud. "You're much prettier than Reinhardt described. But you do look skinny and frail. And the boys are so competitive; we'll just have to toughen you up so you can hold your own against them." She leaned in close. I couldn't help but inhale her perfume. Chanel. I'd have recognized it anywhere. My mom wore Chanel No. 5 when she and my dad went out at night. Tears sprang to my eyes. "Now, don't worry, Ruby," she said, "I'll teach you the ropes and they'll know better than to mess with you."

I roughly wiped my face. What was she trying to tell me? The more she said, the more confused I became. What exactly was she going to "teach" me?

Frustrated, I dropped my head back heavily against the pillow and gave a loud and disgusted sigh. This situation was getting more surreal by the minute. I already knew that my real parents and brother died in that fire, and now suddenly I had all kinds of people around me calling themselves mother, father, brothers. It also appeared that there was extended family and Rose and Rowan were my aunt and uncle. Was Robert part of the family too? Third cousin once removed? All these Rs were giving me a headache. They weren't exactly a creative bunch, I snorted to myself.

Rosalind monitored me closely. Every few minutes, she glanced at her watch, a women's version of Reinhardt's, I noticed, and exchanged subtle glances with Rowan. I wanted desperately to know what I was up against. But I also knew I would have to be patient. She was clearly being selective by revealing only bits of information. She knew exactly what she was doing, her every move and response calculated. Was this all part of a preconceived plan? Physically, apart from being unbathed and drugged and scrawny, I made sure I appeared calm and accepting of whatever these people threw at me, but inside my body and mind were roiling as if storm clouds were taking over inside.

I closed my eyes and lay back. A tear drained down the side of my face and I just left it there to pool up in my hair. I let the sway of the ambulance rock me to sleep.

When we stopped, I woke up and tried to steal a look at Rosalind's watch, but she'd rolled her sleeves down. Rowan climbed over Rosalind's knees and hopped pertly out the back of the ambulance. I could hear him talking to someone. Men.

"We've brought Ruby home," he said. "Are the perimeter and surrounding areas secured?"

"Yes, sir. Air and ground are secure," another man responded. "I'll open the gate."

Rowan stepped back into the ambulance and knocked twice on the side. It started to move again. Another short ride before we stopped again. He clapped his hands on his legs and looked at me expectantly before opening the doors. His expression was kind, sympathetic. It was still pouring, but between two black clouds, the sun glared through, and a single ray pierced into my eyes like a hot knife.

"Ruby, we're home now," Rosalind said, gently nudging my arm. "You're safe and you can start a new life here."

I looked drowsily at her. I didn't know what she meant by "safe," but at that moment, I felt like I was anything but.

Four

I HAD TO MARVEL AT THE IRONY. Since I was a young girl, my dream had been to live on the French Riviera. I used to lie on the living room floor and watch Hitchcock's *To Catch a Thief*, looking past the actors to the sparkling sea in the background. I'd even imagined I might be able to travel there before I started grad school, picturing myself working for some rich and famous celebrity who owned a home there, on my days off pretending to be one of them as I sauntered around beach-side in a floppy straw hat and bright red toenails. When we drove through the gates and rolled slowly over the long gravel drive that led to a massive peach stucco villa, I shook my head. Showing up strapped to a gurney, drugged and on the verge of screaming had definitely never been part of that picture.

Another man crunched up over the walk to join Rowan, rain bouncing off his giant black umbrella. Rosalind ducked out of the ambulance and stood beneath it, and he handed the umbrella to Rosalind so he and Rowan could bring my gurney down from the ambulance.

On the ground, they undid the straps that had held me down. I sat up and put my feet on the ground, but my legs gave way and I started to fall. I cried out, and Rowan caught me in his muscled arms just in time.

"Easy there, sweetie," he said teasingly but kindly.

Once we were clear of the ambulance, it drove away, the back doors swinging closed on their own, and he handed me off to the other guy with the umbrella who looked like he'd just walked out of an Abercrombie & Fitch catalog with his flannel plaid shirt, tousled dark hair and a day's growth of beard.

What an odd batch of people, I thought.

"It's OK," he whispered. "I've got you."

He easily took me around my waist, a gentle smile on his face and began to walk us toward the house without another word.

I tried to walk, but my legs were too wobbly and I fell against his solid body.

He tucked the umbrella into the back of his pants, giving him both arms to hold on to me with, and leaned me against his chest. He chuckled and shrugged. "May look silly, but now I can hold you properly."

I caught his eyes for a second before I looked quickly down; they were nice: brown like sea glass and fringed with dark lashes.

He carefully guided me up a rise of steps toward a massive wooden door that opened as we approached. The rain pelted the umbrella. The noise, our uneven steps over the rocky ground, and the heat of the man next to me were making me dizzy. I'd abandoned the idea of running for it; I couldn't concentrate on any details. Holding me securely, he brought me up the steps, one at a time as if I were a child, until we were through and standing in a dimly lit vaulted vestibule.

He turned to shake his umbrella out the doors and I lost my balance.

Coming from inside the house was another man. Him. Reinhardt. Looking every bit like the gentleman of the manor with his expensive cashmere sweater and pressed pants, he offered me his arm.

Abercrombie man handed me to him and folded his umbrella into the stand by the door. We stood still a moment while he said something in French to him.

While they talked, I lifted my head to have a look. I had to press my oddly full lips together to keep from gasping. The foyer opened to a receiving room with a single round sofa in the centre and an elaborate mosaic scroll emanating from the center. Numerous other doorways led off the receiving room. A large crystal chandelier hung high overhead and reflected off the iron railings of an open hallway on the second floor. All around, the marble walls and floors gleamed.

The tousled and kindly man went back outside and Reinhardt turned to me. "It was a long road, but we made it. Welcome to Fairhaven." His smile was wide, but again I noticed his eyes had a sadness in them. Or I was projecting. He was the one who kidnapped me, after all.

He brought me to the sofa and sat me gently on it. Outside, the rain fell in fat strands. "This is our safe house. You'll be able to rest and regain your strength now." He seemed different, relaxed and at ease in a way he hadn't before. Safe house? There was that word again. Safe for whom, I wondered. I wanted to believe his smile was genuine but nothing made sense and I no longer had any concept of what genuine even was.

A lithe woman clicked in wearing chic heels, a pencil skirt, and bright-red lipstick. Her brown hair was up in a loose chignon and had an elegant silver streak in the front. "Ruby, your room is ready," she said. "Care to come see it?" She had a light English accent and used her arms like a dancer would as she spoke. I felt very dumpy all of a sudden.

"This is Rachel," Reinhardt said. "She'll get you settled. You can trust her. She'll take good care of you. You'll feel so much better after you get some food and have a good night's sleep."

While Reinhardt was talking, Rosalind came bustling in, her chin leading the rest of her. She shook out water droplets from her blond bob with a hand. "Thanks, Rachel. I'll help you."

Rosalind hooked her arm under mine and hefted me from the velvet sofa. For someone so petite, she had surprising strength and resolve. Before I knew it, she had an arm around my waist and was steering me toward Rachel. On one hand, I wondered why she cared so much about whether or not I rested or ate—she didn't know me from Adam—but on the other, there was something so intensely maternal about her that was so strong, I wanted to believe it and just lay my head against her the way I would with my mom.

"Easy does it, child," she said, straightening me.

I tried to stand taller. I had a feeling that I'd need to listen to her or I'd not like the response.

Rosalind and Rachel guided me carefully to a staircase off the side of the vestibule. The staircase took my breath away. It had its own dedicated space away from the other rooms of the main floor and extended up two floors to a masterfully painted ceiling of clouds and sky. Dangling from the gentle blue and white was an enormous light fixture of iron and colored-glass sea birds that glowed from within, lit by tiny fairy bulbs. The marble steps curved like a seashell and ascended alongside a railing of exquisite, scrolled-wrought-iron vines. The marble was cold under my feet. I gripped the railing, scratching my thumb on the edge of sculpted leaf. The tall window showed the tumultuous sky over the ocean. My legs were jelly and my heart heavy, but for a brief moment, I felt like I'd risen into heaven.

Kidnappers maybe, but the women were clucking over me as if I were precious cargo, which was kind of nice. Rosalind took the front and Rachel the rear in case I faltered or lost my footing on the stairs.

At the top, the hallway opened to a hall boasting a floor-to-ceiling Renaissance tapestry, and numerous doors—bedrooms, I presumed—flanked the wall on the right.

Rachel opened the second door on the right and Rosalind led me inside. Against the wall was a rustic, wooden, four-poster bed painted white. The carpeting was soft and thick, and I don't know how they did it, but beside the bed stood a tray with a steaming cup and a plate of biscuits. Rosalind left me and swiftly went to the bed to pull down the duvet. She fluffed the pillows and smoothed the sheets. Rachel pointed for me to be seated and have the snack. I sat gingerly on the edge of the chair while she went to a gilded dresser and pulled out a white linen nightgown.

She returned and set it on the back of the chair. "You need to eat something," she said, moving the tray closer. She went around and took off my shoes. Rosalind was behind me now gently pulling off my leather jacket.

I felt like a doll but was so tired I could hardly sit up. I didn't want to give it to him, but Reinhardt was right. I needed some sleep. I'd ask all my questions later. Not like I was going anywhere.

The ladies guided me over to the soft, cool bed, tucked me in, and I was asleep before my head was on the pillow.

When I awoke, it took me a few seconds to realize that something was in bed with me. It was warm and muscular and moved. Before I had time to register what it was, the thing scrabbled up and stuck its hot face in mine. I shrieked and curled into a ball at the headboard.

"Don't worry," someone in the room with a high, sweet voice said. "He likes you. Don't be scared."

I didn't have the presence of mind to worry that someone had been sitting in the bedroom, watching me sleep. I just wanted this thing away from me. "Get him off me," I yelped.

"Rune, down boy," he said. There was a loud thump as it jumped off the bed and the mattress sprang back. "You, too, Riemes."

Another thump on the floor and the click of nails and I realized that a second creature had been sharing my bed as I slept, too. I pressed my back tightly against the headboard to put as much distance between me and the two large and wiry Dobermans as I could.

"Seriously, the dogs have Rs too?" I muttered under my breath. I rolled my eyes and flopped back into the bed, yanking the covers up to my neck.

I wanted to not look, but I had to; I turned my head to see the kid who was in the room with me. He looked about twelve or thirteen, with freckles and a striped shirt and was sitting in the chair with his arms wrapped around his knobby knees. The two magnificent black and rust Dobermans sat obediently at his feet.

"Ruby," he started, smiling shyly. "I'm so happy you're here." He paused. "I've been waiting for you for days. I'm Roscoe. This is Rune."

He nodded his head at one of the dogs. "And this guy is Riemes." He tickled the dog's ear, and it nuzzled his crossed legs. I bit my tongue against blurting out something caustic about all their idiotic devotion to one lousy letter of the alphabet. Like, why was R so special? Why not B or Q? The boy tugged on my heart, all knees and feet and bedhead. I suspected he wasn't one of the kidnappers, but was a kidnappee like me.

"I could tell they liked you instantly. It's funny because I'm the only man in the household they're friendly to." He emphasized the word *man*. "They've been protecting you all night."

That made me smile, mostly because he said it with a mild degree of pride. He was older than Johnny but he was serious and spindly like him. My eyes welled up. I coughed to cover it. "Have you been here all night too?" I asked.

He shook his head. "I was asleep in my room and only came into your room about an hour ago looking for them." Roscoe laughed as he scratched Rune's ear this time. "You like her better than me, don't you?" He rubbed the dog's head and Rune licked his nose. He got up and sat at the side of my bed.

"Ruby, you can be my sister now." He studied my face for a moment. Even if I hadn't just worked with all those disadvantaged kids in my last school placement, I'd have seen the abject grief in his eyes and marring his little voice. Something told me this boy had seen far more than someone his age should ever see. The heavy look to his eyes was similar to that in Reinhardt's. Maybe they were related, maybe they'd both lost something, or someone.

I was about to start asking him questions when a large man with shaggy, ash-brown hair and a Hawaiian shirt shuffled to the door.

"Roscoe, come on. Rosalind is expecting you downstairs for breakfast. It's on the south terrace this morning." He wore a pocket protector. I almost started crying when I saw that. My dad wore one, and I used to tease him mercilessly for it because it looked so geeky.

Startled, Roscoe jumped off the bed and yanked at his shorts like they were too big for him. Rune and Riemes immediately sprang in front of him, their heads down and ears back, emitting a low throaty growl. Roscoe was right. The dogs didn't appear to like the man.

He didn't seem troubled. "And take the dogs with you," he said, absently brushing an uncombed strand of hair out of his eyes. Unlike everyone else I'd met, all of whom dressed well and expensively and smelled nice, this guy reminded me of all the IT nerds from my dad's firm. Rumpled, big square glasses, and so smart they often forgot about normal things like showering.

I heard the *click click* of ballerina flats on the marble go from tiny to loud and then there was Rose, looking fresh in capri pants and a pink blouse, joining the party. As she came in, her pretty face had a sour look to it. "Renegade, honestly, what are you doing here? Leave Ruby alone. Go on down for breakfast. I'll help her get dressed." She nudged him toward the door. "Go with Roscoe. Rosalind is expecting both of you."

Renegade looked at me curiously and then scowled at Rose before he obediently turned and followed Roscoe and the dogs like a big floppy puppy himself.

"Well, I see the guys are checking you out," Rose said. She rolled her eyes as if they were bothersome. I had to laugh; it was a very sisterly gesture. She saw me laugh and smiled. "Did you sleep well? You look much better. I have some clean clothes for you." She nodded at a neatly folded pile of clothes in her hands. "I hope jeans and T-shirt and sandals are OK?"

What could I say? "Yeah, fine."

"The bathroom is a couple of doors down. You'll feel like a new person…" she hesitated as she squinched up her face. "Sorry. What I meant to say is that a shower will feel good. You'll find everything you need in there."

She led me to the bathroom and stood guard outside the door.

I couldn't have asked for a nicer bathroom and the products were all Aveda, which I loved. At least this abduction offered first class accommodations. Here, too, were marble floors, sparkling porcelain antique fixtures and glistening chrome hardware. A massive mirror over the marble vanity made me stop and stare at the stranger who reflected back at me. I was indeed a new person, but the who and why spooked me.

I turned quickly to get into the shower and drown myself in mint shampoo. I made the water as hot as it would go and enjoyed the scalding cascade for several minutes before drying off and checking out the clothes Rose had brought me. Chloe T-shirt, J Brand jeans, some French designer for the sandals. Expensive, and the perfect size, I noticed as I put everything on. I shuddered momentarily at the reflection in the mirror, then, shaking off my apprehension, I opened the door wide to go to breakfast with the pretty blond prison guard who waited patiently outside.

The second she opened the French doors that led to an outside terrace, the humidity hit me first then the fiercely bright sunshine. I slammed my eyes shut against the light, and when I opened them, I saw what, under different circumstances, would've been a dream landscape: a table laden with pastries and fruit under the shade of a wide white umbrella on a marble deck that looked out over a yacht-dotted bay. A formal and elaborate garden of colorful flowers and tropical plants lay directly ahead between an azure ocean that framed both sides of a narrow peninsula.

"There you are, Ruby," called Rosalind from another table. "Come and get some breakfast." She motioned to a servant to bring me something. "Come and sit down beside me. I want you to meet your brothers." Rosalind emphasized the words *brothers*. She studied my face.

I returned Rosalind's stare, pausing, waiting for what she would say next. But her patience won out over mine and I plunked down into the overstuffed patio chair. The servant placed a plate with a soft-boiled egg in a cup, a bowl of fresh berries and two croissants on the table in front of me.

I looked around the table, first at Roscoe then at the sloppy guy Rose had called Renegade, and then I noticed the good-looking man who'd helped me out of the ambulance across the table from her. Everyone looked so elegant and comfortable together. Anger began to rise in my throat, and I struggled to maintain my composure. But it was enough.

"These people are not my brothers," I said through clenched teeth. I kept my voice quiet and my head down, forking aimlessly at the food on the plate. I felt like a hurricane about to touch down.

"Rosalind, honey," Reinhardt said. "Let's not overwhelm Ruby. She needs time to let the situation sink in. We agreed..." I lifted my head slightly to see Reinhardt raising an eyebrow at Rosalind across the table. He saw me watching him and smiled tightly. "Cook prepares an excellent breakfast. You must be half-starved. Please, eat something." Reinhardt gestured to my plate.

My outburst didn't appear to faze Rosalind in the least. In fact, she seemed satisfied by my response. However, Reinhardt looked concerned and watched me nervously out of the corner of his eye.

"Nonsense," Rosalind said. "You underestimate our Ruby. She needs to know who we are. She's stronger than you think." She looked at me in her evaluative manner and then back at Reinhardt with an *I told you so* determination on her face.

Reinhardt reluctantly nodded his agreement. Rosalind smiled and turned back to me.

Rose interrupted the conversation. "She's already met Roscoe and Renegade. They were snooping at her room," she said disapprovingly. She looked at Rosalind as if for backup.

"Good going, boys. I completely approve of snooping," Rosalind said. She sipped her coffee. "Your last and third brother is Ransom. I believe you met yesterday?" I thought I detected a smirk when she said that. "All in all, you now have three brothers, Roscoe, Renegade, and Ransom." She smiled at me and paused.

That was the final straw. Between her smug face, the idiotic names, and the fact that no one at this fancy table seemed sane enough to belong outside of a loony bin, I'd had it. "Why do you keep calling everyone my brother, sister, mother? Is this a cult? And what the hell is your fascination with Rs?"

A round of grins and snickers rose from the table. I was about to start crying I was so frustrated and confused, and all around me, these wackos were laughing. I looked at little Roscoe, who was laughing, too, and soon I was giggling despite myself. The pressure was too much. It was either that or cry again, and honestly I didn't think I had any tears left.

"They didn't like the names we picked," Rosalind shrugged in pretend indignation. "But really, look at them. Do they look like a Randal or a Russell? Rebus?"

I picked my name, too," Roscoe added. "They asked me what I wanted to be called and I liked Roscoe. It sounds tough to me and nobody messes with a tough guy." That sadness in his voice was back. Rune and Riemes came close and snuggled into his arms as if they could sense when he needed them.

I just stared at them all, waiting, my right eyebrow up in my forehead so high it felt like it might pop off.

"We use the initials RD as our code name," Reinhardt said, his tone turning serious. "It's so no one can track or locate us. Whenever we're away from our safe house, we go by initials only. That way our genders and identities are protected and no one can determine how many of us there are."

"Why don't you want anyone to know who or where we are?" I asked.

There was a long silence as the mood changed and turned dark. Everyone shifted his glance from one to the another. "It's a long and complicated story," Reinhardt finally said after the long moment.

Whatever their private reasons were for not talking was their issue; I had a right to know and was done with sitting by, docile as a lamb being brought to the spit. "Look, you've kidnapped me. You've changed my face. You tell me you're my father, and mother, that I have brothers and that Rachel and Rose and all the other Rs are aunts and uncles. What the hell is going on here? My parents are dead. My life is over. Don't you think that gives me the right to know what kind of situation you've put me in?" I wasn't backing down now. "You keep saying 'trust me' but I don't trust any of you. Why should I?" My temper was flaring. My father always used to say my temper was either an asset or a liability depending on the circumstance. I was about to find out which it would be. "Either you tell me what's going on or I'm getting out of here, unless you're planning on using that thing on me," I arched my eyebrow again and stared at the gun in Reinhardt's belt. I scooted my chair back.

"You're not a prisoner but you would definitely be in danger if you left on your own," Ransom said. "Cold Force has ways of finding us, and when they find you, which they will, they'll kill you. They already know you didn't die in the fire. The body count was short by one. They know Kathleen Jones is alive, and because they managed to locate you at the clinic, that means they also know she's incognito. You're lucky Robert was able to throw them off track; but you need to understand…" He put his hand on mine. "They will never stop hunting for you."

"Ransom," Reinhardt shouted, "never say that name or any of the names associated with our past again. You know the rules and why we can *not* break them. We need to forget our past and only be who we are now. We're Drakers and we will not only survive, we'll defeat that bastard. But not until we're fully ready."

"I know that," Ransom said. "But Ruby has to know the dangers of being without our protection. If she leaves, she'll be putting all of us in danger."

"*If* I leave…" My mind got fixated on those three words. Did that mean that was an option?

"Ruby's not going to leave," Rosalind said. "She's just trying to understand what the situation is." Rosalind looked at me sympathetically, which I thought was rich, since essentially what she'd said sounded a lot like a veiled threat. "Eat your breakfast, darling. This is a lot to take in all at once. You have lots of time to figure this whole thing out."

I forced myself to choke down some of the food, now knowing that it was at least a tiny bit possible for me to get the hell out of there. I'd need to get stronger if I was going to run for it. As everyone chewed in silence, I tried to make sense of everything. I started thinking about the fire, my parents, and my little brother, everything scrambled together and popping around my mind. My heart began to ache, filling me with an empty pain that crept into every corner of my body. They were dead. I had lost my entire family and this whole time, I'd been so drugged and scared for my life, I never got to think about what this meant, never let myself realize it fully. Despair was hitting me full force now; crippling, incapacitating grief replaced the confusion and fear. I wanted my family. I wanted them so hard. I wished I had died with them. The skin on my new face still tugged and stung as the perspiration from the hot sun moistened it and tears formed in the corners of my eyes.

Roscoe was staring at me. I knew he knew what I was feeling. I hoped that he hadn't experienced something similar, that he wasn't grieving a loss, trying to fill a void with these strangers, strangers who forbade him to even talk about his pain. Rune and Riemes came over to my seat and laid their heads comfortingly on my knees, one dog on each side.

He reached out and grasped my hand in his little tanned one. "Let me show you the most awesome view of the garden," he said, standing. "It's like you're at the center of another planet where no one can see or hurt you."

He got up from the table and started walking along a path that led down the narrow garden peninsula, with its tropical flowers and greenery everywhere, and the azure sea on each side.

The dogs paused and looked for me to join them. The Rs at the table watched me closely. Rose reached into her pocket for something. I stood quickly, spilling the cold contents of Rosalind's coffee. I'd be damned if she'd drug me again.

"I'm fine," I muttered and followed Roscoe before I lost control of my emotions. I wasn't going to let the others see me cry.

Five

ROSCOE BOLTED INTO THE GARDEN, the dogs bouncing and leaping playfully after him, one on either side. They played as if they'd invented a new game that involved jumping and pushing each other, the way boys and dogs played. It all seemed so normal, I thought.

Before he got too far ahead me, he stopped and called back. "Come on, this is just what you need."

The dogs looked back as well. Noticing that I hadn't moved far, they sprinted back to the terrace to encourage me to follow, first nudging my leg then running out a few feet only to look back as if to say, "what's the hold up?"

I chuckled and slowly followed.

The dogs ran ahead again to join Roscoe but kept coming back to me, making sure I was keeping up.

The garden path wound uphill, and after a minute I was breathing hard. I hadn't even walked more than a few feet on my own in the last days—or it could have been much longer; I still wasn't sure how much time had passed—let alone gotten any actual exercise. Roscoe was already far ahead but always kept in view so I could see where he was leading me. I was embarrassed that I had to stop so frequently to catch my breath. At least those moments gave me time to appreciate my surroundings and distracted me from the hurt gnawing away at my stomach.

The gardens were arranged almost thematically with spectacular plantings of exotic and tropical foliage, palm trees, rhododendrons, begonias and many flowers and plants I didn't recognize. Reflecting ponds were tucked into each of the gardens, and marble statuary accented the manicured beds. As I struggled to keep up with Roscoe, more garden themes emerged as I went further down the way. The property was on a narrow peninsula walled on each side with terraced overlooks that hung precipitously above the steep cliffs. All around was the vast blue of the Mediterranean and the gentle *shush shush* of the waves that washed up onto the narrow jut of land. Decorative signs in French labeled the garden themes along the way. We walked and walked, past the Japanese garden, the Italian garden, and the Venetian garden, until we reached a rose garden where an open-sided round temple stood, its domed canopy anchored by Corinthian pillars atop a marble platform. It was a reverent and serene monument at the garden's end, high above a cliff that fell treacherously to the ocean. Curved marble steps with elaborately carved rails and balusters sculpted from yet another kind of marble arched up to the temple platform and protected visitors from accidentally stepping out and falling to their deaths.

I struggled to keep climbing. My breath was almost gone and my legs burned. Roscoe and his canine companions waited patiently between the center pillars. When I got there, my energy spent, I tripped at the top step and fell hard on the cold marble floor to my knees. Roscoe teased me for being so fragile, but he came over to help me get up and take me to a bench that faced out to an expanse where only sky and water could be seen.

"We're going to have to get you into better shape than that," he said. "I think a turtle could have outrun you." He punched my shoulder lightly, smiling widely and watching me closely.

I had no breath left for talking so I sat in silence for a long time, taking in the view and the delicate breeze. From where we sat looking straight out, we could see a stretch of sea and sky so wide it was as if we were floating in the air. Roscoe was right. I felt like we were on another planet that was not only extra-terrestrial, but spiritual, reverent, and completely overwhelming in its beauty.

"When I come here I feel like I'm floating above the world," Roscoe said. "Somewhere between earth and heaven." He sat quietly for a while. "Sometimes," he whispered, "I can almost hear them. My mom and dad. They tell me that they're all right and that I'm going to be OK too. I come here to remember." He paused again. His voice softened and went mellow, full of emotion and pain. "I think that's important. So I don't ever lose them." He sniffed and wiped his nose on the sleeve of his shirt. "You know, Reinhardt, Rosalind, my brothers and everybody, they're OK. They're not bad. They made me promise not to tell you anything yet, but just so you know, we're the good guys. There's no reason for you to run away. Promise me that you won't leave us." He grasped my forearm. "I still don't understand everything either but they're nice to me, and they'll look after you, too. We're safe here."

"Rune, Riemes, be good boys and stay with her." He wagged his finger at them as if they could understand his every word. He turned to me, his little face very serious. "I'm gonna go down, but stay as long as you want. If you need us, send the dogs to get us, all right?"

The dogs came obediently and lay down on the hard marble floor at my feet. Then Roscoe turned and bounded back down the stairs like a rubber ball, down to the house which, from up here, looked tiny enough to fit in my hand.

I watched him until he disappeared into the mansion. This was the first time I saw the house in its entirety. The verandas, the large round palladium windows in front of the south terrace, the arched and pillared openings offering a view of the gardens and the azure sea, an inner veranda, cool and shaded, and a solarium with views of the harbor. It was shaped like a salmon-colored clover, balconies off the bedrooms on four sides of the house. My mother had always loved design, and we used to pore over *Architectural Digest* together on Saturday mornings. This was the house of my dreams, the house where I'd wanted to work, a lifestyle I wanted to be a part of. Nothing but the silly dreams of a silly naive girl.

I turned again to look out to sea, at a universe made up of the unknown. Like a blow to the stomach, the grief and loss hit me again and suddenly I couldn't breathe. The sobs came and came and came until they were nothing more than dry convulsions. My eyes were raw, scrubbed of what they used to be familiar with seeing. Standing alone in this temple above the world I could believe that nothing else existed. "Why... Why," I asked over and over. Why were they dead? Who or what could have done such a heinous act? Why would anyone want to kill my family?

And, how did Reinhardt, or whatever his real name used to be, curiously know to be there at the exact time and place to rescue me? And why me? How did these people even know I existed? What if I'd decided to go out with Kim to grab a juice after class instead of heading home? Would I be dead too?

I ruminated over the events and questions that raged through my mind but no answers came. Unlike Roscoe, I heard no voices from another dimension, no words of assurance or comfort. My parents and little brother didn't speak to me from the beyond like Roscoe's loved ones did. I'd never felt more alone.

Finally in exhaustion, I crumpled over on the marble bench, put my head in my hands, and curled into a ball. The marble was hard against my spine and the world and sky tilted dizzily. I had nothing left.

When I woke up, the sun was high in the sky and the day had grown hot. My tongue was sticky and swollen.

I sat up and waited a moment before slowly standing and starting back down the hill toward the manor. I didn't want to run into any of these people, all of them persistent in their ridiculous idea that they were my family. Even if they had saved me, even if they were benevolent, I didn't know them and they would never replace my family who were taken away from me. How dare they erase the identity of who I was, forbidding me to even speak my own name. They had no right.

***

I struggled in the next days, tortured by fear and uncertainty. I grieved deeply for all that I had lost: my family, my identity, the future that once looked so promising and bright. I grieved for myself. But most of all, I struggled to figure out Ruby, that alien that had taken over my body and who stared back at me from every mirror, a stranger who, because I had to pretend to be pleasant about being here, about cohabiting with these people, was starting to infiltrate, to imprint her thoughts and personality on my mind and soul. I tried to keep my guard up against the lies the Drakers may have invented to placate me and keep me docile, but I held firm against them. There was no truth in being someone else, someone whose only reason to exist was to live a terrible disguised reality and to never acknowledge again everything that came before, everything that made me me.

Worst was having to maintain a veneer of calm around them so Rose, with her ever-ready stash of drugs, wouldn't force Prozac or some other mood-altering medicine on me or just tackle me with a syringe whenever she smelled a whiff of rebellion on me. I saw how closely they watched me, so I made sure to move cautiously among them while at meals and afternoon gatherings. I became adept at pretending I was getting used to them and accepting of my role as a member of this manufactured family. I didn't talk much, and when I did, I kept it to topics an old lady at an afternoon tea might cover like the weather or the flowers in the garden. Nothing real, nothing important. And they did the same, never again speaking of the circumstances that had brought us all together. I could tell they were watching me all the time, waiting for me to explode, but I held myself together. I could sit on a bed of nails and smile. Roscoe had learned to accept them, but he was just a boy, and I didn't know how old he'd been when they rescued him but clearly it was some time ago. He truly did need family; his asking me not to leave them tore at my heart. But even though I felt for him—and I was more and more melting toward him like I would my real brother—I held back for everyone else. I didn't need a new family. I would live with the memory of my old one and wait for these days to pass until I could figure out a plan.

Over the first couple of weeks, I spent hours in the pristine and manicured gardens of Fairhaven, walking the carefully designed pathways, thinking at the temple where I tried to will my family to give me guidance and reassurance. But nothing. Still, the sun and warm air soothed the ragged emptiness of my heart. I walked to get away from the Drakers; I walked to forget my fear and torment; I walked to heal; and day after day as I walked, my body gained strength as did my determination to figure this whole thing out.

Soon my legs started to feel a hearkening of the strength I had developed from my years on the college track team. I'd been doing all of my running in the sandals they'd given me and my feet were blistered in several places and the straps were frayed. These people were rich; I couldn't see why it'd be a problem for them to give me some running shoes. I'd say "Ruby" needed them, so she could get strong. They'd like that. They didn't have to know that I was keeping my options open just in case. The only problem if I did have to stick around was that maybe the Drakers would think that once I came to rely on them, feeling more comfortable making requests and becoming dependent on them, that they might think I'd accepted them and my place among them. But, I figured, so what if they did. It was part of the charade. Or maybe eventually I'd just let my guard down and accept them as mine. At some point, I'd have less to argue against. That made me laugh. Calling Rosalind "Mommy." Over my dead body.

One afternoon after I'd been doing sprints up the hills, I came back, sweating and feeling actually pretty great. I figured Rose was in charge of clothes, so I decided I'd ask her about shoes. Why should she suspect anything other than I wanted to get healthier?

I went through the rooms on the main floor, but there was no sign of anyone so I went to my room to shower. I looked out at the sea flanking the manor and felt my heart sink. My plan was starting to seem ridiculous. I had no money, no documents. Where would I go? I felt a moment of disgust for myself; I was buckling. You're weak, a coward, I told myself. I had everything a person needed, the house was safe and I didn't know what dangers lurked beyond the walls of Fairhaven. Ransom's warning was always lingering in the back of my mind.

When I got to my room, the sun coming through the large window felt familiar and comforting in a way that it hadn't before. I was probably just getting used to it. A human being is an adaptable thing; we can get used to nearly anything. I stepped closer to look out at the view of the garden and the sea. Whatever my life was now or what it would become, in this moment, I was in a cool room that smelled of clean linen and salt air, the blue sea stretching out before me. Like my future, I thought, turning around and sneering. Sharks lived in that water, too.

One of the servants had been in to clean and tidy as they did every afternoon. The Drakers had brought me some things over the last weeks they thought I'd like: a leather-bound journal, which I'd nearly filled with writing so small I hoped no one would be able to decipher it, an IPod, a glass water pitcher with cobalt dragonflies etched into the side. These were all neatly arranged on the dresser, and the upholstered chair, its footstool, and the side table were aligned in a perfect triangle. As I looked around, I saw some things on the bed and stopped. There was a pair of Nikes, athletic socks, jogging shorts, a sports bra and a tank top arrayed there as if for inspection. I hadn't said a thing to anyone about this. My skin crawled. I threw everything into the corner, crawled into the bed and fell into a fitful sleep.

Early the next morning I retrieved the new clothes and decided to go for a jog before breakfast. I'd missed dinner and my stomach felt like it was digesting itself. Outside, mist clung to the flowers in their beds and bushes and hung thickly at the horizon. My bare arms and legs tingled in the cool air. I made my way quietly down toward the usual path that defined my walk and started a slow jog. Such a difference having bouncy shoes. It felt great, and I quickened my pace a bit, enjoying the exertion.

A few minutes into my run as I rounded a bend in the path toward the Japanese garden, I blinked through the sweat to better see someone there. Rosalind. She was sitting on the stone bench by the little red bridge that spanned a gurgling creek.

When I got to her, she was tying her shoe. "Morning," she said without looking up. "Mind if I join you?" Her jogging gear was similar to mine.

I was feeling manipulated and didn't answer. I kept running, and Rosalind, without waiting for a response, fell into a jog beside me. We didn't talk, just ran at a slightly picked up pace.

Not far down the path I was surprised again, though I was beginning to see this was an ambush. Reinhardt was down on one knee also tying a shoelace. My annoyance at further intrusion made me speed up and run right past him. I caught the smile and nod he and Rosalind exchanged but ignored them. He took up the pace on my other side. I'd long since stopped being afraid of them, but this smelled bad. They didn't try anything, just ran on my either side, the three of us jogging together as happily as a television family. Maybe they were trying to intimidate me. I tried to ignore them and kept my breathing steady and the pace strong. They were old; maybe I could wear them out.

Ahead at the Italian garden, two shadows sharpened into view as we approached. Ransom and Renegade waited until the three of us silently passed. As if on cue, the two of them fell in behind us. Rosalind and Reinhardt let me take the lead, and the rest paired up in formation behind me. I ground my teeth. I continued to run and let their scheme play out.

We were approaching the rose garden where the mist was heaviest. Obscured dark figures loomed among the bushes on either side and shifted like statues coming to life. More of my so-called extended family waited, and as we passed, the four of them—Rowan, Rose, Rachel, and a beaming Roscoe with his ever-present canine companions—joined our troop. The only thing missing was a military training chant. I kept my mouth occupied with breathing: in through the nose, out through the mouth. They would have to talk first. This was *my* run.

I usually stopped to rest at various points during my runs, but this morning I'd be damned if I was going to stop. I could outrun all of them. What were they trying to do, intimidate me? I'd had enough of being controlled. They had my face, they had my whole life, fine. But I was still me. They couldn't have that.

As we neared the house, they all slowed as one and came to a stop. I paid them no mind and went for another whole round, more than I'd run yet by double, but I didn't care. Anger fueled me and I wanted to run forever. As I raced back around to the Japanese garden, the whole lot of them reared back up and joined me, easily, as if it were nothing for all of them. Meanwhile, I was feeling heavy in the legs but kept going. When we came around for what would have been a third lap, I imagined outrunning them, just sprinting away, hopping a wall and soon being gone, disappeared into France, but my mouth was completely dried out and I was getting light-headed. The Drakers were like robots, fit and strong. I had underestimated their aptness and their determination. I would have to do considerably more training before I could outdo them.

The south terrace had since been set for breakfast. Rather than continue for a fourth, before I stopped, having to admit defeat, the collective merged left and went to the terrace, chatting easily as if they hadn't just exerted themselves or ganged up on someone who, by the way, had up until recently been in the hospital and drugged up to her armpits, I wanted to yell. While they began pouring juice and water, I went to the side of the path behind a bush and bent over to catch my breath. I waited to see if I would vomit, and then when I felt better, I stood. Having nowhere else to go, I decided I'd play their game.

I walked down and poured myself a glass of water. They'd all begun eating and ignored me. I stared at them, waiting for someone to say something, but no one even acknowledged me. Within minutes everyone left, smiling and nodding at me on their way out. I hung back on the terrace and picked at some baguette and cheese until I was sure they were all gone, evaporated into the bowels of the house, the same as every day. When I went inside, indeed, the place seemed empty. As if I'd imagined the whole thing.

The emptiness of the house became more and more intriguing. I suspected everyone had gone somewhere, I just couldn't figure out where. There were no offices in the house, no sounds of typing or phone calls. Roscoe, being little, was around a lot, though he preferred to hang out outside exercising the dogs, or more accurately, with the dogs exercising him. The next morning after breakfast, I found him throwing balls into the bushes. Seemed a weird game to me, but the dogs appeared to love it, flying off to retrieve the balls and returning to plop them at his feet.

"Riemes, your turn. Fetch," he called again and Riemes bounded into action returning almost instantly with the prize.

It was cute but kind of boring to watch, so I was starting to walk back to my room when the dogs began fiercely barking and growling. I ran back to the terrace only to see a startled Roscoe watch his beloved dogs race toward the iron entry gate.

The commotion must have alerted Reinhardt as well, as he burst from the house with Rowan close behind, rifles in hand and already aimed. I froze, then grabbed Roscoe's arm and steered us toward the bushes. We were both shaking. I'd never seen rifles in person before. Ransom's words had seemed almost like a dream, unreal, in the beauty and ease of life at Fairhaven, but now they came rushing back.

By the time Reinhardt and Rowan reached the gate, Rune and Riemes were in a killing frenzy, spiky hair sticking up on their backs and drool dripping from bared teeth, which looked ready to rip into the flesh of an intruder. They growled and barked, insane with rage.

"What have we got here?" Reinhardt asked the guard on duty.

"New gardeners, sir," he responded.

Gardeners? I thought. Who the heck gets out rifles for gardeners?

"Did our contracted company notify you of any change in personnel?" Reinhardt asked.

"No, sir," the guard said. "It's their usual truck, I checked the plates, but the two blokes inside are new."

"New or not, they should've been briefed on the protocol. Call the company and have these guys verified," interrupted Rowan. He squinted without moving his gun, trying to get a look at the men in the cab, who were squirming and seemed very nervous.

Reinhardt raised his to the window and the gardeners threw their hands up. "*Qui est votre employeur? Pourquoi ne savons-nous qui vous êtes?*" Reinhardt asked.

"*Nous sommes temporairement remplacement Giles et Marcel. Ils sont tous les deux malades avec la grippe,*" the driver responded.

"Check out their story and let me know what the company says, but don't give them access until we know everything about them. Also, have their supervisor call me. I want to know why they're not following protocol," Reinhardt said. He snapped his fingers as he turned, and suddenly, docile as lambs, the dogs turned and snuffled after him. They returned to the south terrace where the other Drakers had gathered.

"A change of gardeners. It may be nothing, but they've been sent away until the company verifies the change," Reinhardt said.

Everyone looked incommensurately uncomfortable at this news. Their tension and discomfort were unnerving.

Cold force has a way of finding you… They'll never stop hunting you. Ransom's words whispered in my head. This was real. Why wouldn't a large-scale operation like this Cold Force be able to locate us? How hard could it be? Then again, how many years had these people been walled up here? Why on earth would they suddenly get found out now? I stood there trembling, searching the faces of the "Rs," hoping for answers. "It's just a change of gardening personnel. What's the big deal?" I asked, breaking my silent treatment.

"We can't take things for granted, Ruby," Rosalind said. It was the first time she'd said something to me without smirking.

"You're right, Ruby," Reinhardt said, looking at me. "It may be an innocent oversight on the part of our landscapers. We don't need to overreact. We'll know soon enough who these new gardeners are, and we have their faces on camera. Renegade is running the images through our facial recognition software right now." He looked at me more intently. "We should all relax. We can deal with whatever comes, gardener or not."

Six

Every day I learned new things about the Drakers. And despite myself, I was learning things about Ruby, too. But with all of us standing in the bright sunshine worrying about whether our lives were in danger, I struggled with the hundreds of questions roiling around in my mind, knowing I had to bite my tongue, to wait to ask them. One part of me was supposed to be at the mall with my friends, but this felt entirely like I'd been plunked down in someone else's story, and the other side of me, this new side, Ruby, was taut and ready to spring into a kind of defensive action I'd never felt before. Like protection. Like the way I felt about Johnny. Teeth-bared tiger-type protection.

Their faces and body language told me that there was much more than what met the eye here. We were circling each other, both parties waiting.

We'll deal with what comes, Reinhardt had said. And it turned out to be nothing. They were legitimate gardeners, substituting for the usual guys. But something had awakened in me during those moments when the guns were drawn and everyone's bodies were poised to take action in ways I hadn't seen. Something life and death was lurking on the outside of these walls. And I was slowly coming closer to the idea that

I was a part of this. This was my life now. And, I began to let myself think, I was ready for it. I took to starting my day with power lunges and squats and a hundred sit-ups. In between each rep, I thought, bring it on.

I decided enough was enough. If I was a part of this, if I was Ruby Draker the way they were Roscoe Draker and Rose Draker and Rosalind Draker, then they needed to start being upfront about some things. I'd had enough with being docile and silent. If they weren't going to be forthright with the details, I'd have to find out for myself.

I finished my workout, showered, pinned back my hair, which had grown quite long and highlighted by the sun, and put my damp jogging shoes back on so I'd make no noise. I began investigating the rooms, looking behind panels and paintings. When the gardeners showed up, Reinhardt had emerged from the house carrying a rifle where seconds before he'd seemingly been nowhere.

I closed my eyes as I ran my fingers under antique tables and beneath the staples of sofas. I'd be patient and diligent. I knew also that the Drakers knew what I was up to. I didn't see a soul during my haunts, but I knew they were watching me as I was watching them.

The next morning when I came back from doing sprints, I was caught off guard by Rose, Rachel, and Rosalind, who were looking through the large wooden wardrobe in my room. We stared at each other in surprise. I don't think they expected me to walk in on them. Or maybe they did. I went out for my run at about the same time every day.

"What are you looking for?" I asked.

Rosalind held open the door and pointed into the empty expanse of the wardrobe. They'd increased my wardrobe from one shirt and one pair of jeans to three shirts and two gauzy skirts and that same pair of jeans, but all things considered, it was pretty paltry.

"We're looking at your wardrobe," Rosalind said, winking, "and we're thinking that now that you're settled in, you might want to choose a few things yourself that you like in order to, let's say, round out your options. Are you up for some shopping?"

"There are some lovely places in town you can choose from," Rose said.

"Or, even better, we can arrange for a private showing at Chez Frédéric," Rachel added. She beamed as if going there were her most favorite activity ever. She glanced over at Rosalind with a peculiar tilt of her head, her eyes blinking and shifting among them.

My suspicions were aroused; I took a moment to consider my answer. I wasn't convinced that their motives weren't entirely about the lack of fashion I displayed, although they were always well-attired in beautiful and expensive clothing. I had the feeling I'd been wearing their version of a prison inmate's jumpsuit and now I was getting an upgrade for good behavior.

I decided to play along. "Sure," I said magnanimously. "A day of shopping with my mom and aunties is just the thing I need. When should I be ready?" I opened my new eyelids wide. "Can't wait!"

They glanced bemusedly at one another before smiling at me. A tickle started at the back of my brain. We were going out. In public. They wouldn't dare chain me, would they? And I was strong enough now that I could kick Rose away if she came at me with a needle. I'd never thought like this before. Ruby had barreled in and was in top scheming mode. I nodded and smiled widely in return.

"I just need to discuss with Reinhardt the best means of transportation and cover."

There it was again, the mystery, the secrecy.

I conjured up a vision of armored cars and assault rifles ramming through the glass front of Chez Frédéric, racks of designer gowns thrown into the air, then bolting from our vehicle, go, go, go! like a SWAT team, forming a circle around the saleswomen as Rosalind and her cronies ransacked the racks, yanked out some things, and with their arms full, climbed back into our car, everyone piling in, throwing it into reverse, and racing away, tires screeching, leaving tracks on the exclusive, perfumed street.

"Perhaps we can make a day of it," she added. "Reinhardt and the boys may want to join us. Wouldn't that be fun, a typical family outing?"

I shook myself from my hilarious daydream, still smiling at the thought of it. Oh, yes. I couldn't wait. There was nothing typical about this bunch. But I was curious to see how it would work logistically, what kind of cover we'd have. Couldn't just march this crowd into a store.

"I'm going now to chat with him. We'll leave this afternoon." Rosalind looked me over. "Ruby, darling," Rosalind said, affectionately touching my sweaty hair. "Get yourself ready. We're going shopping."

Obviously this had already been planned. Whatever they had in mind for me, I figured I could handle. I cleaned myself up and pulled on my jeans and one of the T-shirts. I went downstairs to meet up with my fictitious family. Rosalind had mentioned the boys might like to come, but I thought she was just thinking out loud. When the whole crowd was standing at the door with two SUVs already running outside, I was taken aback. I hoped this wasn't an ambush, though if it were, it'd be a jaunty one. Everyone looked enlivened. It could've just been that hanging out at the house, albeit an enormous one, would make anyone stir crazy.

Reinhardt handed me a baseball hat and sunglasses. "Here, Ruby," he said. "Can't be too careful about the sun."

That's when I realized that every person was wearing a hat and glasses; the women in stylish floppy brimmed hats that matched their dresses, and the men in ball caps with yachting logos. A small gesture, but I did notice that the accessories drew the eye as well as hid everyone's faces. I felt embarrassed then to be so under-dressed. Maybe they'd let me wear something out of the store. My mom used to let me do that at Buster Brown.

A lump started in my throat, which I coughed to clear away. Hey, it wasn't my money, so I was ready to do some serious shopping. "Chez Frédéric, here we come," I joked. "Get yourself ready for the Drakers!"

They snickered and Reinhardt pulled the large door shut behind us. Ransom was at the back door of one of the SUVs holding it open for me. I hadn't seen him since the gardener incident. His dark hair glinted in the sun. I looked up into his eyes, but they were trained on my mouth.

"Dibs!" shouted Roscoe who slid in from the opposite side.

I got in and sat in the middle, while Ransom climbed in after me and shut the door. I could smell the heat coming off of his skin. His forearm resting on his thigh was bronzed and smooth. I looked ahead as Rowan jumped into the driver's seat, patted his perfectly coiffed hair in the rear view mirror and adjusted his over-sized sunglasses.

Rose got into the passenger front seat and turned around to look at us. "Oh, look at that tasty little sandwich," she said with a bit of a sneer before letting it melt and turning around. "Sure you won't get carsick sitting in the middle like that, Ruby?"

"I'm fine," I said.

We drove off and everyone, it seemed, slipped into his own reverie as we descended the curved mountain roads. We drove for forty minutes in silence to downtown Nice, the ride feeling leisurely and pleasant as we passed breathtaking scenery of the azure Mediterranean and houses draped with fuchsia and orange bougainvillea.

As opposed to when I first arrived, on this sun-dappled afternoon, Nice was spectacular with its precipitous cliff entry overlooking the harbor and the airport. The main road along the oceanfront bustled with cars, rollerbladers, runners and vendors operating businesses out of neat white tents. A few tenacious bathers braved the rocky beach to work on their tans as yachts, ferries and the cruise liners sailed blithely past.

Rowan turned off onto one of the many streets running perpendicular off the main thoroughfare. Several confusing turns later, we arrived at an imposing three-story cement building and he stopped the car.

The boutique was incongruous to the rest of the area, looking more like an art deco bank than a place to buy clothes. I followed the scroll work and heavy window ledges like eyebrows up with my eye as we parked. At the top of the building, two domes flanking a center obelisk pointing up to the sky made it look as if the building were giving the world the finger. I had a sudden, irrational longing for the Gap.

Rose headed toward the limestone steps before stopping at the top landing and turning to look back at the car.

When Ransom stepped out he offered me his hand to help me from the car. He let his eyes linger on me for longer than necessary. I couldn't help but look back. With him beside me in the car all those minutes, his scent floating out over me, I couldn't help it.

But then I had to look away at Rose's hard tone. "Come on, child. Let's go."

I felt embarrassed then, and trudged up the stairs.

"Ciao, ladies," Ransom called and hopped into the front seat beside Rowan. He saluted through the open window and they drove off. We joined up with Rosalind and Rachel before Reinhardt followed the first car.

"Where are the guys off to?" I asked.

"They're going to shop for clothes for Roscoe," Rachel said. "He's outgrown his pants again and of course his video games."

"Oh, yes," Rose said. "He has a favorite games store here in town. That should keep the fellas occupied for hours while we do lady stuff." They glanced critically up and down the street before we entered the front doors.

The lobby was just as intimidating as the exterior. Marble was everywhere—and gold. And a crystal chandelier hung off a domed ceiling cast a tinkling light over everything, making the lobby look like the inside of a glass of champagne. A glass-fronted elevator pinged across from the entry door.

We went through the foyer to a snipped-looking blond receptionist behind the marble desk. "*Nous avons rendez-vous avec Frédéric,*" Rosalind said in rapid-fire French. For just a moment, my mouth hung open at how easily she and Reinhardt slipped into the language without thinking.

"*Puis-je avoir votre nom, madame?*" the receptionist asked.

"*Il sera répertorié sous les initiales RD,*" Rosalind said.

The receptionist returned a condescending look but picked up her phone and announced that RD had arrived.

"*Oui, je vais l'envoyer tout de suite,*" she answered and then turned to us and said in English. "You may go right up. Please take the elevator to the third floor. Frédéric is expecting you."

Rosalind's disdainful look matched that of the frosted blond Chihuahua's who'd let us up. "How'd she know you were American?" I had to ask.

Rosalind's mouth was in a thin line. "I haven't been speaking French as much lately and slipped a bit on the 'r'."

The elevator doors opened on the third floor with a ping. A man dressed in an impeccably tailored, pigeon-gray suit was standing there to greet us. The left corner of his upper lip turned up slightly, forming a condescending smile as his eyes scanned quickly but obviously across each of our breasts. He extended both of his arms to embrace Rosalind with a kiss before she asserted her right hand within inches of his face.

"Madame Draker, how lovely to see you," he said, sneering slightly at her gesture.

"*Bonjour, Frédéric,*" Rosalind returned, her voice suddenly clipped, all business. "Have you prepared some items appropriate for my daughter?"

"Of course, Madame," Frédéric said. "I believe both you and your daughter will be delighted with our designs this season. And," he paused, "your sisters as well." He opened his lips for a toothy smile, which he flashed at all of us. "Please," he gestured to a beige sofa with claw feet. "Come this way."

Flutes of sparkling water were on a tray on a side table. The room was empty apart from enormous gilt mirrors. "Where are the clothes?" I whispered to Rachel next to me.

A stunning willowy woman wearing a black silk sheath came out from behind a velvet curtain and asked, "May we offer you another beverage, Mesdames?"

I was inordinately nervous and wondered if I should ask for something stronger, but Rosalind was already shaking her head. "Water is fine. We're ready to see this amazing collection of which you speak."

It was clear that Frédéric was no fan of a woman coming into his house and ordering him around. He let his smile drop and his lids fall halfway before he clapped his hands together. "Oui, Madame."

A reed-thin model emerged from behind the curtain, with cheekbones so high, they could have been footholds on a mountainside, and Frédéric took her hand as he described the outfit she was wearing. When he was done, he twirled her around, patted her on her tiny bottom, and sent her back to the curtain. He clapped his hands and another emaciated model strode from behind a curtained area, walked toward us, turned with arms holding open a jacket worn over a silk shirt and purposefully faded denim harem pants. I didn't even see the clothes I was so busy watching this creep.

When the second model arrived, Frédéric had sat beside me on the sofa. He reeked of lemon verbena, and the black curly hairs on the backs of his fingers were growing over his many rings, one of which was a wedding ring.

"Notice the detail to the stitching on the jacket," he whispered in my ear as he put a hand on my shoulder.

Without looking at him, I removed his hand and put it back on his leg. His touch made my skin crawl but I sensed that he enjoyed my uneasiness.

The model retreated and another emerged from the curtain. More commentary about the virtues of the fabric, color and design followed as each model appeared and the former faded away until I noticed on Rosalind's watch that an hour had passed. One of my legs had fallen asleep.

"Mademoiselle Ruby," Frédéric demurred, "do you have any favorites to try on?"

I could barely remember the clothes and grabbed at any images I could recall. "Um, the two denim pant outfits and the sleeveless short white dress with the shirt collar," I said.

He stood in front of me now and extended his hands to mine. I looked over at Rose and Rosalind who were chatting among themselves and let him pull me up to a standing position in front of him. I could feel his breath on my face. A shiver ran down my neck and a knot twisted in the pit of my stomach.

I resented the women for bringing me here and putting me into the hands of this snake.

"We have prepared a private dressing room for you," he said. He put his hand on the small of my back and guided me to a door at the back of the beige room. He opened it and we stepped inside another much-smaller but still plush room surrounded by floor-to-ceiling mirrors.

The clothes I'd picked were already hanging on a hook.

"Yes, you've made excellent selections for your slender figure," he said, positioning himself behind me to look at the two of us in the mirror. He brushed his hands down from my shoulders to my ribcage, then slowly up over my breasts. He sighed with pleasure and I felt him grow hard behind me.

"Ew!" I screamed. That was it. I'd had enough of this guy. This wasn't real, this wasn't my life. I clenched my teeth, turned and kneed him in the groin, hard, then brought my fist into his neck where I felt his throat crumple beneath my knuckles.

I'd never hit anyone in my life like this. It was amazing. My old me would've never been in this situation, in an exclusive boutique with some slime ball trying to rape me in the change room. They don't do that at the Gap.

Rachel burst through the dressing room door first, then Rose who easily stepped over Frédéric, writhing in the fetal position on the floor in front of me.

Rosalind stood calmly at the door and leaned against the frame. "Are you all right, darling?" she asked.

"I hurt my knee," I answered through closed teeth.

I turned to look at him, my unease become intense rage. I twitched and prepared to kick the pile of shit whimpering on the beige carpet.

But before I could deliver the blow, Rosalind interrupted. "Sophie," she called, "please make the necessary alterations based on Ruby's measurements and notify our security company when they're ready. They'll pick them up."

"*Oui, madame,*" Sophie responded, a look of confused horror on her face.

"*Au revoir, Frédéric,*" Rachel scowled, stepping on the soft part of his palm with her high heel.

Rose glared at him as she grabbed my arm to leave the dressing room.

We wasted no time to get to the elevator and out through the front doors where both the SUVs were already waiting with their engines running.

"How did they know to be here to get us?" I asked.

Rosalind held up her phone. "BBM," she answered.

Ransom hopped out and I hopped into the center back seat. The ladies assumed their same seating from earlier.

"Aren't there any normal stores in Nice? I haven't finished my shopping yet."

Everyone laughed.

"In fact, Rosalind has already notified the concierge at Galleries Lafayette," Rose said. "They have a side entrance and women-only staffed private shoppers."

I had to say I felt relieved.

Two hours later when we got back in the car, loaded with bags of beautiful new things, I felt even better.

Seven

IN THE CAR THE WHOLE RIDE HOME, I thought about the new person I was becoming, this hybrid between my old self and my new. Though I still wanted to hold on to Kathleen, the real me, I had to admit that the Ruby in me was gloating at my triumph. I felt so pulled in two directions as I tried to stay connected to my family whom I desperately missed, but with each new experience that the Ruby side of me conquered, I could see Kathleen was fading into the shadows and Ruby, so supported and nurtured by the Drakers, was taking over my personality just a little bit more.

Exhausted and hungry, I dropped the shopping bags on my bed and went downstairs for dinner. Cook had anticipated our late arrival and had the evening meal prepared for us. Dinner was usually in the cozy smaller dining room, but tonight it was set up in the solarium where the windows gave the best view of the sunset, blending on the horizon bright orange against the sea that had already changed from azure to a deeper blue. As the evening waned, the sky flamed with a brilliant magenta that within the following minutes would melt into darkness, leaving only the full moon illuminating the summer night sky over the black waters of the Mediterranean.

The food had been set up on the sideboard in covered stainless steel serving dishes with lit candles underneath to keep them warm. We wasted no time serving ourselves: roast beef, mashed potatoes, spinach with garlic, and roasted baby tomatoes and sat down at the long wooden table, all nine of us, to eat together.

There wasn't much conversation and I noticed the group was pretty jittery and twitchy. I couldn't begin to understand the complicated nature of these people and their motives, so I just tucked into my dinner and tried to ignore the feeling of that man's hands on me. I'd never been touched like that by a boy, by a man, by anyone. I didn't feel violated, I just felt angry. But then I remembered the feeling of his body crumpling over my knee and smiled around my potatoes. Wine bottles were on the table, and though I'd only ever had wine at weddings or a few sips of beer at parties, I poured some into a glass.

Finally, after several uncomfortable minutes, Reinhardt broke the silence. "The boys and I made a bet about today." He pulled twenty Euro from his pocket and handed it to Roscoe who proudly showed it to everyone as if he were Vana White. Reinhardt looked at me and grinned. "He was completely convinced that you'd teach that wannabe Casanova a lesson. Let me be the first to apologize for underestimating you, Ruby. You have truly come a long way. Honestly, I wasn't sure you had it in you."

My heart went cold in my chest. It hit me: I'd been set up. "You knew about that jackass?" I asked.

He ducked his head and put his hands up. "Guilty as charged."

I looked around at all of them. They'd all known. They didn't want to buy me clothes; they wanted to test me, to see how I'd react when I was put into a Petri dish with a sexed-up creep. They wanted to watch and see how I'd rank on some kind of Draker worthiness scale that would either signal that I'd earned a place within their group or... I didn't know what they would do if hadn't "passed" their test, if I'd cowered or cried. Dump me in the river? The Kathleen in me, the nice girl I'd always been, the one who had never been to second base with a boy and always met her curfew, had no intention of succumbing to their influence. So I took on the posture of letting them believe what they wanted to believe.

"Sorry Rosalind," I smirked, "we're probably banned from Chez Frédéric forever." I hated this game; I wasn't sorry at all. Quite the contrary, I wanted to scream at her or throw my plate in her face. She went on and on about being my "mother," but when it came down to it, she was as cold and calculating as the rest of them.

I took a deep breath and stared defiantly at her. My voice was ice cold. I sipped my wine, never taking my eyes off her. I glanced at Rose through narrowed eyes. She had her hands laced together beneath her chin and was smiling, that same smug cat smile as everyone else. I hated her then. Hated every last one of them.

"Not to worry, darling," said Rosalind breezily, waving her hand. "There's always Milan and the selection there is even more superb. We'll take you there sometime."

I rolled my eyes. Great, more shopping! These people were too much. Where they got their money and resources was a whole other can of beans altogether, something I could've cared less about at that moment.

"Of course, next time," she continued, still smiling, "we don't anticipate having to stand outside the dressing room door with our switchblades drawn." She caught my eyes then and laughed.

At first I was confused. Then everyone laughed.

"Darling, did you honestly think we'd leave you alone with that eel? You're a force to be reckoned with, that much we're learning about you, but we most certainly would have put a dagger in his back if we'd needed to."

My anger and embarrassment softened as a round of friendly laughter broke out. Their faces softened, too, almost apologetically. I was still annoyed they'd tested me, but I'd passed, and this celebratory dinner was feeling more and more like some kind of twisted however well-meaning awards ceremony.

Dinner progressed bearing none of the formality and stiffness that was usually present at meals. A round of lively chatter started. We laughed and discussed our purchases, Roscoe's Minecraft game, the Mercedes dealership where the boys wasted time as they waited for us, and restaurants they checked out where we might go out for some fine dining one night. It all sounded so normal, everyone laughing, chatting and sharing our day just like any other normal family. For a time, once the wine kicked in, I relaxed, too, letting myself forget that I didn't trust these people, didn't know them, and despised them for having ruined my life. That in no way were we a family and the circumstances that had brought us together were definitely not normal. For the time of our meal, I decided, even if unconsciously, to let that all go.

Hours passed and the sun had fully set. Only the dim glow of wall sconces in the solarium lit the room now. One by one, the Drakers left the table, calling it a day, until only Rosalind and I remained.

"Ruby, darling," she said, "like it or not, you're a Draker now." She leaned forward and put her small hard hand on mine. "It's not so bad, you know. Of course we all miss the lives we had before, but what we have here is really a very good substitute. We're all happy that you're starting to come around."

I hoped Rosalind's intimate tone meant she was going to start telling me what was really going on, but as I watched her eyes and her steely gaze, I knew she could tell I was still suspicious.

She pursed her lips and pushed herself away from the table. "At some point, Ruby, you will see that our little family isn't just an arrangement by necessity. You may come to realize that we are all we have. And isn't that what family means?"

I stared at her as she left. Alone in the solarium, I looked out at the dark scene beyond the windows, drinking in the romantic setting. Being alone in this mysterious and exotic place aroused loneliness in me again. I hated that emptiness. A part of me wanted to stop pushing these people away. It seemed they were in earnest, but more importantly, it seemed I didn't have a single thing to go back to. Rosalind was right about that.

These people were it.

Back at my room I looked at the bags cluttering up my bed. I was achingly tired and just wanted to sweep it all onto the floor and crawl into the sheets, but I knew in the morning I'd rather not see the mess. I opened the elaborately carved wooden wardrobe and stood in front of its nearly empty space. It was large, over-sized for the room, and I just stood, inhaling the woody smell and admiring the rough boards on the inside. Finally I grabbed the empty hangers and returned to my bed.

After taking off the tags from a polka dot top, I put it on the hangar and buttoned up the top button. When I hung it, the sleeve ruched up so I reached back to pull it down, and the back of my hand bumped into something.

I ducked up and under the shirt to have a look but didn't see anything. Strange, I thought. I stepped into the wardrobe to investigate further. It was dark, so I ran my hands over the protruding wood. There was definitely an open space about four inches wide, creating a false wall. I slid my hand from the bottom to the top where it bumped into an object and clunked loudly. I grasped whatever it was, a handle, maybe, that was latched to a hook by a short cord. I lifted it off and brought the object close to my face. A flashlight. That was weird. I went back inside and felt my way around the unusual design some more. About mid-way in the opening, I felt a metal button. I pulled and tugged, then pushed on it. The closet started to creak and suddenly the panel swung open into an empty dark space. I was both terrified and delighted. This must have been why Rosalind and the others were in my room. Cleverly done, ladies, I thought. I'd believed at the time they were up to something, and sure enough, they were. This time, rather than feel betrayed and manipulated, I actually felt—was it flattered? They seemed to know that I was ready. Ready for what, though, I had no idea.

I fiddled for the switch on the flashlight until it turned on and aimed it at the emptiness: it was a secret passage. Seriously? I leaned in half expecting a monster to jump out, but I was also very curious. Of course I had to go in; it didn't seem I had any choice: the Ruby in me was too strong and seemed to be dying to kick some monster butt.

I felt with my foot and warily stepped inside, discovering a narrow hallway space on the left leading to an even narrower set of stairs about ten feet ahead. I started down the passage a few steps when the same creaking sound that had opened the panel stopped me. I turned quickly, frightened, to exit back to the safety of my closet. The door to the closet was closing. I lunged for it, but it slammed before I reached it.

Panic started in my stomach, and I began banging on it so it'd open. There was nothing there to hold on to, no handle or lever. I trailed the light over the whole panel, but nothing. I was locked in. What if this passage led nowhere? Maybe I'd be locked in here forever to die of thirst and starvation, my skeleton found years in the future by new owners remodeling the house. I punched and pulled and knocked for several more minutes until I finally gave up. I took a couple of deep breaths. I had to calm myself and think. I could only hope that the Drakers were not evil enough to play such a trick on a person. That this was their way of getting rid of me. Even though I'd passed their idiotic test up to this point, they might have figured out they didn't have any use for me.

I didn't have much choice but to go forward and see where the passage led and hopefully find the way out. It must have been put here for a reason. I reassured myself that all secret passages were built to escape some danger, allowing a person trapped in a room to get to a place of safety.

My reasoning comforted me as I inched forward and down the claustrophobic stairwell. I prayed silently that I wouldn't come across any corpses. I would never be strong enough to handle that. no matter how much jogging I did.

I counted thirty-two steps before a wider landing area emerged. I felt around the walls to see if another door would open into another room in the mansion. My hands swept lightly over three of the rough and splintery walls before I noticed another flight of steps that went down further. This stairwell was much darker. I was getting frightened.

Logically I had to believe it descended into a basement, but fear tended to make a person's demons come out. I had to make a choice: either go down further into the unknown or go back to where I started, trapped with no way out.

"Ruby, you idiot," Kathleen scolded me from within, "go back."

I appreciated her caution, but Ruby was my reality right now, and she knew I couldn't go back. The closet door and the portal to the past were sealed. My throat closed tight and my eyes started to tear as memories flooded into the confined darkness of the passageway. Johnny's taunts to chase him, "bet you can't catch me," echoed from behind and faded. I hesitated as I longed to retreat, to return to what was forever lost. My mother's face... I could still see it, but it was losing its shape and contour in my memory. I reached out into the dark, but she disappeared between my fingers. My father's favorite song whistled in my ear, "Ruby, Ruby, when will you be mine," he crooned. Why hadn't I remembered that? The irony stabbed painfully at my gut. It was as if he'd known.

My hands were shaking and sweaty as I tried to hang on to the flashlight. I was so scared, but I inched forward, one footstep at a time, one voice in my head beseeching me to go no further and another louder voice encouraging me, saying I'd find a way out.

In spite of the glow from the flashlight, the musty darkness crowded in around me. I remembered Dante's *Inferno* from English Lit where those who were sentenced for evil deeds received torturous punishments for all eternity. My heart raced and my knees were weak. I started to cry, great heaving silent sobs coming from my gut. I didn't want to die here.

At step number forty, I heard something. Voices. People. I wondered if it were the souls of the condemned, their wails swirling around my head, until I came to what looked like a wall at the end of the tunnel. I stopped crying to listen. I was an idiot. They were people. Real ones.

When I threw up my hand to knock on it, I dropped the flashlight.

"No!" I yelled, and when I bent down to try to find it, my arm hit a handle or something hard off to the side. I stood and put my hand on it, then turned it clockwise.

There was a creaking noise, then the wall began to move, letting in light so bright and white, it pinched my eyes. The wall slid into a pocket in the side wall.

I blinked several times and stared at the room I'd just come into. It looked like the IT hub where my dad had worked: a sterile gray room with very sophisticated computer terminals in each corner, all bearing dual screens. Someone sat at the station closest to the sliding panel that seconds ago had poured me unceremoniously into the room like a rush of water held back by a dam. The door had already slid back into place healing the hole in the wall.

"Took you long enough." My eyes hadn't quite adjusted to brightness of the room, but it sounded like Renegade. He looked at the clock. "Twenty-seven and a half minutes? You'll have to do much better than that in a real evacuation."

"Evacuation?" I said, not knowing where to start lighting into him. "Why the hell would I have to evacuate, and evacuate what?"

Two wall panels opened then and Reinhardt and Ransom came in. They stood still and looked at me.

"What's going on here?" I said throwing my arms in the air. "I feel like I'm surrounded by crazy people!"

"That's one way of phrasing it," said Reinhardt seriously. "In a way, you are. It's just not us. Come," he held out his arm and motioned I should join him. "This is where we monitor where our enemy will strike next," Reinhardt pointed to Renegade's screen. "That's how we knew you and your family were targeted. We tried to save what we thought was all of you, but we were too late for your parents and brother. But because you were late coming home and weren't in the house like you should've been, we were able to rescue you." He smiled. "The ineptitude of the Psych department's ancient electrical system saved your life. And what's more, the people who killed your family didn't notice you were missing; in fact, we didn't know either. It was Robert who spotted you first. Then we had to move quickly before Szabo's assassins noticed that only three bodies would be found."

My stomach plunged. I stared at him. I'd wondered it many times, but now I was exploding. My Dad was a businessman who worked for Intertech and Mom was a real estate agent and Johnny was only ten. I felt like my heart had stopped. I struggled to breathe. I had just started to accept that the Drakers hadn't killed my family, was resigned to the idea that it was a tragic accident. But assassins? Assassins don't happen to real people.

I looked at Reinhardt, trying to determine whether he was being truthful with me or if he were testing me again. If it were the latter, he had some kind of nerve. "How come you were able to save me from a premeditated act, but you couldn't save the rest of my family?" I looked from Reinhardt to the others and then back again with hot eyes.

Ransom's warning flashed through my mind again, as it had been doing throughout every hour of every day of my time with these people. *Cold Force has ways of finding us and when they find you, which they will, they'll kill you. They already know you didn't die in the fire. The body count was short by one female.*

"Why would anyone want to kill us? We were an ordinary suburban family. Who is Szabo?"

"Sit down, Ruby. It's a long and complicated story," Reinhardt said.

I plunked into the closest chair and folded my arms over my chest.

"Felix Szabo was once a powerful man, high in the ranks of the CIA," he started, pulling up a seat to mine. "A man who the American president and leaders of other NATO nations respected. He had great power. He commanded a large team of highly capable agents who had infiltrated the ranks of the Russian government and military, and who secretly accessed information about their nuclear bombs. Back in the '60s, the Russians had prepared for the possibility that, were political tensions to get out of hand, they'd have an inventory of nuclear bombs large enough not just to threaten world security, but to wipe out everyone on the plant. Felix thrived on the power and control that position gave him." Reinhardt sighed. "Felix was orphaned at a very young age and had a sad and lonely childhood. And you're the psychologist here, but it seems that given what he endured growing up, it could make sense that as an adult, he'd try to acquire some power and assert it to compensate."

I couldn't speak. Some guy had a bad childhood so he killed my family? My head was spinning. Reinhardt continued. "In 1991, when the Cold War ended and the threat of nuclear annihilation was diminished by disarmament treaties, the government no longer needed Szabo's department and network of spies, and they dissolved his team. The people were offered buy-out packages that included relocation, which would allow them to live normal lives and have normal careers, all under a government identity protection program. Szabo refused to be 'put out to pasture' or something like this, so to be compassionate, they assigned him an administrative job in charge of keeping Cold War secret documents. He was assigned a minor staff, three agents, who also wanted to remain with the CIA. All of them were retrained as IT officers as their primary function was recording and cataloging data, and that seemed to be that.

"The chief problem is that Felix is a terribly unstable man. Either he suffers from delusion or some equally serious mental condition, or he felt impotent going from being extremely powerful and important to being relegated to head of an archive, but we believe that Felix somehow managed to convince these three former agents that terrorists outside the organization were trying to steal the records they were guarding and start a new reign of nuclear terror. He managed to make them believe the Soviets were still a viable threat and that the 'deserters,' as he labeled them, might sell out American intelligence if offered sufficient remuneration. He even took his concerns to the director of the CIA, but they roundly dismissed his concerns.

"Because the government denied the threat, Felix decided to work in secret right under their noses. It became his mission to eradicate the deserters, along with their entire families, to 'protect American security' he said. He maintained that those people were radicalized terrorists and the safety of the Western World was in his hands alone."

I stared at Reinhardt. He hadn't said the word, but he didn't need to. My parents had been spies. And this guy killed them for trying to move on from that and have a normal life. "All of this," I was shaking my head as if trying to jostle all the thoughts into some kind of order, "is crazy," I said. I guessed by now I could handle my parents' situation, but it was baffling that this person was able to run around killing people. "Why hasn't anyone figured him out? He needs to be locked away!"

"The work he did with the CIA during the Cold War was the only real and meaningful, not just work, but life that Felix had ever known," Reinhardt said. "He stayed with the force rather than risk starting something new." He shook his head. "The guy has never known a life that was normal or happy. And then everything that gave him purpose was ripped away from him. His resentment grew to manic proportions. Not only did he curse the administration who disbanded his department, he conjured up psychotic scenarios that he truly believed in, and swore vengeance on all the agents who took the buyout packages.

"He doesn't have access to the relocation files, which have a much higher level of security clearance above his. Yet as long as he remained employed by the CIA, he has had other ways of getting information as to where the agents have resettled. Felix and his team are masterful at monitoring the Internet, and together with other protected information they do have clearance to access, they've been able to find some of the old team agents. And nowadays, it's nearly impossible to avoid ending up on the Internet sooner or later. And once evidence of a person is found, it's easy to get an address. That's when he arranges 'accidents' that look legitimate and don't provoke further investigation."

"How could the CIA not be onto him?" This couldn't be possible, that this guy was doing all of this without anyone finding out.

Ransom's voice was sharp. "He's clever and so far has managed to stay under the radar," he said. "But there's more. Tell her, Reinhardt."

Reinhardt raised one eyebrow at Ransom. "Let's not get hysterical about this," he said. "We can't verify that Felix suspects that Ruby got away. Even if he knows, he has no way of recognizing her, finding our location, or associating her with us. He has no reason to think that any of us are still alive, looking for him and trying to bring him down."

"It's naive to think that he doesn't suspect anything if you ask me," Ransom said. "I'm still not convinced that the new gardener's incident is what it seems."

"So, wait," I said. "If bringing me here puts you all at risk, then I don't understand why you'd do it. It's not like you owed me or my family anything."

"Almost everyone here has lost family members to Felix's revenge," Ransom said. "He's turned into a psychopathic killer. He's making everyone who 'abandoned him'," he angrily made air quotes, "pay for his loss of power."

"How can you possibly know that?" I asked.

"Because," Ransom said, "I joined his staff in the CIA Archives Department and unwittingly became one of his accomplices. I was hired in 2010, but I had no idea what was going on or how he operated. When I finally put some of his odd behavior together with several odd things I'd come across, I realized what he was doing. I put in for a resignation, but that red-flagged him that I was on to him, so he arranged a car explosion, a 'manufacturer's defect' they determined it was, to kill me. Seems he hired people to rig my car to explode while I was driving home from the agency. But—and here's what he hadn't counted on—for some reason, I hadn't fastened my seat belt yet and was thrown clear of the blast. Reinhardt and Robert came and found me in the scrub brush off the side of the road. I spent months in a private hospital outside of Washington, where I healed." He held up his elbow, which had suture marks in it. "Pins," he said somberly. "And they got me facial reconstruction. I know how his mind works, and let me tell you, this man will stop at nothing if you're on his hit list."

Just then, a wall panel on the opposite side to the secret passage buzzed open and Rosalind entered. She strode into the room straight-backed, her ample chest leading the way, high heels clicking loudly on the tiled floor. A serious look lined her face. "I trust you've filled her in," she said. She looked at the three men as she went to Renegade's computer station and motioned that he should get up. "I'll take a four-hour shift now. You can get some sleep."

Renegade stretched and stood to make room for her.

"How much time do you spend down here, and what exactly are you watching for?" I asked.

"Apart from meals or special occasions like today, we make sure someone is here around the clock," Renegade said. "And even then, the system notifies our cell phones if the facial recognition program sees a match. Come on, Ruby. I'll show the not-so-secret way out."

"Ruby," Rosalind said with her back to the room. "Now that you know everything, tomorrow you begin your training. We've developed a training program very similar to the one used by the CIA to train their spies. You've shown us you can handle yourself under pressure. We know you're ready." She turned around to face me. "But it takes a lot more than being a good runner able to find secret doors to survive in this world. You'll receive self-defense maneuvers to start and will learn to use a gun. Your life, and ours, may depend on it."

I put up my hands. "Oh, no, I'm not shooting anyone," I said. I was surprised, given all that had happened over the last weeks, to hear that come from my mouth. Maybe Kathleen was asserting her pacifism, the girl who liked to scout the neighborhood for wounded birds and insects so we could set up a hospital. Her voice was getting quieter and less in control. I could quiet her; the Ruby in me couldn't wait to start. I could already feel my palm wrapping around the cold steel of a pistol.

"And, Ruby," Rosalind said as Renegade was guiding me to the main exit that led back to the house, "don't forget to put the flashlight back in the closet. Trust me. You might need it someday."

Eight

I TOSSED AND TURNED ALL NIGHT. There was so much that my parents
had kept from me, secrets that festered like an unattended sore. I tried
to imagine what Felix Szabo looked like, what made him so hateful that
he'd kill innocent people, their families, and their young children. I was
beginning to think of myself as two halves of one person. The person
I'd always been had empathy and compassion for people even when
they were at their most troubled, the chief reason I chose to go into
psychology. Oh, man, I thought, my Abnormal Psych class would have
had a field day with this guy.

I had to snort at that. I'm sure I would've made them salivate as
well, considering how my life had changed. Over the last few weeks I'd
become harder, stopped feeling pitted and gauged by circumstances, by
my grief. I knew that in the face of extreme loss, when "the everything"
that holds your world together is suddenly gone, your values, morals
and humanity can get lost as well. The inability to grab onto a thread of
something that makes you feel secure and valued fills a person with ugly
feelings, often a desire for revenge, which cheaply and easily fills the
empty shell that's left behind. That's how people who suffer often
morph into a distorted and ugly version of the people they once were.

I hit my pillow. Was that what happened to Felix? Was that what was going to happen to me?

Sleep refused to come. I fought with docile, peace-loving Kathleen who would never so much as look at a gun let alone use it to shoot someone, even in self-defense. But I knew that Kathleen wouldn't last long in this reality. The world we lived in now was a very dangerous place. It wasn't a place where Kathleen would want to be.

So it was agreed. If I were going to protect any last vestige of who I was, I had to put her away. At least for now. Where she'd be safe.

I jogged the next morning to the temple, the place that had become my sanctuary, where I searched and waited for messages of hope and deliverance. The sun was rising over the water and the warm breeze blew my ponytail gently over my face. I jogged slowly, busy with the conversation that played out in my head. At the rose garden, I paused and carefully bent the thorny stem of a white rose until it peeled away from the plant. I took the dewy flower and walked slowly up the steps to the temple precipice and sat down. I marveled how one place could so easily separate two worlds: the corrupt world of human transgressions, and the sea, where nature simply existed, ambivalent to people and their ridiculous machinations.

A single tear slid wet, warm, and slowly down my cheek. For several minutes, I stared at the rose in my hand without seeing it before I kissed the velvety, pure white petals and threw the flower forcefully into the wind, into the peace and the beauty of the universe beyond, letting it carry into the water. A thorn tore the skin of my pointer finger releasing bright red blood that dripped and was also carried away.

"Goodbye, Kathleen," I whispered as it disappeared from view. Maybe I'll see you again someday, I thought. But I knew I wouldn't.

Free of the crippling doubt and fear that I had harbored all this time, I decided from there on in, I would only look ahead. The past just held grief and memories that hurt; the future needed more attention. It was daunting and precarious, and it depended on secrecy, physical strength, and above all, a keen sense for danger. I took my time returning to the manor and walked over to the side yard where the Drakers had set up a shooting range.

Rosalind was waiting for me. I wasn't surprised by this; hers and the Drakers' innate ability to understand me had become a comfort rather than a surprise. I welcomed seeing her face, kind but also extremely serious.

On the green manicured lawn of Fairhaven cluttered with effigies and bullseye target circles, I began my practice. We used a variety of weapons to take down the artificial representations of our enemy. Rosalind didn't allow even the smallest infraction. She was a relentless drill sergeant demanding a perfect aim and hit every time, and soon, she wanted to see more: stealth and cunning, finesse, and an ability to find an alternate method should the first fail.

This became far more than just target practice. She trained me physically as well, defining my body, upping my speed and agility. Every day I was exhausted, but thrilled. Poor Kathleen had always wanted to be able to do the splits. All those years at the community gymnastics classes and she could never quite get her hamstrings to go down all the way. Now I melted into splits easily as if I were sitting in a chair. Rosalind forced me to go further, harder and faster, reminding me that my life might just depend on it one day.

Renegade came to watch one afternoon and chuckled. "You and Rosalind doing a little cat fighting?" he asked, munching on an apple.

I smiled sweetly and flipped him onto his back before he could finish his bite. I then turned to the punching bag and delivered a series of kicks and a roundhouse to the side for good measure.

His eyes were big and he was grinning widely as I helped him up.

Even though Ruby was ready for it, when Rosalind put the first gun in my hand, I felt nervous in a new and awful way. I didn't feel the same kind of control I felt when I was using my own body. It was heavier than what I'd expected, and when I squeezed the trigger the first time, the shot went wildly off the target even though I'd thought I had aimed perfectly. The force of the bullet as it exploded through the shaft threw my hand astray and I dropped the gun like a scalding pot. Rosalind's quiet disapproval aside, the smell of it, the pungent hot metal, sickened my stomach.

She brought it back to me and positioned it in my hand. "Try it again," she said firmly but gently. "Concentrate. Hold it with respect. Keep your feet planted, and recognize the power you have."

It was weeks of this kind of training, probably thousands of bullets, Rosalind patient and firm like a parent, until I felt like it was an extension of my arm, like it was mine. My aim became excellent. Then I learned to fire the others' weapons, too, in case mine was ever taken from me.

Where earlier, when I was still new at Fairhaven, it seemed the other Drakers just disappeared during the day to do who knew what, now I saw how busy and committed they were. In addition to keeping watch in the control room, each kept his defense skills sharp, the lawn serving as their practice field as well an underground gym. Renegade, who'd let me take him down without a fight, was actually a martial arts master; Rose and Ransom excelled at Krav Maga; and even at thirteen, Roscoe was an excellent marksman. I hated that his young mind and spirit had to be inculcated in this way, growing up under Felix's searching eyes and constant watch. We had become very close, and I opened my heart to him. He felt like a brother to me. I watched his sad and grieving personality turn from innocence to determination, his self-confidence growing with the knowledge that he might have to one day act to protect his family—his pseudo family—but nonetheless the only family he had. For him, the price to pay seemed small in comparison: he just had to lose his childhood in the process.

Some weeks into my training, Rosalind brought me a revolver she felt was suitable for me. It was little, sleek, and very dangerous. I hefted it and liked how it fit comfortably in my hand. She gave me a waist and calf holster so I could see where I preferred to carry it, and I found I liked it at my waist and began wearing it every day. I especially felt ready for anything on our rare trips away from Fairhaven. Our lot in life as Drakers meant being ready for anything. The more I learned about Felix, the more I learned about the complex web of people he maintained over the globe. His eyes were everywhere. And though he was insane, he was no fool. He knew what he was doing.

When we weren't training, we took turns watching the computers for matches from the Facial Recognition Program. Renegade was our resident computer expert. He showed me how to run daily backups freeing up the hard drives for the constant influx of new data. This came easily to me as Dad had always showed me things on his own computer. He'd been proud of me no matter what, but I'd always known he had secretly wished I'd go into computer science because I loved all things technical and I think he wanted us to share that. The summer before, he'd gotten me an internship in his department at Intertech and I think he'd hoped it would ignite the fire in me to change my major.

The day after day monitoring, the constantly searching for clues that would give away Felix's next target, was tedious, but this was how they knew who the next victim might be. And so, we sat.

I'd been on surveillance for about a month, only and always seeing "no matches found." It seemed like such a waste of time when there had to be other methods out there for intercepting this guy. But finally, one afternoon, the program found a match. On the monitor was a newspaper picture of four men in a dimly lit bowling alley in Portland, Maine. Their arms were around each other's shoulders and a trophy stood on the table in front of them. The caption read, Bunions Win at Pins and listed the names of the team: Henry Adams, Sam Newman, Reggie Ragusso, and in the corner darkened by shadows, Lenard Johnson, proudly holding a bowling ball at his chest, an eagle tattoo spanning his upper arm. Lenard's image was in shadow and a casual observer wouldn't be able to recognize the nose on his face, but the program corrected the image's light and found it a perfect match. His real name was Pietre Vanitch, Szabo's most successful soviet infiltrator. Vanitch's CIA file image came up on the display opposite the photo.

"So what do we do now?" I asked. "Is there any reason to suspect that Szabo will order an attack on him?"

"Szabo no doubt has already ordered his accidental execution," Ransom said dryly.

"The only thing we can do now is try to get to Lenard before Szabo's hit men do," Reinhardt said. He stood and looked at his watch. "It's an eight-hour flight plus we need extra to prepare the plane."

Renegade was already dialing. "We can probably be on our way to Portland within an hour," he said. He held up a finger. "Yes, this is RD. Right, a Challenger. As soon as possible."

My chest began to thump. "I want to go with you," I said. "I want to help you catch this guy, put him away in some dark deep hole where he'll rot for the rest of his life. Do you think that if we caught the assassins in the act and turned them over to the authorities, their testimony would be enough to arrest Szabo?" I was trembling and on the verge of tears.

Rosalind put her arm around my waist and squeezed. "That's my girl," she said. "But Ruby, we've been at this for a while." Her voice was quiet. "He's clever and very slippery. Not an easy man to catch. We don't take anything for granted. Every one of our rescue missions has been dangerous, and as you saw with your own family, only partially successful, if at all." She shook her head. "Felix is very good at what he does. He's in and out before anyone has a chance to blink."

"Rosalind, are you su—" started Reinhardt, looking at me, his brow furrowed.

She smiled a cat's smile and squeezed my waist again. "Go get yourself ready, darling."

I looked at the men. Reinhardt and Ransom didn't look comfortable, but I was right about Rosalind: she was not someone you argued with. I wondered how she held such authority over the Drakers.

Renegade hung up. "OK, so, the charter service has a plane and they'll have it ready by the time we get there." He slapped his hands to his thighs and stood. "I'll get the car."

"I'll just pack a few things," I said as I prepared to leave the room.

"No need, darling. I suspected this day would be coming, and I've already looked after that," Rosalind said. "Your bag is waiting for you in the foyer."

Reinhardt and Ransom were already on the move to the door. This was happening so fast. My stomach dropped. Everything we'd prepared for was actually happening. I wasn't entirely sure I felt ready to do this, whatever "this" was.

But Rosalind was. "Ruby, just one thing," Rosalind called after me as I walked out of the monitoring room. "Try not to get yourself killed."

***

It was already dark when we landed at Portland International Jetport. I was amazed at the precision of all the arrangements. The Drakers had clearly done this several times before. We cleared easily through immigration; nothing in our forged passports was questioned, and within minutes of landing, we walked out of the terminal doors into the brightly lit pick-up area where Robert was waiting with a black SUV, the same kind I'd first been brought to the airport in. I had a brief flash of residual fear getting into the car but shook it off. Things were different now. We jumped into the running vehicle and drove off into the night.

"There are already cars casing Lenard's house," Robert said. "At the very least, Szabo has him on watch. If we go now, we have a small chance of intercepting him. I have your weapons in the back."

My stomach went into a knot. We hadn't flown with our weapons, obviously, and I'd childishly hoped we wouldn't need them once we got to the U.S. It's not that I was worried about my ability to use mine. Rosalind had perfected my aim so I could shoot the nose hairs off a fly. But the thought of having the bullet connect with a real person, possibly an innocent person, made me feel sick.

"How long before we get there?" Reinhardt asked.

"It's only a ten-minute drive, but given the activity at the house up to now, it's a strong possibility that the job's already been done."

"Another fire?" Ransom asked, glancing at me.

"I doubt it," Robert said. "You know Szabo. He'll make it more interesting than that."

The highway sign read Congress Street and we drove only a few minutes before taking the Edwards Street exit into a residential area. It was just after 11:30 p.m. The street lights glowed and only some of the clapboard and brick houses had lights on inside.

We drove up to a simple gray colonial near the end of the street. A white sedan was parked in the driveway and another dark Ford sedan was parked across the street, but the house was dark.

Robert rolled to a stop, evaluating the scene for anything suspicious. "Ransom and I will cover the house from the back," Robert said. "You and Ruby knock on the door and see if Lenard answers."

We gave Robert and Ransom a few minutes to get into position behind the house before Reinhardt and I left the car. We approached the front door with caution, carefully scrutinizing any street activity or noises behind us. Everything seemed quiet, just a normal evening. Behind us, a cat yowled. We rang the doorbell and waited. After a few minutes, when no one answered, we rang it again. This time, there was movement inside, some scuffling. The door opened, and an irritated man who looked like the man in the bowling picture stared back at us.

"Do you guys know what time it is?" he asked.

"Lenard Johnson?" Reinhardt asked.

He hesitated. "Who wants to know?"

"I can explain everything, but if you are Mr. Johnson, your life may be in danger."

"I'm not going anywhere, with anyone," he said. "Now get the hell out of here, or I'll call the police."

I noticed that while Johnson's tone was brusque, his eyes were wide. There was fear in them. He knew we weren't there to rob his house.

"I suggest that you come quietly," Ransom said. Robert and Ransom had entered the house from a back entrance. Ransom locked him in a grip from behind with a gun poking into his back.

"Let's go," Robert said. "We've gotten here before Szabo's men."

"Szabo?" Lenard argued. "How do you guys know about Felix? What's going on here?" Lenard paused then elbowed Ransom, freeing himself while Ransom bent over and gasped, but Robert was ready as back up and knocked him off his feet. He held Lenard firmly with his face tightly against the floor and a gun to his head.

"Lenard," Robert said. "We don't have time for this."

Lenard was yelling, becoming hysterical, so Reinhardt nodded to Ransom who despite looking quite nauseous, quickly pulled a hypodermic needle from the pouch on his belt and jabbed it into Lenard's thigh. Within seconds, Lenard flopped over, and the men lifted him like a sack of grain and took him to our waiting SUV. We drove off with me in the front and Reinhardt and Ransom in the back with Lenard slouched between the two of them.

"I have a motel room on Westbrook just outside of the city," Robert said. "We can hole up there while we monitor Lenard's house. If we need to get out of there immediately, the airport is just a couple of minutes away."

The Congress Motor Inn was a shabby bungalow-style motel just off the highway. We drove up to the unit at the end of the building, parked in front and quickly went inside, the boys depositing Lenard roughly on the first of two double beds.

I looked around at the rust and lamé wallpaper, the warped wood paneling, and the coin slot beside the bed, and decided that though I didn't want to, I had to use the bathroom at some point. I was glad when I got inside that at least it was clean and had soap and white towels. When I came out, Ransom was perched on the second bed, atop the 1979 style bedspread with a sunflower motif. He was flicking through the TV channels with an aged remote until he landed on the local news. A small bar fridge nestled into the cabinetry hummed noisily between the drawers. I settled into a peeling beige recliner near the window while Robert opened the fridge and pulled out a plastic triangle.

"Sandwich?" he asked, holding it out to me.

I was hungry, but something about what had just taken place made me uneasy and my stomach was rebelling. I waved it away.

"There's lots. I put everything in before I picked you up," he said, unwrapping it for himself. He then threw Ransom and Reinhardt cellophane-wrapped triangles and Cokes. I turned and kept a finger on the curtain, which vibrated every time a car drove by on the road. The feeling that something wasn't right lingered uncomfortably inside me.

I must have dozed off because when I awoke, the clock on the bedside table showed 12:30 a.m. Lenard was moving around and moaning. I was surprised to see Ransom sleeping like a baby in the second bed. I wondered, as I let myself look at him for a second, what his face used to look like. When Reinhardt and Robert, who were watching Lenard with their pistols loosely in their hands, saw that I was awake, they stretched and straightened their backs.

"Did you find it strange that Lenard's place was so quiet? You'd said you saw all kinds of activity earlier. And we were at least twelve hours behind the photo appearing in the newspaper. Wouldn't it make sense that Felix would beat us here? Especially since he's only like an hour away?"

"You're right, Ruby," Ransom said from the bed, his voice as bright and alert as if he'd been awake the whole time.

I was horrified; I prayed he hadn't seen me watching him.

He swung his legs off the side of the bed and looked at us for confirmation that Lenard's actions were not what were expected.

"That is suspicious," started Reinhardt, "and something else that's bothering me is Lenard should have recognized me. Years ago, we worked a job together. My face is the same. I didn't have any facial reconstruction to change my appearance. He may have been in shock or too caught off guard, but he seemed to have no idea who I was."

"Well, you are twenty years older," Ransom said. "And anyway, he probably doesn't even think much about his past."

"Let's not kid ourselves," Robert said. "We may not talk about it, but we always remember our spy days."

"Does anyone have access to that bowling photo?" I asked.

"The laptop is locked up in the car," said Reinhardt, "but here," he said, pulling out his cell phone. He held up the digital image, placing it next to Lenard's face. The shadow of the photograph made it difficult to confirm that the man lying on the bed was, in fact, Lenard Johnson.

Then I remembered. "Roll up his sleeve," I said.

Robert grinned at me, surprised that I had noticed a detail they'd missed. He roughly yanked the sleeve upward to reveal the man's arm. The tattoo of an eagle on his bicep would have confirmed his identity if it weren't for the clarity and brightness of the colors.

"Very pretty," said Robert, sighing. "Looks like he just got it yesterday."

"Shit," the men said in unison.

"Well, then who is this?" yelped Ransom. "Damn it. We should have searched the house." He turned and began pacing, his hand raking through his thick hair. On the TV, the muffled voice of the newscaster came on. We turned in time to see the headline scrolling at the bottom of the screen: MAN FOUND DEAD ON EDWARD STREET. BEDROOM WINDOW BROKEN AND HOUSE CONTENTS DISRUPTED. POLICE SUSPECT A CONFRONTATION WITH AN INTRUDER TO BE THE CAUSE.

The man on the bed moaned and tried to get up. "Whaa… going on?" he muttered.

We just sat there trying to catch up. Our rescue mission had turned into a sting. "So this means Felix Szabo is on to us? He knows that someone is interfering with his killing raids?" I asked. "This changes everything. He's trying to figure out who we are."

"Our fake Lenard knows what we look like," Robert said. "Our identities aren't secure any more." He looked at the man and drew his gun.

That woke Fake Lenard up; he began to scream, but then there was a screech of tires and car doors slamming. We all drew our guns at once. Robert and Reinhardt flattened themselves behind the motel room door, and Ransom waved me over, so we dashed into the bathroom and peeked through the crack in the door. A second later, the motel door burst open and two men in black, their faces covered with balaclavas, blazed in shooting their automatic pistols everywhere, including at a now very dead fake Lenard. They turned, not expecting to find Robert and Reinhardt, who fired into their faces. The men sank to the floor and Reinhardt sprang over to check each for a pulse. "We're good," he said. They were dead.

We grabbed our things and bolted from the room, shutting the door on the messy scene. The four of us coolly walked to our car. If someone were watching, he would have never suspected that we were escaping a crime scene. We casually opened the doors and took our seats inside, taking care to shut them quietly and moderate our purposefully convivial conversation. Robert maneuvered our SUV slowly and casually out of the motel parking lot and headed to the expressway that would take us back to Portland International Jetport. Maybe I wasn't as ready for this as I'd hoped. I didn't realize tears were streaming down my face and falling onto my lap until we were belted, the radio was tuned to a slow, sad country and western song, and we were already driving down the dark road.

Nine

OUR RESCUE MISSION HAD GONE very wrong, yet I saw no signs of panic in Reinhardt or the others. They moved robotically and carried on as if it were business as usual showing no sign that they were moved by the vicious events that had just unfolded. Rosalind had trained me well. I subtly dried my eyes and followed their lead so no one would know that inside I felt stained and ruined. I had helped kill people. I told myself that it was self-defense, which it was, but the thud of our weapons as the bullets entered and exited their bodies kept playing over and over in my mind.

I tried to do the math on how long it would take before the bodies would be discovered and how soon following that the police would be looking for us. I hoped the silencers on our guns had bought us time until the housekeeping staff would discover the gruesome scene in the morning.

No one in the car spoke. Robert kept his eye on the rearview mirror; Reinhardt watched for any activity from the passenger side mirror, and Ransom sat in the back seat across from me, his back stiff and his hands tightly clenched at his side, ready to draw his pistol again. Any second, I expected to hear police sirens. But nothing. Even as we drew closer to the airport, every minute putting distance between us and the incident, I had to keep reassuring myself that we would be OK. These were people who truly knew what they were doing. Robert had led us out of danger when they rescued me from the clinic. I hoped that he had this situation under control as well.

"Szabo was waiting for us," I broke into the silence. "We walked straight into his trap."

"He must have planted the bowling photograph to lure us to Lenard," Ransom said, shaking his head in disbelief. His eyes darted from side to side as if he were trying to figure out the miscalculation in the plan. What signs had he missed?

"How would he know we'd take the bait?" I asked.

"It was just a matter of time before he caught on to us," Reinhardt said. "I let my guard down and didn't suspect a thing. I just thought that we got lucky and arrived before Szabo. Lenard's double was convincing. I didn't think about searching the house further." His voice was low and quiet. "It all went too smoothly. I should have suspected the sting."

"Szabo wanted us to be the bodies lying dead in that motel room. But he's underestimated us. Now he's got a mess to clean up," Ransom said, a light smile flickering over his lips.

He caught me looking at him, and I looked away. I was too empty to even think about anything but what had just happened.

Robert sighed. "Which also means he's probably watching the outgoing flights in the Portland area, especially charters," Robert said. "You'll have to camp out here a few days before you fly back to Nice."

"So what do we do now?" I said. "Where will we stay, or should I say, hide?"

Seeing the emotionless acceptance of the failed situation in Reinhardt and the other guys helped ease my guilt. My question came out strangely unemotional. I didn't feel the same fear and panic that gripped me when Reinhardt and Rose had rescued me from the clinic in New York this time; instead I began to feel a sense of satisfaction that we had outsmarted our clever adversary. Eat that, Felix, I thought. He couldn't hurt enough to know how I felt. But more, I felt something new. Concern for my new family. I wanted to protect them, these strangers who were growing more important to me every day.

"It's time we stop doing damage control and start doing what we can to get this miserable slug behind bars," Ransom said. "If we can connect him to the accidents and deaths, we can turn him over to the CIA and let them deal with him. Then we'll all finally be safe."

"How are we going to do that?" I asked.

"CIA Headquarters are located in Langley, West Virginia," Ransom said. "We can drive there and find a way to lure him into our own trap and tip off the CIA of illicit activity, let them catch him in the act."

"Felix would never fall for that," Reinhardt said. "He's far too distrustful of anything out of the ordinary. It's better that we let him think he's luring us. He knows we're out there now and that we'll try to intervene in any attempt he makes on the lives of the other ex-agents he's hunting. Robert, did you have somewhere in mind where we can stay for a few days?"

"I have a place just outside of Springfield," Robert said. "It's off the grid and held in my partner's name. The added benefit is it's only twenty minutes from Westport County Airport, so we could have a plane ready in the time it takes to drive there." He smiled. "I don't get there enough, but it's always great to go home."

Reinhardt looked at him inquisitively.

"It's my childhood home, our farm. I pay the taxes and Myrtle keeps it up. That's our agreement. She's a bit of a recluse, so it works for her. She only goes out for supplies, keeps to herself otherwise. When we get there, I'll let her know she's going to have house guests for a few days."

***

The road was pitch black, lit only here and there by the few cars that passed. We kept our eyes open, but it seemed no one was following us: no hired assassins, no police, no rogue agents, nobody. It was almost unsettling. It seemed too easy. But, for now, we had to roll with it. Felix had the upper hand, and until we figured out how to turn the tables, it looked like hiding out for a bit was a good idea.

Springfield was six hours away. None of us had slept or eaten apart from the men with their triangles of sandwich. I was shaken and felt brittle, but I looked at Robert, so sturdy behind the wheel, and Ransom, whose wounds ran deep in his own heart but whose passion was fierce, and felt my resolve strengthen. Hour after hour we drove, stopping just a few times for gas and bathroom breaks.

***

The sun was coming up on the horizon as Robert pulled off the main highway onto a county road. He slowed down considerably; the road was curved, very bumpy and thickly shadowed by trees. "We're almost there though this part seems the longest," Robert chuckled. "I hope Myrtle is up. I don't know about you, but I could eat three breakfasts."

As if on cue, my stomach growled loud enough for everyone in the car to hear. Ransom snorted and then we all cracked up.

Half an hour later, Robert turned right and drove down a long graveled driveway. I wondered if he had taken a wrong turn. It looked like he was driving on a narrow pathway into dense woodland. The rough potholed lane jarred the car and bounced us roughly around on our seats. But he kept on for several more minutes until soon a house appeared in a clearing.

It was a two-story Georgian, a particular favorite of my mom's, with white clapboard siding. A centered front door, painted charcoal gray, stood beneath a roof-covered veranda that ran along the lower first floor. A large barn, partially shrouded in mist, poked up ghost-like behind the house to the left.

As soon as we pulled up, a light came on in the big picture window downstairs and a person stood in it, watching us approach. The driveway circled in front of the old farmhouse and then rejoined the narrow gravel drive that we had come in on. Robert stopped and parked directly in front. We got out and stretched. It was so quiet, too early for birds but too late for crickets. I felt the hush of the forest suck out all the sound. I didn't dare speak. But no one had followed us. We seemed to be safe, at least for now.

"You didn't say that you were coming," Myrtle said. Her voice was low and melodious but creaky like it didn't get used much. She stood at the open door with a sour look on her face. Even though it was just past dawn, she was already dressed in loose-fitting blue jeans with a plaid shirt serving as a jacket over a snug jersey shirt underneath. She looked to be in her sixties, her gray hair neatly combed and tied at the back of her neck in a bushy ponytail. She came slowly out to greet the car, her step firm and solid. One look at her brawny physique and I almost jumped back into the car.

"Hello, Myrtle." Robert greeted her cheerily. He came around to give her a hug, which she didn't return. "It's nice to see you again. Sorry we couldn't give you any notice. We just suddenly felt like we needed… a few days of country retreat. I'll make it worth your trouble." He cuffed her arm like she was a drinking buddy. She let out a huff and rolled her eyes and cracked a tiny smile. It seemed she understood what "a few days of country retreat" meant. I could see that they indeed did have an arrangement. Myrtle knew her obligation.

"How long will you be staying?" she asked.

"Four, maybe five days," Robert said.

"Put the car in the barn, out of sight. Don't want any looky-loos getting ideas. The rest of you get your things and come inside while Robert attends to the vehicle."

Her words and facial expression were neutral and deliberate. I couldn't tell how much she knew about Robert or why we might be here.

We grabbed our bags, trudged up the veranda steps and entered a warm and charming country living room. An overstuffed sofa and two matching chairs were arranged on either side of a heavy square wooden coffee table supported by a wagon wheel. A large stone fireplace took up almost the whole back wall. And the smell: bacon and coffee. My appetite was ignited and I was sure Myrtle could see me sniffing at the sensual aroma. I was so tired and hungry but happy to be somewhere that seemed so comfortable and safe.

Robert stomped in, his boots heavy on the planked hardwood floor, and smiled as he looked around. "Myrtle, this is my brother Reinhardt, and his son Ransom and daughter Ruby," Robert said. "We don't mean to be impolite, but we've been on the road all night and need some sleep."

Myrtle huffed, walking off to the kitchen and started to noisily clunk and whisk and mix things. "Can't go to bed on an empty stomach," she said from the kitchen. "I'm not much of a cook, but I'll whip you up something to eat. Go pick out a bedroom, get settled, and I'll have it ready by the time you come down."

I sighed with gratitude I was so hungry.

She came to the kitchen doorway and looked sternly at Robert. "The bedrooms are clean and ready, just in case someone's needing a few days of country retreat," she said archly. She walked back into the kitchen muttering to herself and making even more racket than before with her breakfast preparation.

We climbed the stairs to the upper floor of the farmhouse. The top landing opened up to a hallway on either side. "The guys can take the bedrooms to the left and Ruby, you take the bedroom on the end beside Myrtle's," Robert said.

My bedroom was painted rose pink. It had a single bed up against the wall. topped with a ruffled, cream bedspread that matched a cream-painted dresser with a ceramic wash bowl and water pitcher on it. Frilly white curtains fluttered over the wooden window that was open a crack at the bottom. I wanted nothing more than to fall into this sweet little bed and sleep forever, but the clawing in my stomach won out and I clunked back downstairs. The guys were already at the table gobbling down large platefuls of eggs, bacon and biscuits, washing down the food with gulps of hot coffee.

"Gee, thanks for waiting for me," I said, plunking down into a chair. Ransom winked with his mouth full.

Myrtle wordlessly handed me a plate and a cup of coffee and I joined the men. Either I was beyond starving, or she was a much better cook than she professed to be, but the food was wonderful. Myrtle didn't join us but stood at the kitchen counter and nibbled on a section of toast.

When we were done, Reinhardt got up and went to his bag on the sofa to bring out his laptop. "I'll stay up and keep Myrtle company while the rest of you get some sleep," he said. "I'll catch up on the news."

Myrtle opened up a broom closet, pulled out the hunting rifle and plopped it noisily on the counter.

Robert laughed when the three of us jumped and looked at her in shock.

She shrugged. "I'm perfectly capable of keeping watch over things myself." She patted the barrel of the rifle. "You never know when a cougar might be lurking about."

"I can see that you are," Reinhardt replied.

It was clear Myrtle was not your typical house-sitter. The arrangement that Robert and Myrtle had was an interesting one. There was probably a reason he described her as a recluse. I guessed that she had a past that needed to remain secret. I wondered if she was connected to the retired agents whom Felix was intent on eradicating.

"OK, Myrtle," Reinhardt said. "I see you have things well under control. The news can wait. But wake me if you have any problems with… the cougars." He closed the laptop and got up from his chair.

No one spoke as we all filed back up the stairs. I felt secure knowing Myrtle was in charge, and I figured the boys felt the same. Still, I knew that all of us would be sleeping with our guns beneath our pillows. Just in case.

I woke up from a noise. At first, I couldn't tell where it came from. I had been in a heavy and dreamless sleep. Then I recognized the sound;

someone was knocking on the bedroom door. The door opened and Ransom began to enter. Still half asleep, I slipped into danger mode, threw off the covers and sprang out of the bed.

He paused, taking in my body.

I was only in my bra and underwear. I fumbled to pull on my shirt.

He ducked his head, smiling. "Sorry... I just wanted to see if you were OK. You've been asleep for eight hours. We got up an hour ago. Supper is ready. You should come downstairs."

"Yes, OK, sure, I'm fine," I said, now fully awake. I jammed my legs into my pants and drank some water. "Wow, I can't believe I slept so long."

Ransom was still grinning. His eyes hadn't left me, and though I had my clothes on, I felt as naked as before.

"What?" I yelled and tossed a shoe at him.

He threw up his hands in defense and turned out to the hallway but I could hear him laughing as he left. "Sorry, sorry. But I really like your reindeer undies. They're very cute."

My face burned.

"I'll tell them you'll be down shortly," he said, starting down the hall. "We need to get you up to speed on our plans."

I sat on the bed a moment to regroup. I still felt his eyes on me. I tried to assess how I felt about that. It was confusing; we were just thrown into this, he was my "brother." I'd seen how he'd looked at me. I'd been thrown by his smell, the heat of his skin, several times already. "Ugh," I said out loud. "Whatever." I buttoned my shirt to the last button on top before getting up to retrieve my shoe from across the room.

A savory aroma greeted me as I hurried down the steps to join the others in the kitchen. They sat around Reinhardt's laptop, open on the table.

I looked around. "Where's Myrtle?"

"She's gone into town to get supplies. There weren't enough groceries to feed all of us for next couple of days," Robert said.

"Is it safe for her to do that?" I asked. It wasn't just that we'd killed

Felix's men and he might come after us; he could turn the whole thing around and we'd be the criminals, the police on the hunt for us. "After all, she is harboring fugitives."

There it was again. This new way of speaking that suggested I had developed some kind of hardened shell that protected me from thinking about the real danger. I hardly recognized my voice as the comment left my lips. And yet, this was accurate. We were fugitives, and we were on the run, hiding from the police as well as from an adversary with a nasty vendetta against us.

"Good point. I suppose that it will look suspicious that she's buying more groceries than normal. But she knows how to be discreet. I'm sure she'll be fine," Robert said.

"Anything show up on the news?" I asked.

"I've been checking out all the Portland local papers," Reinhardt said. "There's nothing reported. Nothing at all."

"Szabo must have sent a clean-up team to the motel before the bodies could be found," Ransom said. "That bastard! He's planned for all contingencies. I think we can be sure that he's looking for us."

I let this sit with me for a minute and wondered which was worse: being wanted by the cops or being wanted by a crazy person.

Reinhardt's laptop pinged. He clicked on the message. "It's Renegade. There's another facial recognition. This time the photo is from Erie, Pennsylvania. Well well! How convenient that it's so close by," he said, raising an eyebrow. "OK, Felix, bait taken. We can be there in four or five hours."

The photo was also from a newspaper article, Locals Raise Money to Restore Library. Five men and women were standing in a line for the group photo. The face highlighted was of Margaret Warren, the last name in the series. Felix's next target. Unlike Lenard's, her face was in clear view. Her CIA profile appeared to the right on the laptop screen.

"But this looks too easy again," Ransom said. "Felix really wants to flush us out. How do you think we should handle this?"

"Do any of you know her from the Cold War days?" I asked.

"I do," said Reinhardt. "Margaret worked stateside and decoded secret messages for the CIA. She was never stationed in the Soviet Union. If I remember correctly, she and Felix worked together closely on protecting the agents' undercover identities."

I stared at the photo. "Something makes me wonder if she's still working with him."

Reinhardt smiled slowly. "I strongly suspect you're right, Ruby." He patted me on the shoulder. "You're certainly getting the hang of this."

Ransom scowled slightly and hastened to add, "Only her real name isn't Margaret Warren. It's Magda Worchenski. I recognize her from archived photos I handled before Szabo turned on me," he said. "I'm the one who archived her file." He paused. "This might mean that he's made a connection to me as well. Even though it was widely reported that I'd been incinerated in the explosion, Felix would've had to trust that information, and trust isn't his strong suite. Let's see if Renegade can come up with more information on her before we get ourselves into something we can't handle."

Another ping on the computer answered that question. Reinhardt opened the email.

"Renegade came up with over twenty *Margaret Warrens* in his search. None of them has ever lived in Erie," Reinhardt said. "I'll bet that Felix is deliberately making this too easy for us. He wants us to know that this isn't what it seems to be. Maybe he hopes that the confusion will make us careless. Or maybe he really thinks that we're stupid enough to fall for this one."

Another ping. "Rosalind's charter will land in Grove City, which is just one hour from Erie, at 7:00 p.m." He laughed. "The only noteworthy thing in Grove City, apart from the local airport, is an outlet mall. Not exactly her style, but I guess she's going shopping!"

The thought of gorgeous, expensively dressed Rosalind going into a discount mall made me smile, too, until I considered the bigger picture. "Oh, no," I said. "She's walking into a trap. We have to stop her."

Reinhardt sat back in his chair. The big smile on his face turned into a roaring laugh. Robert laughed with him while Ransom and I looked on in horror. "Felix will kill her," Ransom said.

"What are you two laughing at? Do you want Rosalind to die?" I said. My blood began to boil.

"I'm sorry, Ruby. Don't worry," Reinhardt said. "Felix is looking for us to barge into Margaret's apartment in Erie and save her while his thugs lie in ambush. I suspect Felix even has a second line of assassins set up in case his plan goes sour again. But Margaret *works* at the outlet mall in Grove City… So, little will Felix know that while he thinks she's at work, the couple of motorcycle gang members Rosalind has hired will have already abducted her and have her safely tucked away until Rosalind arrives."

"How can you possibly know that?" I asked. I could not understand why he was making light of this very serious situation. My hands tensed up and I waited, my whole body prickling.

"Ruby, it's truly all right. Come here. Look at the bottom of the email." Reinhardt pointed. "RD - VAIC."

"What's that supposed to mean?" I asked.

"RD. Rosalind Draker. VAIC. Victim already in custody," Ransom said, starting to smile.

"I can meet her at the Grove air strip with a Cessna to bring them back here," Robert said.

"But wait a second. If Margaret is actually still working with Szabo, she'd lead him right to us," I said.

"That's the plan," Reinhardt said. "But we'll be ready for them."

"And if Margaret is legit and she's not collaborating with Felix?" I asked. "We're making that assumption because she worked closely with Felix and isn't listed publicly as living in Erie. Maybe she's recently moved and her information hasn't caught up to her yet."

"Then we wait a few more days before we fly back to Nice?" Ransom suggested.

"I don't think so," Reinhardt said. "We want to keep our home base anonymous. But we might consider bringing Renegade and Rowan over. Rachel will need to stay with Roscoe. We can't bring a youngster into this dangerous situation."

A late-model pick-up truck rolled up the driveway and stopped directly opposite the front door. Myrtle stepped out and went around to get two large bags of groceries.

Robert met her at the door. "Were you able to get everything?"

"I have the surveillance cameras and software to run them as well as enough ammunition to start a war. It's all in the bed of the truck. I also have the new hunting rifle that I ordered last week. No night vision goggles, though. Weren't available." Myrtle shrugged. "And I had a chat with Pete, owner of the tackle shop, as I was buying the stuff. Told him all about our terrible 'deer infestation,' them eating away all our electrical. He's had that problem too, he said." She twisted her mouth. "He liked my idea of cameras so much, he ordered his own. After all, can't sit outside all night and wait for 'em." She folded her arms over her chest and cast a sly look at Robert.

"That was good thinking, Myrtle," Robert said. "Anyway, I can get some goggles in Erie when I pick up Rosalind and Margaret." He turned to Reinhardt. "Can you let her know I can be there in two hours?" He was dialing before he finished his sentence.

Reinhardt typed the coded message into his laptop, and I helped Myrtle put away the groceries while Ransom unpackaged and started assembling the electronic surveillance equipment. I felt slightly better now that we had that. We could spot anyone before he realized he was being trapped.

"And if you guys have to make a run for it," Myrtle said. "I'll leave the SUV hidden out in the back forest. There's a rough pathway that leads to a rarely traveled country road."

"I'll take Myrtle's truck to the Westchester," Robert said. "She has a couple of escape routes if you need them. But I don't imagine that anyone will be around until Margaret is here. If she is linked to Szabo, she'll probably have some kind of GPS device on her."

The men nodded to each other. They were ready. Without another word, Robert left in the old pick-up truck.

"Are you ready for this, Ruby?" Reinhardt asked, a concerned look shadowing his face.

"She'll be fine," Myrtle said. "Come on, Ruby. Let me show you how to use a rifle. I have a target range set up behind the barn."

I picked up the new rifle and followed her outside. She had spring-loaded targets set up in among the trees. Myrtle had an impressive rifle range complete with practice targets all ready for me.

"The target you miss will be the one that kills you," Myrtle warned. "So stay sharp."

She sent me out on a predetermined path. The first target shot caught me off guard and would have grazed my shoulder if the bullet had been real, but my adrenaline was heightened now and I landed a fatal bullet into each of the remaining targets, obliterating them into splinters of wood and plaster board.

"This is a good rifle Myrtle," I said. "No cougar out here stands a chance." I gave her a triumphant smile as I took a last shot.

"Impressive," she said. "Someone's trained you well."

I could tell she was trying hard to maintain an impartial expression, but I saw the corner of her mouth curve upward into a half smile as we walked back to the house.

Ten

FOR THE NEXT SEVERAL HOURS, Ransom was busy programming and installing the surveillance cameras at strategic points along the driveway and other possible access points around the barn and back of the property. His expertise was evident. He was meticulous in his setup and fine-tuned the settings until the monitor images sequenced exactly as he wanted, giving us a different view and exposure of the property every three seconds. We would be ready for any unwelcome guests.

Myrtle, too, was constantly on the move checking the barn and the woods just beyond the back lawn but mostly she carried on with her household responsibilities, cooking and cleaning, always with her hunting rifle in short reach. For a house-sitter, she certainly had talents that extended far beyond all things domestic. I wondered what circumstances had brought her and Robert together and the real meaning of what Robert and Myrtle's arrangement involved. No doubt it was an interesting story, but one that would have to wait for another time. Today, we were too occupied by much more immediate potential danger.

I suspected that Reinhardt's outward calm demeanor was a facade and he was feeling the same tension I felt. He watched the clock intently and took laps around the house to secure the perimeter, like a security guard on duty. Occasionally, his path would cross Myrtle's and they'd pause and discuss something before he'd continue on his rounds. He cautiously and routinely looked for any signs of movement or unusual activity. His hand was always near his hip where his revolver rested, always ready to take down any intruder.

My own tension came out through pacing as well. I walked around and around the farmhouse, frequently peering out the windows, also looking for anything that might indicate danger. Like the others, I just couldn't sit still. Although I didn't know details, I sensed that any minute, there could be an attack that could take all of our lives.

"What time do you expect Robert and Rosalind to be here?" I asked.

Reinhardt looked at Ransom, their body language stiff and tense as they glanced at their watches, then at the computer monitor, nervously shifting in their chairs before getting up and pacing the room as I was doing.

"It's only been five hours since Robert left for the airport," Reinhardt said. "If everything goes smoothly, they should be back here by eleven tonight. They'll need at least eight hours for travel and maybe little longer for… incidentals." Reinhardt looked away trying to hide his concern. His voice had lowered to a whisper with "incidentals." I could tell he didn't mean stopping to pick up a bag of chips.

I felt my face tense up. What he really meant was if there were unexpected trouble. Felix had a way of delivering surprises.

"How are we going to handle this Margaret person?" I asked. "Do we let her know we suspect she's Felix's mole?"

"We can't know for sure what her role in this is," Ransom said. "She could be working for Felix or she could be one of his victims. Even though she hasn't seen field action, she is a trained CIA agent and is skilled in the art of deception, so we'll have to watch her closely. Let's just hear her story and assess the situation after that."

"Rosalind and Robert will set up the ploy," Reinhardt said. "Maybe, by the time they get here, they'll know what her game is and tip us off.

If she doesn't show her hand, we'll just play along and watch her closely."

It was just after midnight when Ransom alerted us to an unfamiliar dark vehicle approaching the house from the main driveway. On the monitor, we watched it, with the three passengers, bouncing and jostling over the pocked road and determined that the driver was being deliberately careful so as to minimize the impact of the potholes on the suspension of the car and the passengers. It stopped in front of the farmhouse. Two people stepped out and started walking toward the steps of the porch.

"It's Robert and Rosalind," Ransom said, sighing with relief. "The other woman must be Margaret, but I can't tell for sure."

We went to the front door to greet them.

A third person, a small woman, stepped out of the back seat. She stumbled and fell to the grass as she tried to put weight on her left leg. Rosalind and Robert came to her side, helped her to her feet, then supported her as she limped with them up the steps to the open front door.

"You're later than we expected," Reinhardt said.

He looked at Margaret and down to her leg where her shin had several deep gashes; her ankle was bruised and swollen. He turned to bring Rosalind to him.

"It seems that Margaret doesn't do well with motorcycles. Hello, darling," Rosalind said as she embraced and kissed Reinhardt. "I see our children are in one piece." Rosalind looked over at Ransom and then to me, winking with a bright smile. She reached for my hand, which surprised me, and pulled me close for a brief hug before returning her attention to Margaret.

Robert helped Margaret inside to the sofa in the front room and propped her battered leg on the ottoman.

She settled with a grunt of pain into the soft seat, took a moment to look around the room, and stopped when she spotted Reinhardt. "Well, well," Margaret said, a smug half smile growing on her face. She took a moment to study him.

"And what do you call yourself now?" she asked.

"Call me Reinhardt." He bent down to his old acquaintance and cupped her hands in his. He held them carefully as he sat beside her. "Magda Worchenski. It's been a very long time, hasn't it?"

"Margaret Warren, if you please," she retorted.

He looked down. "What happened?"

"Strangest thing, you know," she said with mock sarcasm, "I was on my way home from my shift, when two rather rough-looking biker guys grabbed me, put me on the back of a Harley, my first time on one— *imagine!*—and drove off at breakneck speed."

She let out a vexed chuckle as if she wanted to laugh about the seizure but was also clearly uncomfortable how it had gone down and with the outcome.

Reinhardt and Rosalind were looking at her kindly, but I could see she wasn't sure what kind of company she was in yet.

"So these nice gentlemen drove me to the Grove City airport where they deposited me on the runway in front of a Cessna. Just for fun, I decided to have a bit of a jog to get away from them. However, I tripped and hurt myself. When I looked up from the asphalt, these two familiar faces," she gestured to Rosalind and Robert, "were standing over me. They grabbed me and commandeered me into the plane, which took off immediately, and now, here I am, abducted into the company of an old CIA comrade."

Her stare lingered again over the occupants of the room. She seemed like she was being cautious, secretive maybe, certainly not showing her hand or allegiance.

"Might you have any whiskey?" Margaret said. "For the pain, of course."

Myrtle snorted as she walked over to a side cabinet and pulled out an amber-colored bottle of liquor and a glass tumbler. She poured a half glass of whiskey and handed the drink to Margaret who slammed it back in a few big slugs to our surprise and amusement.

"Is there somewhere where I can rest?" she said. "It's been a long day. Unless of course, you intend to kill me, in which case, I'll have another whiskey."

She handed the empty glass back to Myrtle who rolled her eyes, reluctantly refilling it as before.

Myrtle handed the glass back to Margaret, and she polished it off as quickly as the first. Margaret plunked the glass onto the table and sank back into the sofa, closing her eyes and sighing. Several minutes later, she was out cold.

I shook my head. Some CIA agent. Passing out with a circle of vultures standing over her body. Didn't seem the smartest move. Or, after I thought about it, maybe she was smarter than I gave her credit for. I poked her foot with mine. She did look pretty asleep.

"Put her in the bedroom between Myrtle's and Ruby's," Ransom said. "Robert, would you help me carry her up the stairs?"

"Ruby and I will check her for wires or tracking devices," Rosalind said.

The men carried her up the stairs and placed her gently on the bed. I helped Rosalind take off her shirt and pants. No electronic or wireless devices were visible on her ample person, and all she had left were her industrial-strength bra and granny panties. I lifted my eyebrows and looked at Rosalind, but she shook her head no. We covered her with a warm wool blanket and left her to sleep off her drunken stupor.

"But it could be in there," I whispered as we left.

"Ruby, sometimes as women we have to trust and hope that by honoring a code among women of not violating her at that level, she wouldn't stoop so low as to violate herself at that level." I have to say, while it was risky, I admired Rosalind's stance and didn't push. We rejoined the group downstairs.

"She's unconscious, in her underwear, and without any obvious tracking paraphernalia," Rosalind said. "If Felix is monitoring her location to get to us, he's either being very disgusting or very crafty about it."

"Easy enough to figure out which one," grinned Ransom. "I've installed a camera in her room. We can watch to see if she's up to anything." He pressed a button on the keyboard and a snoring Margaret appeared on the screen, lying in exactly the same position Rosalind and I had left her in.

"I can't tell from her behavior if she's on his team or not."

"Guilty until proven innocent," Rosalind said. "It's safer for us to go on the premise that Felix already knows our location. We're ready for him. The laneway, house, and surrounding grounds are all covered. Who's on surveillance duty through the night?"

"Ransom and I are reasonably well-rested. We'll take the night shift," Reinhardt said. "The rest of you should get some sleep, but you should definitely keep your weapons handy."

We went upstairs to our rooms. I stopped at Margaret's door, opening it narrowly to peer in. She was still lying on her back with her mouth open, snoring softly, oblivious to the world. I started to feel sorry for her, but I stopped myself. Guilty until proven innocent. If we kept that mindset, we'd stay alive a lot longer.

***

At the moment, sleep was the furthest thing from my mind. I was wide awake, feeling tense and agitated. I supposed impending danger had a way of doing that to a person. I looked anxiously at my window, knowing that even a child could get in, so I glanced around the room and found some usable things: a glass fishbowl of marbles and a game of *Candy Land*. I emptied the marbles into the box and put the box under the window. Then I took my pistol out of my waistband, the silencer still screwed on from the previous shooting, and put it under my pillow. I positioned myself on top of the covers, my back to the wall and my face to the door, Myrtle's new hunting rifle was cradled in my arms. I knew I wouldn't sleep; my senses were prickling. I heard every creek and snap the old farmhouse made and the incessant *tick tick* of the windup alarm clock on the night stand. I began to feel like my eyes were darting around the room with each and every minute going by.

A loud whapping woke me from an unanticipated deep sleep; my breathing was rapid and my heart pounded in my chest.

I jumped from my bed with the hunting rifle firmly in my grip and pointed it as I looked around the room. It was still dark outside but a light was strobing through my window, the *whap whap* breaking the silence of the night.

I released one hand from the rifle and reached back under my pillow for my pistol, returning it to the waistband of my jeans and then slowly got off the bed, forgetting about the marbles, stepping into the box and scattering them everywhere. "Damn!"

By now, I heard a scrambling noise down the steps to the den where we'd left Ransom and Reinhardt keeping watch at the computer monitor. What happened that they didn't alert us to danger? Did they fall asleep?

I heard the front door burst open and loud footsteps of what sounded like several people barging into the den.

"Hands in the air!" a man shouted.

It was too late to help Reinhardt and Ransom. If they were still downstairs, they were being held at gunpoint.

In spite of Ransom's meticulous positioning of the cameras, ground surveillance hadn't alerted us to an airborne approach. Felix's men had attacked from above without warning, falling like God's wrath from the sky.

My first thought was they didn't know I was up here, so I froze, considering what I should do.

Margaret.

I ran to her room on the balls of my feet and opened her door.

Her bed was empty, and her clothes were gone.

Damn it, I cursed her. I admired Rosalind, even pedestalized her, but her sense of honor had cost us. Bitterness stung my eyes. I wanted to get this man, wanted him dead. Now he was going to win.

Or maybe I was underestimating Rosalind. I knew better than to do that. I hoped that my pounding heart and quick rasping breath couldn't be heard as I crouched at the top of the stairway to listen for clues as to what might be happening downstairs. But the noise had stopped. The whole place was as quiet as it was the day we arrived except for the slow whir of helicopter blades as they came to a stop. No gunshots, no movement. The strobing light still pierced the darkness through the window of the upper hallway in the boys' wing. I listened for several minutes and then just as I mustered up the courage to go down to investigate, someone grabbed me from behind, and with a hand pressed firmly against my mouth, lifted me backward and pulled me into Reinhardt's bedroom.

"Ruby, don't make a sound." It was Rosalind. "Stay quiet when I remove my hand."

She released me from her hold, and I turned and looked at her in surprise. She had remained back as well. This didn't add up. Then I started to panic. She had to have known the woman would have a device in her underwear. And how was it that she was still upstairs, her hand over my mouth? I couldn't believe what I was thinking, but here she was.

She pressed her index finger to her lips and then cocked her head to the side toward the bedrooms back in Myrtle's wing. She wasn't going downstairs to rescue the boys. She took my hands in hers as if she could sense what I was thinking. "Ruby, we're going to get the boys," she whispered. "I have a plan."

I had to trust her. She was Rosalind. I'd come too far with her to believe she'd betray me, or any of us.

We slipped quietly out the bedroom door and crawled along the hallway floor to Myrtle's room. The soft summer evening breeze tickled her curtains around us as we climbed out onto the porch roof and shimmied down the posts to the lawn. We dropped down and crawled over the edge of the driveway, the gravel digging into our knees and scrubby low branches catching in our hair and scratching our faces.

When we reached the perimeter of the forest, we scrambled into the dense thicket behind the farmhouse.

In the clearing, we went around to the back of the barn and entered through a window. I was breathless and bruised but couldn't think about that as we jumped through the open window and landed hard on the straw-covered wooden floor below. Rosalind motioned to me that we should put our backs to the wall to wait for our breathing to stabilize and listen to what was happening outside. There was nothing—someone had cut the engine of the helicopter—and now only the chirping of crickets broke the stillness.

We saw through the window a short, slight man in horn-rimmed glasses hop down from the pilot's side and pause as if he heard something..

I held my breath.

But then he turned and dashed into the house through the side kitchen door.

"How many are there," I whispered.

"Two men are already inside. He makes three," Rosalind said.

"I didn't hear gunfire. What are they doing?"

"My guess is that they're waiting for another member of their team."

"Felix?" I suggested. I felt cold saying his name.

"Who knows... but probably."

Just then a car bounced up the drive and stopped in front of the farmhouse in a cloud of dust.

A big burly man emerged from the house, a gun in his thick hand, to greet the car. The person in the car rolled down the window and the two men's voices carried through the still night air.

"We're holding three men and Margaret Warren inside," the man from the house said.

A muffled response came from within the car and the man returned to the house.

Rosalind and I looked at each other. "They don't have... but where's Myrtle?"

"Let's just say that night time is the best time to hunt for cougars," muttered a woman from behind.

Those could have easily been Myrtle's last words. Startled, we both pointed our guns directly at her.

"Take it easy. It's just me," she said. We couldn't see her only hear her. A door creaked and she emerged from a horse stall and joined us by the window.

While my heart continued to pound in my chest, we turned our eyes back to the house.

"Do you have a plan?" Rosalind asked. She looked as startled as I was, but her voice was as razor sharp as ever. Rosalind usually didn't let things surprise her. She seemed angry, and if I had to guess, I'd suppose it was at herself.

"I figured that they'd attack while we slept, so I came out here just after you went to bed." Myrtle kept her eyes on the house.

"Do you think they know we're missing?" I asked.

"Not likely or they'd be looking for us," Myrtle replied.

The slam of the front door directed our attention back to the porch and the unfamiliar car parked in front. The same large man appeared again, this time pushing a struggling Margaret out of the front door. Her hands were tied behind her back and she limped awkwardly and painfully as he pushed her forward toward the open back door of the car. The person who had stayed inside motioned to Margaret through the window.

"Felix," she said flatly. It was more of a question than a greeting, as if she were surprised to see him.

"Get in, Magda," he said, his voice reedy and gruff.

"Not a chance," she said. "I don't want anything to do with you, nor do I have anything that I want to say."

She yanked away from her captor and stepped back as a tall man with buzz-cut hair stepped out of the car.

"Leave me with her," Felix said. He nodded to the other man gesturing that he should return inside. The man turned and went back into the house. "So, Magda, tell me what you know about the people who brought you here," Felix said.

"I don't know who they are or why I'm here. But I see that you do. What have you gotten me involved in, Felix?" Margaret demanded. "I'm retired from the agency and want to be left in peace."

"Retired," Felix huffed. "You and all the others are all traitors. You abandoned the agency and you betrayed your country. You're all cowards leaving before our job was done. Now I'm going to make sure that you're all going to pay for abandoning your country—and for abandoning me."

Felix and Margaret stared at each other menacingly, facing off in a meeting of wills, their faces firm and lined in shadows by the bright moonlight. Felix towered over her small frame. Although he appeared to be of mature age, he seemed strong and muscular. Margaret, by comparison, appeared diminutive and frail even though she kept her posture firm and didn't back down when he stepped toward her. I was impressed by her tenacity.

"Tell me what you know and who these people are!" he demanded.

"I don't know anything about them. Why don't you go in and ask them yourself," Margaret shouted defiantly.

Felix's man lumbered out of the house again to check on the confrontation unfolding outside.

"Everything OK, sir?" he asked.

"She needs a bit more persuasion." Felix motioned with his head toward Margaret and shoved her. She stumbled and fell to the ground.

The man came over and grabbed her arm behind her back and pointed a gun to her head.

"Tell me who they are!" Felix shouted.

"Go to hell, you bastard," Margaret said. The man hit her roughly on the head with the butt of his gun. She fell motionless to the grass. Felix looked down at her without emotion. Then turned and calmly re-entered the back seat of the car. The man stood over Margaret's motionless body for a moment then returned inside again.

"We have to do something," I whispered.

"Not until the proper opportunity presents itself," Rosalind said. "We can't help the boys if we're dead. Let Felix regroup and make his next move. It sounds like he's flustered that Margaret isn't cooperating."

"Where's Myrtle now?" I looked back around the dark barn but she was no longer with us.

"There," Rosalind said. She pointed to the helicopter where Myrtle was stealthily creeping along on the grass on all fours to the helicopter. We watched as she attached a box to the fuselage then slid back into the bushes.

Two minutes later, she came back in through the same window we'd used, a Cheshire cat grin on her face. "We need to figure out what's going on inside," she said. "There are three of them plus Felix and a driver. If we take them one at a time, we shouldn't have any problem neutralizing them."

The big man left the house again and walked over to Margaret's motionless body. He hefted her over his shoulder, wavering somewhat beneath the weight, then went to the back of the farmhouse and deposited her in the helicopter. Moments later, the pilot came out of the back kitchen door and the two men exchanged nods. "Felix wants us to take all of them back to Washington for interrogation," the man said.

"I'll get the chopper ready for take-off," said the pilot. He hopped into his seat and the blades began to whir. "We only have a few minutes," Rosalind said. "They're taking the boys aboard. We'll have to ambush them as they come out."

"I'll offer a distraction from the wooded area," Myrtle said. "You two take down their man at the rear just before they try to load our guys onto the helicopter." Myrtle quickly slipped through the window again and back into the bushes.

Rosalind and I followed, creeping closely behind her, then passed her as she staked her defensive position. Rosalind and I continued running to the tail of the helicopter and dashed across the lawn, our bodies low, and ducked under the deck beneath the kitchen door.

The burly man, who seemed to be Felix's main associate, came out first and headed to the passenger side of the helicopter. Reinhardt, Robert and Ransom emerged from the door next, walking slowly and looking around at the evolving dark scene and the whapping blades of the craft. Another man followed behind them, his gun pointed at their backs. As he came into full view and I had clear range, I aimed and took my shot. He fell to his knees, blood trickling from his shoulder. He writhed on the porch, his gun thrown from his hand.

Robert quickly scooped it up.

Reinhardt, realizing we'd escaped and managed to derail the intruder's plan, looked around.

"Over here," I called in a hoarse whisper.

The three of them leaped over the deck railing and started for us. The burly man, realizing they'd been ambushed, ran to the chopper. He threw open the pilot's door, got a hand up, and disappeared into the craft.

Seconds later, the night sky erupted with light and thunder, and gun shots exploded along the tree line to the woods. Myrtle had indeed been busy and must have set up explosives to add to our fire power. The boys reached us, we handed them revolvers, and now five of us squatted down and fired at the helicopter.

Despite our hitting the chopper—I could hear the pings in the metal—it was still able to take off. It gained altitude quickly and soon disappeared into the darkness leaving only the whapping sound behind. It seemed they were going to get away, but then, just beyond the tree line, there was a bright flash and a loud rolling boom. Myrtle had detonated the charge she'd attached to the helicopter's fuselage.

I felt a curious pang of guilt and unease: Margaret. But there wasn't any time to worry over her now. We had to deal with Felix and his driver first.

We raced around to the front where his car was parked, but we were too late. Felix's car was already racing away, faster than the bumps and holes allowed.

But Myrtle wasn't finished yet; seconds later, another blast lit up the lonely pot-holed lane and metal burst into the air like shrapnel.

Dodging the fiery projectiles, we ran to the scene, guns in hand, ready to investigate the damage and apprehend our enemies. I ran hard like an animal chasing its prey. Revenge raged in my heart; I snorted it with every breath I exhaled. I was so close to the beast that had ruined my life, ruined all of our lives. A savage rage filled me with an uncontrollable need to avenge my parents and Johnny.

The smell of hot metal and burning gasoline drew me like an incantation toward my enemy. I ran harder, then harder still. When I arrived, followed by the others, we saw a broken and steaming car blocking the lane, the driver lying hunched and bleeding over the steering wheel, and an empty back seat.

We heard someone coming up from behind. It was Myrtle, her cougar rifle aimed at the car. "Did we get them?" she asked.

"Felix got away," Reinhardt said.

"He has to be near. Let's hunt him down," Myrtle said. She wasn't going to give up.

"No, we have to get out of here now," Robert said. "I'm sure there's been enough noise and explosions to get everyone in the county nervous. Our neighbors no doubt have notified the police and the fire department. They should be here shortly. We can figure out our next move when we're somewhere safe, but definitely not here. Anyway, Felix is probably long gone by now."

"I'll stay to clean things up and handle the police," Myrtle offered.

"It's too dangerous, Myrtle. Come with us," Reinhardt said.

Myrtle lowered her gun and looked around the chaotic scene slowly before nodding.

"OK," she said tersely. "You're right. It would take a sizeable clean-up crew to cover this up."

We ran back to the house and got our things, regrouped in the kitchen, then left by the back door. We walked over the short stretch of back lawn behind the farmhouse where the helicopter had been and disappeared into the thicket of trees and brush. The moon couldn't penetrate the forest here, but soon we made our way to an obscure lane-way where our SUV waited. Myrtle had planned for any contingency, which we surely needed now.

Taking the lead, she clicked the fob she had pulled from her pocket and then threw it to Robert who got in, started the car, and as soon as we were all piled inside, tore away, tires spinning. He took the car over the rough terrain for several minutes in silence until he reached the back road that seemed to lead to a main highway, and, I assumed, the airport, and hopefully to safety.

I was clammy from dried sweat in the air conditioning and felt like I hadn't had a shower in months. "But won't Felix know that we have a charter plane waiting at Westport?" I asked.

"We're not going to Westport," Robert said. "I have somewhere else in mind where we can go until we figure out Felix's next move."

Eleven

ROBERT, EVER STALWART, drove for hours, through the night and into dawn. We were the only car on the road as the sun was just coming up, but I still didn't feel safe that we hadn't been seen. In the last three days, we were either hiding, being shot at, or running for our lives. But apart from poor Margaret, the rest of us were safe—although I knew that for us, safe was relative. I reflected on her heroic efforts to keep our identities anonymous. She was a victim after all and paid the ultimate price: her life. How senseless it seemed; how hopeless I felt; how ashamed I was of being caught up in such primal emotions that would have allowed me to kill Felix. Had the opportunity presented itself, I would have pulled the trigger without thinking. The day before, I relished the thought of the vibration that would ripple up my arm as the bullet fired through the barrel. I could almost hear the thud as it landed in the soft tissue of his chest. I considered that I had changed so dramatically I didn't feel even a shred of remorse at imagining the delight I'd feel from killing him, from watching him die.

We drove for several more miles before Robert stopped at a deserted gas station. He drove the SUV to the back of the derelict building where it couldn't be spotted or seen from the road. "We're changing cars," he said. "They might already be looking for this one."

Another of Robert's many talents was his ability to plan ahead. He always seemed to have an alternate plan that he could put into place at the exact right time. Waiting at the far end of a clearing behind the abandoned lot, barely in sight, was a tan SUV, larger than our old one. Robert drove into a hiding spot behind a fenced barricade and we switched cars, everyone taking the same seat as before. With all the unpredictable events of the last several days, this tiny bit of consistency and order offered at least a small feeling of security. Within minutes, we were back on the deserted highway again.

"Where to?" Reinhardt asked.

"I rented a hunting cabin about a hundred miles from here in upstate New York. It's remote, and it will give us some time to rest and decide what to do next. We can get supplies and food along the way. Then, I suggest, we stay put for a while to let things settle down," Robert said.

"What do you think happened to Felix," I asked. "How could he possibly have gotten away? At the very least, he must be injured."

Now that we were away from the farm and I had some distance to the person I'd been there, the person I'd become, guilt and shame were flooding into me. I needed some time to understand what was happening to me. Maybe in a remote country cabin surrounded by the solitude of nature I could remember who I was, excise this new vindictive me. Johnny's laughter rang in my head. His innocence, his gentle eyes. I let myself remember our family camping trips, the campfires we helped build, the songs, the scary ghost stories that made Johnny pull tightly into my lap. *Remember your humanity,* Kathleen was pleading. I brushed tears from my cheeks hoping the others hadn't notice.

"Don't assume anything about Felix," Rosalind said. "That bastard has more lives than a cat. I guarantee he's not through with us yet."

The sun had topped the horizon when we pulled onto a dirt road. Dew shimmered on the leaves and deer scattered as our car startled the morning calm. We drove on deeper and deeper into the remote landscape. When a lake came into view in front of us, Robert stopped and got out of the car. On the side of the road was a hidden lane with a fenced gate whose sign said, 'No Trespassing.' He keyed a number into a large lock and the chain fell to the ground. Robert swung open the wide metal gate, returned to the car, rolled into a forest lane so densely wooded it was as if we were being swallowed into another dimension, got out and secured the lock, then got back in and into the dark woods we went.

Branches swished and scraped against the sides of the car as we slowly drove down a dirt road that seemed barely more than a path. We could only see a few feet ahead of the car and the path appeared to lead to nowhere. There was no sign of human life, only trees and more trees. If Robert ever wanted to turn on us and kill us, this would be a perfect spot. I had to laugh; Kathleen would've probably thought of a Disney movie, with squirrels gathering around to sing and birds alighting on our shoulders.

Finally, after interminable scraping, bumping and undulating, we came to a clearing where a bucolic log cabin stood. It had a roof of darkened cedar shakes, walls of rounded logs, and a moss-covered cedar deck framing a roughly hewed front door. I wouldn't have been at all surprised to see a woodsman wearing a mack jacket and holding an ax come out and start splitting logs or something.

Robert drove the SUV around to the back of the cottage. It seemed unlikely anyone would ever be by to see that a car was here, but he didn't want to take any chances. He turned off the engine and we all sat a moment, dumbfounded, adjusting to the silence.

We got out, stretched our stiff legs and went inside.

The cabin looked like it hadn't been used in some time. Cobwebs hung in every corner and the moss from outside was creeping in through the window panes and door frame. But it had a big fireplace and was charming and rustic and frankly I was just glad to be somewhere.

Robert went back to the car to get the groceries and supplies we'd bought at a general store just off the Interstate. Reinhardt and Ransom followed him to help.

Rosalind, Myrtle and I dropped our bags and went further inside to explore.

The place had a piney musty smell. I pulled the gingham sheets off the sofa and chairs and tossed them onto the tree stump serving as a coffee table and sneezed.

"Bless you," called Rosalind from another room. She came out and laughed ruefully. "I never thought at my age I'd have to sleep on a bunk bed again. Or use an outhouse." She nodded out the back kitchen window at a little wooden shack with a moon cut into the door.

"Least there's water," said Myrtle, who was inspecting the wood stove.

And a fireplace, I thought. I couldn't wait to sit by the licking flames and let my thoughts organize themselves.

Myrtle had found a broom and a light switch and went to work. Rosalind scurried around the bedrooms pulling blankets from a closet and tucking them into the bunks. I poked around the kitchen cupboards to see where I should put the food, and the men prowled around outside. Even though it was summer, the shade from the trees and a light wind made our sanctuary feel chilly.

"I'll get the fireplace going," Ransom said when he came back. He went to the wood pile under a lean-to and got an armful. I admired how deftly he built the fire; he must have been Boy Scout in his youth. Within ten minutes, the fire had started to warm the cabin, its crackle and glow making the place feel welcoming and comfortable.

The ladies gathered along the kitchen counter to prepare breakfast. It had been a long time since we last ate and everyone was starving. Soon we had a simple meal assembled of canned minestrone served in mugs and bologna sandwiches.

Reinhardt set up the laptop on the kitchen table and checked the local news reports for information on the helicopter crash and explosions at the farmhouse. He scrolled through every major paper, but there was nothing. We were stunned by Felix's adeptness for obliterating every trace of the messes he made that might lead back to him. "I wouldn't doubt if he had the local law enforcement in his back pocket," muttered Ransom, leaning over Reinhardt's shoulder. It did make sense, and also sent a chill through me. More people on his side who should have been on ours.

The food and warmth of the cabin made me feel much better. Everyone was animated and chatting easily while I curled up on the sofa. I didn't know how the others could stay awake for such long periods of time, but I was exhausted. I said my good-nights, which made everyone laugh since it was only late morning, went into the bedroom, climbed the ladder to a top bunk, and settling into a surprisingly comfortable mattress and pillow. The pistol at my waistband poked uncomfortably into my side, and as had become my nighttime routine, I took it out and put it under my pillow. I covered myself with the warm wool blanket and didn't even remember falling off to sleep.

It wasn't the noise but the lack thereof that awakened me. Judging by the sunlight, it was late afternoon. A delicate wind picked up a branch of a tree outside of the bedroom, and began scratching it rhythmically at the window. I stretched in the bunk feeling refreshed, and when I heard the voices of everyone outside, I felt enlivened and much better. As I climbed down from my bunk perch, I noticed that Myrtle was asleep in the lower opposite bunk. I tiptoed out of the ladies' bedroom wondering where Rosalind was.

The fire was still crackled cheerfully in the fireplace of the common room, but the room was empty. I opened the door to the cottage to see where the rest were. The cool fresh air and musky aroma of the forest was intoxicating. I breathed in deeply, welcoming the calm and peace.

"Did you have a good sleep?" someone from the side whispered. Ransom was carrying an armful of firewood he'd retrieved from the lean-to. "I'm stocking up the firewood so no one has to go out after dark."

I smiled and nodded. "Where is everyone?"

"They're checking out the lake," he said. "It's pretty down there and just a short walk through the trees." He pointed to a path just ahead with his chin. "I think they might be fishing for trout."

I started to walk away, when he stopped me. "Just watch out for garter snakes. They're not poisonous but they're very slimy." His eyes were glinting mischievously.

My heart jumped at the mention of snakes. "Very funny," I added, rolling my eyes at him. "I'm not afraid of garters."

"Really?" Ransom said. "Could've fooled me. Your whole body bristled when I said the word!" He hissed the "s" and laughed as his foot rustled the grass at his feet.

I deeply regretted that I was surrounded by people who had trained themselves to notice every single thing all the time. I couldn't help but notice myself how red his lips were, shadowed in the forest light. How olive his smooth skin was. "No need," I said, flipping my hair back. "I'm fine." But I wasn't fine. He was right. I was absolutely and unequivocally terrified of snakes, a phobia I'd had since I was little girl when my parents had taken us camping and we'd accidentally walked into a nest of them.

I flounced away as he chuckled, "Suit yourself."

I walked cautiously, scanning the ground and keeping my ears on alert for any sound or movement. When I saw the sparkling blue lake in front of me, I was relieved. I hurried until I came to a rocky shore, the sun instantly warm on my skin and the breeze blowing my hair over my face. I tucked a strand behind my ear and looked for Rosalind, Reinhardt and Robert. They were just up ahead on a rocky outcropping, all three of them with fishing poles in the water as they lounged in the warm sunlight.

Rosalind waved me over. "We're going to have fish for dinner tonight," she said. "Look. The boys have already caught some." She pointed to basket where three fish half-heartedly flopped on top of each other.

"Do you want to try, Ruby?" Reinhardt said.

"No, I'm not much of an outdoors kind of gal," I said, trying to be cute. I had no interest in touching a fish. "You didn't see any snakes on the way down here, did you?"

The three of them eyed me before breaking into a hearty laugh.

Rosalind came over and put her arm around my shoulders. "Let me guess. Ransom?"

I shrugged and smiled sheepishly.

"He's just trying to tease you," she said, "like brothers do."

My throat filled up at her compassion and the thought of my own brother. He teased me like crazy, but he was terrible at it. Rubber mice on the floor, pennies coming out of my ears. My clumsy little angel. I thought about the hardened person I'd become and held her up in my mind against who I was when I was Johnny's sister. She didn't look a thing like me. Not a thing.

Rosalind's fishing line jerked and she yanked on it with a whoop. "Ah ha! I've got one too." I was impressed by her yet again. I'd never caught a thing in all the times I'd fished with my dad upstate. Though it was probably on purpose, now that I watched the half-dead fish in the basket glisten in the sunlight.

"There's more than enough for dinner tonight. I'll get to cleaning them," Robert said as he placed Rosalind's catch in the basket and picked it up. He started to head for the cottage then turned around and grinned. "Don't worry, Ruby. I'll clear the way for you. There won't be a snake within miles of here after I shake the bushes." He chuckled all the way back to the path entrance where he disappeared into the trees.

"Ha, ha, ha," I said. I didn't actually mind the teasing. It was a welcome break from the fear we'd been flooded with the last few days. A couple of harmless snakes, I could get over that. But unlike garters, Felix was lethal.

I sat down with Rosalind and Reinhardt on the large bolder that served as their fishing perch and tilted my face up to the warm afternoon sun to enjoy the tranquility and solitude of the nature around me. It had a sort of healing power that felt like it was renewing my strength. I felt better, like I had a new energy for whatever was to come.

Later that evening, when the sun had set and the cabin was cloaked in darkness, we ate by candlelight on blue-speckled, enameled plates, using mismatched cutlery, the kind used for camping. The fireplace crackled and made shadows dance along the walls of the common room. A feeling of gentle camaraderie filled the cabin. Protected and peaceful in this serene environment, it seemed inconceivable that in reality we were fugitives on the run and in hiding from a man who posed as an American security officer, albeit an agent falsely using his power at the CIA to go off the rails.

I had to shake my head when Myrtle served us the dinner. Not an expert cook, my behind. She was amazing, and tonight's trout, made with limited ingredients, would have rivaled any restaurant's in New York. She served the fish with a creamy sauce with tarragon she'd plucked outside the house, sweet and crisped roast potatoes and a salad with lemon vinaigrette she made herself. I looked across at Ransom and his eye caught mine. He lifted his fork as if to say "cheers" and I laughed. Life in this remote cabin could have been idyllic, under different circumstances, if only I could shut out Felix and the fear he created in our lives.

Reinhardt opened the laptop again and checked the headlines. Still no news of gunshots or explosions at the farm and nothing about a helicopter crash. It defied explanation.

"Maybe we can charter a plane back to France in a couple of days," I said. "We could use a different airport, one we haven't flown out of before." I felt like a child who wanted to go home.

"Ruby," Ransom said, "Felix won't stop trying to find us. He's obsessed, and unless we stop him, we'll be running for the rest of our days." He came over and sat on the arm of the La-Z-boy I was sitting in, his arm resting on the high back of the chair like he was protecting me. Maybe my insecurity was showing. He looked at me reassuringly but I quickly looked away.

"Most of the retired CIA agents are here in the U.S.," Reinhardt said. "We know Felix will plan another hit, and we can reach them faster if we're already here. Plus, Ransom's right. It's not a good idea to draw him to our home base when he's this focused on figuring out who we are."

"It just seems like he has us on the end of a string, getting us to follow him," I said. "If we're going to stay here, is there a way we can get two steps ahead of him to stop him? He's going to keep killing people otherwise."

"It's hard to be patient, I know," said Reinhardt. His eyes had their sadness back in them. "But he'll make a mistake somewhere along the line. We've evaded him twice now and very soon, his anger and frustration will make him lose his focus. That's when we'll have our opportunity to take him down."

"But if we kill him, in the eyes of the law, we're just murderers," I said. "His own people have to stop him. What can we do to draw attention to him from within the agency?"

"That's my girl!" Rosalind said. "We might have to fight him on two fronts, letting Felix think that we're falling for his clues and drawing us into his traps while we're alerting his commander of his actions and causing an internal investigation. Now with this last altercation between us, we have something we can bring to the CIA as early proof that Felix isn't just sipping coffee at his computer terminal in the archives all day. I'll get Renegade to tip off his direct superior, make him aware of the things Felix has covered up in Portland and on the farm. We can start by using the disappearance of Margaret Warren. Surely her employer wondered why she went AWOL. She's not exactly the type to just stop showing up to work."

"And as long as we keep up the pretense of interference," Ransom said, "by showing up to rescue the next agent he's going to kill, I'm sure he'll keep trying to set us up."

Rosalind went to the laptop and sent an email to Renegade. It read: RD6 - ch/o△.

Renegade would know that this said there were six of us who needed him to deliver names of the reporting hierarchy, the chain of command. The triangle represented the top down reporting structure.

I marveled at the complexity of it. "How does Renegade know this code?" I asked.

"He worked for Felix too," Rosalind said. "He came to Cold Force much later than Reinhardt and I, about fifteen years or so, but still long ago enough to have qualified for the buyout package. His family is gone, too. But Renegade never saw foreign action. His job was to decode the secret messages the undercover agents slipped back to the department."

It made sense to me then how Renegade knew so much about computers and the inner workings of the CIA. I was relieved. If we were going to stop Felix, we needed the help of the agency. It was shocking to me that Felix was able to operate at such a level without anyone finding out. Who would ever suspect a benign records department director, someone in charge of a department the CIA paid very little attention to, to be conducting covert operations?

It'd only take Renegade a few hours to get us the information, but until then, we had to wait. I was fine with that; I honestly wasn't too keen to leave this little cabin and go back out into Felix's territory.

"I just don't see how Felix could cover up evidence of a helicopter crash. The debris, the people, if there were no survivors…" I tried to visualize the area. It was so densely wooded. "You know, he would have had to have missed something. He moved too quickly. What if some of the helicopter debris flew off into the woods?" I turned to Robert. "Can we go check? See if we can get some evidence?"

"The problem is that the wreckage could be anywhere within a wide range," Robert said. "It would be problematic if we were seen poking around. Our trip back to Springfield has to be quick and quiet."

"It's a good idea, but I have to agree with Robert. Springfield is a small place," Myrtle said. "The residents are a tight bunch of busybodies. I'll bet the explosion was heard by many of the locals. Even if it weren't reported on the local news stations, there would be all sorts of wild speculation. And if someone found the crash site, it would be the talk of the town. But…" She pursed her lips and nodded, thinking,

"Felix wouldn't be able to squash idle gossip. Maybe I should consider doing some hometown grocery shopping. Also, it might be a good idea to see who's at the coffee shop. There is always a bunch of nosy Bettys there who want to draw me into conversation. And they do love to talk."

Rosalind was nodding, too. Of course it made sense that the explosion would've been heard by the locals. Felix couldn't erase sound. Myrtle, just like Robert, was always a step ahead of all of us. She had been listening closely while she was washing dishes at the sink, but she had already figured out a possible next move. It was vital that we find out what became of the intruders at the farmhouse and if Margaret had survived the crash.

"Excellent. We'll go back to Springfield and participate in some… gossip," Reinhardt said, grinning. "But Robert's right, we'll have to be as discreet as possible so no one starts asking questions about us, or this could turn around and end badly."

"You guys should go back to the farmhouse and stay out of sight," Myrtle said. "I'm the best for this. No one will think it's unusual that I'm doing my regular grocery shopping. While I'm there, I should be able to get a very detailed scoop."

"Well, now that we're returning to the farmhouse, maybe I'll be able to pull down the footage from the surveillance cameras," Ransom said. "They bashed up the equipment, but the hard drive is buried inside. With any luck, I can get some images."

Rosalind was frowning. "No. Felix will have someone watching the place." "He knows we're looking for him and also for clues as to his next move."

Robert was shaking his head. "If we're going to get the CIA to recognize what Felix has been up to, we'll have to risk it. I think this is our best chance. I can sneak in through the back path we left by. I'll grab the busted-up surveillance equipment and leave. And just to be on the safe side, let's find another place in town to sleep."

A *ping* sounded on the computer. Renegade had probably found the information Rosalind wanted. We gathered around the laptop, all of us anxious to see his message. It read "RD" with only a link to a classified government CIA site. Rosalind double-clicked a home icon, and the National Archives page appeared on the screen. Felix Szabo was identified as Director of Classified Records. As we suspected, records access was restricted and anyone wanting to view the documents would require written authorization from the secretary of the Defense Department, whose name was not provided.

"Not a problem," said Ransom, grabbing the mouse. A few clicks later, we got the name: Charles J. Hollinger, along with his designations, titles, and responsibilities including secret record retention.

"Old records would be of little priority or interest to the Defense Department. It's quite possible they don't pay much attention to Felix," Reinhardt said. "I'm sure that Hollinger has no idea what's going on or what Felix is doing."

"I think it's time we give Felix a higher profile," Rosalind said. She almost hissed as she spoke his name. "I've always liked Washington. That's where we'll go after we get what we need from the farm and the helicopter crash site." Her eyes had narrowed. I could see myself in her at that moment: the desire for his blood coursing through her.

"How can we find out who Felix's next target is?" I asked.

"Oh, don't you worry, Ruby," Rosalind said. "He'll make sure that we know where his next victim is. He's as interested in luring us to his next target as he is in killing us. Two birds with one stone, that's what he's after. But Reinhardt is right. His ego will get the better of him. It won't be long before he shows his hand."

While we had originally planned to enjoy the peace of the cabin for a couple more days and let the dust settle, it was suddenly urgent that we leave and look for any remaining evidence. But evening had come, and in the dark, it would be unreasonable to set out, so it was decided that we would leave as soon as the sun rose.

Wordlessly, we all got up and began organizing our things for the early departure.

Twelve

THE SIX OF US COLLECTIVELY TENSED UP as the last tree branch slapped us onto the main road. Keenly aware that we were out in the open again, we sat stiffly and hyper watchful as we started the six-hour drive to Springfield. The dense forest had given us protective cover for the last couple of days, and being on this eerily empty road felt uncomfortably vulnerable. The tires screeched as Robert accelerated off the dirt and onto the pavement. Again we were the only car on the road. I so wished for a good old traffic jam, horns honking, people screaming out of windows, so I'd feel like I was back home. This quiet was unnerving.

Finally, about mid-afternoon, we arrived at the outskirts of Springfield, a small rural town nestled among the hills and trees of Massachusetts. Robert pulled off the highway into a motel parking lot. The sign above the office blinked, VACANCY, a fact that was more than obvious as our SUV was the only vehicle in the lot. These Drakers had a knack for finding the motels no one else wanted to step foot into. I had to give them that.

"Wait here while I get us some rooms," Robert said. He cut the engine and headed to the office reception area. A few minutes later he returned with a single key, got back in, and drove us around to the back of the motel where a laneway led to a cottage hidden in among shrubs and tall maples. The exterior of the cottage was so cute with its white siding and curly cued trim with hearts in it, I half expected to find three bears living there.

"This is it," Robert said. "Home sweet home for a day or two. I paid for two nights in advance, with cash so there's no record."

I was grateful to get out and stretch. Everything hurt. I hadn't realized how clenched up I'd been for most of the drive, if not all of it. We all gathered our bags from the narrow space behind the SUV's third row of seats and went in. The first thing that hit us like a wall was the cinnamon air freshener. Rosalind tidily went to the far wood-paneled wall and plucked a cartridge from the outlet. I set my bag down on the plaid sofa and marveled at how the cottage must have been decorated in the '60s: avocado fridge, wood paneling, and a tube television, which I'd only ever seen at the Smithsonian.

"Adorable," said Rosalind dryly. "At least it's private."

Robert did have a nose for finding just the right places for us. This cottage was set apart from all the others and I could barely hear the rare *shush shush* of a car going by on the road. And though we again had to bunk in together, in some way that made me feel safer than if we each had our own separate room. I was glad for the company; my nerves felt jangled and I wanted to be around the others. Their sturdiness and confidence warmed me.

It was agreed we would take turns keeping watch. None of us would put it past Felix to know exactly where we were. We had been careless before and had no intention of being surprised again. Robert and Myrtle agreed to keep guard while the rest of us showered and napped. I was grateful for their heartiness. I'd be flopping over my own feet while those two never seemed to get bogged down by something so pedestrian as fatigue.

Just after six, we headed to the motel's restaurant and sat down at a large round table conveniently set up for all of us. The large window in front looked out onto the empty highway. While we waited to be greeted, only one transport truck and a police cruiser went by. Mournful country music crooned in the background, and one of us occasionally murmured something to the other, but apart from that, we were the only customers and didn't hear any sounds of life: no cooking, no waitresses snapping gum, nothing. Finally, a slender woman with her gray hair done artfully up with a black lacquered chopstick sticking out of it at a peculiar angle approached us with menus. She had on a green and white striped chef's apron, and I wondered if she were the cook too.

"Hello, Helen," Robert said. "You run this whole place, do you?"

She chuckled. "I like to keep busy. Plus it's my motel. I want to keep track of what's going on in it." She winked. "Also it's been quiet like a cemetery around here for the last week. Some loud noise spooked people off, got a bunch of cancellations, and now no one's traveling through here. Word does get around quickly. Oh, but here's something interesting." She lowered her voice to a whisper, "Two government men have been coming around telling people that the Department of National Defense is investigating reported UFO sightings in the area. But no one is supposed to talk about it." She winked. "Top secret, they said."

"Anyway…" She straightened up and cleared her throat, "I've got meatloaf tonight, with veggies and mashed. Dessert is lemon pie, and that's included."

We all ordered the Special and let Helen go off to prepare our meals.

"Government men, UFOs, top secret?" Rosalind said. She barked out a laugh. "That's rich. Felix is so good at this!"

We all shook our heads and snorted as we shifted uncomfortably in our seats, searching the corners of the room and then scanning the highway for cars or unusual activity.

"That's not going to stop the gossip club from talking," Myrtle said. "There's more to this, and my money is on the coffee shop busybodies. Let's see if I can learn anything more and maybe get a location on the crash site. These folks are like aliens themselves. Their antennae are always up."

Helen soon returned from the kitchen with a trolley loaded with plates that were piled high with food. She placed a huge platter in front of each of us. None of us had eaten since breakfast and the aroma of the steaming meatloaf made my mouth water.

We clinked glasses, and I gorged myself on the delicious home cooking faster than my brain could register how full I really was. I looked around the table and saw everyone quietly shoveling down the dinner as well. By the time we finished, we were all groaning happily. Helen returned to clear away the plates and offered us pie.

"Couldn't do it if I wanted to," said Robert, and we all agreed.

Helen grinned. "People can't usually manage dessert after the size of my meals," she said. "I'll pack it up so you can make coffee in your cottage and have it as a midnight snack." She went off and returned with two large boxes.

Robert pulled out his wallet and paid the bill in cash again along with a very generous tip.

Helen beamed.

We got up to return to our cottage. "Helen, could you make sure we're not disturbed," Robert said as he slipped an extra twenty-dollar bill into her hand. "We've had a very long drive today and really need to get some rest."

Helen cocked her head to the side and looked at him strangely. She glanced at the generous tip money in her hand and then back up at Robert. Her face changed and she took on a thoughtful, serious expression as if she'd just understood something. I felt a chill go through me.

"It's been very quiet around here," Helen said again. "But if those government men come around snooping again, I'll tell them that the motel is unoccupied."

He'd been here, looking for us. A shiver of fear tingled down my back; I just needed this to stop. I was so tired. Now someone would have to remain on guard all night.

When we got back, Reinhardt and Ransom took guard watch for the early night shift, and Rosalind put her hand on my shoulder, as if she could sense what I was feeling and was trying to give me strength.

"Ruby and I will take over at four a.m. We'll watch the sun rise together, won't we, Ruby?"

It was raining and a chill wind was beating the drops against the window when Rosalind and I awoke. Ransom was slouched over the laptop and looked tired and frustrated.

"Have you found any information about the UFO sighting?" I asked. "Or Felix's next target?"

"Nothing," Ransom replied, raking his hand through his hair. "I can't understand it. Maybe he hasn't found his next victim yet?"

"Or maybe Myrtle's ambush injured him when he left the farm and he's taking some time to recover," I suggested.

"Get some rest, Ransom," Rosalind said. "Ruby and I will take over your post. We can figure out what Felix is up to later."

Ransom stalked off to the bathroom while Reinhardt quietly gave Rosalind a kiss and went into the bedroom.

We sat down and looked out of the front and side windows at the surrounding grounds. It was too dark and the rain was coming down too hard for us to see anything. That state of "nothingness" gnawed at my stomach. It was like a horror movie where you walk along a dark lonely hallway knowing that someone or something that you can't see is going to jump out and grab you.

I needed to move; I couldn't just sit still. "I can't see anything. I'm going to take walk around the building just to check it out," I said.

"I'm feeling it, too," Rosalind said. "I don't like feeling like a sitting duck."

It was just an urge I had, to be alone with my thoughts, my body. "It's OK, I'll just take a quick check and be back in a minute."

I was just starting for the door when Rosalind grabbed me with both arms and shook me once, sternly. "Rule number one," Rosalind said, "don't do surveillance alone. I'm going with you. Where's your gun?"

My pistol was my constant companion these days. I had it securely tucked into my waistband. I was fully aware of the danger we were in and also knew that my life might well depend on being armed against someone who might be staking out an attack on us.

Looking out onto the soggy night, we realized that we'd be soaked in seconds, so we went to the closet where we found two umbrellas and three rain capes. Helen knew what she was doing; no guest would want to show up to breakfast on a day like this soaked like a wet dog. Rosalind and I slipped on the clear plastic ponchos and put up the umbrellas before venturing outside.

A quick walk around the house convinced us that we were alone. No one was hiding in the bushes or waiting in ambush—or not at the moment anyway. Felix was at least sensible enough to stay out of the rain. I wanted to go back inside and drink coffee, but wanted to be extra sure before we returned.

"Let's take a quick look at the front of the motel and check out the traffic on the highway," I said.

"Indeed," Rosalind said. "It's a lovely morning for a stroll."

I smiled; her sarcasm was her way of saying she agreed with me.

Taking the lead, Rosalind walked cautiously close to the tree line, her gun drawn, as we made the short walk toward the line of dark motel rooms. I pulled out my gun and followed closely behind. In front of the motel, we stopped short, concealed in the shadows of the trees. A light was on in the reception office and in the adjacent restaurant. We looked at each other. Dawn was still a long way off, not a typical time for travelers to need motel rooms, especially around these parts. I wished it were just that Helen was already up and baking scones or something, but the black sedan parked outside the restaurant made my heart sink. It looked like she had company.

We moved in for a closer look and saw two men seated at a table by the front window. Retreating back to the office door, we peered through the window at the reception desk. The room was empty, but a side door that led into the restaurant kitchen was open; light was streaming through and casting shadows of a person moving about beyond the door. In the office, the only light came from a dim wall sconce and a computer screen that was still illuminated. We stole into the room like ghosts, hugging the dark corner of the room and tried to see whose shadow was inside.

The tantalizing smell of bacon wafted into the office. We approached the kitchen door and cracked it open it a bit further.

It was Helen; she was cracking eggs onto the hot grill beside a huge pile of wrinkly, sizzling bacon. She turned to slip bread into a toaster, but we couldn't catch her eye. We had our suspicions, but we needed to find out for certain whom she was serving at this early hour.

We holstered our guns, knocked softly on the door and returned to the reception desk. Thankfully, Helen heard us, and she came out to the desk to find the two of us standing there.

"Government men," she whispered, pointing to the restaurant. "I woke up to noises in the office and when I came in to investigate, they asked if I would open up and serve them breakfast." She leaned in. "They're big and mean looking," she said. "They might be from the government, but I don't trust them. They probably have guns and who knows what their real motives are. One of them had been snooping around at my computer. UFOs indeed! But what are the two of you doing here? I thought you needed to sleep and not be disturbed."

"We saw lights and wondered if you were OK," Rosalind said.

"Did you ask what the men are doing up and about so early?" I asked.

"I didn't want to look like I was prying," Helen said. "I just laughed and called them early birds and told them that I'd be happy to make them some breakfast. They started asking questions about hotel guests, but of course I told them that the motel was empty. They acted very gracious, and the older little guy, Felix, his friend called him, said he'd leave me a big tip for my trouble."

My eyes widened as Helen mentioned the name. Rosalind nudged my thigh with the back of her hand as if to remind me to act casual.

But Helen had noticed my face and cocked her head at me. "You two know this Felix guy?" It was more of a comment than a question. This woman seemed fairly adept at reading people, probably from her years of owning this place and dealing with all the different types coming through. Just my luck; for once it'd be nice to be around someone who didn't notice a thing.

"Helen," said Rosalind calmly stepping to the office door and shutting it against the restaurant. "Let's just say that the men out there aren't legitimately associated with the government. You're right that they're not investigating UFOs. You're also right that we know him. We have to warn you that Felix is a dangerous man. It's important you don't raise any suspicion. Just serve them their breakfast and let them be on their way. Everyone's life depends on your discretion."

A noise from the office door startled us. We turned sharply around and pulled our guns.

Helen gasped.

"What's going on here?" Robert demanded, glancing at Helen.

Myrtle was right behind him, pointing a pistol at the three of us.

At the door, Reinhardt and Ransom looked nervously into the office, looking like they were waiting for an explanation as to why Rosalind and I had left the cottage.

"Hi, guys," whispered Rosalind effusively. "Our friend Helen is making breakfast for Felix and his companion."

"Helen, go attend to your customers and keep acting like everything is normal. We'll protect you, but you can't let them know we're here," Robert said.

Helen looked shaken, but she turned and went back to the kitchen.

We followed her, keeping tight to the wall, in case the men came in to investigate why their eggs were taking so long.

She gave us a worried look as she slipped through the swinging door into the restaurant dining room.

"Here you go, fellas," Helen chirped as she brought out the food. "Can I get you more coffee?"

They shook their heads. "Just the bill," Felix said.

Helen hastened back to the kitchen to tally up the breakfast items on a small pad and poured two coffees into Styrofoam take-out cups with lids. Her hands were shaking.

I felt sorry for her that she'd gotten mixed up in this.

She returned to the dining room. "Two coffees for the road. My compliments," she said. "Thought you might like something hot on such a miserable morning. You sure I can't get you anything else?"

Felix pulled out his wallet and threw a fifty-dollar bill on the table. Without a word, he and the other man abruptly stood up and left the restaurant.

We heard the sedan doors slam and the engine rumble to life. Watching from a dim corner of the dining room away from the window, we breathed sighs of relief as the headlights pierced through the large front window then dimmed as the car turned and sped out onto the highway.

"Charming fellows, that Felix and his friend," Helen said. "I sense that you guys are in some kind of trouble?"

"Let's just say that we need to stay away from them," Robert said. "It's a complicated story and the less you know the safer you'll be. Do you have any reason to think they knew we were here?"

"No..." Helen said, as if she were considering whether that was actually true. "Well, like I told these ladies," she nodded to me and Rosalind, "I did notice that the computer screen was lit up when I came into the office. They must have been checking the guest list. But I don't log in guests who pay in cash, keep it between you and me. No need to involve Uncle Sam, if you know what I mean—" She stopped and panic went over her face. "You won't report me to the IRS, will you? What they would have seen on screen is that the motel is empty, exactly like I told them. I promise."

Robert pulled out his wallet and peeled off several one hundred-dollar bills. He placed them securely in Helen's hand, which he cupped gratefully in his. "Your secret is safe with us," Robert said, "but it's important that no one, especially those two guys, know that we were here."

"So can we ask you about the UFO reports?" Reinhardt asked.

"What do you know about them?"

Helen snorted and laughed. "Firstly, I went to school. I know that there is no such thing as UFOs," she said. "The coffee shop regulars in town have blown the story completely out of proportion. I guess some retired folks have nothing better to do than to argue and gossip over things they don't understand. Some say that they're even scouting the countryside for signs of a burned-out fire or maybe a crash site. If you want information, Tim's Diner is the place to ask questions. But be careful," she cautioned with great seriousness. "They'll try to draw you into their suspicions. Once they have your attention, it it's hard to break out of their clutches. We don't get much excitement around here so this has become quite an obsession with them."

Myrtle didn't have time to suffer even a conversation about fools. "We should leave immediately," she said.

"The coffee shop club, as we call them, meets at eight every morning, just like clockwork. Let me make you something to eat. You have lots of time for breakfast," Helen said. She scurried off to the kitchen.

Ransom went over to the window, drawing the heavy drapes tightly shut. "Just in case our friends drive past again," he said. "Maybe nothing too fancy for breakfast if that's all right? We can't stay long. My guess is they'll drive around town for a while and then go back to the farmhouse to see if we returned. We need to get out there so we have a chance at grabbing the surveillance equipment before they do."

"The last thing we want is another encounter with Felix and his accomplices," Robert said. His face looked lined and heavy. "You're right. They'll probably head over there. I'm not in the mood to meet up with them again."

"They might even be staying there," I said. "It's isolated and it would give them more freedom to poke around. Do we need to go there right now?"

"It may be smart to begin by getting some information at the diner. One should never underestimate the value of a group of keen seniors.

And if the local coffee club went a step further than gossip and actually investigated the area, they'd surely have found where the helicopter crashed. After all, they've had a couple of days." She smiled. "I can't wait to meet these people. Then it's just one more step to Hollinger knowing about Felix's involvement."

Ransom was frowning. "I know it's dangerous, but I still want to recover the surveillance cameras," he said. "Robert, why don't we drop Myrtle and Ruby off at the diner? The locals will be less inquisitive about Myrtle and maybe—a niece?" He nodded at me with a smirk. "Rather than the whole gang of us snooping around. The four of us can slip back to the farm by the back pathway. If Felix is there, we'll hide out in the bushes until they leave. They're probably taking routine drives along the highway to look for us. I know exactly where the cameras are mounted. It would only take me a few minutes to grab them."

A clatter of dishes diverted our attention to Helen who emerged from the kitchen pushing the same stainless steel cart that delivered our dinner last night, only this time, it was loaded with bacon, eggs, toast and coffee.

The scent of comforting breakfast foods filled the room as she laid the large oval plates in front of us.

We dug in with vigor but ate in silence, fearing what the day would bring. We still had hours before things opened in town, so we had to be patient until the next part of our plan could be put into action.

"When you get to the diner, let them overhear you talking about the UFO," Helen said. "They might be elderly, but their hearing is as sharp as any Doberman's. They'll start right in with details of what they think caused the flash of light and loud noise last Tuesday. You won't have to work hard at all to get information." She brought out some brown paper bags from the lower shelf of the cart. "I also packed you some sandwiches and soft drinks in case you don't get a chance to stop for lunch." Her brow furrowed. "Good luck and stay safe."

We all knew that our being there had put Helen in danger. If Felix found out that she had helped us, he'd kill her. Not sharing that realization, we thanked her for her kindness and headed back to the cottage. We quickly gathered our few things, piled ourselves into the SUV and drove off toward town.

Thirteen

THE DAY HAD DAWNED GRAY AND DULL, the driving rain lightening up to a fine mist. We'd taken as much time as we could at breakfast and getting into town, and by now, a few of the locals were out with their umbrellas and Wellington boots, going grocery shopping or ducking into the hunting supply shop where an antlered deer head guarded the door. I noted its sign, which indicated that the store carried a variety of electronics in addition to ammunition and other weaponry. It was a charming downtown, the kind I used to read about in books; the stores' facades were painted in soft country colors of blue, ocher, lavender and heather, many like our cottage with gingerbread trim at their peaks and wood-carved doors with bells on the knob that tinkled when anyone went in or out. Large glass windows, some with striped overhung awnings, displayed the wares sold inside. I craved just resting on a bench to admire the hanging flower baskets, but there wasn't any time to linger. Tim's Diner was located just beside the supermarket and we had some coffee to get.

"Good luck at the farm," Myrtle said. "But be careful. How will we know you're safe?"

"We'll be back in a couple of hours," Robert said, looking at his watch. "By lunchtime. If not, get out of town and find Hollinger."

"Rosalind should stay back in the car," I said, then bit my tongue. It hardly sounded feminist of me to suggest the men do all the work and the woman stay in the car. I just instinctively wanted to protect her, even if she were the last woman in the world who needed protecting. It was just that being typically clear headed in a crisis, she would be helpful if they ran into trouble. Yes, I was sure they'd realize that's what I meant.

Robert dropped Myrtle and me off at the grocery plaza and the two of us went inside to shop for a few things, though, as we idly grabbed bottles of water and some fruit for the car, we mostly just wanted to kill time while the locals settled in to order their coffees. When we'd stalled enough, and had seen enough people through the wide front window go into the cafe, we paid for our items and then headed over.

At the diner, Myrtle and I exchanged a small glance of triumph. We took a table just a few tables over from four gray-haired elders—two men and two women—all of whom were already chattering enthusiastically. The busybodies, as Myrtle called them, seemed to be two married couples enjoying their regular morning coffee while munching on sticky donuts and holding newspapers they weren't reading. They eyed us as we sat, their conversation stopping abruptly as they checked us out.

"What can I get the two of you on this soggy morning?" the waitress asked.

"Just two coffees, please," Myrtle said. "So, have you recovered from the shock of the alien invasion?" she laughed amiably. "You know what I mean—the report of the UFO sighting that everyone is talking about?"

"Can't say that I've seen any little green men around here," the waitress said. She gave an amused snicker and left to get our coffees.

"Hello, Myrtle," said one of the four, a hunched-over man in thin-rimmed glasses. He was dressed as if he were about to go hunting, in a camouflage green-and-gray-pattern hunting jacket and matching brimmed hat. "Surely you'd have seen the bright flash and heard the sonic boom from your farm?"

"Hello, Amos." Myrtle nodded to the couple. "Hannah."

"Why don't you come over and join us at our table," Amos said. "I'm sure Norm and Alice are interested in what you saw last Tuesday as well." He gestured to his friends who nodded. "Might as well tell all of us at the same time. And who is this charming young lady?"

"This is Ruby," Myrtle said. "My niece from Portland. She's staying with me for a few weeks."

Amos pulled up two chairs and slid the adjacent table over to theirs, making room for us. We got up and seated ourselves with them. Amos settled back onto his chair, fidgeting with excitement for details that we might have to offer about that previous day's unexplained events.

The four of them leaned in tightly as Hannah whispered, "Myrtle, did you actually see the spaceship?"

"I just thought it was some lightning and thunder. Didn't really think much more of it," said Myrtle with an innocent face.

I held back a laugh.

They leaned back looking disappointed.

Myrtle smiled sweetly, baiting them. "We didn't hear the UFO story until we got into town this morning!" she said. "But I have to ask…" She whispered, "There's nothing about it on the news, so what makes everyone think it's from outer space?"

"Because men from the Department of Defense are all over the town asking questions about it," Norm said. Taller than Amos with long, dark hair and a rough patch of whiskers on his chin, Norm was dressed in similar hunting gear as Amos. "They don't come around and do that for thunder and lightning."

The others laughed.

"They're telling everyone it's top secret," Alice said, "and not to talk about it to anyone." She made a defiant face. "The heck with that! This is a free country and no one is going to deny me my freedom of speech."

They all nodded vigorously as they sipped their coffees.

"But how do you know it's real?" I asked. "Like, maybe they're making it up to scare people for some reason. I mean, if it was a crash, wouldn't they find pieces of the spaceship or whatever?" I could sound like a teenager if I wanted to, but I'd have died if anyone I knew heard me.

"Well, that's just it," Amos said. "I don't think they know. The two agents keep asking people if they've seen anything. The one his crony called Felix gets kind of threatening when you ask questions back at him about where it might have landed." He whistled. "That guy is fierce. I wouldn't want to meet him in a dark alley."

Hannah added, "They were here at the diner yesterday morning, questioning people. Nobody knew anything. Or at least nobody told him that they knew anything. I acted like I needed to get something at the store and followed them out. The hard little one, Felix, said to the big one, "They're lying. They're all lying.""

"Well," Myrtle said, "have you in fact seen something?"

Amos winked and all four looked smugly into their cups. Amos put his down, leaned in again and in a hushed voice started to explain. "Can you two keep a secret?" he asked. "We know exactly where it is. But." He paused and crooked an eyebrow at Myrtle, "I'm surprised you don't know. It's in the forested area just a couple of miles behind your property."

"Amos," Myrtle said, slapping his arm. "How on earth would you know that? It's purely dense forest out there, just trees, deer, and maybe the odd cougar or two. No one goes in there and expects to find his way out."

Amos pointed back and forth between his and Norm's shirts. "Hunters do," he boasted. "Norm and I go in there all the time. Got ourselves many a deer. The further into the bush we go, the more chance we have to land a kill. But we've never come across a single cougar. Have you?" He looked at Myrtle to see if she was joking.

"What makes you think I've seen cougars." Myrtle laughed.

"Well. You just mentioned 'cougars' and because you bought a new hunting rifle perfect for shooting large game... you must do some hunting. This one is your second rifle."

"You know how many guns I have?" she asked, looking at me as if to say, *See? Told you.*

"Shucks, Myrtle," Amos said. "You know Benjamin is Hannah's brother. Sometimes we talk. I like to know who else might be out there hunting, and I privilege myself of this information, being related to the owner of the gun shop and all. We just wondered why a woman would have several firearms is all."

"I've seen large paw prints around the barn," Myrtle said. "I wanted something with enough fire power to bring down a large animal just in case I did actually spot it roaming about."

"Shut up, Amos," Hannah said. "It's none of our business. Myrtle has the right to protect herself. We all do."

"Sorry, Myrtle," Amos said. "I didn't mean to be nosy, but something isn't right about those two guys."

"What do you mean?" I asked. I appreciated that at least Felix was consistent and we weren't the only ones who thought he was a nut-job.

"We've asked," Amos said, "and they're not staying in any of the places in town or around the area, but instead they just drive all over the highways, back and forth and around, like they're looking for something, or maybe someone. And people are sayin' how they're pretty mean and nasty. Maybe that's why everyone's keeping quiet.

"Myrtle," he added, muttering and leaning in close, "you should be careful out at the farm. I think they've been checking out your property. Norm and I were out hunting yesterday and we saw their black sedan at your place. Didn't you see them?"

"No," Myrtle answered. "I drove up to Maine to pick up Ruby and slept overnight at my brother's. We're just on our way home now. But don't worry, Amos. You know I have my hunting rifles. And that I'm a damn good shot."

I thought about Robert, Reinhardt, Ransom and Rosalind at the farm and closed my eyes quickly to make a wish that they'd be all right.

"Your property, your right to defend it," said Hannah firmly.

The others nodded.

Then Amos started laughing, "I'd love to hear that conversation, *'Honestly, officer. I thought they were cougars!'*"

The others burst into laughter.

I looked up and saw our tan SUV driving past the diner. It was Robert with the others, back from the farm. I exhaled and smiled as I watched them park in front of the supermarket.

Myrtle saw them, too. She stood up. "Well, we really have to get back to the farm," she said. "I'm sure everything will be fine. It was nice chatting with you folks." We started gathering our grocery bags.

"Take care, you two," said Alice.

I could feel eight eyes drilling into my back as we left. We walked to the supermarket parking lot where Robert was waiting safely outside of the range of prying eyes from the coffee shop.

Myrtle and I hopped in, put our bags of groceries in our laps, and buckled up.

"Let's get out of here before anyone notices that Myrtle and I have company."

Robert reversed the SUV and drove us out onto the highway. We were several miles out before anyone asked questions. "Did you get any useful information?" Reinhardt asked.

"Amos says he knows that the crash was a couple of miles from the farmhouse in the forested area of the hills," I said. "They also saw Felix's car at the farmhouse while they were out hunting yesterday."

"We know," Robert said. "They were away when we got there, but there were definite signs that they're staying there."

"Did you find the surveillance equipment?" I asked.

"No," Ransom said. "Felix must have found the cameras. If he's able to recover any files, he'll know that you ladies are with us and…" He paused. "And now he'll know what you look like."

I felt instantly furious. My new face, all the surgery, the whole ordeal, would be for nothing. "Yeah, but you protected the hard drives with passwords or codes or something, right? Don't you need special drivers? Something?" I was desperate. I wanted to scream.

"Ruby, prepare yourself for whatever will come," Rosalind said. "We can't look back, only forward. He won't be able to get into them on his own here in Springfield, which buys us some time, but he definitely will be able to extract the footage back in Washington." She didn't look at me.

"Fine, then. At least we know what he looks like," I said. "So we're even. I just hope we can find some important evidence at the crash site. I want to turn him in and be done with this already."

"Amos says it's only a couple of miles into the forested area," Myrtle said. "But I doubt that we'll find anything from the ground. An aerial view would be very helpful."

"No, too overt," said Robert. "Felix would know we're looking if he hears or sees a helicopter or small aircraft scouting the area. Doing a ground search might be our only option."

I remembered, then, an article I'd read in *Entertainment* magazine about how they shot some of the footage when they filmed *Harry Potter*. "A drone," I exclaimed. "That could do it. They have a range of several miles and could point us in the right direction. Do you think we could trust Amos to take us there?"

"Yes, but it would put not only him, but all of them at risk," Reinhardt cautioned. "Felix would kill them in a heartbeat if he discovered they were involved. We don't want to be responsible for any more casualties."

"A drone is a good idea," Rosalind said. "I'll get Renegade to locate one for us."

Rosalind typed a message into her phone.

A moment later, a *ping* alerted us that Renegade was on the task and would notify us shortly.

Then he messaged again right away to say it would take a few hours to find one and then have it couriered to a nearby location. In the meantime, we had to find somewhere to get out of sight. If we kept driving around on the highway, sooner or later, we'd end up crossing paths with

Felix, a happy coincidence Felix was probably counting on.

Minutes later, I saw on the shoulder of the road, an old pickup truck listing to the side. An elderly man in a hunting jacket got out of the truck and walked to the rear to investigate his back wheel. It appeared he had a flat.

"Oh, Robert, that's Amos," I said. "One of the men from the diner. Can you pull over?" I'd liked Amos. He was a character. And I suspected there was a lot more to him, to the group of them, than met the eye.

Both Reinhardt and Robert looked back at Myrtle in the rear view for confirmation.

"He'll ask us all kinds of questions," Myrtle said. "He'll want to know who you are. At the coffee shop, I let them believe that Ruby and I were alone."

Then I noticed Hannah's poufy blond curls in the cab of the truck. "But if Felix happens to see them first and suspects they're headed to the crash site, or have any investment in that situation personally, they might be in danger. Can we just help them change their flat and then be on our way? We'll just tell them that other family members showed up unexpectedly. Maybe they won't ask anything else."

"Don't count it," Myrtle said. "There's sure to be an interrogation. It's just the way those busybodies operate."

Robert reluctantly pulled over the SUV and got out to help.

Hannah retreated to behind the truck by the passenger door, and Amos stayed put, squatted down by his tire, but his expression was wary. Until Amos saw Myrtle and me get out of the back seat, that is. Then he stood.

"Funny meeting you out here. And you have friends with you?" He looked over at Reinhardt, Robert and Ransom with suspicion.

"You looked like you needed help," Myrtle said.

Amos looked shiftily at Myrtle and then at me, his eyes full of questions but neither he nor Hannah said a word, which, I suspected, was unusual for them both.

Myrtle smiled, laying her hand reassuringly on Amos's shoulder. "Family," Myrtle said. "Ruby's people."

"Humph."

Hannah looked on sullenly from the passenger door. She was clearly uncomfortable being outnumbered by this group of strangers.

"Allow us, please," Robert said. "It's no trouble. We'll have you on your way in no time."

Robert and Ransom tried to be amiable and chatty as they set about the task of jacking up the truck while Reinhardt rolled the spare into position. Rosalind looked nervously up and down the highway before offering Amos a warm beaming smile. Amos didn't seem at all comfortable with our companions, but anxiously and distrustfully stood by as if waiting for something to happen.

Suddenly he and Hannah looked at each other, and she grabbed her rifle and pointed it at Robert, Ransom and Reinhardt. "Myrtle, Ruby," Hannah yelled, "step behind the truck, now!"

Robert, Ransom and Reinhardt, who had just finished installing the new tire, stood and slowly put their hands in the air.

Amos scurried to the driver's door, jerked it open and yanked out another rifle from the rear rack. He joined Hannah in pointing it at us. "You too, Blondie," he said, motioning Rosalind should join the men.

"Amos, what are you doing?" Myrtle asked, glancing at our group as she and I rounded the front of the truck. At Hannah's urging, we hopped inside. Amos waited until we were squeezed in tight, clumsily fumbled into the front seat, started the engine, and sped us off onto the highway, shooting loose gravel over the others left standing on the shoulder of the road.

I was dumbfounded. I had no idea what these two old farts were thinking or why they had pulled weapons on us. Maybe their minds were going, dementia or something like that. We sat quietly. I was afraid to speak, not wanting to say anything that would set them off again.

"Were those folk with the Defense Department men?" Hannah asked.

Amos jumped on his wife's question. "Something's not right about them, Myrtle," he said. His chest puffed up. "Good thing we were in the right place at the right time to help you." Amos looked at us. "We'll turn onto the side road up just ahead and should lose them as soon as we pull off onto the laneway to our house. You'll be safe with us there."

Myrtle had had enough; she was breathing hard. "No. No, you don't understand. They really are our family, or as much as a kind of family as family can be. Amos, they're good. Really. Please stop and let us out. We're in no danger. I promise."

"I don't know about that, Myrtle," Amos said. "They had this strange look about them. They're hiding something or not telling something. Hannah and I both felt it." He looked at Hannah and she nodded, her eyes wide. "We're pretty good at reading people. Kind of like a sixth sense."

This situation was bizarre. Two backwoods seniors thought they were rescuing us from danger. Once, I'd have been grateful for them. Now I knew they couldn't have been more wrong. I frowned at Myrtle.

She rolled her eyes and shrugged her shoulders.

"Amos, Hannah, we're running from the Defense Department men as well," I said. "When we saw it was you with the flat, we wanted to get you off the highway just in case Felix and his sidekick drove by again. He's unpredictable, and we care about you. Now stop and let the others catch up. We'll explain."

Amos looked over at us, almost driving off the road as he shifted his gaze toward us, his eyes wild with the excitement of the moment.

"Watch where you're driving, Amos," Hannah scolded. "You'll kill us all."

"Wait," Amos snapped, "you actually mean we pulled our guns on your kin?"

"Yes, they're our people and they are our family," I said. "Pull over and we'll explain the whole situation." I didn't feel stupid for saying it. On the contrary; it felt right.

Amos pulled off onto a gravel road and idled on the side so Robert could see us. We got out and waited for Robert and the others to catch up. They pulled up, jumping out of the SUV with their pistols drawn.

Amos and Hannah looked at us for assurance. "They have guns. What aren't you telling us?" Hannah demanded.

I took her soft arm in mine. "I promise they're good. We carry guns just like you do. To protect ourselves." I leaned forward and showed her mine poking up from my waistband. I hopped out and moments later, she and Amos shakily climbed down, too.

"Don't shoot, don't shoot," Amos yelled. "It was a mistake."

Some sixth sense; it was more like a .05 sense. That said, in all fairness, we were a fairly unique situation.

"It's OK, Robert," I said. "They thought you kidnapped us, that you were with Felix and his partner. They were trying to protect us. Put down your guns."

The apologetic seniors lowered their arms and walked over to Reinhardt and Robert. "Look, I'm sorry," Amos said. "We thought we were helping Myrtle and Ruby. But if those guys are looking for you, you need to get out of sight. Come back to our place. You'll be safe there."

Rosalind narrowed her eyes. "Provided you don't pull guns on us again, we do need somewhere to stay for a bit." I guessed she meant until Renegade found us a drone. "Let's get off the road before someone really dangerous finds us."

We got back into the vehicles and followed Amos and Hannah a couple of miles down the dirt road and turned onto another hidden laneway masked by trees and bushes. Several hundred feet into the rough, a small house appeared in a tightly treed opening. The house with its rough-cut lumber siding looked more like a garden shed than a house. Amos parked his truck under an attached cedar-shingled carport. Robert parked behind him.

I was relieved that like the cabin we had stayed at in upstate New York, it was well hidden from the road, but more importantly from the air, which I was sure Felix would take to in order to find us if he wasn't getting anywhere on the ground. Still, we got out of the SUV to consider our surroundings tentatively, not trusting that Felix or his thugs weren't hiding among the trees ready to ambush us again. Our hands were close at our sides ready to go to our weapons. Amos and Hannah lifted their rifles from their truck before approaching to talk to us.

"Come inside," Hannah said. "Strange things have been going on here in Springfield, and if you folks are involved and plan to hide out with us, you owe us an explanation." She gave us a piercing critical stare. No one wanted to start so we all said nothing. Frustrated, she walked into the shack, disappearing beyond a creaking door flaked with blistered paint.

Reluctantly, we followed and entered the shabby dwelling.

"Sorry about the mess," Hannah said. She was already over at the stove putting on the kettle. "I'll make some coffee. Make yourselves at home."

It was difficult to decide where to sit. Newspapers, magazines and miscellaneous papers were strewn over the tables and chairs, their jackets and sweaters draped over the sofa and other upholstered recliners. Myrtle huffed at the disorderly clutter and started to gather the clothes to hang in the closet by the door. I cleared the table to make room for coffee. Hannah was now running hot water from a rusted tap into the sink and washing the cups that had been sitting dirty in the basin. Amos appeared at the door with an armful of firewood and dropped it into a bin by the wood-burning stove.

"I'll just get a fire going," Amos said. "Will take the chill right off. Just make yoursel…" He paused, noticing everyone busying himself with bringing order to the chaos. Amos cast a momentary judgmental look at Hannah, still busy washing dishes. He huffed and resumed his attention to the fire. Ten minutes later, coffee was ready and we were all warm and seated comfortably but were waiting anxiously for an intense interrogation from our meddling hosts.

Amos broke the silence first. "So you say that you're running from the Defense Department men," he said. "Why are they looking for you?

You guys some kind of spies?" Hannah and Amos looked at us with unveiled elation, enjoying the intrigue of the moment.

"Look," said Myrtle, splaying her square fingers over the top of her cup. "The less you know, the better off you'll be. The two of you are in danger just for having us here. You should have let us change the tire and be on our way. This makes things complicated."

Ransom leaned in. "We're waiting for the delivery of a drone, which will help us survey the crash site by air. As soon as we hear from our contact, we'll be on our way."

"Shucks," Amos said, "it's not that far from here. I can show you where it is. You'll be there and back long before your high-tech contraption even ships out."

"No. We can't let you get any more involved," Reinhardt said.

"Well, if you don't come with me, I'll just have to go on my own and see what all the fuss is about," Amos countered. "This is America. We have the right to defend our territory, you know. Stay if you want, but I'm finishing my coffee and then I'll be on my way."

Amos gulped down the last of his hot brew and went over to the door where he had dropped his hat and hunting jacket on the floor. He dressed quickly and grabbed his rifle that was propped up against the wall. He gave us a long final stare and headed out the door.

Rosalind sighed. "I guess we're going hiking."

We rushed after our determined host who was waiting by his truck. When he saw us pouring out of his house, he grinned. "The easiest access is by a trail Norm and I call Hunter's Pass," Amos said. "It's a couple of concessions over on a dirt road that's rarely used. Norm and I usually drive right into the bush a ways. It's easier on our old legs and then no one sees when we're hunting out of season. Besides, that Felix scoundrel won't spot our vehicles from the road if he does happen to drive up there. You'll have to follow me."

Myrtle and I went with our fellow Drakers and followed in the SUV over the rough country gravel roads that crisscrossed the outlying areas of Springfield. He was right. It wasn't very far. Minutes later he had pulled into a thicket of trees that swallowed his truck completely. We stayed on his tail, slipping the SUV precariously among the trees and brush well back into the forest. When we came to a stop, Amos was waiting for us under a grove of pines waving our SUV into tall grasses where, in this dense bush, our car would be impossible to spot even if someone were looking for it.

"It's a half hour north of here," Amos said. "There's lots of wildlife. You might see deer or wolves. But Myrtle, I've never seen a cougar." He winked. "Unless you mean my wife when she talks to some of those young bucks in town," he looked at Hannah. "She's really an incorrigible flirt."

Hannah snorted.

"Lead on," Robert said.

Amos headed off into the trees carefully noting landmarks that indicated the direction north toward the helicopter crash site. I was impressed that someone his age could hike with such agility and strength. The only times he stopped were to check the ground for tracks. I, and it seemed the others, on the other hand, found the trek arduous. We were good runners, but we weren't used to the rough, uneven ground, and going almost entirely uphill. We trudged on, each step more uncomfortable than the one before. I figured fate worked in mysterious ways; sure, it'd been a weird morning, but then again, we'd have never found this spot even with a drone and its GPS.

We had fallen back from Amos's lead, all of us not talking, breathing hard. He stopped to call back to us. "We're almost there. Only another quarter mile up that hill." He turned and started to climb a rocky path.

That quarter mile was painful and sapped the last of my remaining energy. When we finally reached the summit, we stopped and flopped onto the soft, moss-covered earth to rest. Amos, however, went another five hundred feet until he disappeared beyond more brush and trees.

After several moments, hearing nothing, we wondered if something were wrong.

"Where is he?" I asked.

"Maybe he's left us stranded, trying to lose us. I don't trust that old man," said Ransom.

We pulled ourselves off the ground and walked into the bushes where Amos had disappeared. We pushed past a distance of undergrowth that scratched and brushed against our skin and clothes before finding our way into a clearing where broken tree limbs lay scattered on a large, burned patch of grass.

This was it. The area looked like a demolition zone. In places, the ground had been cratered; exposed roots and bare dark soil on which burned skeletons of bushes and trees lay, indicated that a catastrophe had occurred. We looked around, but Amos was nowhere in sight. Then on the far side of the disaster zone, the bushes moved. We took cover and drew our guns.

Amos emerged from the brush dragging a large narrow piece of metal behind him.

"The helicopter is gone," Amos said. "How the hell does something the size of a chopper disappear from a remote hillside? Something is definitely wrong here." Confused, he looked questioningly at us for an explanation.

He'd known all along there was no UFO. "Was the whole helicopter here a few days ago? I asked.

"You bet. Norm and I just about had a heart attack when we saw it," Amos said. "Couldn't have been more than a few minutes after the crash. We came in for a closer look to see if anyone was still alive."

"And?" Reinhardt asked.

"Not a one," Amos said. "Just the helicopter, parts of it on fire, but no one inside or around the area. Norm and I looked around real good. It was like the chopper flew itself."

"What have you got there?" Robert asked, looking at the metal in Amos' hand.

Amos held out a flat charred piece of metal several feet long. "Don't really know," he said. "Maybe a blade from a propeller, definitely nothing that should be out here on its own."

"If they missed that, they'd have missed other things. Let's check out the area a little more," Robert said. "There have to be signs as to how Felix moved the helicopter."

We paired up and started to search the surrounding area. A few bits of glass and metal lay strewn around the perimeter. There was no question that this was the site of the crash, but apart from this standard detritus, nothing remained to identify the specific circumstances of the crash. Felix must have done an aerial search for evidence and had probably lifted out the craft with hoists the same way. But where would the bodies have gone? It'd be a special person who could have people buried and so well-concealed that they couldn't be located by these two geezers just minutes after the craft went down. Still, we hunted for possible grave sites. But there was nothing.

"There's nothing of use to us here," Rosalind said. "Let's get back to town." We had to agree; Amos had found the only interesting piece, and it was too small and inconclusive to get Hollinger's attention.

Half an hour later, we were back at the SUV still carefully hidden among the grasses.

"Amos," Reinhardt said, "it might be a good idea for you and Hannah to get away from Springfield for a while." I could tell just by looking at him and hearing what he wasn't saying that because they'd helped us, if Felix had spotted them with us, they'd become targets, too.

"Don't you worry none about Hannah and me," Amos said. "We know how to look after ourselves." He patted the barrel of his rifle. "Any unknowns come nosing around our place will be shot first and asked questions later. Our Constitution guarantees our right to defend ourselves. You all be careful now, and good luck finding your evidence to get that scoundrel."

We thanked our rugged old friend and fought our way back to the car among the tall, tussled grasses. It was more difficult getting the SUV out of the grassy bog than it had been to get it in, but after much gear shifting and rocking, a vehicle so dirty it was unrecognizable emerged from the forest onto the remote gravel road that led back to town.

It had been a hard day. I'd let myself feel sure that we'd find something, and now I felt extremely disappointed that the crash site hadn't yielded anything useful. Moreover, Felix was closing the noose. Not only had he taken over Robert's farmhouse, leaving us homeless and forever infecting Robert's childhood home with his presence, he had limited the places where we could hide. There were a few motels along the strip of main highway he and his companion were patrolling, which meant if we stayed in Springfield to find him, it was just a matter of time before he found us first.

"There's nothing more we can do here," said Reinhardt. "I'd like to get us to D.C. where we can just meet with Hollinger and appeal to his sense of reason. Not much else we can do without walking in there brandishing a twisted wreck of a helicopter."

"That's a good idea, Reinhardt," said Rosalind, reaching up to where he sat in the front seat and entwining her fingers in his. A *ping* came from her pocket. It was Renegade confirming the delivery of the drone. It was waiting for us at the local post office inside a gas station just off the highway at the top of the main street.

"Great timing," scoffed Ransom.

"Well, it's here now, so we may as well pick it up," said Robert. "It might be useful later. Anyway, we need gas, so the timing is actually perfect. I hope they have a hose, too. I can barely see through this muck. Can't roll into the nation's capital looking like we've just come out of the swamp."

***

The sun was blazing now, having burned off the fog from the forest. I relaxed in my seat and enjoyed the countryside.

A couple of miles before we got to town, Ransom pointed out the window. "An auto wrecker," he said. "Robert, turn in there."

The wrecker's front yard was piled so high with rusted vehicles, we could see them heaped up over the place's corrugated metal fence.

As Robert pulled in, Myrtle sat up. "If ever I wanted to get rid of a crashed-up helicopter," she started, "I believe I'd discard the wreck at a junk yard." She pointed to the back where a strange-looking piece of metal peeked above the fence. "Maybe Felix isn't so smart after all."

Robert parked, the car creating a cloud of beige dust. Approaching us was a tall, hefty man with salt and pepper hair wild like desert brush, and a chin and neck sporting several days' growth of whiskers. The smell of oil and gasoline on his overalls met us before he did. He waddled over to greet us and waved at his stock with a hand holding a half-consumed Budweiser. "Looking for anything in particular?" he asked grandly, his eyes half-lidded.

"We noticed your collection of vintage vehicles from the road," Reinhardt said. "Do you mind if we have a look around your yard? We're collectors and sometimes we just get lucky and find a treasure in among the... thorns." Reinhardt had started to say "junk," but he caught himself.

"Be my guest." He rattled a jumble of keys that hung on a heavy chain from his pocket, selected the right one and walked over to the sliding panel door in the fence. When he unlocked it and yanked hard on the door, he exposed what looked like the aftermath of mechanical warfare. Tall, precarious piles of twisted, rusted and dismembered auto corpses filled a vast arena like a maze. The narrow paths snaking through the debris were dotted with puddles ribboned with petroleum rainbows. In here, there was no sound, no wind, all blocked by the towers of cars. The smell of old metal, rubber and gasoline bit sourly into my nostrils. Each of us wandered in among the car towers, not really knowing how we'd identify a crushed helicopter.

After several minutes, I heard a small voice. "Over here." It was Myrtle.

Everyone came to where she was standing and found her proudly holding her hands up to the destroyed remains of a helicopter cockpit. The upper shell and window framing were intact, but the undercarriage had been blown open, revealing thick jumbles of wiring spilling out like spaghetti. The mid-section was missing, but the rotary blades of the tail protruded straight up from the tangled mess. Ransom and Robert climbed the pile of rubble carefully to look inside the remaining portion of the cabin. My heart surged with hope; maybe this was it, maybe this would be enough to link to Felix.

The skeleton creaked and shifted hazardously as they crawled inside. Rosalind and I took photos with our phones. I felt like paparazzi. But then I thought about it; how could we prove that this chopper had been used to target Margaret Warren?

"It's Felix's helicopter for sure," said Robert. "I found stuff inside. And bingo! Forensic samples!" He held up a blue rag. "This looks like a shred of the jeans Margaret was wearing. And it has blood stains on it." He grinned and wiggled the fabric.

I felt happy then felt conflicted for feeling happy. Not much I could do about the past. I shrugged. We had no choice but to look forward and try to make things right.

"That's a relief," said Rosalind. "Even if this isn't enough to prove Felix killed her, it's certainly enough to start an investigation about her death that could eventually lead to Hollinger's finding that Felix killed her." She produced a clean Ziploc baggie from her bag and leaned on her tiptoes to hand it to Ransom, who passed it to Robert.

"But it would be so much more effective if we could tie Felix to this evidence," I said. "Somehow we have to prove that he's here snooping in Springfield, telling people that he's with the Defense Department and making up stories about UFOs. If I were Felix's boss, I'd want to know why my Archives manager had found himself a new hobby."

Ransom punched himself in the thigh. "I hate that we don't have any of the video from the farmhouse," he said through clenched teeth. "That would have been more than enough for the Defense Department to put him under surveillance, start watching what he's doing."

Then it occurred to me. "Maybe some of the places in town have security cameras. You know, to catch shoplifters or something, Felix and his buddy have been masquerading as government agents. Maybe they've been caught on film. Plus people in town have seen them and talked to them, so we have witnesses. We should go back and find out."

"That's a good idea," said Robert. "The only problem will be getting access to shopkeepers' files without telling them everything and possibly ruining our plan. Or worse, one of them is under the thumb of Felix and rats us out."

"Leave that to me," Ransom said, smiling. I hadn't seen him smile in several days and it caught me off guard. He saw me looking at him and stared back at me. I looked away and busied myself with the rough edge of my fingernail as we left, retracing our steps to the gate.

On the other side, Reinhardt waved to the man.

"Did you find anything you're after?" he asked. He took a long slug of his beer, teetering slightly as he came closer to discuss business.

"Lots of interesting stuff in there," Reinhardt said. "How late are you open? We might want a second look."

"Nine p.m.," the man said.

"Oh, that's perfect," Reinhardt said. "That will give us time to call our clients and see if they're interested."

The man grunted, threw his empty over the fence and took another Bud from a long pocket on the thigh of his overalls, twisted the cap and slugged back half the bottle. "Yeah, right, I'm sure you'll be back," he muttered. He flung his arm in a good riddance wave as he turned to go back to his tin-sided shed.

We piled into the muddy SUV and headed to town. The car may have weighed more for all the dirt on it, but I felt lighter like I'd set down a rock I'd been carrying for a long time.

Fourteen

I MULLED THINGS OVER on our way to the gas station. The problem with Felix was that he was irrational; he was after us for something that in his twisted mind was a very good reason. I worried that if we even chatted with any of the locals and he found out, he'd be after them, too, innocent people, maybe people with families, children. And the way he was going about his cat and mouse game was just that, it was a game to him, as though hunting us down was sport. We had to find some surveillance footage, hard evidence that placed him in the location of the killings that he so cleverly covered up and kept out of the news. Then we'd all be safe. As it was, I knew he'd infected sweet, sleepy Springfield with fear.

The gas station was huge and its logo and plastic brightness made it look like an oasis of civilization with its bathrooms, car wash, a convenience store and a post office.

Robert pulled the SUV into the first lane of pumps and a teenaged gas station attendant burst out of the door. The sign said self-serve, but the young man seemed bent on being helpful. He was awkward and geeky with spiky white-blond hair that had far too much gel in it. I got the feeling this was his first ever job or maybe even it was his first day on his first ever job the way he kept tripping on the hose and bumping into the cement curbs. On his chin was a cluster of very angry looking acne. My heart just broke; that could have been my brother in a few years if he hadn't been murdered.

He yanked on the hose and jabbed it into the tank. "My name is Spike. Can I fill it up, sir?"

Robert cracked a smile. "Yes, please. Listen, a package was delivered here for us today. Is the post office inside?"

"Yes, sir," he said proudly. "I run that too. I'll be in as soon as your tank is full. Want me to clean your windows? Looks like they need it." He snorted. "I'll just finish up here and be right in to get your mail. If you want, go on in and have a look around. Feel free."

"Well as kind as your offer to wash the windows is, I'm thinking a full car wash might be more effective," Robert said. "I don't see anyone over there." He looked at the boy. "Or are you in charge of that, too?"

"Yep," Spike said. "I'm a one man show." He cracked up again. He looked into the back window and seemed startled to see me. I smiled at him and he blushed furiously and looked down intently at the gas nozzle.

"But we'll get the package first," Reinhardt said, leaning over Robert to tell Spike.

"What? Oh, sure, sure," he said, staring now at the gas meter.

Rosalind and I giggled. He was so cute.

We got out and went inside. When we walked into the air conditioning, I felt instantly comforted by the terrible familiar smell of rotating hot dogs and bad coffee, the rows upon rows of snacks, DVDs, tourist trinkets, and clothes. There was a sign at a counter at the far end that said, U.S. Postal Service.

A few moments later, the young man hurried back inside the variety. He stubbed his foot on the threshold, which caused him to lose his balance and he knocked over an orange pylon. He carefully replaced the cone to its corner and came over to the postal counter where Ransom and Reinhardt were waiting.

"Just hold on a second. Only one package came in today, so it must be yours. Be right back."

He bound with a loud thud through the swinging doors into the back room. A series of bumps and bangs and muttering came from behind the wall. I wondered what the problem was. He said he saw it there earlier.

Behind us, I heard the ding of a bell. I hadn't seen anyone else come in and flipped around, startled. I couldn't believe it, but going to the convenience store counter was the burly man from the helicopter, Felix's assistant or friend or whatever he was, who had lifted Margaret into the helicopter. He rang the bell again looking annoyed and very much alive.

"Shit," I whispered under my breath. I glanced around the store to see if Felix was with him. Through the window I spotted a black sedan at the second line of pumps. I couldn't see his face but I knew it was Felix from his small tight form and jerky gestures. He was at the gas pump fumbling with the hose, trying to awkwardly insert the nozzle into his car's gas tank. I watched him from the safety of the chip aisle then saw him finally get the nozzle in and turn to look inquisitively at the dirty SUV at the next pump over.

I slid as silently and inconspicuously as possible from the bags of Doritos and Ruffles to the postal counter. The others had also noticed Felix's crony. Without a word, we stealthily moved through the swinging doors to join the store clerk in the back. The puzzled look on his face could have as easily given way to him exclaiming something, but fortunately Rosalind could be gentle and maternal when she wanted to be.

She went to him and put a soft hand on his shoulder, while putting a finger to her lips. "There's a man wanting to pay at the counter." Her voice was as calm and sweet as a summer's morning. "He's one of those government Defense Department men who have been scaring the town's folk." She stepped forward and whispered right into his ear. "We really don't want him to see us nor do we want to talk to him or have him ask us any questions. Can you go be a good boy and take his money and get rid of him? Let's not let him know we're here, OK, love?"

Her enunciation was so precise and direct, it was as if he'd been hypnotized. He nodded, his eyes glazed over.

"That's good, Spike. Very good." Without looking down, Rosalind reached into her bag and pulled a hundred-dollar bill from a zippered pocket inside and pressed it to his sweaty hand. Spike would have known all about the drama that was unfolding in his small town—at least up to a point.

His eyes sparkled when he looked down. He pocketed the bill and grinned wide. "You bet!" he whispered.

He opened the door narrowly and peeked cautiously at the counter where the bulky man fumed and dinged the bell again. Spike nodded back at us and went to the counter to serve his customer.

"About time! Here," the man said, throwing down some items. "And pump two." The man jerked his thumb out toward the pumps. "Whose car is that?"

The lad hesitated and glanced at the postal doors. I thought for sure the man would know something was up then, but he was staring at the boy.

"Just some customers, sir," he said as he shrugged his shoulders. "I think they're thinking about getting a car wash. They're probably wandering around outside waiting for me to start up the wash center."

"How many are there?" Felix's man asked.

"I don't know," the store attendant said. He punched the numbers into his register. "That'll be sixty dollars for the gas, the soda and chocolate bar. Anything else, sir?" His voice squeaked on the last "sir." I cringed.

The man stared menacingly at the youth for a moment, but Spike held his ground. Felix's man grunted and rudely threw money at him before leaving the store, looking over his shoulder and scanning the aisles.

Once the burly man had gotten back to his own car, Ransom muttered, "Watch the door. This is going to take a few minutes." Ransom had scooted over to a cluttered desk in the corner where an ancient desktop was humming, its screen green and covered with dust.

He inserted a thumb drive into the USB port and in seconds, a pop-up appeared: files being copied.

"I can't believe our good luck," Ransom said, "but speaking of surveillance cameras, we've hit the jackpot." He pointed to the first of four screens on another monitor on the desk, all of which were trained on various areas of the gas station and store. "Look at that. There's Felix... See him? He is watching his man come out of the store... and... bingo. He just looked right into the camera. I've got it."

Ransom tore the external drive out of the slot and put it back into his pocket.

"Good luck?" I said. "Are you crazy? One mistake and Felix will know we're here. I think all the luck is on his side. We need to get out of here, now!" Felix's face was staring directly at me from the monitor. My heart was racing. I didn't know which emotion inside of me was stronger: fear or hatred. I pulsed with emotion but my body had grown numb. I couldn't move. His face, so close, held me in a trance.

Just then, Spike returned to the back room. The wide smile on his face indicated that he was pleased with his performance at the register. He looked at me and cocked his head. "If those guys are looking for you, I can help," he said. "I'll put your car through the car wash, get it all cleaned up and drive it over to the diner in town after I get off my shift. You can take my van and we'll switch when I get there. I'll put your package in the car." He threw us his keys.

"Are they still out there?" Reinhardt asked.

"They poked around for a while but then drove off up Main Street. But they have to come back this way to get on the highway. That sedan has been seen driving up and down the highway throughout the day and sometimes at night. Everybody's been talking about it in secret. Pretty clear that those guys are looking for someone." He paused. "The man asked about your car. I'm, um, actually saving up for a car of my own. So I promise to take real good care of it." He whipped his head around dramatically. I had to laugh; this kid clearly watched a lot of movies. "You can leave by the back door," he whispered. "I'll be there in less than an hour."

Spike's enthusiasm was intense. While this may have been a lark for him, like a movie come to life in his otherwise boring existence, and a lucrative gig to boot, this was so real to me, I worried if we screwed it up, we'd all end up like Margaret: a torn piece of bloody pants in a junkyard.

"You're getting a bit carried away, Spike," Robert said, laughing off the moment's intensity. "We just weren't in the mood to talk to them. Our friends have told us that they're kind of mean and nasty. So, while we appreciate your help, we won't need your van. But we'll accept your offer to wash our car." Robert threw Spike's van keys back at him. "I've got another fifty for you if you can do it now."

I looked at Robert and realized what he was doing. If this kid got tangled with us, he'd be trapped in the web, too. He had his whole life ahead of him, a car to save up for.

Spike glanced at me, and I smiled encouragingly.

"Yes, sir!" He pocketed the cash and sprang to the task of getting the SUV over to the car wash. "It'll only take about ten minutes," he said. "Maybe they won't recognize your car when it's clean. I'll have it looking like new in no time at all." He looked at us, seeking approval. Getting none, he glowered for a second. I knew that face and wanted to say to him, adults definitely do not get it. I did, but I had to side with the grown-ups on this one.

We remained in the back room out of sight while he burst through the door like a cowboy into a saloon, the energy of youth and motivation of money charging his every move. If Felix and his friend drove past again, the car would be either in the car wash or parked out back and they wouldn't see us through the store windows. Reassured we were safe for the moment, we took to rummaging through the storeroom for the drone.

Ten minutes later, true to his word, Spike tore in through the back door of the office. In what I gathered was his usual clumsiness, he caught his foot under a large box on the floor, falling to his knees on top of it. I had to wonder how he ever managed to get anywhere without breaking half the bones in his body.

"Careful, buddy," Reinhardt said. "Are you OK?"

"Yeah," Spike replied looking down at the box. "Oh!" he laughed. "Found it! You'll have to sign for it. RD. Is that you?"

The box was addressed to RD, c/o Postal Station 52, Springfield MA.

Spike got up and fetched a courier delivery receipt form from the drawer and handed it to Reinhardt who discretely signed it with illegible initials: RD.

"Your car is parked right outside the door," Spike said. "If there's anything else you need, I'd be glad to help." Spike was obviously enjoying the intrigue, but we'd involved him enough. His safety depended on his knowing as little as possible, and on us leaving discretely and soon.

"Spike," Robert said. "Remember. We were never here." Robert winked at him. "This is for the car wash." Robert passed the delighted youth another fifty and we left without further conversation out the back door to a sparkling clean car parked right outside.

"Bye," said Spike a bit solemnly. He waved until we were long gone.

"Let's get something to eat before we head for D.C.," Reinhardt said. "It will be a long drive, and we don't want to make too many stops along the way."

As our SUV pulled around to the front of the station, a black sedan passed going in the opposite direction. After it had disappeared from sight, Robert stomped on the brake pedal and our car skidded to a stop.

He let out an enraged groan. "I know I seem as impenetrable as Fort Knox, but Washington is a very long drive, and frankly, I feel like a good night's sleep would better prepare not just me but all of us for a fresh start tomorrow morning. I'm going to suggest we go back to Helen's place. She's an ally, a good cook, and we're familiar with the terrain."

"Good idea," said Rosalind, stifling a yawn. "I could use some of her home cooking. If I stay awake that long."

***

The afternoon sun was casting shadows on the store fronts along Main Street. Some of the shops had started closing down for the day and were dragging in outdoor tables and displays. There were only a few people on the street and even fewer cars. We stuck out like sore thumbs among the locals, and I suspected we should've pushed on to the Capital, but it wasn't my call. Anyway, one last night would probably be all right. The risk of running into the black sedan was high, but Felix had already checked out the Inn and would have reasonably figured we were long gone. I hoped so, anyway. Trying to stay one step ahead of him was proving to be tricky.

A light in the reception office at the Inn indicated that it was open for business but the parking lot was as empty as it had been the last time. Robert drove up close to the office door and all of us went inside, hoping that Helen had already started her dinner special.

She was at the computer and looked distressed as we entered. She got up and shut the curtains. "You should put the car around the back where it won't be seen from the road," she said. "I wasn't expecting to see you back here. Those government men have been patrolling the highway all day."

"Our hope," said Robert, "is that he'd believe we wouldn't dare come back here given that he's patrolling the area so intensely. Sleeping right under his nose might be safer than trying to outrun it, especially since I don't think I can drive another mile today." He smiled wanly. "Should we assume you have a vacancy?"

Helen and Robert exchanged a mischievous laugh.

The rest of us were too tense to appreciate the humor. Helen nodded and lightly touched Robert's hand. He looked down at it and after a moment, put his other one on top of hers.

"I'm sure I might be able to find something for you," she said. "Plus, you already paid me for a night you didn't use. The cottage is clean and ready. So get yourselves settled, and I'll have dinner finished by the time you get back here. I hope you're hungry!"

She pulled a key from a drawer and handed it to Robert. Her brow tensed. "Or maybe you should eat in your cottage? Might be safer."

Robert grabbed the keys. "We'll take our chances. I'm tired of having to tiptoe around because of this guy."

He left brusquely and drove off behind the motel to where our cottage lay hidden among the trees.

The rest of us decided to do a thorough inspection around the motel and the grounds before joining him. Apparently, I wasn't the only one who felt uncertain about our decision to spend another night at the cottage. We took our time scouring the grounds for signs of anyone in hiding or clues that someone had been lurking about.

It was getting dark by the time we joined Robert at the cottage. He had already brought our stuff inside and was sitting in the dark checking for messages on the laptop that he had set up at the kitchenette table. "I've emailed Renegade," he said. "I'm getting an address for Hollinger. I think it will be better to courier the thumb drive and fabric sample. I'll ask Helen to FedEx it."

"So then we won't really need to go to Washington," I said, feeling hopeful. "Maybe we should find a way to slip away from Felix for a while. Get back to Fairhaven. It's obvious that the authorities aren't looking for us. Felix has made sure of that. Robert, you did it last time, made our charter disappear off the radar after take-off. Can you do that again?"

Rosalind came over to me and put her hand on my shoulder. I knew she could feel my anxiety. She nodded over to Reinhardt. "OK," she said. "But I want Ransom to touch base with Renegade and make sure that nothing on our monitoring system has come up on this side of the pond. Felix must be frantic by now because he hasn't found us. I can't help but think that he's working on another plan to try to draw us out."

"Of course he's planning something," Myrtle said. "And I don't like being the one who's hunted." Myrtle moved from window to window, nervously looking for signs that we were being watched. She looked like I felt.

"The courier package to Hollinger should do the trick," Reinhardt said. "We can always send more anonymous evidence later. In fact, repeated inferences to Felix will have to be investigated by Hollinger who fortunately has enough sense to be discrete. Hopefully Hollinger will blindside Felix."

"Do you think that video of him in Springfield and blood on a scrap of denim will be enough?" I asked.

"If anything, they will certainly make Hollinger wonder why Felix is lurking around here and not in Washington doing his job," Reinhardt said. "I doubt he called in sick," he said dryly. "Hollinger will check to see if he's been at work, and when he sees Felix hasn't, his unauthorized absence will be suspicious. He may not be able to pinpoint the reason for the wrecked helicopter photos, but the fact that no mishaps of that kind in the Springfield area were reported would be curious. As for the blood on the fabric sample, it will be tested. And if we include an anonymous note in our package of evidence about Magda Worchenski, who has most certainly been reported missing by now, that should really rouse Hollinger's interest."

"We'll have to print out the photos," Rosalind said. "Emailing them from one of our phones will tag our location. Helen has a printer in the office. Let's put the package together and get a courier envelope from her when we go for dinner. Right now, I want to take a shower and freshen up a bit."

Rosalind took a shower so long and hot that steam came out from under the door of the little bathroom. When we finally heard the hair-dryer's high-pitched whine, Myrtle and I knew we'd soon get our turns. Myrtle perched on the edge of the bed holding her towel, ready to pounce into the bathroom.

I couldn't sit still. Immobility heightened that feeling of impending catastrophe and it gnawed inside my belly. Darkness had fallen, but I decided I wanted to have a quick look around the cabin. I figured I knew the area well enough, and if I stuck close to the cabin, I'd be fine. I knew if I didn't get some air or do something useful, I'd lose my marbles.

There was no light on the little porch, but my eyes adjusted quickly to the shadows. I stepped off onto the grass and began to stalk around the perimeter. My paranoia must have been getting the better of me because I couldn't help but feel that I was being watched. I scolded myself as I remembered Rosalind's rule number one: never do surveillance alone and immediately regretted my decision and started to head back inside. I felt around my torso; at least I still had my gun. Just to be sure, I pulled the weapon as I rounded the cabin and returned to the front door.

A shadowy movement down the lane caught my attention. I crouched close to the safety of the front door and watched a moment longer. Maybe it was my imagination. Unnerved, I grabbed the door handle and was about to dash inside and slam the door behind me, when I was greeted by a stern-faced Rosalind who had everyone ready with guns drawn to come outside and look for me.

She immediately launched into a tirade. "What the hell do you think you're doing," she yelled. "Didn't I tell you not to go out alone? That kind of stupidity will get you and the rest of us killed."

"I thought I saw someone down the lane," I said. I hadn't gotten over the adrenaline rush yet and blurted out my finding. "It was just a shadow, and I only spotted it for a second. It spooked me, so I came in to get you guys. Maybe it was just my imagination. I've been jumpy since we left the gas station."

Myrtle burst out of the bathroom, still fully dressed. She grabbed her hunting rifle which was propped against the wall by the entry, and checked out the window. She had that same look she'd had when we were in the barn trying to free the boys from Felix's capture, that look she had when cougars were afoot. "I don't see anything," she said, "but we need to check it out. Form two teams of three and approach the restaurant from different sides."

Rosalind, Reinhardt and Ransom left the cottage first. They skirted behind the bushes on the opposite side of the lane from the motel and approached the restaurant.

Myrtle, Robert and I left behind them and snaked through the tree line to join up with them at the restaurant. Robert took the lead. Myrtle followed, stalking with her cougar rifle, and I stayed close behind in the rear. I could almost feel the breath on my neck of the person who belonged to the shadow I'd seen earlier. The snap of a twig caused me to stop and look back at the cabin. "Myrtle, I—" I started to say, when someone grabbed me from behind with one bulky arm, and pressed the other to my mouth. I instinctively jerked my gun behind me to the side and squeezed the trigger. The sound of the bullet made a low thud as it came into contact with something, I didn't know what, before I was held in a strangling grip and dragged off to the bushes.

Fifteen

WHOEVER HAD ME WAS TALL AND STRONG with arms as solid as tree trunks. The more I struggled, the tighter his grip became. After the initial shock wore off, I didn't have to see him to know who it was. He lifted my body as he forced me further into the bushes, my feet barely touching the ground so I couldn't get enough of a foothold to anchor myself sufficiently to launch a blow or kick against him. So I did what I could and wriggled and squirmed and kicked my feet to at least make myself difficult to hold onto. I cursed myself for my weakness. Rosalind would be furious that I allowed myself to be overtaken this way. If only I had paid attention to her warnings. I should have stayed closer to the others and not put so much distance between us. I'd basically handed myself to whomever this was before Myrtle or Robert even had a chance to come to my defense. My carelessness would draw them into having to rescue me, which was exactly what Felix wanted.

After several moments of tousling and struggling through the woods, the bush opened up to the road where the black sedan was sitting calmly, waiting for us. I recognized Felix right away: his stiff brush cut and short stubble of a beard on his chin, his tense face. He got out and held open the back door like a maître d'. At the car door, the burly man released his grip and shoved me into the back seat. I landed on my face. Felix's assistant pushed me further in, plopped down beside me and slammed the door shut, the same maneuver the Drakers had initially used with me. What is it with abductions and back seats of cars? I wondered. I tried to open the door on my side but it was child locked. I was pissed off and panicked. I kicked and punched and twisted trying to free myself but the man beside me was too strong. In a second, he reached out with a big hairy paw and smashed me across the back of my head. I sank to the floor, my vision blackening until everything went dark.

When I came to, we were driving down an exceedingly bumpy road. I was on the car floor and the man had his heavy foot pressed to my back. I didn't have to look up to know we were going up the farm laneway. Felix and his man were taking me back to the farm where they knew the others would try to rescue me.

"Nice work, Slade," Felix said. "They didn't even see that coming. Keep her down and quiet."

"How long before you expect they'll come after her?"

"Not long at all."

I noticed Slade's body language change when he realized he hadn't been apprised of Felix's plan until just now. Note to self, I thought, their relationship may not be all roses. I could hear everything but knew I should stay down if I expected to piece together any snatches of information I could use for later. I could tell without feeling around to the back of my waist that they'd taken my gun. Information would be the only weapon I'd have. Though I had no idea how I could warn the others, I knew Felix was right. Reinhardt and the rest would come after me even while knowing that Felix had set a trap, maybe several, one to cover every contingency. Some last few deep potholes bounced me painfully against the car floor, and I knew we were near the farmhouse.

The car stopped and Slade grabbed me roughly by the arm, yanked me up, and pulled me out of the car. He manhandled me up the porch steps to meet Felix, who was already there, again holding open the farmhouse door, this time staring at me with a pleased and evil grin.

Slade thrust me through the door and shoved me onto the living room floor with a heavy thump. I could have stopped the fall and flipped around with an acrobatic rebound but decided it was futile at this point, so I broke the fall with my hands to prevent me from hitting my head on the hard surface. Once on the floor, I turned to look at him and noticed that he was limping and blood was dripping from his shoe. I snickered to myself. At least my gun had found a target in his shin.

Felix noticed it, too, and snorted a complaint. "What's wrong with your leg?"

"The bitch shot me."

"Well that's damn inconvenient. How bad is it? I need you to be in good shape."

"I don't fuckin' know," Slade said. He sat on the sofa and pulled up his pant leg to examine the damage. He winced but said, "A flesh wound. It just grazed my calf muscle. A bandage should do the trick, nothing to worry about." Slade sneered at Felix. "But thanks for caring about me,"

"This was entirely your doing. You grabbed my hand and made it discharge," I said. "Don't you know enough to knock the gun away before the grab?"

"Well, well," Felix said. "The little bitch is scolding you. What's your name?" It sounded like he was giving a military order, brusque and directed.

"Bitch is good enough for me," I said. The less he had on me the better. The last thing I needed was for him to try to figure out my identity, not that my identity was solid anymore.

It seemed Slade was trying to be stoic about his wound, but there was a look of pain and distress on his face, and I could tell that he felt rather aggrieved at Felix's indifference. There was definitely tension between the two of them. I knew already that Slade needed kindness. He craved it. I could try to gain his trust while simultaneously further irritate Felix. I decided to use this to my advantage.

"You're bleeding all over the floor," I said. "If you want, I can try to find some bandages for you. Where's the bathroom?" This was my chance to test whether they knew Rosalind, Myrtle and I were the ones who got away the night of the crash. I opened my eyes wide and waited.

Felix was cleaning his nails with the edge of his Swiss army knife and nodded toward the staircase. "Upstairs," he said, "but I've secured all the windows, so don't think you can get away. If you try to break the glass, we'll be there before your pretty little feet touch the grass, and I'll make sure that you need more than what's in any first-aid kit for the effort."

"Don't be such a jerk. Slade needs medical attention. Don't you care that he might bleed to death? At least I'm trying to help your friend, which is more than I could say for you."

I went to the stairway, trying to appear unfamiliar with the house. I looked back at the odd pair as I climbed. Felix looked unsympathetic and Slade, who appeared to be in considerable pain, glanced at me as I went up with an expression that suggested he was heartened by my kindness. *Good,* I thought. There didn't seem to be any love lost between these two. In fact, it seemed they didn't even remotely like each other.

I thought out my options. There were only two of them and while one was hurt, it wasn't critical and he could still shoot a gun or hurl explosives so I couldn't count him out. Soon there would be six of us, and I had to wonder how these two men thought they were going to deal with being so outnumbered. I remembered Rosalind's warning, "Don't underestimate Felix."

When I got to the bathroom, the first thing I did was to check the window. It didn't budge. It wasn't the best escape route anyway; the window was small and because it wasn't over the porch, it'd have been a long jump to the ground. I grabbed the first-aid kit from the bathroom closet where Myrtle kept it and started back down to the living room where my unlikable patient waited for attention. Before I got to the stairs, I tried to remember if Myrtle had tucked away any weaponry in the upstairs bedrooms. There wasn't time to check right now, but knowing her, I suspected she was crafty enough to have squirreled away something for an emergency. This certainly qualified.

When I got back downstairs, Slade's pant leg was black with blood. It might have been a flesh wound, but I must have hit something important because it was bleeding profusely. I knelt down in front of him and lifted the sticky fabric above his knee. He winced at my touch. It was pretty gross, and I got a cold shiver looking at it; the bullet had torn a three-inch gash into his calf that looked deep but at least the bullet had not embedded itself. Basically it was just a really bad cut which, under normal circumstances, would clean up with some stitches. But Felix wasn't about to get his companion medical help any time soon.

"Looks nasty, Slade," I said. I took the bottle of alcohol out of the kit. "This is going to hurt." I poured a generous amount over the wound.

Slade screamed obscenities at the ceiling and gripped the chair.

I quickly put a thick wad of sterile dressing on it and pressed. "It needs pressure to stop the bleeding," I said. "Hold this while I wrap an Ace bandage around it."

The sterile dressing in his hand was already red and soggy. I opened more dressing packets to soak up more of the blood then unwrapped a rounded roll of Ace bandage. I replaced the dressings and bound his leg securely. It'd probably bleed through in a minute, but this was all that was left in the kit. "Is Slade your first or last name?" I asked.

"Christian. My first name is Christian," he said quietly.

Felix had been ignoring Slade, oblivious to his discomfort and was peering out the window, probably looking for a car coming up the lane, when he turned to us and said sarcastically, "Suck it up, *Christian*." He pulled a face. "Did the Band-Aid make the boo-boo better?" I looked at Felix, confused he'd act so hostile toward someone who'd gotten hurt. But then I remembered the lecture we'd gotten right before spring break on sociopathic behavior. Of course: Felix was incapable of caring about anyone except himself.

Slade glared at Felix then turned to me with a cautious smile.

"Thanks," he said. "It already feels better." He got up to try to walk.

"Is he always like that?" I asked out of the side of my mouth.

"You could say so," he said ruefully.

I tried not to smile at this. I knew I could totally milk the tension between them.

"Anyway," I said, "you should keep your leg elevated until the bleeding stops or else it'll just keep on bleeding." I never thought in a million years that what I'd learned in first aid, which I'd always assumed I'd use for my family or to be a good Samaritan, would be to clean up a kidnapper whose job it was to deliver me to the man who had killed my family and now probably intended to kill me and my other… family. I thought the word again. My family.

"How sweet. The bitch is so concerned about your welfare," Felix said.

"So what do you intend to do with me?" I asked, standing up.

"To kill you of course," Felix said. "But not before your band of treasonous friends bravely comes to your rescue." He wiggled his fingers in the air and took some mincing steps. "I'm so glad this worked out so well! It will save me from the further aggravation of coming after them. It's so much easier if they come to me." He chuckled at whatever secret evil plan he had agitating around in his head, searching my face for reaction or emotion.

I gave him neither. "Exactly why do you want to kill us? What have we done?"

I wanted to affront him a bit. I wanted to draw him into a tirade. I wanted to get him unbalanced in his delusion, to throw him off his game so his decision-making would become faulty, hopefully to give me an advantage. I needed to know how he perceived us and the situation he believed we were in.

"I don't know who you are or how you fit into this whole puzzle, but I don't care. You chose the wrong people to keep company with, Missy. Cold Force needed to remain intact." He spat out the word and pointed his pencil-thin finger in my face. "If all of you would have stood with me, they would have listened and kept us active. You and your kind deserted your country." He was shouting now and seemed ready to grab me by the throat. "So we had 9/11 and now Putin has invaded Crimea. He probably has infiltrators among us right now." His nostrils flared and his breathing was so erratic I could tell he was on the verge of losing his grasp of reason. His eyes rolled into his head. He was lost to his paranoia. "You deserted me, all of you, and I had no one left to stop the communists. I was relegated to a shit job with no authority or power to stop our enemies. This was supposed to be my job, and they stole it away from me. Now communists and other terrorists target Americans everywhere. They strike when and where we least expect. This is your fault that they're here on U.S. soil. I'll make you pay and I won't stop until every one of you gets what you deserve."

In a way, he was so demented, I wanted to laugh, but I suspected that was not the best way to go. I turned on my teenager voice again and made myself a little younger. "So, just so you know, I'm only twenty-two. The only job I've ever had was as a counselor at Oaks 'N' Sunshine day camp? I don't think we're who you're looking for."

Felix's eyes narrowed. "I don't make those kinds of mistakes," he said. "I know who my enemies are. I know there is someone who interferes with my justice raids and I've followed them here to this place. The one who calls himself Reinhardt is the leader. I can't figure out why you're with them, but time will tell."

"They're just my family, innocent bystanders," I said. "What the hell do you think we are?"

"Maybe you're all double agents masquerading as Americans," Felix said. "I know what you're up to. You want to stop me from protecting our country against your terrorist attacks. That's why someone is always there to interfere with my important work." It was clear to me that he believed everything he was saying. I worried I'd pushed him too far. He looked like he was close to having a psychotic episode. His eyes were wild and he began muttering, off in a world all his own as he paced the room looking for dangers that weren't there.

I glanced at Slade, who was leaning back, looking shocked. I was surprised he'd not seen this side of his boss, but the look on his face suggested he hadn't experienced this before. He caught my eye and widened his own as if to say, *Stop baiting him!*

I held up a hand to placate him; I'd gotten what I needed to know from Felix. What my fellow Drakers had said about him was true: he was a psychopath and there was no reasoning with him. The problem with that, of course, was that people out of touch with reality were vulnerable to their own non-reasonable ideas. They saw only what they wanted to see and heard only what they wanted to hear, regardless of what was true.

"Maybe I could make us a nice cup of tea?" I asked. "Wouldn't that be soothing?"

Felix had his arms crossed tightly over his chest and grunted. He stood at the window and had his eyes trained on the laneway that led to the house.

"Kitchen?"

"Back there," Slade called over.

Surprisingly, they didn't follow me. Once inside and out of their view, I tried the door but it, too, had been barred shut. The windows, same. The men had turned the house into a prison. I started rifling through the cupboards and drawers for anything I could use: a knife, a fork, a bottle opener. Then I looked at the stove. Boiling water.

I lifted the kettle and was on my way to the stove when Felix barged in. "It's no use trying," he said. "I heard you. Everything is locked. You're trapped and at my mercy. What do you think you're doing anyway?"

"I don't know what you heard, but I'm making tea. Like I said. Or are you worried I might poison you?" I filled the kettle and placed it on the stove. Still playing the act, I started looking through cupboards for tea bags. "Oh, here they are." I grabbed a box of Earl Grey and found a ceramic tea pot on the counter and plopped two bags into it.

Felix snorted. "Bring in an extra cup."

For whom, his second personality? I laughed to myself.

I prepared a tray with three cups and took the tea with milk and some sugar I'd put into a bowl into the living room, where I poured each of us a cup.

"If you don't mind," Slade asked, "would you pour me something stronger?"

"Name your poison," I said. I snickered and looked at Felix who peered into his cup then set it down.

"Scotch," Slade replied. He pointed to the bureau where I knew Myrtle kept the liquor. I poured him a large glass and handed it him.

"Thanks again," Slade said. "I don't know why you're being so kind. You should hate me."

"She's a traitor just like the others," Felix said. "For God's sake, Slade, can't you see what she's doing?"

Outside, I could faintly distinguish a buzzing hum from overhead, sort of like an aircraft, high-pitched but not as throaty, as if it were lower in elevation. Could Felix and Slade hear it as well? Maybe Slade missed it, so distracted by pain and his own buzz that his extra-large shot of scotch had produced, but Felix, keen to both real and imagined perceptions in his state of paranoia, should have detected the threat. Luckily, he was still in the midst of some kind of episode and was muttering to himself and gesticulating. I looked at the coffee table. The TV remote. I grabbed it and turned on the television, hoping to mask the barely distinguishable sound.

Then I realized they were using the drone. I thought about what they'd be seeing through the drone's camera. It was evening, so it would deliver only darkened images. But maybe with the light shining through the windows, the footage would at least show that the house was occupied and there was a sedan in the driveway. Maybe they could swoop down and get a picture of the license plate. I wished I could text Rosalind about this, but she would surely have thought of it. I also had no doubt that Reinhardt was orchestrating my rescue again and doing it while knowing full well that they were walking right into Felix's trap. I knew my job was to help throw Felix off his attack plan. Our lives would depend on it.

I considered baiting him some more, since I hadn't found any other way to distract him. But when I turned to talk to him again, he went outside, fussing about something "checking the set-up for readiness."

"What's Felix up to?" I asked, trying to keep my voice calm.

"Oh, you name it. Everything from guns to explosives. He has booby-traps everywhere," Slade said. He looked at me with a placid but not unkind face. "Your people don't have much of chance and neither do you," he said practically.

"Why do you go along with him?" I asked. "You don't seem like you're out for blood like he is."

"He might be a nut-case, but he pays me well," Slade said. "I'm starting to feel sorry for you, though. You seem... nice. People aren't usually nice to me." His words were slow now. The scotch was taking effect. I poured him another.

"Is that the only reason you do his dirty work?" I asked. "Doesn't your conscience bother you?"

"An ex-con can't exactly be choosy about jobs especially the kind that pay good money," Slade said. "Felix and I seemed to like each other as soon as we met. I liked the money he was offering and he liked... something about me, I don't really know what, but he didn't seem to care about my past or my qualifications or anything. I didn't ask questions, I was glad for the gig. I also knew he'd keep me from going back to the pen. He has a way of making things look like they never happened." Slade gave a pleased chuckle. "So I drive him around, scare some town folk, wait on him, but nothing that would send me back to jail. He has other people do the real dirty work and then a bunch of other guys who are his clean-up crew. I just turn a blind eye and he pays me. And as long as he pays me, I do what he says."

I topped up his glass again. He seemed to be a sympathetic drunk, something I hoped I could use.

"How's the pain?" I asked. "Looks like the bleeding has stopped.

Here, this will help." I nodded at the scotch. He smiled wanly and took a long slug. His eyes were swimming and his head was lolling around.

"Do you want a pillow?" I asked, starting for the stairs then stopped. "There must be one upstairs."

"A pillow sounds great," Slade said, his words starting to slur. He lifted a finger. "But don't count on me nodding off and giving you a chance to escape. It takes a lot more than a couple of drinks to put me out. Anyway Felix will be back in here soon."

I laughed lightly. "Oh, that's OK. I'll get you the pillow anyway," I said and tiptoed up the stairs again. I figured that Myrtle's room was the best bet for me to find a hidden weapon somewhere. At the top of the steps, I stopped and looked back in case Slade had decided to follow, but I only heard slow heavy breathing.

I opened the door to Myrtle's room. Hers was nearly double the size of the cute one I'd slept in. Her double bed was centered on the back wall with night tables on either side. I opened the drawers to check for pistols or revolvers or knives but found none. I looked under the bed and behind the pillows.

Disappointed, I went to the closet. It was a disorderly mess full of clothes and blankets and shoes, not at all in keeping with her meticulous character. I shuffled through the hangers and my hand bumped on something hard in the pocket of a jacket. Bingo! I pulled out a small pistol and quickly shoved it into my waistband. I shuffled the hangers back into position when my foot bumped another object at the very back corner. Good old Myrtle. Sure enough another hunting rifle was cleverly propped up behind extra pillows. I grabbed the pillow and the rifle and headed to the stairs where there was a storage bench on the landing. I carefully opened it up and placed Myrtle's rifle inside trying not to make a sound.

The moon shone brightly through the window at the end of the hallway in the boys' wing. I thought, if necessary, I could break through the window by shattering it with the butt of the rifle before leaping onto the side porch roof and jumping to the grass below into the protection of the wooded area behind. Just thinking that plan through made me feel much better.

I was starting down the steps when Felix came in the front door. "What the hell are you doing upstairs?" he asked. His face turned red as he caught sight of Slade slumped comfortably over on the living room sofa. "Slade, you idiot," Felix shouted, storming to him and kicking him in his wound. "Is this how you watch a captive? By giving her the run of the house?"

Slade's face crumpled with pain. "Relax, Felix," he said, struggling to sit up. "She's not going anywhere. We've got this place sealed up like a tomb. Anyway she just had to use the lady's room."

I was surprised that he made up a lie to settle Felix down.

Felix looked at the pillow in my arms. "What? Are you thinking you can suffocate us?" Looking particularly amused, he broke into a condescending laugh.

"I just wanted to make Slade a bit more comfortable," I said. "I'm sure if you were injured, you might appreciate that, too."

"What I'd appreciate," Felix said, spittle coming out of his hard thin lips, "is getting rid of you cowardly traitors. When I do, they'll see that I was right." His smile became a vicious sneer. He grabbed my arm and pulled me roughly into the living room and tossed me into the upholstered chair beside the sofa. I glared back at him in defiance and stood again, taking the pillow over to Slade. I placed it attentively behind him.

I watched Felix's reaction. My attention to Slade infuriated him. My plan was working. With his mania well-nourished, I knew he was thinking that everything and everybody was conspiring against him.

Just then, a whirling noise penetrated the outside air.

Felix dashed to the window, knocking over a wood chair in his haste. He ripped back the curtain and strained to see where it was coming from. He grunted a string of obscenities and stormed out the door to get a location on the source of the sound.

Slade staggered to his feet to also look out the window. We exchanged a worried look.

"Slade," I said. "You've got to help me. Tell me what Felix is going to do."

He looked outside, surprisingly calm, or it was the scotch that kept him unruffled.

"Your friends are probably near or approaching the house," he said. "Felix wants to see them get blown away by the land mines he set all over the laneway and yard." He looked down. "I helped him plant them. Listen, I told you that you and your friends don't have a chance." He paused. "Hear that? That's Felix taking up a sniping position on the porch roof. He'll pop off anyone who gets through to the house."

A gunshot boomed out front. I should have ducked, but instead I ran to the window alongside Slade to see what was happening.

"Get down," Slade yelled. "Are you trying to help Felix kill you?" He pulled me back from the window and tucked me behind him. His gun was drawn as if he were defending the two of us.

"Slade," I said. "We haven't done anything wrong. We're innocent. You know Felix is crazy. Whatever your past, you're clearly not a cold-blooded killer like him. You actually seem really nice. Please, help me warn them?"

Slade paused and looked sympathetically at me as I pleaded with him. He looked like a big, sorry, teddy bear then. I had a strange urge to hug him.

"This can't keep going on, you know, him covering up explosions and hiding bodies. Sooner or later he's going to get caught. You'll go back to prison. You know that," I said.

Slade's eyes narrowed. "Upstairs," he said. "Take the pillow and kick through the side window. I'll show you a safe route to the barn."

I ran up the steps with Slade stumbling up behind me. At the top, I grabbed the rifle from the storage chest. Slade backed up a few steps, his face awash with confusion.

"I found it when I was looking for a pillow," I said, shrugging. "Maybe we can use a bit of extra fire power. Let's go."

I headed to the window and kicked out the glass, the pillow in front of me, shielding me from the shards. I climbed out onto the porch roof and Slade followed close behind. An explosion lit up the tree line along the lane, causing us both to fall flat. I looked back in horror, wondering who had detonated the explosion, then down to the ground. "I can jump this, but maybe you should slide or climb down the post because of your leg." It was bleeding again. I could see the shine had returned to his pants. "I can help you when you get to the bottom."

I jumped to the grass with a thud and waved to Slade that he should ease his way down the post. He was quite drunk and slipped down quickly, crying out in pain as his wounded leg hit the porch railing. When he was on the ground, I put his arm over my shoulder and tried to support him as we started for the barn. He was having a hard time speaking, either from his pain or inebriation, and just pointed us in an irregular zigzag direction so we'd miss the explosive devices. We maneuvered our way across, and in less than a minute we were safely under cover inside the barn.

"I'm going to circle around the back behind the woods," I said. "I have to try to reach the others and warn them. You stay. You'll be safe enough in here."

It didn't seem to occur to him that I wouldn't be able to speak to my plans if I'd never been here before. He smiled wanly. "You're a silly little bitch," Slade said. "You really are trying to get yourself killed, but you're feisty and brave and I like you." The whiskey on his breath was strong; I wondered if he was lucid enough to keep us from being blown up while on the way to the barn. "I'll try to offer whatever distraction and gun cover I can from here. I can't move fast enough to go with you. Good luck. You'll need it."

I smiled at Slade and spontaneously gave him a quick hug and then slid out the back window we'd used the night of the attack. The bushes and trees offered me cover as I circled to the front where I figured Reinhardt and the others were trying to approach the house.

I could hear the panicked pounding of my chest and tried to remember all that Rosalind had taught me. Her warning of "our lives might depend on it" played over and over in my mind. I had to be careful because I didn't know where Felix had positioned himself. I knew he'd have perched someplace where he could get a clear view of anyone who might have cleared his mine field. I stayed as close as I could to the ground so he wouldn't see me.

There was a creak at the house. Then I saw him. He was standing on the roof of the front porch. In front of him, mounted on some kind of holding stand, appeared to be a heavy-duty automatic rifle he'd aimed toward the laneway. If the Drakers got through, Felix would spray them with sufficient rounds of gunfire to finish them off. I hadn't heard an explosion for a while. Then I heard Robert's voice from somewhere in the darkness. I was so awash with gratitude at the sound of it, my breath hitched and I had to swallow my emotions to keep from coming apart.

"Felix," Robert shouted, "let her go. She hasn't done anything. It's me you want."

"And me," Reinhardt shouted. His voice echoed from a different point beyond the trees.

"And me," Rosalind called. Her voice seemed very close, within whispering distance.

Then Myrtle emerged from the bushes, her cougar rifle aimed directly at Felix on the roof. I felt deep relief. Myrtle never missed. As she stepped away from the bush, I watched with horror as she tripped on a root. She never got to take her shot. A hail of gunfire sparked through the darkness and Myrtle fell first to her knees then onto her face into the roadway mud. Even in the dark, I could see the black inky liquid pooling around her. I stared at her fallen body. She didn't move. I knew Myrtle was gone.

"No," Robert cried as he ran to her to pull her fallen body to safety. Another volley of bullets ignited the air, and when the noise subsided, Robert was lying on top of her motionless and bloody.

I was paralyzed. If I tried to help on the slim chance that Robert was alive, Felix would mow me down like the others and add me to the pile.

"Felix!" Another shout from somewhere in the dark came in the silence after the last barrage of bullets. It was Slade. "Stop this madness. I'm not with you on this crazy rampage any more. Put the weapon down and give yourself up, or I swear, I'll go to Hollinger and tell him what you're up to. You need help, man, serious help. What did these people ever do to you, really? Or this girl? You've never even met her."

"Slade, you're a traitor just like the rest of them," Felix answered. "The bitch got to you and now I have to kill you, too." He raged on. "Your life is meaningless anyway, you idiot. You're nothing without me."

I winced hearing Felix's vindictive words but knew I had to use this time to get out of here. "Rosalind..." I whispered, "it's me, Ruby. Where are you?"

"Over here." She was only a few feet away. Through the dark scrub I crawled to where I thought she was, but she got to me first and grabbed me similarly to how she had that night on the stairs, except this time, she had both arms around my chest and squeezed me tight. "Stay calm. You're with me now."

We remained crouched, both of us shaking with fear and rage from our hiding spot against the dark, fetid earth. I wondered if she had a plan for how we would alert Reinhardt and Ransom as to where we were. I looked back at the crumpled bodies of Robert and Myrtle, two of the most honorable, dedicated people I'd ever known. There was nothing more we could do for them. I knew entertaining the idea that they might be alive was ridiculous and if we didn't want to wind up the same way, we needed to regroup with Reinhardt and Ransom and get out of here.

In the darkness beyond the house, a burly figure came limping out of the barn with his arms in the air and his eyes scanning the ground as he weaved around what I knew were his planted explosives. Slowly, he made his way over to Felix. "Felix, we need to talk," Slade said. "This needs to be over."

I wanted to shout, 'No!' but I couldn't.

"Where's the girl?" Felix asked.

"She's gone, got away," Slade said. "She's too young to be one of your traitors, she's nobody important. Give it up, Felix. Just give it up. You're not thinking straight."

"Never," Felix shouted. He aimed the automatic rifle in Slade's direction.

I understood then that Slade was trying to distract Felix so we could get away. Maybe he knew he wasn't going to get out of here alive, or maybe he was just trying to do the right thing, but even I could see that Felix was in a killing mood and no matter how much Slade tried to reason with him, it would end the same for him as it had for Myrtle and Robert.

While the two men faced off, gunfire erupted, this time coming from the bushes and aimed at Felix. Felix ducked and retaliated with a round of shots sprayed in every direction.

Rosalind and I flattened ourselves against the ground until the rhythmic staccato of the bullets subsided.

"What on earth are they doing?" Rosalind sputtered into the dirt.

I was surprised that Reinhardt and Ransom would intensify an already volatile situation by shooting at Felix

Another volley of bullets was fired at Felix. Slade looked behind him to determine from whom and where the gunfire was coming. He hit the ground and crawled to the bushes.

A terrible popping commotion that sounded like firecrackers erupted from behind the barn. Rosalind and I looked at each other, our eyes wide with fear and questions. Our men were in the bushes in front of the farmhouse and Felix was on the roof. It was someone else adding to the mayhem. But who?

"I'm going back to the barn to investigate," I said. "Rosalind, cover me."

"I'm right behind you," Rosalind said. "Your forgetting rule number one is what got us into this mess."

We were behind the house so at least the chance of Felix noticing any movement from the back bushes was small. Still, we stayed low to the ground to make sure we were keeping out of sight and gun range.

Until we knew who this other shooter was, we weren't taking any chances.

At the barn, a small man was down on one knee scattering something on the ground. He got up and did it again in another spot about fifty feet away, and then another, each time crouching and linking together whatever he was scattering with rope or wire. We followed. When the moonlight caught his form, showing a green and gray hunting jacket, I gasped, calling his attention to us. The man looked up and cocked his rifle at the bushes in front of us.

"Amos," I whispered. "It's Ruby. What are you doing here?"

"Ruby?" Amos said, lowering his rifle. "Meet me in the barn."

Rosalind and I scurried to the back window of the barn and jumped inside. Amos followed. For a few seconds we just stared at each other, breathing in the tang of hay and dust. I had to admit I was very glad to see him, but I hoped he'd brought reinforcements.

"Well, at least the two of you are OK," Amos said. "Where are the others?"

"Felix, the government man, shot and killed Myrtle and Robert. And Reinhardt and Ransom are somewhere out there hiding among the trees," Rosalind said.

Amos's voice quivered. "That bastard." He hung his head. "We should have acted sooner." Amos pulled another string of fireworks from his hunting jacket. Even in the dark, it was obvious he was holding back tears. I looked away. I didn't need to start crying either; it wouldn't help any of us. "Fine, then what about that other government man?" Amos asked. He sniffed and wiped his face on his sleeve. "The one who tried to talk the idiot off the roof, didn't I tell you that something wasn't right about them? Who the hell are they, communists or something?"

"Amos, don't think we're not very grateful you're here, but why are you here?" I asked. "You're going to get yourself killed. These people are very dangerous."

"Don't you worry about me," Amos said. "Anyway I've been watching the place. I could see that something was up. And I'm not here alone. Norm is staking out the back trail, and Hannah and Alice are waiting with our trucks on the back road for a getaway. I was just going to set up enough commotion to throw them into a spin. Figured if you were actually here, it would give you a chance to get the hell out."

"We have to let our guys know you're here," I said. "Otherwise they might think you're working with Felix and shoot."

"I have an idea," Rosalind said. She grabbed a bucket and crept out the window. At a tap, she poured some water into the bucket and returned with it sloshing out. She grabbed some of the mud and went back outside to smear "RD" on the barn's wall then came back in again.

Amos and I watched the bushes intently from the window to see if we could detect any movement. We waited. Nothing moved from the front. Then there was activity at the back window again: two dark figures jumped through and landed perched on one knee with pistols extended, pointing into the darkness of the barn.

"Thank God they're all right," whispered Rosalind under her breath. Reinhardt and Ransom came to us.

In the darkness, I felt Ransom's arms go around my waist. "I honestly thought we might have lost you too." He hugged me tightly, and I realized that this was not just a brotherly embrace. I curled into him, breathing in the scent from his neck.

Reinhardt and Rosalind were murmuring together a few feet away. "We've lost Myrtle and Robert," I heard Reinhardt say to Rosalind. I looked over and saw him break away from her embrace, straighten up and set his jaw. His eyes were blazing.

"Yes, hate to break up this family reunion, folks," Amos said, "but we should get the heck outta here."

"The SUV is at the back road. We'll take the same trail Myrtle showed us," Reinhardt said, his voice breaking.

"Less good," Amos said. "I have another way out. Norm and I use it when we hunt for wild turkey. No one except the two of us knows about it because it crosses over private property. You won't tell anyone that we're trespassers, will you? Just let me get some fireworks going and then you can follow me." He pulled a match from his pocket and struck it to light a line of fuse that ran to a large mound of firecrackers.

Once the spark started running along the wire, he took a hand grenade from one of the pockets of his hunting jacket, pulled the pin and threw it at the porch roof.

Seconds later, a boom shattered the stillness again and debris flew everywhere as we dashed from the barn and scurried into the woods following an ever-surprisingly agile and quick gray-haired senior in a hunting jacket. I'd never been so glad to see anyone than I was this group, for all their various reasons and talents, however quirky.

Another volley of bullets erupted from the house. My heart sank. The grenade hadn't killed Felix, but as we dashed out, I saw Slade who had run from the protection of the trees lying still and face down on the grass. I wasn't able to go back and look.

More firecracker noises erupted. Amos had them set up in sequenced intervals with the lit fuse running from one spot to another. No sooner had one spot finished when another burst into sparks and pops.

Amos's distractions did the trick. We were well into the woods with no signs of Felix following us. Anyway, Felix had killed his only assistant. Now he was alone and left with another messy clean up to look after by himself. I wondered how he would be able to cover up the bloodbath this time.

We continued running and just when I was nearly out of breath, the path opened up to a gravel road. An old pick-up truck waited a few feet down the road, and as soon as we were close, the engine started. The men jumped into the bed, joining Norm who was already there, and Rosalind and I climbed into the cab with Hannah. Hannah floored the gas pedal and we drove off, leaving a trail of dust in our wake.

"Where's Alice?" Amos asked, calling through the back window slider.

"I decided that while they were busy shooting at you, she should tow your SUV back to our place. She's probably already there making us coffee and putting out the donuts we bought this morning."

"Hannah," Amos said, "what we've seen calls for something stronger than coffee."

Amos grinned sadly at Norm whom I had barely noticed. Norm grinned back looking exhilarated from the adventurous caper that had just unfolded. I thought it would've seemed fun, too, if I hadn't just seen my friends die.

"Yep," Norm said, "calls for some of our special homemade moonshine, I think." The two of them chortled, clutching their hunting rifles as the old pick-up shot up dirt and rocks and sped over the deserted gravel road.

"To Myrtle and Robert."

"To Myrtle and Robert."

Sixteen

THE OLD PICK-UP BUMPED and swayed up the hidden driveway. Every time it bottomed out on the deeper ruts, I could see in the rearview the boys getting bounced into the air and scrambling to grab onto the sides, and the branches slapping the side of the truck, periodically catching them in the face. I didn't want to keep an eye on Ransom, but I couldn't help it. My heart thumped harder when I thought about how he'd held me in the barn.

When we pulled up to Amos and Hannah's old house, it was clear that Alice had accomplished her task. Her pick-up sat in front of the woodshed, the tow bar still attached to our SUV. Hannah pulled up and parked behind it and we tumbled out. I felt numb but relieved that for at least a short while, Felix would be too occupied to come after us.

It was calm here among the trees, but a tight painful knot ached in my stomach as I realized that Myrtle and Robert weren't here with us. To save ourselves, we had abandoned their bodies, the whole bloody affair being something that Felix would certainly—Slade or no Slade—manage to erase into oblivion before the authorities or media could report on it. I could see the same pain in the eyes of the others, eyes where the massacred images of our loved ones were indelibly burned.

"Come inside, you folks," Alice said, leaning against the doorjamb. "Coffee is ready. And it was smart of you to pick up donuts, Hannah. I can see that we won't be going to the diner this morning," she joked sadly.

Everyone shuffled into the small house. Inside was overly warm and when I got a whiff of the overwhelming smell of freshly brewed coffee mixed with the sweet sugary donuts, I felt my stomach coming up. I covered my mouth with my hands and looked with panic at Hannah. She calmly put a hand on my lower back and steered me to their bathroom.

She lifted the toilet lid and held my hair as I knelt down and vomited, over and over. The gripping emptiness of loss strangled me. I gasped for breath, suffocating. *Breathe, breathe,* I told myself, but the grip wouldn't release. My head pounded with the strain.

Hannah stood and then Ransom was at my side. "It's OK, it's OK," he whispered, holding me.

It was too much, his compassion, my grief. I was powerless to stop it, this force that had been welling up in me for too long. Finally, I let out the cry I'd had lodged in my throat since my parents were killed. The air was filled with it, my lungs wide, and uncontrollable tears flowing down my face and onto my shirt. My body had no strength, and I clutched Ransom's firm arms, aching for every bit of his tenderness. There we sat in front of the toilet, and rocked together as he whispered words of comfort to me through his own tears. Reinhardt and Rosalind joined us, linking their arms around our bodies, the four of us letting our collective tears wash over our pain.

We were sniffling and starting to crack jokes to ease the tension through our wet faces when Alice came to the door. "Sorry to interrupt," she said gently, "but I think you guys need to see this." She pointed to the flickering TV in the living room. "There's a news report."

Alice's interruption jolted the four of us back to our present situation. Just because we had escaped Felix's treachery, it didn't mean we were safe. I looked at Reinhardt; Robert had always been the one who looked after everything and made sure we were safe. I felt suddenly very vulnerable.

"We need to pull ourselves together," said Reinhardt, carefully looking at each of us with tenderness and a firm jaw. "We ran away from Felix who is still very much alive. I don't doubt that his rage is eating him alive for his failure to kill us. The longer we hide out, the greater the chance for him to close in. As long as he is alive, he will never stop hunting us. I don't want to see any more of us..." He stopped, his chin quivering.

Rosalind took his hand in hers, and we all silently walked into the living room where Amos had turned up the volume on the television. A gas-line fire had been reported by a non-resident driving by on the highway. The fire department and police found three people deceased on the scene as a result of an explosion. "No foul play is suspected but an early investigation by the local gas company reports that poorly main-tained gas lines are responsible for the unfortunate and fatal mishap." The reporter shook her helmet of blond hair and cleared her throat. "The victims' bodies have been taken to Erie for an autopsy and a coroner's report. The deceased had no family."

I was stunned. And furious. "Obviously he's paying off the local sheriff's office. He couldn't have covered up the killings this quickly." I looked at Reinhardt helplessly. "Right?"

Reinhardt turned. "Amos, I don't think you and your group are safe in town. If Felix saw you, you'll be his next target. You really should consider getting out of here as soon as you can."

Amos grimaced. "I'll be damned if I let that slime chase us out of our home." He nodded at his wife and two friends. "We know how to defend ourselves."

I remembered that Felix and Slade would have met the four when they were poking around the diner asking questions. I thought about the patriotism our seniors were so proud of, and suspected the one and only way we could get them to leave their home was by asking them for help. And I also had to admit I really liked having them around. They were funny and kind and interesting. Plus we owed our lives to them.

I looked at Rosalind with a face that begged her to do something. She smiled. "We really could use your help, Amos," she said, "and your instinct that something's off here is completely right."

Our four seniors leaned in closely. "Felix has a vendetta against us. He's lost touch with reality and is using all his resources to get at us. It seems his boss is unaware of his criminal activities, but now we've gotten some important evidence that will implicate Felix for these and other crimes, evidence that will cause his superior to take action. Here's where you come in." Her expression was utterly serious. "We had intended to courier that evidence to Washington, but on our way to send everything, Felix kidnapped Ruby. We would just take it ourselves, but Felix has eyes everywhere and will be looking for us. But... even though he's seen you before, you'd be able to melt into the crowd in a way we could not." Ruby saw Amos's eyes begin to twinkle with the possibility of another adventure. "Would the four of you be willing to take the evidence to a man named Hollinger? He's Felix's boss and the head of the U.S. Defense Department. What we have could very well be the thing to bring Felix down."

Amos looked skeptical. "You mean to tell me," he bellowed, "that our own Defense Department doesn't know what's going on? How the hell does this guy get away with it?"

"Here's where the story gets interesting," said Ransom, cocking an eyebrow. "He used to be the head of an international security operation during the Cold War. When the nuclear arms race ended, the government didn't have a need for his department anymore and disbanded it, retiring all the secret undercover agents. Felix, however, was not about to retire. He used some of the high-level connections he had and called in some favors—or maybe even threatened to go public with some of the classified information he'd been privy to. His whole world was the CIA and he'd be dammed if he'd slink off to Florida in a Hawaiian print shirt. So to keep him happy, they gave him an administrative position in archived records. Not exactly an illustrious position, but he took it. So even though he got what he wanted, something about that whole shift rattled him, changed him, made him angry, suspicious. He never 'bought it' that the Russians ended the nuclear arms race." He paused and added with his arms open. "And he's been on the rampage ever since."

I wondered if Amos would be so enchanted by Felix's stealth that it wouldn't occur to him to ask how we came to be targeted by Felix who, from this story, just sounded like he was paranoid that the arms race was still going on.

I looked at him and could see his wheels were turning. "Sounds like this guy has to be stopped," Amos said slowly. "The way I see it, it's our patriotic duty to help you folks."

"Darn right," Norm said. "And this Hollinger fellow is in the capital?"

"That's right," Rosalind said.

I let out my breath. We just couldn't tell them everything. It was too dangerous. Plus Amos was a bit of a loose cannon and could've taken it upon himself, vigilante style, to storm in and do something rash. "We'll arrange for somewhere safe for you to stay. It would be best for you to be incognito for a while. Have you ever been to D.C.?"

"We stay pretty close to home these days," Hannah said.

Both Alice and Hannah stood up and nodded at each other.

"Amos, I'll get us packed. Do you think we should take our rifles?" There was a mischievous twinkle in Hannah's eyes. I caught the brief shift of her eyes and a wink as well as the smallest curl on her lips. Amos gave her an equally discreet look. They had told us repeatedly how they sensed that something wasn't right about the government men in town. Now I was feeling like I should feel similarly about our seniors.

At the thought of these country folk sauntering into a high-end hotel, rifles in hand, I had to stifle a laugh. Their headstrong belief that this was the land of freedom and everyone could enjoy his constitutional right to bear arms and other things might not go over so well there.

"You might want to bring something a bit less conspicuous," I said. "Didn't you say your brother-in-law owns the gun shop in town?"

"Sure, sure," nodded Amos. "We should be more subtle, I get it. How about something like this?" He went over to a drawer at the far end of the kitchen and pulled out a hand pistol and waved it around over his head. Hannah and Alice were at the closet. Each grabbed her purse and pulled out a smaller version of her husband's and plunked them down onto the table.

"My hand revolver is in the glove box of my truck," Norman said. "It's good to be prepared, just in case. You know what I mean?" He had that determined look on his face. Indeed, I knew exactly what he meant.

But the look of shock on our faces must have been hilarious because our hosts started into a round of boisterous laughter. What was it about these seniors that made them so suspicious? Before we showed up, I had the feeling this was a very sedate place. But they seemed to be able to sniff danger out and where they caught the scent, they didn't hesitate to jump in. I used to hang out a lot with my grandparents and their friends, and they didn't have a shred of resemblance to these four.

"It's settled then," Rosalind said. "I'll text Renegade and he'll make all the arrangements for your accommodation in Washington." She took out her phone and began typing. She paused. "I also have to tell him about…" She looked at Reinhardt.

He nodded sadly. "I suppose so. And he should also make travel arrangements for us." He clenched his hands together. "I relied too heavily on Robert. He knew what we needed even before we needed it."

"It's done," Rosalind said as her message sent. "It won't take long for Renegade to take up the reins."

"No use letting coffee and donuts go to waste," Alice trilled. Her voice was cheery but her face revealed that she knew how we felt and that we were fighting with our emotions.

"We need to get moving," Ransom said. "Felix is going to lose his mind now that he missed us. Getting away from him this time will be more challenging than ever. We know he'll have all the airports covered, especially charter flights."

"Let's just see what Renegade comes up with. He knows what we're up against," Rosalind said. "I doubt that he'll arrange anything out of the local airports. We're probably in for a long drive, my darlings."

I shook my head. She was trying to be reassuring, but we all knew that Renegade would opt for the fastest escape route, which was Westport. Renegade would leave it to our shrewdness, trusting our stealth to get past Felix.

Where earlier the smell of coffee and donuts made me sick, now it seemed a comfort. Our plucky hosts lost no time busying themselves with preparations for an extended absence away from home. While we ate, Alice went back home to their house. Apparently, it was just a short walk along a path that only they knew about and used. She said she was just going to pack a few things.

When Alice returned, it took me a second to realize it was her. She had transformed herself, clothes, makeup and hair. She looked ten years younger dressed in black tight-fitting jeans with a snug fitting T-shirt that showed off her ample chest and tiny waist. She'd topped it off with a black leather jacket, a far cry from the frumpy and meddling old lady she had seemed to be at the diner.

Hannah came out of the bedroom shortly after, also similarly transformed. Seconds later, Amos emerged from the bathroom, clean shaven and looking quite dapper for a gentleman of his age. Our jaws dropped.

"Norm, you need to change, too," Alice said. She handed him the backpack she'd brought with her. Without a word he left the room to change in the bathroom.

"You guys look so... different!" I exclaimed. "No one would recognize you as the same people."

"That's the point," Amos said, winking at me. "We know Felix would be out to kill us, too, if he realized who we were." He glanced at his cronies and sat down. "Listen, our whole thing here..." He gestured to his cabin, his hunting jacket, "Let's just say this. We knew who he was. Felix Szabo was our commander when we worked for him during the Cold War days."

I wasn't the only one who gasped.

Amos smiled and continued. "Those were dangerous times and we were glad to turn a page in our lives when the government offered us the opportunity to leave, kind of like a witness protection program but only for spies." He paused for a bit to make sure that we understood what he was saying.

I looked at the others to see their reaction. They held their faces steady.

"It took us a while to figure it out because some of you folks are so young," Amos continued. "But as soon we heard the explosions and later found the helicopter, we realized that something other than alien invasions was up. It wasn't until we got a good look at Felix that we knew it was him and that he was on the hunt for someone. We knew he hadn't identified us. You said it yourself, we were unrecognizable.

"One evening, we followed the sedan and it turned off onto the farmhouse lane. We wondered why the farmhouse had been targeted. Then we put two and two together and realized we'd always found it strange that for a person who liked to be on her own, Myrtle sure had lots of company."

"Oh, man!" said Ransom with a rucful laugh. "The four of you worked for him? I worked for him, too, but years later, after he was demoted to Archives. Worst boss ever, right?"

The five of them laughed.

"You're lucky you got out when you did. By the time I was working for him, he'd already lost most of his sense of reality. When I got suspicious about why he'd be out of the office for such extended periods of time and started asking him what he was doing, he must have worried that I'd report it, and that's when he arranged my 'accident.' It just didn't work. He didn't manage to kill me, and Reinhardt and Robert rescued me and arranged a new identity for me." He tapped his cheek. "This is not my original face."

The elder four looked aghast but also sympathetic as if they knew all along what Felix was capable of.

Amos looked at me. "But you're so young. How did you get mixed up in this?"

I swallowed. "He killed my parents and little brother. Reinhardt and Robert knew he was coming for them and managed to snatch me out of Felix's raid on my family, a house fire." I was crying again. "This isn't my face either. But in the end, it was for nothing, because by the time I recovered from the surgery, Felix's men had found me. At the time I had no idea what was going on." My throat was thick with emotion. Telling my story, saying the words aloud, made it all so real I stopped talking.

Rosalind's phone pinged. "OK. You'll be staying at the Hilton Garden," she said, reading the message. "The reservation is for four adults under the initials RD. It's already paid for, so the hotel doesn't have any need to ask you questions. Fortunately, hotels in D.C. are accustomed to practicing a certain amount of discretion."

"Forward the reservation confirmation to my phone," Hannah said. "That's all we'll need. From here on in, we'll be practically unnoticeable." Rosalind held her phone up to Hannah's, making a BBM link. Rosalind clicked out a text, and it pinged on Hannah's phone seconds later.

It was like the foursome had never ended their spy careers. They were still as sharp as ever, right on top of their game. They would know how to find Hollinger and once they filled him in, Felix's deadly pursuit of us would be over. Their aptitude wouldn't stop me from worrying about them though. In my mind, even though they were dressed in leather and had dropped their hokey accents, I still saw them as the delightful. albeit meddlesome, old farts they had passed themselves off as here in Springfield. I hated that they were about to put themselves into danger for us. But then again, Felix's wrath was like a raging forest fire and would eat everything in its path. It was probably for the best to get them out of Springfield. And it seemed they'd know how to handle themselves in Washington just fine.

A ping signaled another message. "Renegade has set up a private charter out of Westport," Rosalind said. "The flight number is IC20. It will land in St. John's, Newfoundland, but then will continue on to

Iceland. He will keep track of us and will advise further plans when we get there."

"Amos," Reinhardt said. "Email a coded message to Rosalind when you find Hollinger." They created a BBM link with their phones too.

Hannah laughed. "At least now our phones are intimately acquainted," she said. She stood. "We're ready to go. We'll look after Hollinger. You guys be careful at Westport. Szabo will be tracing all flights. He'll know you'll try to get away from here."

"We've done this before, but you're right," Reinhardt said. "We'll stay alert to even the slightest sign that he's tracking us, which no doubt he is."

Amos and Hannah scurried around the little house pulling plugs from sockets and extinguishing the fire in the wood stove. They gave a final look around and grabbed the bags they had packed.

"We should all get going," Amos said. "Good luck to you."

We followed them out to the cars. One of them had unhitched the SUV from the tow bar and reoriented it so it pointed out to the lane. After handshakes and hugs, our small convoy of two pickups and an SUV scraped past branches and brush. The dirt road was clear, although everyone was on high alert as we watched for a black sedan.

On the highway, we turned west for Westport airport, only twenty minutes away, and Amos and Norm, who took the wheels of their respective trucks, turned south for the long drive to Washington D.C.

For us, the short drive seemed to pass in slow motion. We scoured the countryside, looking for anything that seemed out of the ordinary. We saw nothing, but my gut told me that Felix knew our every move. Perhaps it was paranoia, but then again, Rosalind trusted instinct over reason and over the last couple of weeks, our instincts had served us well.

***

The parking lot at Westport was fuller than it had been during our last visit. The runway, which could be seen from the parking area, was clogged up with aircraft of various sizes and configurations awaiting clearance for take-off. People with baggage moved in and out of the terminal. I thought at first that it was good the terminal was so packed, but then again, all the people might prevent us from seeing Felix or some other men coming after us as easily. We moved quickly among the crowds, trying to be unnoticeable, just another group of travelers going somewhere.

I marveled at how the place teemed with people whereas it had been so quiet the last time. I scanned the long lines snaked in front of the airlines' check-in counters. It made me nervous seeing a man holding up his newspaper and looking around strangely. A security guard with a walkie-talkie looked straight at us as we passed. Any one of these people could've been working with Felix. I could see that the others felt the same.

We quickened our pace to the charter corridor. When we got there, we paused at the change of energy. It was empty. The one we wanted, NY Charter Services, was located at the far end of the terminal, down a long hallway, a distance away from the check-in counters.

A lone attendant was working on something at the computer and didn't notice us approaching.

"You have a reservation there under RD for four people," Reinhardt said.

The man jumped. He shifted his irate expression to a smile. "Name, please."

Reinhardt paused a second, looking straight into the face of the young man. "RD," Reinhardt replied. He studied the man's face. He was a different person than had been there the last time.

"Did you lose your name tag?" Ransom asked.

The man looked down at his shirt, moving his hand over his breast pocket. "It's… It's Jim. Sorry. I forgot to put it on. I was called in at the last minute. The regular guy phoned in sick."

"Sorry to hear that," Reinhardt said. "Tell Adam that we hope he gets better soon."

"I'll be sure to tell him," Jim said. "He was in a really bad way this morning. OK. So. Your plane is ready for take-off. You can board right away." He pointed to the side door that led out to the tarmac where our charter craft sat considerably further from the terminal than usual.

The stairs of the charter plane were already lowered and a uniformed co-pilot descended the steps and waited at the bottom for us to board.

Reinhardt and Ransom's brisk walk slowed noticeably as we approached the plane. The co-pilot was fidgeting with his hat and looking around.

"Sir, how are you today?" he asked Reinhardt when we got there.

Reinhardt stayed close to Jim, who had accompanied us out to the plane, another unusual new protocol, and Ransom moved in to greet the uniformed co-pilot with a handshake. Out of the corner of my eye, I saw Rosalind's hand hovering over her gun. I immediately did the same.

"All new staff today?" said Reinhardt with forcible cheer as he approached.

He looked at Rosalind. "Now!" He stopped abruptly, causing Jim to bump into him. Reinhardt reared back and elbowed Jim in the diaphragm then delivered a striking blow to the co-pilot's head. Ransom grabbed the co-pilot's hand, pulling his body forward, and as his head lowered to waist height, he jammed his knee up into the man's face. The man fell to the pavement with a thud and lay there motionless, blood streaming from his nose. Reinhardt threw another punch at Jim who was starting to recover, and he, too, fell to the ground and didn't move.

Around us on the noisy airfield, planes taxied and luggage trolleys zipped between planes. The airport was abuzz with activity. As we dashed back to the terminal, I hoped that by the time anyone noticed two bodies lying on the tarmac, we'd be inside, indistinguishable from the rest of the travelers.

In full survival mode, my body pulsed with adrenaline as we sprinted back to the terminal.

Once inside, we paused and caught our breath. We had to act normal so we wouldn't draw any attention to ourselves.

Ransom dashed to the now-unattended computer terminal and punched at the keyboard to clear our information from the screen and delete our reservation before joining us again. He grabbed the charter service employees' blazers hanging on hooks behind the check-in counter and handed them to us. I tied my hair back with an elastic I'd had on my wrist and put on my sunglasses; Reinhardt and Ransom put on the pilot caps from behind the counter; and Rosalind wrapped a print scarf over her head she'd had in her bag.

Staring at each other for a second, we all took a long, deep breath. Rosalind nodded and we moved as a unit calmly through the terminal and out the sliding glass doors and back to the paved outdoor lot where we had parked. It wasn't until we were inside our car that the loud blast smashed through the air and the night sky was instantly bright. We didn't stay to investigate.

"He's getting sloppy," said Ransom through his teeth. "This one can't be anonymously cleaned up without a thorough full-fledged investigation."

I had to wonder whether that were true—that he was just getting sloppy—or whether his desperation had taken on a whole new tactic. He'd shown his hand; an aviation disaster would make the news, possibly be looked at as an act of terrorism. Hollinger would have no problem seeing the truth now. So what was Felix's game plan, I had to wonder. This new territory frightened me. Now I couldn't begin to guess what he'd do next.

Slowly and calmly, we left the parking lot along with dozens of other vehicles on their way back home.

"What made you suspect that something wasn't right?" I asked Reinhardt.

"There's no Adam who works for them."

"Renegade will find us another way home," Rosalind said, her face to the window.

"Felix will have all airports and flights covered," Ransom said, leaning forward to talk to her in the front seat. "We won't get out of the country without him detecting us."

I'd had it. It was the same feeling I'd had before: trapped. "Since we can't run, let's chase him. We've got to stop him. We can't run for the rest of our lives."

"If we're lucky, Felix will think he blew us to kingdom come today," Rosalind said. "If not, maybe the plane explosion will buy us a little time."

"What if this time we arrange a surprise for him on his own home turf?" I asked. "Only we'll be armed with the best weapon, one he won't be able to escape from."

"What, Hollinger?" scoffed Ransom. He put his hand on my thigh. "It's a great idea, but it won't be that easy. Felix has a very loyal and well-paid crew. They'll cover for his absence, and I'd bet they even have proof that he's been at work all along. Only that surveillance footage will prove anything different. But even then, it will be a stretch to incriminate him. I know how he works." He shut his eyes. I could feel his frustration because it was mine, too. We had lost too much to let this bastard win. I put my hand on top of his, and he turned his around and weaved his fingers through mine.

"All the more reason to go to Washington and help our seniors," I said, though now that we'd seen them all tarted up and looking sexy, it made me laugh to call them that.

"And all we can do is try," he said, looking at me and smiling devilishly. "After all, I still have the thumb drive with the gas station surveillance footage in my pocket."

I laughed, not just because I was happy we had something powerful on our side to use, but also because Ransom was making really silly suggestive faces talking about the "thumb drive in his pocket."

"But seriously," he went on, "they can lie for him all they want, but we have all the proof we need to show he wasn't hard at work."

That decided, Reinhardt programmed the GPS for Washington. Except, this time we were running toward Felix instead of running away from him. I hoped his ego was so inflated he considered us eradicated. So when we showed up in Washington with our seniors as reinforcements, we'd throw him. I could only imagine his rage when he found out that we were still very much alive and this time were directly challenging his game.

***

Washington was a city always on the move and even though it was the middle of the night, the traffic on the expressway and streets remained heavy. When we entered the city limits, I just shook my head. We used to come to the city a lot when I was younger because my mom "loved the energy," she said, and how educational it was. Now I suspected that when my parents said they were going to see a show or have dinner, they weren't doing either. I never saw this coming. What kid imagines that when her parents say they're going to have a walk down at the Lincoln Memorial, they're actually going to meet with a bunch of ex-spies to exchange Intel or something? I sighed loudly and rolled my eyes at myself. I'd seen too many movies.

Ransom had taken the wheel. He was accustomed to Washington traffic, which Reinhardt wasn't. We were missing Robert and his expert skills of always so deftly getting us to where we needed to go. With only a few wrong turns due to the confusing Washington traffic circles, after seven hours in the car, we arrived at the Hilton, where Renegade had made reservations for us, also under RD. We checked in quickly and quietly. We had time to get a few hours of sleep before meeting with Amos and the others for breakfast. The next day, we would find Hollinger and fill him in on how he had a rogue agent on a killing spree and hopefully help him disarm a very dangerous and villainous maniac.

After the modest and dated accommodations in Springfield, the Washington Hilton was a treat with its luxurious white duvets, plush carpets, sparkling bathroom fixtures and thick terrycloth robes. The card key elevators were a nice security feature as well, though getting around that would've been child's play for Felix. We were given adjoining rooms. I'd wondered before why Rosalind didn't choose to sleep with her husband, but by now I understood that she wanted to look after me; plus, by this point, it'd have been awkward if Ransom and I had to share. But we did leave the inner door open between our two rooms so we could talk easily. We locked the outer doors with their chain locks, plus, for extra security, we propped the plush easy chairs from our rooms against the doors. Then, physically and emotionally exhausted, we all fell into our respective queen-sized beds and quickly fell asleep.

It was the first time since we had arrived in the United States that all of us slept at the same time without someone being on guard. We slept like rocks until Reinhardt's alarm woke us at 7 a.m.

I groaned and stretched.

Rosalind laughed. "No moaning, darling. A whole night of sleep without anyone trying to kill us? We should be celebrating."

I laughed. "Good point. Though I still think I'm going to need some coffee."

We showered and went down to the restaurant where the room had been set up with a silver service buffet of bacon, eggs, waffles, cereal, you name it. My stomach growled and I couldn't wait to eat. In the corner behind a half wall topped with tall potted plants, Amos, Hannah, Norm and Alice sat at a table already set up with extra chairs.

"I see you had a change of destination," Hannah said, her eyebrows high over her coffee cup.

Rosalind laughed. "Our charter plane encountered a few problems. Actually, it just exploded. So we thought we'd join you. No use letting Felix blow up every charter flight in the area trying to keep us in the U.S. Ruby thought we should meet him on his own turf. If he thinks he can get rid of us that easily, he might want to think again."

"He's getting reckless now," Ransom added. "Have you been able to reach Hollinger? How were you planning to tell him about Felix and what he's been up to?"

"Well," Amos said with a slow smile. "Felix didn't realize it, but when Norm and I realized it was our old boss scoping out the diner, we got a few pictures of him on our phones along with some we took at the helicopter crash site. We emailed them to Hollinger this morning. Then we called and said that Armond Flemming was requesting an appointment with him. When he puts that name together with the photos, I'm pretty sure he's going to want to talk to me."

"Armond Flemming?" I asked. "Is that your real name?"

"Well, no," Amos said. "None of us used our real names during the Cold War spy missions. The Bureau didn't allow it. Too much chance of something bad happening to our families if the Russians actually found out who we were, so we were all assigned bogus identities."

"Would Hollinger know that name?" I asked. "I thought all of you and your Cold War identities and records were sent to Archives to be sealed and forgotten forever in order to protect anyone who left the force."

"Yes, and Hollinger signed off on each record," Amos said. "You see, I'm the one who demanded new and hidden identities for all of the spies who were out of a job when the Soviet Union collapsed in 1991. The buyout package costs were staggering. Oh, no, Hollinger will never forget the name of Armond Flemming. He took a lot of heat from Congress and the President. Anyway, in the end it was decided that it was the best thing."

Amos's phone buzzed on the table. "Well, speak of the devil." He picked it up and put it to his ear. "Hello, Hollinger, it's been a long time! Oh, good, good. You? Excellent. She's fine, yes, yes." He saw us all staring at him and made an exasperated face. "OK," he whispered and put his mouth back to the phone. "So, I'm sorry to cut this short, but I have some information that I think you'll be very interested in. Yes, I'll meet you in one hour, but not at your office." He laughed. "It's a little early for beer, but our old pub is perfect."

Seventeen

We drove to Upper Malboro to Jasper's pub. When we arrived, Amos told us that back in the Cold War era, they'd picked it because it was far enough off the beaten path that you wouldn't run into coworkers from Bureau. Amos told us that Hollinger introduced him to it as he badgered the Bureau for anonymity during the buyout negotiations.

Amos had led Hollinger to believe it was a private meeting, just an old acquaintance coming by with some unfinished details to discuss about the protection program, unforeseen issues that had come up and needed further attention. On the drive over, everyone was jumpy. We were counting on Hollinger's cooperation. On his integrity. We counted on him being on our side to help us stop a crazed psychopath. It was important that we didn't overwhelm him though, and agreed that Amos would explain everything. The last thing we needed was to make him think we had some ulterior motive and were unreliable, all of us leaping in with our two cents. But we weren't fools; there was, of course, the likelihood that Felix would have discovered where we were or what we were doing, so we stayed together, our weapons loaded, every one of us on alert.

"The beer's handcrafted on the premises," said Amos affectionately as we entered. In contrast to the slickness of our hotel, this place was rugged and down to earth with its long wood bar and rough-hewed tables. We split up and took a table in the corner and another table against the wall and kept our eyes open.

Amos dialed Rosalind and put his phone in his pocket. She put in one of the headphones and gave me the other. Every time Amos moved, we heard loud static from his shirt fabric, but otherwise, it was a perfect connection.

"Armond," Hollinger said after he came in and they shook hands. "What do you retired agents need money for this time? Face-lifts, hair transplants, how about liposuction? I'll tell you right now, the answer is no! You're always a sign of trouble. Costly trouble!"

"All right, Hollinger, you're very funny. Listen," Amos said, "you can't even imagine the trouble we've encountered."

"We?" Hollinger said. "What do you mean 'we'? Who else is involved in this trouble you're talking about?"

I sneaked a look over. Hollinger leaned back in the booth and glanced around. There were only a few tables filled in the place, and the way he paused on us made me think he knew we were with Amos. I sipped the weak coffee and tried to look normal.

"You saw the photos I emailed?" Amos asked.

"What do you want me to say?" Hollinger said. "We both know who it is, that he's my Archives manager of Cold War records, and an old boss of ours put away to pasture. Are you trying to allege that he has something to do with this helicopter crash? I'm supposed to wonder why he was in a diner in Springfield, Massachusetts, when he was supposed to be behind his desk? So that's our mystery, I gather. How Springfield, a crashed helicopter, and Felix Szabo have to do with your 'trouble'."

Amos leaned in and tapped his fingernails on the table. "Not only is he involved in the crash, he has been involved in multiple other so-called 'accidents' in which people—who just happen to be ex-agents—have lost their lives. You might also want to do some investigation into agents Magda Worchenski, Adam Jones and Robert Draker, all deceased under strange circumstances. And that charter plane explosion at Westport yesterday? Worth looking into as well."

"These are very serious allegations, Armond," Hollinger said. "Why would a quiet old man counting down the days to retirement and in a secure government job with an excellent pension want to do these things? Besides, wouldn't the local authorities have been suspicious if they suspected any criminal activity?"

"Our friend Szabo has a wide reach. Somehow, he's managed to cover them up," Amos said. "Other than his last few hits, none of the accidents or deaths even made the local news. He also has the Springfield sheriff's department under his control. Together, they've terrorized the local residents who are now walking around fearful of arrest. Or worse if they talk about the crash because they've been told it's a secret government UFO investigation. The Springfield authorities covered up several murders that took place just a few days ago. The three bodies of Myrtle Hamilton, Robert Draker and Christian Slade were supposedly taken to Erie for autopsy, but I checked. They never got there."

Hollinger went silent.

I cheeked to see Hollinger taking out his phone and begin scrolling through the photos.

"These photos prove Szabo played hooky from work, nothing more," he said. "I need more than this to launch a murder investigation against him, and I certainly couldn't arrest him on this. His lawyer would have him out in no time."

"Hollinger," Amos said, his voice deepening. "We need your help. People's lives are at stake here. He's killed several retired agents already and the rest of the agents who took the package are on his list. No one is safe. One by one he's bent on killing us all, says we're traitors and deserters working with the Russians to terrorize Americans. He's psychotic and very dangerous. My wife and I, my friends, we've all been targeted and he's after us even as we sit here. He's already made several attempts to kill us."

"Do you know what you're saying?" Hollinger said. His doughy face had gone beet red up to his sandy hairline. "You're telling me that we have a killer in the Defense Department, operating right under my nose, and I haven't been aware of it. What kind of an incompetent do you think that makes me?"

"I can see that it doesn't look good for you, but it's understandable why you haven't known about this. Why would you pay much attention to an old records administrator just putting in time until he chooses to retire?" asked Amos. "But it's important now that you watch him. We know without a doubt that he'll make another move soon. If we're smart, and have your support, we can catch him in the act, preventing a crime that you discovered and put an end to. That would make you a hero, don't you think?

"And further," he said, taking a deep breath, "the ultimate heroism will be not just that you prevented more killings of ex-agents but that you saved their children. Felix Szabo doesn't discriminate. He wipes out the whole family when he moves in for the kill. There are eight of us here in the city right now who are being targeted, whose families were killed but they managed to survive. One of the survivors had a ten-year-old brother. Do you want the blood of innocent children on your hands?"

Hollinger rubbed his eyes. "Armond, I've known you a long time. I trust you. Always have. Bring me something I can work with, and then I'll stop him."

"Will you at least assign some surveillance on his activities?"

"I'm not promising anything without proof," Hollinger said. "But I can have someone audit his department for expenses. If all you say checks out, they'll find some discrepancies, and that will give me entry into their records. He won't know anything is up. An audit is annoying but routine and perfectly normal. How do I get hold of you?"

"You have my email, but don't worry, Hollinger," Amos said. "I'll stay in touch. "If you don't hear from me... well, then you'll know I was on to something."

Amos stood and left the pub and we watched to see what Hollinger would do next. He drummed his fingers on the table, looking pensive and worried. Then he took his phone out of his pocket and held it to his ear. "I want an audit on the CW Archive group, all travel and expenses," he said. "And put a mole in their midst who reports directly back to me only." He hung up and shuffled out of the booth. He stopped in front of the table where I was sitting with Rosalind and nodded knowingly to each of us. We said nothing, just lowered our heads and continued sipping our cold coffee. Hollinger turned and left the pub.

***

We regrouped back at the Hilton in the seniors' suite. Renegade had suggested that our seniors enjoy the highest level of accommodation to keep them willingly in Washington. Not that without marble tiles and a personal butler they wouldn't have stayed. But Rosalind agreed that they deserved it for being so willing to help. There was safety in numbers and numbers stacked the odds in our favor. Felix needed to feel overwhelmed with opposing forces. He either had to orchestrate a major disaster to wipe out the lot of us, or try to eliminate us one at time, leaving him vulnerable as we closed in on his next attack. It wouldn't take him long to realize what he was up against and that we were worthy opponents. This time, he had no element of surprise. We fully expected his retaliatory actions. But did he expect us to offer a fight?

We decided to stay in the hotel until Hollinger had time to think about the situation and make his decision as to what he would do.

"Hollinger has already arranged an investigation of Felix's department," Ransom said. "Sure, he knew we were there, so he could have called his girlfriend and pretended to be calling the CIA for all we know, but in time, we'll know whether he is taking Amos's plea seriously or not. And if he actually did issue the audit, that will keep Felix close to Washington. The distraction should give us some time to figure out how to get that solid proof Hollinger is looking for. And the mole he requested should definitely source something interesting."

"Can Hollinger just arbitrarily put a person into his department?" I asked. "Wouldn't Felix know immediately that he's being watched?"

"Szabo always has an open requisition for extra staff," Ransom said, "and he usually gets someone. Archives is a good place for interns looking for work experience. Don't worry. Hollinger is no fool. He'll make it look and feel legitimate."

Amos's phone buzzed. "It's Hollinger already," Amos said. "That didn't take him long." Amos put the phone to his ear and after a few "yeps" and "OKs" hung up and put it back into his pocket. He was grinning. "It appears that Felix isn't at work," Amos said. "And the building's mail delivery hasn't seen him for over a week. But the interesting thing is that his assistant said that he *was* there and would get him to call Hollinger when he was free. When Szabo returned Hollinger's call, it was traced to Springfield, and when Hollinger had the IT department confirm by checking the IP address on Szabo's laptop, it was also in Springfield. Bingo!"

Ransom laughed. "He's so old school. He can clear away bodies and pay off cops, but masking his IP address wouldn't ever even occur to him?" He paused and looked at Amos. "Oh, sorry, man."

Amos laughed. "I don't even know what an IP address is, so no apologies necessary."

Ransom smiled and went on, "Anyway, this is great. Now Hollinger has his own positive proof."

"Which is all we need to get the ball rolling," said Amos putting on his glasses to look at his phone. "He says he wants to meet with all of us before he meets with Szabo tomorrow about the audit. He's suggesting the Jefferson Memorial." He looked at us over his glasses. "I didn't bother suggesting he just come here. He knows we wouldn't want to reveal our location. But at the same time, if he doesn't know it yet, he's got his intelligence team working on it and will soon enough. Anyway, since I've known him, Hollinger has liked to take a break on nice days by having a walk along the pathway that leads to the Jefferson.

It's within his normal routine so no one will think it's unusual, even Felix if he's watching. As for us, we'll pose as tourists and blend in with the others at the site. Ruby." He looked at me. "Have you ever had a chance to visit Washington before?"

"We used to come a lot." I paused. "It was a long time ago." I had to fight hard to prevent the memories from stirring up all my tumultuous feelings, feelings that were better kept hidden.

"Well, it's a lovely day and a walk would do us all good," Rosalind said. "Ruby, we need to get some sunglasses from the hotel gift shop, and maybe a hat." She probably saw my eyes getting dewy as I remembered my past. She grabbed my arm and pulled me away from the conversation. Rosalind always seemed keenly aware of my emotions, and she had a knack for helping me carry on despite them. I was grateful to her for that, time and time again.

The Jefferson Memorial was visible for miles before the walking path widened at the steps of the portico that opened up on the man-made Tidal Basin of the Potomac. I'd forgotten some of the details, like the rounded colonnade of Ionic columns that surrounded the famous bronze statue of Jefferson, or the way the water played at the base of the white marble. There were tourists chatting and snapping pictures but the whole atmosphere felt serene, like a place of peace and reflection. I knew that peace could be shattered in a second if Felix decided to attack. My conflicting senses tore my attention from the beauty of the place to a guarded unease as we looked for Hollinger among the throngs.

We found him standing in front of a panel inscribed with the famous quotation: "*We hold these truths to be self-evident: that all men are created equal, that they are endowed by their Creator with certain inalienable rights, among these are life, liberty, and the pursuit of happiness, that to secure these rights, governments are instituted among men.*"

We came up and stood behind him. "Doesn't seem right that we have to fight so hard for life, liberty, and the pursuit of happiness,"

Hollinger said without turning around. "It always makes me humble when I read those words." He turned then and smiled as we drew in close to greet him.

"The coffee at Jasper's is horrible, isn't it?" Hollinger said. I and the others all tried to look like we didn't know what he meant, but he put up his hands. "You were pretty obvious. The fact that all of you were there was one of the things that made me listen more attentively to Armond's story. I always check things out even when I don't really believe they're true." He sighed. "It seems that I've got a real mess on my hands."

He was going to help us. The relief that washed into me nearly knocked me over. I felt like a child being rescued from a tree or something and wanted to hug him, hard.

"Felix Szabo killed my parents and my little brother," I said. "I want to stop him from doing that to any other families." It was all too much for me, the memories of a wonderful time spent in Washington with the people I loved most. I couldn't bury the hurt any longer. My voice softened and a tear ran down my face.

Hollinger's stern demeanor mellowed when he answered me. "I'm sorry that he's caused you such loss and pain. I know you probably want to be nameless but who are you?"

"Jones," I said clumsily as if it were a foreign language I hadn't spoken in a long time. "My dad was Adam, my mom was Marie and my brother was Johnny. He was only ten."

"Adam Jones?" Hollinger said. He stared at me for a moment and took a deep breath as he turned again to look at the inscription on the panel. He remained silent for a few minutes, gripping the back of his neck. Finally he turned. "And what about Kathleen?" Hollinger asked, staring into my eyes.

"Kathleen doesn't exist anymore," Reinhardt said firmly.

Hollinger stared hard at me but said nothing. It was obvious who I was, but if he didn't acknowledge that I was her, he was allowing for her to stay nonexistent and possibly save my life—again. He walked over to the bronze statue then over to the other inscribed panels. We stood in place as he pretended to view the historic importance of the words memorialized in marble.

He returned to our group, his face expressionless. "Armond says he's still out to get you and it appears that's accurate," Hollinger said. "If you want my help, this has to stay confidential. The Defense Department can't be made to look negligent. And I have no intention of having the media portray me as an incompetent bureaucrat who can't see the very thing the department is supposed to protect against." His face grew steely. "I already know that Archives has been covering up Felix's operations. But it's going to be tough to link him to any crimes unless you have some other evidence that irrefutably implicates him."

"Good you asked," said Ransom, pulling a Ziploc out of his backpack. "I have some surveillance video that shows him at a gas station in Springfield, and a piece of fabric with Magda's blood on it that we found on the wreck of a certain helicopter that was brought to a junkyard in Springfield. One of the photos shows the spot where it was found on the wreckage."

"This is good. Not conclusive," Hollinger said, "but the more we have, the better our case will be. I'm meeting with Szabo at his office tomorrow. He must have rushed back here from Springfield when his assistant told him about my phone call. I'm going with the audit team. I don't know if he'll think there's more than just an audit going on, but I don't care. If he is guilty of these horrendous actions, I'm going to make sure he's stopped and punished to the fullest extent. In the meantime, I think it wouldn't hurt if you had some extra protection."

"Thank you, but no," said Reinhardt. "If Felix finds out or sees that we're protected, it'll confirm that we got to you. It's best if he still sees us as somewhat vulnerable. We'll stay alert and notify you if he makes any moves on us."

Hollinger was staring at me. "What's your name, then?"

"Ruby."

"Ruby, just so you know, Adam and Marie Jones operated under the names of Lawrence and Patricia Slade when they worked at the Bureau.

I knew them very well. The three of us were a team and we worked undercover in Russia on several missions. Almost lost our lives twice before being recalled back home. They continued with the Bureau and I transferred to the Defense Department shortly after. I don't think Szabo ever forgave me for my promotion."

"Slade?" I said. I felt like I'd been slapped. "Does the name Christian Slade mean anything to you?"

Hollinger paused for a moment and looked up at the sky.

"Mr. Hollinger?" I asked again.

He sighed. "One of the reasons Lawrence and Patricia remained stateside was because she was pregnant. She gave birth to a son. A son they named Christian. It wasn't a planned pregnancy and they knew they could not successfully parent a child and continue to…" He paused as if trying to find the right words. "… to honor the commitment they'd made to the government, so they gave him up for adoption at birth with the condition that his name be kept in case they could reconnect with him later, when they were sure his life wasn't going to be in danger for his association to them. Though it was against policy, the adoption agency agreed." Hollinger looked almost fearful as he turned to me. "Why do you ask?"

I felt like I'd been plunged into ice water. "Christian Slade was Felix's hit-man and constant companion while in Springfield," I said. I was shaking as I began to understand the story. "It was Christian who helped Felix threaten the local townspeople and it was Christian who grabbed me that night and kidnapped me and took me to the farmhouse to lure the others so Felix could kill us all, but my gun went off and shot him in the leg. Felix wouldn't help or care for him, so I dressed his wound. He appreciated my kindness. I wonder…"

An urgent look from Rosalind to say no more cut off my sentence.

Hollinger looked dazed. "What happened to him?"

His voice was so encouraging and kind, I couldn't help myself and kept talking. "Felix shot him down and the last I saw of him he was face down on the lawn at the farm. Slade helped me get away from Felix and distracted him so we could escape. He sacrificed his life to save us."

Hollinger was visibly moved, his voice wavering with emotion as he took my hand and looked into my eyes. "Do me a favor," he said. "Stay safe. Don't do anything that's going to get you or the others killed. I'm only a phone call away. I'll deploy help within minutes."

"Thank you," I said, "but you don't even know where we're staying."

He continued his gentle hold of my hand, smiling warmly. "I know exactly where you're staying. I'll do what I can to keep him away from you." With that, he released my hand and continued his walk along the Potomac like he had never met with us.

I had another brother. Slade had been my brother. Felix took him away, too. I seethed with anger as the hurt burned in my soul, corrupting whatever moral thoughts I had left inside me.

"Let it go, Ruby," Ransom said. He stood close and his voice was gentle. He had taken my cold hand into his and I hadn't even noticed. "Let's get back to the hotel. We've all had enough excitement for one day." He continued to hold my hand as we walked back.

Eighteen

IT KEPT GOING THROUGH MY HEAD. Christian Slade had been my brother. I wondered if he had felt some kind of connection to me. Was that the reason we seemed to bond so quickly despite our strange circumstances? The painful memories of all I had lost became fresh again. I struggled to push them back, the conflicted feelings of losing a brother I never even knew existed who tried to help kill me then saved my life. The others saw the torment this new information gave me. The Drakers were supposed to be my family now and superficially I had accepted them because I knew we shared loss as a common bond. Yet my pain stayed with me, haunted me, as I'm sure it stayed with the other Drakers, and it would forever. Our connection was a strange one, a common understanding and certainly a common enemy. They left me alone to sort my feelings out. What else could they do? I saw their caring glances, especially Rosalind's, and appreciated them, but they couldn't do more than that. So Rosalind kept a close eye on me just in case I needed her.

Somehow, the distance they gave me to deal with my feelings started to endear them to me even more. I had resisted adopting them as family even though they fully had accepted me from the very start. But this strange turn of events made me consider a new definition of family more intimately.

We waited for Hollinger to update us on Felix's reactions about being audited. The audit wasn't scheduled until tomorrow and the process was intended to take two days, one for expense and financial records and another for procedural records. I found the wait intolerable because it left me with too much time, time to wallow in unproductive and tortured feelings of who I was and the kind of person I was becoming. The rest of our group looked restless as well. It drove us all crazy just sitting around our hotel rooms, trying to stay out of sight, working out in the tiny gym and watching movies on the hotel television. There wasn't much else we could do.

"I feel like we're in prison," Ransom said, pacing around the room like a bored tiger. "I'd imagine Felix is scrambling to prepare for Hollinger's audit. Even if he does suspect we're in Washington, I'm sure covering up all his extra-curricular activities is occupying his time, and if he had people out looking for us before, I'd imagine they'd have all been reallocated to keeping Szabo out of prison by falsifying records and receipts. What do you say? Let's do some sight-seeing!" he said, jumping into the air.

"Well, it's a dangerous idea but an excellent one," Rosalind said. "I love Washington. So much history, so much architecture, all the wonderful restaurants! We'll get ourselves some minor disguises and then have a day's outing."

"All right," Amos said, "but we'll take our guns. At least we can put up a fight if Felix or his field goons happen to find us."

"Yay! A day's outing in Washington with guns," I said. "Just like a normal family." A cynical glance from Reinhardt made me laugh.

"Disguises are my specialty," Alice said. "Nordstrom, here we come! It'll be fun! Then we can go out for a nice dinner tonight and tomorrow we can do the Smithsonian or Georgetown or check out some of the other sights."

If Alice were responsible for the transformation of Amos and their four into the country busybody guise that fooled the Springfield locals, she could certainly transform our spy-like fugitive look. I had to admit we did look rather grim dressed in black leather and dark shirts. I felt my mood lift at the thought of doing ordinary activities. The others grabbed their jackets and started for the door of our hotel room. Maybe, I thought as we walked down the hall, this time, I wouldn't get molested in the change room. Of course, ordinary people didn't go shopping with guns in their purses or tucked into their pockets or waistbands. I chuckled. Or maybe they did and we just didn't know it. Didn't everyone have his secrets?

Alice and Rosalind had a grand time in the department store trying clothes on the rest of us like dolls. In the end, I found some nice things, even a flirty skirt and cute top I thought Ransom might like, then blushed to even consider it, and headed back to the hotel loaded down with bags to get ready for dinner.

Hollinger called just as we were leaving. He had news about the audit that would take place the next day. Amos answered his cell phone and put the call on speaker. "Szabo's assistant has been in contact with my assistant, asking lots of questions about the expense audit," Hollinger said. "He's befriended people in my department and become quite chatty with my staff asking unusual questions, making jokes about Archives and illicit goings-on. He's sleuthing for information, trying to figure out the reason for the audit. I'm afraid that Felix and his team are on to us."

"That's OK," Amos said. "It's good that they're on the defensive. It will keep them busy for a few days. I'm sure you'll find something anyway and when you do, we can lead him into a sting operation where he'll have to show his hand. Got any ideas?"

"Felix won't be happy to see me there with the audit team," Hollinger said. "He might even be belligerent. He wasn't happy when I was recruited by the Department of National Defense and even less happy when I was promoted and became his boss. It should be very interesting tomorrow."

"How long will the audit take?" I asked.

"Long enough to look official," Hollinger said. "But I'll make it last at least a couple of days, longer if I can. That should keep him away from you all and give you a breather. You probably need some time to get yourselves together after what happened at the farmhouse. But I still recommend you stay out of sight. No use inviting trouble."

"Don't worry," Alice said. "We've all spent years going incognito. You keep him occupied and we'll take whatever precautions necessary to disappear into plain sight."

"Humph," Hollinger said. "Don't listen to me then! I'll stay in touch. You know how to reach me. Call if you need help." He hung up.

We looked at each other, everyone dressed nicely: the men in suit jackets and shiny shoes and the women in skirts for a change, and hesitated, considering Hollinger's advice.

"I took the liberty of making dinner reservations," Norm said as if we hadn't just second guessed going out. "A place called the Occidental over on Pennsylvania Ave. You don't eat anywhere here in Washington without reservations. Bring your credit card, Reinhardt."

Reinhardt pulled a credit card from his wallet and waved it at us in a gesture that said, "sky's the limit!" We all laughed but when he put it away, his brow was furrowed. "I suppose we can't hide in here forever," he said. "What name did you make the reservation under?"

"RD of course," Norm said. "Spelled the last name as D E E. They didn't ask for more."

**

The carpeting of the restaurant was so thick, the heels from my new shoes sank in and I stumbled. The sound of conversation and silver against china was muted from the carpeting and the upholstered walls on which paintings of all the American presidents as well as other prominent bureaucrats hung. There was a large glossy mahogany bar where elegantly dressed people were sipping martinis. The restaurant had both private and public dining rooms and a large open patio outside.

Although we didn't dare sit outside, we decided to risk sitting like normal people in the dining room.

As we were led to our table, I didn't think I'd ever seen so many suits in one place except for at a funeral. We took our chairs and apart from an occasional glance, a look of disapproval, and one downright snub from a busboy when Ransom asked him for water, against the political elite and power players around us, despite our nice attire, we could've recently walked in from the Appalachian mountains for all they thought.

More than half an hour passed and still the waiter remained elusive. Reinhardt and Amos were shifting in their chairs tilting and turning their heads looking for someone who would take our order.

A few minutes later, Hollinger showed up. Immediately, a waiter came to the table and pulled up an additional chair, handing him a menu and fussing over him and whether he needed anything to start. Hollinger looked around and noticed we were still holding our menus. "Three bottles of Chateau Montelena from Napa and bread for the table, please," Hollinger said.

The waiter bowed and scurried off.

"How did you know we were here?" I asked. I looked at Rosalind and Alice who shrugged their shoulders, crooked smiles on their faces.

"I hope you don't mind that I'm joining you," Hollinger said. "I have more information on our mutual acquaintance."

So Hollinger was having us watched. That could only mean a couple of things: either he thought we were suspects or we were in imminent danger.

"Has the audit revealed that Felix has done anything questionable?" Ransom asked.

"Hard to tell," Hollinger said. "Bankers' boxes have been moving in and out of the Archives building all day designated for 'off-site storage,' and it seems easy enough to see they're clearing out material they don't want us to get our hands on."

"You've seen this for yourself?" Reinhardt asked.

"No," Hollinger said. "One of my interns has been reporting their activity to me. The boxes are marked 'Redundant,' and were this normal circumstances, I wouldn't suspect anything. I did however get an unannounced visit from Szabo himself. Said he wanted to say hello to me, his old acquaintance." He snorted. "First time in fifteen years? Not at all unusual."

"That had to have been interesting. What did you talk about?" Amos asked.

"Thought I'd push him a bit," Hollinger said. "Started to talk about the Cold War days and the dangerous times we encountered on our missions. We talked about Adam and Patricia and her pregnancy. I asked him if he remembered the name of the couple who adopted Christian. He said he didn't but he's the one who arranged it. My guess is that he followed Christian throughout his youth and later hand-picked him to help him with his dirty work."

"Slade told me that he had spent some time in prison, and the reason he worked for Felix was the money," I said. "But why would Felix care so much about Christian if he was Patricia and Adam's son?"

Hollinger took a deep breath. "He wasn't their son," he said quietly. He looked at me. "But he was Patricia's."

I waited for Hollinger to stop being so vague, but he was looking down, ringing his wineglass with a finger. I tried to think: so this meant my mother had had a baby before my dad was around? No, the timing was wrong. Then I stared at Hollinger, horrified. She had the baby while she was with my dad. My mother cheated on my father? How did Hollinger know? I felt sick. There was so much that I didn't know, so much my parents had kept secret from me and Johnny. That must have been why Christian was given up for adoption. "You know who Christian's father is, don't you," I said coldly. I knew the answer; I could tell I was right from Hollinger's behavior. My blood froze in my veins.

When he looked up, I could see his eyes were sorry. "Those were treacherous times," Hollinger said. "Women particularly were always targets for men, not only from our enemy but from our own. Patricia did what she had to do to keep us safe. We were undercover in the Soviet Union and arrested for espionage. Szabo got us released, but he was no philanthropist. He had his price. Patricia didn't hesitate. She couldn't hesitate. It was that or a Russian firing squad for all of us."

"Szabo? He was Christian's father?" I whispered hoarsely. The words caught in my throat. I had a half-brother, the son of the maniac who had killed my family. My mother had cheated on my father and made a baby with the man who killed her, my whole family, and was trying to finish the job. "He gunned down his own son."

I was raging inside, and my voice rose. People in the dining room looked over at me. But I didn't care. I was on the verge of losing it. I wanted to lash out, my anger and disgust getting the better of me. I couldn't storm out, so I grabbed my wine glass and drank the whole thing down. Alice and Hannah came to my side and had their gentle hands on me before I could make a scene, and from her chair beside me, Rosalind put her arm around my shoulders and held me close to her. It was a tableau of empathy and anger, our table. I was touched by every-one's reaction but was suddenly too drunk and upset to appreciate it. Ransom snaked his hand into my lap and gripped my hand.

"So what do we do next?" Amos asked Hollinger in low undertones.

"I have a staff member who is retiring this week," Hollinger said. "Retirement always seems to bring out the worst in Felix Szabo. Just the word irritates the hell out of him. I'll invite him. It's going to be a big deal, a black tie gala affair. Maybe in a weak moment he'll let something slip, something about how he feels about the people who choose retire-ment rather than serve their country, or something about how he deals with his department being dissolved, and if I'm lucky something about how he deals with people who retire."

"Better yet," Amos said. "Why not let him know that you've also invited Armond Phillips and his wife. We should be on his hit list."

"Niles and Alicia Hetterman might also stir up his ire a notch or two," Norman said. "Since we're the group who pushed the buyout package and identity protection program, he would probably salivate that we're nearby."

"That would make you easy targets," Hollinger said. "But it would also give Felix lots of opportunity to show his hand."

"I'm the one he really wants," I said. My eyes felt hot. I looked around the table, my face tight. Or Ruby's face tight. "Let him know that Ruby Draker is your special guest, a daughter of an old acquaintance who happens to be in Washington looking for work. You offered to take her to the gala to network with important people you know in government positions. Let's take a selfie. You can show it to Felix when you see him at the audit."

Reinhardt and Rosalind looked horrified that I had let my name slip. I saw the tiniest gesture, a sideways shake of their heads, their lips formed to create a subtle *shh*. But it was too late. I'd said it aloud, and now it was out.

Hollinger looked uncomfortable with the suggestion. But there was no denying that it offered the best enticement for Felix to move to desperate action. Felix might not associate Kathleen with Ruby Draker, but "the bitch" who'd gotten away from the farm was a loose end that could expose him and would need to be eliminated.

"Ruby Draker," Hollinger said. He held that name in thoughtful silence contemplating possibilities, wondering what kind of connection drew the lot of us to Washington in pursuit of a dangerous killer. I could sense that he was trying to make the connection to Kathleen or perhaps to an unknown daughter of his own, a consequence of his own work during the Cold War. I looked away in disgust. God knows that he and my dad probably had sex with every Russian agent in the Soviet Union to extract intelligence information or maybe just because they could. Who knew? I could have siblings all over Russia. The thought made me feel sick.

"Draker," Hollinger repeated. I was sorry I'd let the name slip. Now he'd run an investigation on it. He wouldn't find anything, but he'd try. I could feel Reinhardt and Rosalind's disapproval radiating off of them like heat.

The waiter brought more wine and took our orders. The rest of the evening was spent in casual and strained conversation about the weather and Washington gossip. Hollinger's eyes danced from person to person but his gaze frequently lingered on me. Was he trying to distinguish some resemblance, some trait or mannerism that might give him a clue as to who I really was? I felt the whole night like he was trying to determine whose daughter I was. I didn't want to give him the satisfaction of saying it wasn't him. Then again, now that I understood the conditions he and my parents worked under, who knew? I could've been his.

***

The next two days passed, but painfully slowly. We visited the Lincoln Memorial with its reflecting pool, the Washington Memorial, several of the Smithsonian Museums and dined out at all different types of restaurants. I didn't care anymore if Felix knew about us. I wanted to be discovered so Felix would make his move. Out in the open here, we were safer than if we were in hiding where he could arrange an accident, or make it appear that we had encountered just plain bad luck that the police would attribute to misfortune. Hollinger must have also kept Felix sufficiently engaged in the audit because the days passed pleasantly without consequence. Nonetheless, while we had a good time and explored the city, we remained vigilant. We were also heartened to know that Hollinger's people had our backs and were so good at their jobs we didn't see any sign of them.

By the end of the week, Hollinger and his team had completed the audit and told Felix that everything looked good, saying nothing of the inconsistencies they'd found. Hollinger knew the dates when Felix had been in Springfield. Felix's records indicated that he was at work on those same days, meaning his attendance records had been falsified, which the surveillance tapes would prove. There were no travel expense records or hotel receipts, both of which Felix would have received, so even if he had destroyed them, the originals could be easily gotten. Since the Defense Department recorded all incoming phone calls,

Hollinger had records of suspicious inquiries made by Felix. Lastly, Szabo had his assistant try to pull some strings to avoid the inspection altogether, calls which had also been recorded and noted. But Hollinger kept everything to himself and instructed his review team to report a clean record of department expenses back to Szabo.

Hollinger's private investigation of the helicopter at the wrecker in Springfield was also yielding some interesting results. Further forensics on the helicopter found more evidence of blood, and blood meant injuries, injuries not reported along with the crash. In a few more days, the forensic report would be completed. Hollinger would know who the helicopter company was and to whom it had been contracted. Not that he didn't already know.

"The retirement gala is tomorrow night at the Weston, one of Washington's most prestigious hotels," Hollinger said. "The security level will be high, which Felix will know. Amos, you and Hannah will be my personal guests. Ruby, you'll be their niece, a newcomer to Washington."

"How did Felix react when you told him that Amos and Hannah were coming?" Reinhardt asked. "Did he remember them?"

"Oh, yes," Hollinger chuckled. "He went into quite a tirade. He called them cowards, traitors and an embarrassment to all things American. Asked about the niece as well. I showed him a photo of you, Ruby. His eyes went big as saucers. He looked at the photo a long time then accused me of being involved with communists. 'Communist sym-pathizer,' he called me. Muttered it under his breath thinking I wouldn't hear, then started yelling orders at his staff to clean up the mess left by the audit, to get everything filed away and back to normal. He can be one nasty bastard when he's feeling threatened."

"Good," Rosalind said. "He took the bait. I hope you're prepared for fireworks, Hollinger. He might be crazy but he's remarkably crafty. He has lots of tricks up his sleeve and if he suspects that he's being set up, he'll take extra precautions."

"You forget that I worked for him too," Hollinger said. "And today he demonstrated, without any shred of embarrassment, how mistrustful he is." He shook his head. "I honestly don't know how anyone continues to work with him. His behavior is… uncomfortable to be around, to say the least. Anyway, I certainly hope he suspects he's being set up. We want to drive him to the point of paranoia where he can't think straight. His twisted mind will be his Achilles heel."

"What do you have planned?" Reinhardt asked.

"I plan to let the evening unfold exactly how Felix Szabo wants it to," Hollinger said, shrugging. "Who knows what he'll do. We'll arrange the cars that will bring you to the gala, but we'll use decoys just in case he rigs explosives. In the actual cars you'll be in, we'll have sensors that detect tampering. And we'll do a thorough pre-pick-up inspection. And if all that fails, our drivers will be prepared for the worst."

Reinhardt nodded with approval.

"As for gunfire," Hollinger went on, "I've planned for extra security. If we suspect he's going to open fire, we'll need to apprehend him before he can get to his gun, so all of us will need to be on guard the whole evening, watching his every move." He sighed. "Unfortunately, there's no way to guess what a nut-case like him will do. We'll just have to wait and see and be ready for anything. And cross our fingers that no one dies."

"Well, on that happy note… Ladies and Gentlemen," Rosalind said, "looks like we're heading back to the store. We're going to a party."

Nineteen

THE GROUP OF US RUSTLED IN OUR SATIN, silk, and other stiff fabrics. We smelled elegant. I hardly recognized any of us. I hadn't worn a gown and high heels since my prom and felt both a little ridiculous and also kind of sexy. Our attire distracted me from my nerves and what could transpire later on.

Rosalind came clacking out of the bathroom fastening on an earring and Alice put the finishing touches on Hannah's lipstick. The men came in, pressed and slick in their black tuxedos and crisp white shirts. Once we were collected together in the suite's living room, we admired each other. Reinhardt whistled as he came over and took Rosalind's hand, planting a tender kiss on her cheek then standing back to take in a full view of his gorgeous wife. Amos and Norm did the same, Alice and Hannah doing a curtsy twirl as the men stepped back to admire them.

Ransom stood back, leaning against the wall by the bedroom door. He was absolutely dashing, strong and sexy in his tux. I tried not to stare and looked quickly away. He grinned back at me but said nothing. He didn't need to. His eyes said it all. His gaze trailed slowly from my head down to my shoes and then back again. I felt like he was undressing me. I wondered if he found me as desirable as I found him.

Finally he came over and stood in front of me. "Ruby," he said, "looks like you clean up OK. The men at the gala won't be able to take their eyes off you."

I wanted him to tell me that he couldn't take his eyes off of me but was glad he didn't. Not exactly the kind of thing a brother is supposed to say to a sister even though I ached to hear him say it. I'd been very proud of myself for distracting my attention away from him, day after day, but in these brief moments, when my heart felt like it was turning itself inside out, I couldn't help but cave in.

Fortunately there was a knock at the door of the suite. Ransom hesitated a moment, then turned to go answer it. I took a deep breath and brushed off my satin gown. It was form fitting and lower cut than anything I'd ever worn. I had to confess to myself that I loved it. I just hoped that if it came to it, I could run and leap over things without tearing it up the side or falling out of the top. I yanked it higher up and hoped no one noticed.

Hollinger entered without a word, not even a hello, and strode anxiously to the window to look out at the street six stories below where a uniformed limo driver stood beside a black Lincoln town car.

"The limo is out front," Hollinger said. "Amos, Hannah and Ruby, the limo is for us, and it will drive around to the alley where another DND vehicle is waiting. We'll change vehicles there and this one will carry on to the Weston using a different route." He looked over to Reinhardt, Rosalind, Ransom, Norm and Alice. "The five of you will take a cab that's waiting in the hotel's underground parking. I don't want anyone to associate you with us."

Hollinger was wearing a military dress uniform and looked quite impressive. The navy blue jacket had epaulets piped in gold with matching buttons at the shoulders. Four gold embossed buttons were done up tight down the front though his slight belly strained the last one. In his hand was a brimmed hat with the American eagle insignia at the peak.

Hollinger pulled back from the window and gave us a once-over.

"You all look... fine," he paused as if he were inspecting his troops. He turned back to the window, pulling the outer shear curtains narrowly aside to see if any new activity were happening at the limo. He pressed a button on his phone, and after a few grunts and an "OK," he hung up and returned it to his pocket, which was adorned with gold crests and an assortment of flags. He patted it and adjusted the stiff fabric. "We should get going." He strode to the door.

The four of us went down and slid into our Lincoln town car. It coasted quiet as a shark through the dim and empty hotel alley, until it came to a stop. We got out and switched to an SUV that said *United States Department of Defense* on the side. The limo drove off, exiting the alley onto 13th Street and headed west to the river, supposedly making a more circuitous route to the gala. The vehicle we drove away in emerged back onto 14th Street in front of the Hilton. The Weston was only a few blocks away up on M Street. Traffic was heavy, but Hollinger assured us we'd be there inside of ten minutes. As we neared the Weston, the driver brought our car into the queue of limos waiting to pull up and let their passengers out.

Twenty minutes later, we were out in the exhaust-scented air and climbing the three cement steps to the glass entry doors held open by doormen.

A quick glance around inside filled me with dread. There was abundant opportunity for us to be ambushed. The large lobby was crowded with party-goers, nearly everyone wearing black, and only the occasional woman standing out in a red or blue evening gown. We inched our way among them, trying not to bump or jostle anyone in the closely gathered crowd. I couldn't imagine how we could distinguish danger when we could hardly see two feet ahead of us. It would be ridiculously easy for one of Felix's men to move about with a silenced pistol, pull it discretely from a pocket, or from inside a jacket, and simply pop off an unsuspecting target, then carry off the slumped-over victim, explaining that the person suddenly became ill. It wouldn't be the noise of gunshots to watch for; Hollinger's people would be looking for anyone who seemed to be moving quickly or standing in an unusual position, or who looked like he was having trouble standing. But so far, everyone was upright, laughing and chatting and sipping on cocktails.

I walked in beside Hollinger. "He's here. I can feel it," he muttered. I knew that, too, but didn't reply. The massive rectangular ballroom with its bright red print carpeting and enormous glittering chandeliers hanging from the coffered ceiling above was set up for more mingling and cocktails. A raised platform designed to serve as a stage with a podium and microphone was set up at one end, and tables with white linens and floral centerpieces were set up over the floor. Hollinger, Amos, Hannah and I staked out our spot at a table near the stage, pausing to scan the room for Felix.

The room buzzed with conversation, but Hollinger must have had his phone set to vibrate because suddenly he was putting in his earpiece and straining to hear someone on the other end. Within a few seconds, his forehead was wrinkled and his mouth parted in a look of distress.

"What happened," I asked when he hung up.

"The limo—the decoy—was ambushed," Hollinger said. "The driver and the car are at the bottom of the Potomac." His face was purple. "There's our confirmation. Felix is going to try to come after you tonight." Hollinger's posture stiffened as he searched the crowd.

With so many people around, it was hard to imagine that Felix would want to try anything in here. After all, if he were clearly identified as trying anything, he'd be taken out and all his careful efforts would come to an ugly end. He was smarter than that. I looked at one of the potted palms around the room's perimeter; he could have a shooter do his work and discard a weapon in one of the planters and slip away undetected into the crowd, perhaps to a guest room in the hotel before anyone were the wiser. I glanced at Amos and Hannah; their expressions were serious and their eyes were sharp and attentive.

Across the room, I saw Reinhardt, Rosalind and Ransom. They were making casual conversation with a distinguished older couple, the man also in military dress. They were standing at the side of the ballroom, away from the thickness of the crowd, near a table at the far wall.

Rosalind spotted us first and nudged the men to look over at us. She cocked her eyebrow at me, then they excused themselves and slowly moved our way, circling the perimeter, their eyes scanning the people now so tightly packed into the room. It took several minutes before they reached us.

"What's happened," Reinhardt asked.

"Szabo ambushed the limo," I said. "Arranged for it to drive into the river. The driver is dead."

"I knew there was no way he would miss this opportunity," Rosalind said, her voice a grim, thin line. "I can't see him, but I can feel him here. Dammit. He's like a snake slithering underfoot." She looked at me, Amos and Hannah. "Watch where you step tonight. And take care of yourselves." She scanned the crowded room. "Best that we split into two groups again."

Without another word, they turned and left.

Hollinger was supposed to give a congratulatory speech on the retirement of his employee, but after the phone call, he handed his speech off to his assistant who would tell the guests that Hollinger had come down with laryngitis, leaving Hollinger available for action.

He reached into his breast pocket and inserted a device into his ear. "Hollinger one, do you copy?" Hollinger pursed his lips. "Reinhardt saw Szabo in the hall," Hollinger said. "He was talking to several men who dispersed into the crowd, and now he's headed into the ballroom. We should spot him shortly. It's show time."

As if on cue, I saw a man with a graying brush cut and stubbly but trimmed facial hair inching through the crowd. A few people tried to stop him to chat, but he brushed past them, shaking his head and pointing to us, his smile turning into a sneer as he came closer.

Hollinger spotted him and waved him over.

Felix flashed a smile that said "gotcha," the kind of expression a person uses when he catches someone breaking a rule. Then his face relaxed, and his posture became even more confident.

"Quite a turn out," Felix said. "Baxter is a popular guy."

Hollinger and Felix shook hands, hard, before Felix turned to Amos and Hannah, the sneer returning to Felix's face. "Armond, you look good," Felix said. "'Retirement'," he said archly, making air quotes with his fingers, "seems to agree with you. How do you live with yourself knowing you deserted your country?" Felix laughed and slapped Amos on the arm. He turned to Hannah, took her hand in his and kissed it before cupping it in both of his and glaring at her menacingly. "So nice to see you again," Felix said, his voice syrupy. "And how are you enjoying your retirement?"

Hannah nodded at Felix with a guarded smile but didn't speak.

"And this charming creature must be... Ruby, is it?" Felix said. Felix's eyes flitted back and forth between Hollinger, Amos and Hannah before locking his stare directly onto me. He didn't reveal in his expression that we'd met before. I returned his stare with a confident and determined smile that made his smile wilt somewhat. I wondered whether that was the right move or whether I should have pretended to be nervous, fearful or intimidated, but even though I was the child of spies, I wasn't exactly seasoned as one myself and just went with my gut. Of course, my demeanor would make no difference to the outcome. Each side expected to win.

I remained cordial but kept my hands tightly at my side refusing his handshake.

"Good evening," I said. I had no intention of entering into to an exchange of sarcasms with him. But Felix, I knew, loved mind games and continued to press for triggers that might unsettle me or the others.

"How exactly are you related to these fine people again?" Felix asked, his voice overly sarcastic.

"Felix, don't you remember? I told you she's their niece?" Hollinger answered. "Maybe it's time you thought about retirement, too."

Hollinger, Amos and Hannah chuckled.

I watched that comment hit a nerve. Felix's smile turned sour, and his eyes went dark. "You'd like that, wouldn't you, Hollinger. Discard those who serve and protect the American way of life, who keep us safe, and keep the commies and towel-head terrorists out of our midst. Maybe you're on their side. At least you still have me to look out for American interests." Felix laughed again without mirth, punching Hollinger a little too hard on the shoulder.

"Just how are you doing that from Archives?" Hollinger asked. He confronted Felix with a mock accusatory gaze and wagged his finger. "Do you have some kind of secret mission going on there that I don't know about?"

They both laughed heartily.

"Ah, the Cold War days," Felix said. "Our team was the best America had to offer. You know that, don't you, Hollinger? The president depended on our efforts and we came through for him. I reported directly to him back in those days. The head of the Defense Department at that time respected my position. He had to or the president would have had him fired. And between the president and me, we singlehandedly kept the Russians under control. We kept the nukes in their silos.

"And now," Felix added. "My team is disbanded, all of them gone soft, enjoying early retirement, raising their little families, going to *Disneyland*." He spoke as if the words were poisonous. "How does that happen, Hollinger? Just tell me how that happens? The world isn't any safer today. In fact, it's a much more dangerous place. And the department, my department, the most experienced and able, America's best bet at keeping our enemies at a safe distance, is suddenly closed down, disbanded? You don't think that our enemies had something to do with that? And my people take the buyout... Cowards, deserters, all of them! For all I know, they've been bought out by the enemy, on their side, working against us. But I'm onto them and they'll have to reckon with me." Felix was sweating profusely now and yanking on his shirt collar.

Hollinger had been successful in irritating him into a rage, perhaps a manic fury.

I glanced at Hollinger, who winked at me. With Felix off-kilter, we'd have an advantage.

Hollinger pressed him further. "Reckon with you," Hollinger said. "Exactly how are they 'reckoning' with you?" Hollinger's playfulness had disappeared along with his smile. "No one even knows their identities. How can you say that?"

"I have my ways of knowing," Felix said, "and one by one they're all going to pay for their duplicity."

"How are you going to make them pay?" Hollinger asked, stepping forward.

The vein in Felix's temple pulsed so hard I worried it'd burst. "Like this!" he said. He grabbed my arm and yanked me forward to his body, then thrust a gun into my stomach. Hollinger reached for a weapon in his side pocket, not withdrawing it into the open but pointing it in Felix's direction, which was my back as I was standing between Felix and Hollinger.

Felix whispered into my ear. His breath made me shudder. "Now turn around and walk slowly and calmly in front of me," he said.

I turned around and he moved the gun slowly down to my lower back. He ran his other hand over my front and I felt an electric shock of fear jolt inside me, his nasty hard hands on me. "One wrong move and she's dead."

"Take it easy, Felix," Amos said. "Let her go. She has nothing to do with this."

"She's with the likes of you. She has everything to do with it," Felix said. "And she's the reason Christian is dead. I had to kill him because she turned him against me."

I could feel the adrenaline pulsing in Felix's grip, an excited surge of *now you're mine, you bitch* feeding his mania. With the gun poking into the small of my back, he pushed and pulled my body through the thick crowd of people to an exit door.

The door opened to a back hallway where a few guests had found a quiet corner to chat, but when we arrived, they quickly moved to the nearest door and disappeared into the main ballroom, leaving me alone with Felix. I felt panic begin to rise in my stomach, but I knew that Hollinger had the hotel swarming with security of his own. It took all of my resolve not to try and flip him or kick him in the groin, but I knew this capture had been carefully calculated by both Felix and Hollinger, and I needed to wait and see who would move next. My adrenaline had kicked in and my senses shifted into overdrive; as if in slow motion, I heard the clanking of dishes in the hotel kitchen and the scuffle of a shoe in the hall. Someone was smoking a cigarette.

And then, as if someone had pressed fast forward, everything burst into action like a bright white star exploding. Felix had been pushing me forward down the long hallway but the noise from behind caused him to spin me forcefully around, using me as a shield.

I tried to blink away my dizziness and realized it was Ransom with his gun drawn and aimed in our direction.

He took slow, threatening steps forward, which made Felix grab me around the chest with one arm, and bring the arm holding the gun at my back up to my right temple. His breathing was coming in rough, raspy grunts, and his hot, foul breath on my cheek was like the snorts of a feral beast.

Strands of my hair were caught in my mouth and eyes, but I couldn't move them away.

"Felix," Ransom yelled. "Let her go. It's over for you. Don't make things worse for yourself."

"Worse?" Felix said. "Worse for whom, me or for Ruby Draker! So the bitch has a name, probably not her real name, but I'll find out who she is and what she's doing with you clowns."

Ransom took several more steps toward Felix. Felix's posture stiffened and he pressed the barrel of his gun harder to my head. He clutched me tighter around the chest, and I could feel his labored breath whining in his lungs even though he stood at my back. "Stop where you are," Felix shouted, "or you'll both be dead."

Ransom's eyes darted around, moving to both sides of the hallway and then over Felix's shoulder.

I could feel the situation changing, becoming increasingly tense and probably lethal.

Then the hallway came alive, bristling with movement, some in the open, others hidden and unseen.

Soldiers in combat gear, with bulletproof vests, helmets, and carrying high-powered automatic rifles roared out of every doorway and positioned themselves along the hall, their weapons pointed at us. From behind closed doorways burst snipers. Hollinger probably had the hotel surrounded by now, his men in every door waiting for just the right opportunity to explode with gunfire as they rushed the scene to take down Szabo.

As much as being surrounded ought to have been a relief, I couldn't exactly celebrate with Felix still holding his gun to my head.

Ransom took two more steps forward, pressing his luck.

I tried to signal with my eyes that he should stop, but he kept on.

Felix started moving us backward one slow step at a time but we were running out of hallway. A few more steps and all that was left was a large palladium window at the end.

"Felix," Hollinger yelled from down the hall, "you might think you have the upper hand, but you're wrong. Let her go. She's an innocent American. A good citizen."

Felix brought us a few more steps back until we bumped into the window. Before us, the hall had filled with dozens of men dressed in fatigues, holding what Rosalind had taught me were M4A1s used for close quarters and confined areas.

A swarm of soldiers moved in from the left, their rifles aimed in our direction. More from the right advanced toward us in short and slow steps. Still others crouched down on one knee close to the hallway walls to look for more of Felix's men who were mysteriously not in residence.

I absently wondered whether they'd shoot me to get to Felix. I didn't see another way. I squeezed my eyes shut.

Then behind us, a shot from outside broke the glass window and found a target in one soldier at the front.

He fell to the floor, and bullets started to fly.

Felix yanked away his gun from my temple and shot several rounds of bullets into the hall.

I jammed my elbow into his ribs, which made him let me go, and I dropped hard, flattening myself to the floor.

Now, with Felix fully exposed, the SWAT team should have had a clear aim. But in the volley of gunfire, there was a loud crash and glass shattered like rain down on top of me. I threw my arms up over my head and neck, and sharp nicks pin-pricked down onto my skin. When the glass shower ended, I saw that Felix had jumped through the palladium window down to a parking lot behind. A few seconds later, a motorcycle screamed away. Then I was surrounded by men in black.

"Ruby," Hollinger shouted. "Are you shot? Can you get up?"

I shook off the largest shards of glass and slowly sat up. A warm rivulet of something slid down my neck from my head, but I didn't feel any pain. I wondered if I were in shock, but I felt fine. Maybe a little numb, but fine.

"I think I'm OK," I said. I looked down the hallway and Rosalind and Reinhardt were crouched over someone lying face up, a pool of dark red blood growing around his head like a halo beneath him. Amos, Hannah, Norm and Alice had their arms out and were barking back hotel and party guests who were trying to see what was going on.

The man on the floor was struggling against Reinhardt, trying to get up, but Reinhardt urged him to stay down, telling him that help was on the way. His voice was thick with concern. That's when it hit me. This wasn't a hotel guest. I looked harder and realized it was Ransom. I screamed out his name and scrambled to my feet, slipping on the glass, as I raced to his side.

Hollinger chased after me and grabbed me into a bear hug before I could get there.

I struggled like a caught animal to get to Ransom, but by now the paramedics had arrived and were clustered around his body, working on him. All I could do was stand there and watch in horror. A few minutes later they loaded him onto a stretcher and rolled him away.

"He'll be all right, Ruby," Hollinger assured me. I hadn't noticed before but he was stroking my back trying to comfort me. I must have looked at him with some kind of face because he broke his resolve and softened to the point where I thought he'd cry. "I'll take you to the hospital," he said. The tears in his eyes scared me more than Ransom's blood pooled up in a quiet lake around where he'd been.

Twenty

THE AMBULANCE SPED THROUGH the Washington night traffic, lights blinking, flashing, sirens wailing, followed by a DND vehicle with Hollinger, Reinhardt, Rosalind and me inside. Fortunately, we had an emergency light Hollinger had popped onto the roof, which enabled us to evade traffic lights and forget the speed limit as we kept up with the ambulance ahead.

Speeding along, I prayed to God, anyone, my stomach aching, my heart thumping in my chest, so afraid Ransom might not make it. I hated that I wasn't next to him in the ambulance. I felt impotent as we watched the traffic and raced through the streets. We couldn't do anything but look out at the cars we were passing, concern and helplessness coursing through all of us in the car.

There had been so much gunfire.

How many bullets had Ransom taken. The blood beneath him was immense. I wondered what his condition was and prayed he'd hold on. Idiot, I thought. Why did he confront Felix alone without back-up from Hollinger's men? Then I grew cold. Had he taken those bullets to save me? Was I the reason he was fighting for his life? Another casualty because of me. I should have been the one in the ambulance.

Hollinger sat silent in the front seat, his face twitching. I looked at him and felt angry that he had lost control of the situation tonight. He knew the risks. He was supposed to have taken Felix down inconspicuously without casualties. He'd really screwed up. I vindictively hoped his superiors would make him accountable for a ruined party, which was the least of his worries, property damage to the hotel, and for the injuries sustained by a civilian, an injury that had been caused by one of his own people, an employee he had neglected, and who'd been using the CIA as his own personal database for a big game hunt.

The SUV made a hard left into the emergency entrance of Washington Memorial Hospital, where an emergency medical team was standing at the entrance waiting for the ambulance.

We screeched to a stop and I threw open the back door and jumped out. Ransom's bloodied body was being rushed inside, one paramedic pumping air into his lungs from a bulbous device attached to a breathing tube that snaked from Ransom's slack open mouth, another pushing on his chest in rhythmic thumps to keep his heart going. The medical team swarmed around shouting orders at each other as the wheels of the gurney rolled over the cement. Seconds later, the swarm buzzed through the automatic doors and disappeared into the hospital.

"I'll let the reception clerk know who we are," Hollinger said, running in after the melee. "He's in good hands. He'll be well looked after." Clearly, he was trying to sound confident and comforting though his blank expression told us that he thought the situation was grim.

He walked over to the desk where a woman in scrubs sat behind a glass enclosure. He said a few words to her, and she pointed us to a waiting room down the hall.

"We're supposed to wait down there," Hollinger said, turning to us. "We'll be more comfortable there. Can I get anyone a coffee... or anything?"

We all shook our heads no and followed him to a room framed by low-backed leather chairs, to wait—for how long, we didn't know.

I didn't let myself think about anything and idly picked up the first magazine in the pile on the table beside my chair.

"I told the paramedics to list his name as Arthur Day," Hollinger murmured, though we were the only ones there. "With Szabo still out there, it's best we use a new alias."

Reinhardt huffed, looking at Hollinger with pursed lips and narrowed eyes. "R—thur?"

I glared at him with vitriol. He couldn't even get our code initials right? Not that it mattered right now. I was just acting out. But still.

A round, stainless steel clock on the wall loudly ticked out every second. Every tick a knife to my heart. I waited and paced over the hours. We took turns pacing and looking at the door.

Hollinger occasionally left the room to go to the reception desk for an update, only to be told that the doctors were working on Ransom and that they would let us know his condition as soon as they could.

I didn't know how many hours it was of this, but finally someone did come to the door. It was a doctor in a blue surgical cap and scrubs. I didn't think doctors talked to patients' families themselves unless it was serious. My heart froze.

"Are you Mister and Missus Day?" the doctor asked.

He looked at Rosalind and Reinhardt and they nodded numbly.

"I'm Doctor Marsh. He's stable for now so we can take him into surgery. We'll let you know more as soon as we can, but it's going to be a long night for you. I won't lie. His situation is critical."

"Thank you, Doctor," Reinhardt said.

Reinhardt choked back his emotion and put his arms around Rosalind whose face was wet with tears. She wept softly on his shoulder. I was numb in my body, but my extremities were straining; my eyes bulged, my breathing sputtered in quick gasps, and a horrible tight lump in my throat prevented me from speaking, which I was actually grateful for because I was sure that the first sound out of my mouth might release a torrent of uncontrollable cries.

The doctor left and we waited again.

The earlier rustle of our elegant evening wear now just reminded us of the disconnect between feeling hopeful and possible and our now-tense state of suspended animation. No one spoke much. Hollinger paced, taking the occasional phone call, which he stepped out into the hall to answer.

When the door opened again, it was four-thirty in the morning. Doctor Marsh walked in. He looked tired and his face was thickly lined. "He made it through the surgery," he said, rubbing his hands. "But he's still very critical. We almost lost him twice. It will be several hours before you can see him. He's still in post-op being watched closely. If he stays stable, he'll be moved to intensive care. It's still touch and go. You should get some rest and come back in four or five hours."

"I have to see him," I said. My voice was smaller than a whisper. I hadn't realized how my body was pulled into this, how much I needed him.

"Ruby," Hollinger said, "my men are posted here at the hospital. If anything changes, they'll call and we can have you back here inside of a few minutes. The doctor is right. We should all get some sleep."

Reinhardt and Rosalind came to my side and put their arms around me.

The door opened again and Amos, Hannah, Norm and Alice came in. "What's the word on Ransom's condition? We stayed back with the investigation team at the Weston," Amos said. He ground his teeth and looked furious. "He got away again. It's like he vanished into thin air."

"Ransom's still in post-operative recovery," Reinhardt said. He didn't say more. The look on his face said everything.

"We'll stay here a while," Alice said. "Go back to our hotel and get some rest. Ransom will need you when he comes around. There's nothing you can do for now. No use running yourselves into the ground. He'll need your strength later." Her voice was so soft and comforting, I nearly began to weep.

"The car's waiting," Hollinger said. He motioned for the three of us to follow him.

Within minutes of Hollinger's dropping us at the hotel, I fell into the bed. Rosalind sat down at the computer and typed a message to Renegade as I drifted off into a fitful sleep. We napped until early afternoon, had quick showers, and after throwing on whatever normal clothes we could find, Reinhardt, Rosalind and I were ready to go back to the hospital.

Hollinger himself came to fetch us, also having changed back into his office clothes, a suit and shirt with no tie. He seemed to be keen to take charge of our safety himself.

Sometime in the early hours of the morning, Ransom had been moved to intensive care. Only authorized visitors were allowed on that floor. We hurried to the specialized unit, anxious to see him and met up with Amos, Hannah, Norm and Alice in the waiting area close to the nursing station. Amos updated us with what he knew. He said it was around six a.m. when Ransom was released from post-op, but they still hadn't been allowed to see him.

At that, Hollinger strode to the nursing station, flashed his badge, and the nurse conceded that we could go in.

The unit was busy with beeping and hissing and flickering lights. Ransom was at the end of the hall, room 24A, and we walked down the long corridor, peering into the small narrow rooms, each housing a person lying motionless in his bed. About mid-way down we passed a second nursing station where only one nurse sat, ticking away at a computer.

When we got to Ransom's room and I saw him lying there, I hesitated at the door. To see him reduced to a motionless and bandaged body with tubes and lines hooked into it, nearly broke me. I barely recognized him but for the tattoo of a bleeding rose on a heavily thorned stem on his bicep, which confirmed that it was him languishing in the bed. A breathing machine was hooked up to his face because, the nurse who slid in around us quietly explained, he wasn't able to breathe on his own yet. I grew cold. If Felix were to get in here and unhook the machine, Ransom would be dead in a minute.

All around his body, the room worked: oxygen hissed loudly, the heart monitor beeped, clear liquid dripped through intravenous lines—one in each arm—and another larger tube with bright yellow fluid snaked out from under the white sheet at his groin. He was so still; we might have thought him to be dead except for the rise and fall of his chest as the ventilator breathed for him, hissing loudly with each inhalation. His skin was pale and almost transparent. I feared that he was just too fragile to make it.

I slowly walked over to his side and took his hand. It was cold and limp but the touch caused his eyes to flutter. "Hi, Ransom," I whispered. "You're doing fine. We'll have you out of here in no time." Tears, several of the many I'd been holding back, now rained from my eyes and landed wet and warm on our hands.

His eyes fluttered open.

"I've been so worried about you," I said. "I need you to get better." My voice was hardly more than a whisper. "I love you." I didn't even know if my words were audible. I may have only mouthed them, but Ransom must have read my lips.

He lifted his thumb and gently pressed it to my hand. I knew that he understood.

"You gave us quite a scare, Ransom," Rosalind said, smoothing his forearm. "Don't worry about anything. You're getting excellent care. The doctor tells us that you're going to be OK." Rosalind bent down and kissed him on the forehead. Reinhardt was on the other side of the bed holding his other hand.

Ransom must have needed to hear those assurances because he was able to keep his eyes open now. A tear ran out of one of his eyes and landed on the pillow. I felt his hand relax in mine and could tell he was trying to smile.

A nurse came into the room to check on him and asked us to step out for a minute. "You don't have to go far, just in the hall is fine," she said kindly.

More tears formed in the corners of Ransom's eyes, and I brushed them away for him.

"Don't worry," I said. "We'll be right back."

I hadn't noticed that Hollinger hadn't come into Ransom's room with us. When we stepped into the hallway, I saw him talking to a man near the entrance of the ICU. He stopped his conversation when he noticed us, said a few more words to the man, and came over to greet us. He glanced into Ransom's room before returning his attention to us. "My men have checked everywhere," he said grimly. "Szabo has vanished, no trace of him at the Archives, at his home, at the airport. Nothing on his email, phone or credit cards. We're watching all of it. He's just disappeared."

"Does any of his staff know where he might have gone?" I asked.

"He has five staff members," Hollinger said. "Two are temporary interns. Two are part-time clerks. The only person who might be an accomplice is his assistant, the one who phoned my office assistant and asked all the leading questions. He's now saying that he only acted under Szabo's orders, that he never realized his boss was a killer. We have nothing to hold him in custody for, but he's under surveillance as well. We'll know if he gets in contact with Felix or tries to tip him off. Hell, we'll know if he takes a shit."

"Are you putting another manager in the Archive Department?" Reinhardt asked.

"I've shut the department down for now until we finish our investigation," Hollinger said. "All the employees are laid off with pay until we find out what has been going on. So even if Felix does come back, he has nothing to come back to. At least that will keep him from using government records for finding more victims. Unfortunately, and this is something we can't control, he's probably managed to duplicate his records and is still able to continue to hunt for all of you."

The nurse came out of Ransom's room. "Sorry to interrupt, but Mr. Day seems to be doing well enough to see you again. Just not too long."

Everyone grinned at this good news, but when we went back in and again saw all the machinery, it was all so hard to swallow. We hovered close, hoping that he could draw on our strength.

"Is he able to talk yet?" Hollinger asked.

"No," the nurse said. "Because of the ventilator, and it'll be at least twenty-four hours before we even attempt to wean him off." Hollinger nodded and the nurse returned to the station in the middle of the ward.

"I have plain clothes men stationed all throughout this hospital," Hollinger said, "just in case Szabo tries anything else."

Hollinger's statement jolted us back to the seriousness of our situation and reminded me how vulnerable Ransom was. How it would only take one small slip for him to die. Even though we knew Hollinger's men were vigilant, we decided that one of us, or someone from Amos's group, would stay with Ransom at all times. We'd take surveillance shifts again.

"As soon as Ransom is able to be moved, we want to take him home," Reinhardt said. "Renegade can have a private charter on stand-by. Rose, who is a trained nurse, is already packed and ready to fly in to care for him during his transport."

"I hope Renegade knows how to take same precautions Robert used to take with erasing our flights," I said. "If he found out about Fairh—" I realized I shouldn't say the name of our home aloud. I missed Robert, how cleverly he managed to keep us safe. I hoped Renegade had the same skills. I felt homesickness then, which surprised me. It wasn't for my home with my parents, but for Fairhaven.

"When Ransom is stable enough, I'll have a DND helicopter take all of you to a private airfield," Hollinger said, "which will make your flight nearly impossible—or at least significantly harder to track—if Szabo is looking, and I'd put money on it that he is."

We made the mistake of assuming that Ransom was half unconscious, but he seemed to hear everything and made some agitated noises and tried to move. That spiked his heart rate, setting off an alarm.

Two nurses rushed into the room and pushed us aside to administer to him. One injected something into the fluid bag that hung from a pole feeding into his IV tube. In no time at all, Ransom was anesthetized again, his eyes closed, the ventilator pushing oxygen into his lungs, making his chest rise and fall. I felt terrible shame for putting him through that. If I'd jeopardized his health, I'd never forgive myself.

After that, we only discussed Felix and our getaway plans when we were away from his bedside. But there was a lot to do. Rosalind and Renegade suddenly became very busy making preparations.

For the next twenty-four hours, we carefully coordinated our efforts. Amos and Hannah took shifts at the hospital as well as did Norm and Alice who spent the night. The fact that everything was so quiet became more and more nerve wracking with the passing minutes because the probability that Felix or some of his hired goons were near was high.

***

The next morning erupted bright and sunny. When we left our hotel, a stiff breeze nipped at my skin, giving me goose bumps, and I wrapped my hands around my arms. The wind blew my hair into my face, and I shivered as we made our way to the car, not sure if it was the cool late summer morning air that was making me tremble or if my worried and restless sleep still had me agitated. Being away from the hospital was a loss of control. I didn't know what had happened, though we'd not heard anything. But if Ransom's condition had worsened or if Felix had slithered in like a poison in the air conditioning vents, Ransom would be in danger. Ransom's warning echoed in my mind as we passed one government building and then another on our way to the hospital to relieve Norm and Alice. "He'll never stop hunting you…"

"Good morning," a cheery nurse said as we passed the nursing station. We didn't recognize her, so Reinhardt, Rosalind and I stopped to assess if she was really a nurse or someone planted by Felix. "You're quite the early birds," she added and smiled as she continued to type on her computer keyboard.

The nurse still on duty from the night before came into the station and picked up her sweater from the back of a chair. "Sarah, Mr. Day, will probably be moved to the floor today," she said. "He's doing much better."

"Sounds good," Sarah said and continued with her keyboard input. "Has he been taken off the ventilator?"

"Yes. We just finished the procedure. He's breathing on his own and seems to be doing fine," the nurse said. "He needs to be monitored for the next couple of hours, and if everything stays stable, he can be moved out of intensive care."

We should have been relieved to hear that Ransom's condition had improved significantly, but the fact that this unfamiliar nurse didn't look up at us, or the other nurse, was suspicious. Her demeanor differed from that of the other nurses.

Just then the elevator dinged, and Hollinger emerged onto the ward. He seemed hesitant as he looked at the nurse, Sarah. Why did he look uneasy all of a sudden? He pulled us over to the side where the nurses couldn't see or hear us.

"Sarah is one of ours," Hollinger said. "She reported unusual visitors on the ward, two men looking for a 'brother' who had been shot accidentally, the brother's name not on the intensive care patient list. Then they asked if there were any gunshot victims by another name. I'm afraid that Felix has located Ransom. We need to get him out of here immediately."

"But he may not be ready to be moved," I said.

Sarah approached Hollinger, the two of them checking the long hall for other staff and visitors. "He's been sedated. We'll move him, bed and all, to the service elevator," Sarah said. "Do you have everything ready?"

There it was again, that hesitation.

I could see that Reinhardt and Rosalind noticed it, too. We looked at each other. Something was going on.

"There's an ambulance at the emergency entrance waiting to transport him to a private clinic," Hollinger said.

That confirmed it. Hollinger hadn't briefed us about moving Ransom to another facility. I stared at him, wondering just who was orchestrating this. Was it Felix or was it Hollinger who couldn't be trusted? And why did it seem that this Sarah was in charge?

"He's not going anywhere," Rosalind said. "Where are Norm and Alice? Why didn't anyone let us know that Felix had made a move? That was our deal, Hollinger."

"They're still with him in his room," Hollinger said. "Look, you can ride with him in the ambulance, but we have to go now." Hollinger was fidgety and really pushing the issue without his usual matter of factness, and Sarah was already on her way to Ransom's room.

Having no choice, we followed.

Norm and Alice were sitting in chairs at Ransom's bedside as we burst into the room. They jumped at our abrupt entry then looked at Reinhardt, Rosalind and me with dazed expressions. They didn't speak. They just sat straight in their chairs, their eyes moving from ours to the bed where an unconscious person lay, someone of the same size and build as Ransom, but clearly not him.

"He's doing just fine," Sarah said. "The clinic isn't far from here and when he wakes up he'll be safe. He won't even know that there was a problem." She smiled at us but her eyes were searching our faces as she clumsily unhooked the probes that monitored his vitals.

Hollinger remained surprisingly neutral. Why wasn't he helping and where was Ransom?

She pushed the bed on its wheels down the hall to a service elevator. The doors opened and all of us crowded inside. We watched the floors count down to the parking level where the doors opened, and we were greeted by the smells of rubber and gas fumes.

An ambulance was waiting with its doors open, and the driver, and another man dressed as a paramedic, ran over to the open elevator door and took over, pushing the bed to the ambulance.

Sarah hopped inside. "I can make room so all of you can ride with him," she said.

The paramedic jumped out to make room and walked around to the passenger side.

"Might be a bit crowded," Norm said. "Our car is in the parking garage. We'll follow."

The driver nodded, closed the rear doors and hurried to the front, jumping into the driver's seat. He started the engine and screeched the tires as he made his way to the parking exit.

Our group, still standing in the parking garage, ganged up on Hollinger. "Where the hell is Ransom?" Reinhardt demanded.

Hollinger looked reluctant to answer, his face looking grim and uncertain. "When we came to relieve Amos and Hannah last night," Alice said, "we noticed that three people were on the ward: two men and a woman. They seemed to be looking for a patient. The nurse came over and told them to get off the floor. They argued with her, but she called security and they were escorted off."

"It smelled of Felix," Norm added, "so we took matters into our hands. I notified Hollinger and he sent one of his men into the room to take Ransom's place in the bed, pretending to be him. Alice and I put Ransom into a wheelchair and took him to the emergency entrance where Hollinger had a private service ambulance waiting for him. Right now, he's safe at a private clinic just outside Washington."

"But," Alice said, "when that other nurse, Sarah, came onto the scene, more men dressed as hospital orderlies came with her. They didn't see us, but they had guns and took Amos and Hannah. They're holding them hostage."

"They also have two of my men," Hollinger said. "Right now, they don't know that the man they've taken away in the ambulance isn't Ransom. We made the switch before Felix took Amos and Hannah and my men. But just after, I got a text that said they'd kill them all if I said anything to you or anyone else. They wanted you to have access to Ransom. Felix knows you'll come to the rescue."

"But we're not following the ambulance. Shouldn't we make it look like we're playing into Felix's plan?" I asked.

"I have a car following their ambulance," Hollinger said. "Hopefully, they'll think it's us. It's what Felix wants. If they realize it's not us, I'm afraid Amos, Hannah and my men are as good as dead."

Reinhardt looked fiercely at Hollinger. He tensed his jaw and turned away. Hollinger had lost control of the situation again. I knew Reinhardt well enough to know he was having a crisis of conscience: he wanted to help Amos and Hannah, but he also needed to get us all out of Washington, including a very fragile Ransom who probably wasn't ready to travel.

Hollinger stood with his head hung down, looking at the cement floor.

Reinhardt spoke through his teeth. "Ransom needs to be our first priority. We won't have much time before Felix realizes that his plan didn't work. Goddammit, Hollinger, handle the hostage situation and buy us as much time as possible. And don't screw this up!"

Hollinger nodded meekly. "You have to know I'm doing all I can."

Rosalind had her phone in her hand. "Renegade has a charter on standby. Where's that private air strip you talked about?" She stared at Hollinger. She and Reinhardt were on the same page. She knew her priorities, and family came first.

"Go back to the hotel and get your things," Hollinger said. "There's a helipad on the roof of the Hilton. I'll have a DND chopper dispatched to take you to a military air strip. It's a secure airspace and the DND will notify the charter company of the coordinates."

Twenty-one

WE BLEW IN AND OUT OF OUR ROOMS at the Hilton in less than fifteen minutes and rushed to the roof where the helicopter was already waiting to whisk us off to a remote airfield.

Norm and Alice were hovering in the elevator vestibule, but they didn't have any bags with them. They seemed particularly calm and smiled sadly as we approached, but didn't press the button. A melancholic feeling gripped me. I knew what they were doing.

"We're staying," Norm said. "Hollinger will need help finding Amos and Hannah, and there is no way we can just leave them."

I felt sad, like rocks were in my gut, but I understood, of course. None of us tried to argue. We just took turns hugging them and wishing them luck before we stepped into the elevator. We had no time to waste. The longer we delayed, the more chance there was that Felix would find us.

The elevator doors closed in front of us, the car now taking us to the roof and helipad. It felt anticlimactic leaving them. It seemed ungrateful to just walk away but Ransom's life depended on our getting him away, away to a place of safety, to a place where he could recuperate and regain his strength and health. We needed him to recover so we could keep up our fight to bring down Felix. Or for other reasons, I thought.

We stepped out onto the roof and were met by a frenzy of noise and wind. The DND chopper blades whapped loudly, wildly stirring up the air. We bent over and braced ourselves against the torrent, our hair and clothes flying.

Hollinger opened the chopper's doors and we hurried to climb inside. Because it was a military craft, Hollinger was there sitting up front with the pilot. They were discussing something over their headsets while we got settled behind them.

Within seconds, the pilot lifted us up into the evening sky deepening with blue, leaving the bustle of the Washington streets below us. Instead of a military base, we were on our way to Hagerstown Regional Airport, a small facility used by the Washington and political elites especially for private business flights.

Rosalind had alerted Renegade to have a charter waiting for us there, and Hollinger had made sure that Ransom was already en route. Another private ambulance was speeding down Interstate 81 and would arrive at Hagerstown approximately at the same time as we did.

I hoped.

Our charter's destination was to be listed as Heathrow, but Renegade would do some magic and scramble the flight numbers so the plane would disappear from the flight records and become untraceable. A fueling stopover in St. John's, Newfoundland, is where the computer glitch would scramble the flight information. In reality, our charter was on its way to Reykjavik. That way we didn't have to risk Felix's finding our home in Nice, and Ransom wouldn't have to endure the long flights and a stopover. In Iceland we'd have a condominium near a private health clinic where we could cool off—the pun making me laugh ruefully—for a little while, just long enough to confuse Felix.

***

Hagerstown was mass of glowing runway lights, some flashing and others steady. The chopper set down on the tarmac and we disembarked quickly. The blades slowly came to a stop as we put distance between us and the craft. The chopper remained grounded because it would return Hollinger to Defense Headquarters where a rescue mission under his management was underway, a mission that he was coordinating even now.

But Hollinger seemed even more than before personally committed to our safety, which we appreciated. He planned to stay with us until we were safely in the air. When our C600 series Challenger left his sight, Hollinger would have to turn around and save other lives, not only Amos and Hannah's, but some of his own men's. His phone buzzed regularly as the mission updates became available to him, his face never wavering from intensely serious. The burden of his negligence was weighing heavily on him.

Fortunately, the DND chopper had made good time. We waited uneasily on the tarmac for our charter plane to arrive and for Ransom's ambulance. My stomach was in knots, Ruby's former bravado now melted like butter. This was a difficult plan to get away with; innumerable pieces had to come together without a flaw for us to escape before Felix realized that Hollinger had outsmarted him. Unfortunately, I knew with regret, that Hollinger's involvement put him on Felix's hit list as well. Another possible casualty. I didn't know whether he had any family, and now, given that he was a target, I wasn't sure whether I wished he did or didn't.

A few minutes in, we saw a plane circling the airfield. We strained our eyes against the dark sky as we watched the plane descend. From its size and markings, we determined that it was our charter. Minutes later, it made its final approach and was taxiing down a runway to its designated stopping spot. Hollinger took another phone call.

"The charter will taxi and stop a few hundred feet away from here," said Hollinger. "We're not even going to check in at the terminal. They know it's an emergency medical operation. My people tell me the ambulance is just coming off of Interstate 81 and will be here in twenty minutes, maybe less. We're breaking all radio contact now with the ambulance just in case Felix is already tracking you guys."

That was the worst news. If something happened, we'd be powerless to help. The next minutes seemed like hours. Every minute that passed gave Felix more time to find us, to close in on our location, to finish the job he was so intent on completing. We had evaded his plans several times. I couldn't help but feel that our luck was running out.

A terminal worker stood ahead with light batons waving the plane into position. It finally came to a stop and the stairs dropped down. A uniformed man emerged and waved us over while he waited at the bottom of the steps on the tarmac.

We hurried to greet him.

"Are you folks… RD?" the man asked.

"Yes," Hollinger answered. "We're waiting for an ambulance, an emergency evac."

"Yes," the man said. "The nurse had special medical equipment put on board."

A smile of relief formed on Rosalind's face as a statuesque woman appeared at the top of the stairs. It was Rose. She had flown in to help as soon as Rosalind had notified Renegade to make the arrangements. Rose wasn't always the warmest person, to say the least, but seeing her after all this time, I was comforted to know that Ransom would have her to care for him during the flight. Now all we needed was for the ambulance to show up.

"Rose, darling," Rosalind said. "How are things at home? Let me tell you, we're quite ready to get away from here. Far away."

"From the sound of your messages, it seems things have been a lot better for us than they've been for you," Rose said. "Where is Ransom? I would have thought you'd have him here by now." She gave everyone a disapproving glare which softened as soon as we noticed an ambulance racing up the tarmac, heading in the direction of the C600 that was being fueled up and stocked with food and drinks from the charter company.

The ambulance stopped twenty feet short of the aircraft. We hurried over and opened the back doors, even before the paramedic had a chance to jump out and help remove the gurney from inside.

Ransom winced from the jarring bump on the pavement, but he was alert, and I was happy to see that his condition had improved since we'd last seen him the day before at the hospital. It was pretty incredible that just forty-eight hours after lifesaving surgery, Ransom was sitting up on the gurney, and in spite of his still-critical injuries, he was ready to come aboard with us for a speedy escape. His eyes widened and a narrow smile of relief formed on his face when he saw us and he lifted his hand to give a tiny wave.

I ran to his side and gently took his raised hand while Reinhardt, Hollinger and the paramedic pushed the gurney to the steps of the aircraft.

They realized it wouldn't fit through the door, so Ransom was going to have to walk aboard. Ransom let out a painful groan as Reinhardt and the others helped him to his feet.

"Just take it slow, Ransom," Reinhardt said. "Easy, my son."

The men carefully guided him up the steps into the aircraft to where Rose had already set up a bed.

"We don't exactly have all the time in the world," Rose snipped, "so let's put some effort into this. Don't worry, Ransom, I'll give you something for the pain once we're on board," her voice turning floral when she spoke to him. "You'll be comfortable before we even get off the ground."

Once he was on board, Rose settled him onto the special stretcher, strapping him in securely and then injected something into his buttock. He lay back and closed his eyes, pale from the exertion. As Rose busied herself checking his vitals, he drifted off into a peaceful unawareness.

Hollinger's phone buzzed again and he quickly raised it to his ear, listened, grunted and returned it to his pocket. His jaw was set tight in rage. I looked at him closely. This hadn't been easy for him either. His eyes were bloodshot and his face was drawn as if he hadn't been eating or getting any fresh air.

"My two men have been found dead outside a Washington warehouse," Hollinger said. "A note was pinned to one of them that read, 'Don't look for me. If you do, the other two are as good as dead.'"

Immediately after, Reinhardt's phone buzzed. It was a text message from Norm, which Reinhardt read out loud. "They're on a yacht. Naval intelligence is trying to find their location."

Hollinger sighed. "Looks like you're ready to take off. I have to get back to headquarters." He shook Reinhardt's hand and turned around. "Good luck. We'll be in touch."

Hollinger returned to the chopper, which lifted off as soon as he was inside. A few whapping chops of the helicopter blades, a roar of the engine, and the DND helicopter was on its way back to Washington, leaving us on our own. We went inside, the doors came up, and soon it was our turn to fly.

As we took off, I picked up some of the brochures on board about Iceland. I'd always thought true to its name, it'd be one big glacier, but I read that that was a misnomer: Iceland was actually green and Greenland was the country full of ice. The pictures of the midnight sun were stunning, and I wondered if we'd get to see it. Reykjavik looked like a really cool place. Lots of restaurants, hot sulfur springs, nice people. It was a bigger city than I'd have thought, with a population of two hundred thousand. I hoped we'd get a chance to check out some of the sights, though I knew we'd probably not get to see much. We were going there expressly to hide and to heal. Whale watching or hiking would have to happen in another lifetime.

We were going to be staying at a rented condominium, a "guesthouse," the locals called it. There wouldn't be any receptionists or hotel staff to ask any questions or get in the way. A medical clinic was nearby just in case Ransom took a turn for the worse, but Rose would be managing his pain and his wounds so we hoped he wouldn't need it. But just in case, it was good to know it'd be nearby.

The six-hour flight was harder on Ransom than we expected. Take-off and landing were especially bad; I supposed the change in pressure bothered his lungs or affected his internal wounds though I couldn't really tell because he had a hard time speaking through the morphine. When we got into the guesthouse, the men carried him to a proper bed and he fell into a drug-induced sleep for the next eight hours.

***

The next day, Ransom was feeling stronger. He was able to sit up and actually refused additional pain medication. Rose hovered over him relentlessly, but he didn't seem to mind, even walking slowly to the window a few times to enjoy the beautiful scenery. The condo had enormous windows overlooking the mountains and the bay that bustled with ship traffic. If it weren't for the direness of our situation, Reykjavik would have been a fascinating place to explore. But as soon as Rose gave Ransom clearance to travel, we would be on another charter to Fairhaven.

I had dropped all pretense of our being brother and sister and didn't care what anyone thought. I sat by his bedside while he slept and held his hand, stroked his hair, and kept his blanket tucked in around him. I was confused about what was happening, but then again, only because I was worried it would be seen as wrong. On my end, it actually felt completely right.

Rose watched me for several days, saying nothing. Finally, she said offhandedly as she was walking into the kitchen, "I'd thought it was my job to nurse him back to health." She feigned a laugh. "You're being very... loving to your brother."

I didn't have time for her passive-aggressive comments. If she wanted sole control of him, she'd have to inject me, too. I wasn't going anywhere. I only knew I didn't just want to be with him; I had to be with him. My whole body ached to be by his side. I knew my emotions would change the order of this family's relationships, planned and specific relationships that gave us order and protection in their orchestration. But I couldn't help it.

Rose studied my face for a moment then returned her attention to

Ransom who was starting to wake up. "How are you feeling," Rose asked. "Do you need anything for the pain?"

Ransom stretched gingerly. "For God's sake, Rose! Don't jab me again. My arm and chest are sore from the bullet wounds, and now my butt is sore from your injections. But I'll tell you what I am feeling. Hungry." He was grinning. "Is there anything to eat around here?"

"Well, that's a good sign," Rose said. "It's near dinner, so I'll talk to Rosalind and see what she wants to do." She scurried off to the kitchen and talked to Rosalind. I overheard her say she'd ordered in and the food would arrive shortly.

"You don't need anything for the pain?" I asked him quietly.

"Nothing I can't handle for now," Ransom said. He stared at me with his big brown eyes. "Have you been here long, watching me?" He put his hand over mine and watched my face, his smile lingering as he waited.

"It's the least I can do for someone who saved my life," I said. I leaned over and kissed him on the forehead, and then pulled back, our faces only inches apart.

My heart was beating like crazy as he reached around and pulled me to him. Our lips met and I tingled all over. I pulled back slightly and looked at him again as if to ask him with my eyes, "are you sure?"

He smiled and kissed me again, this time longer, deeper. His mouth was warm and soft.

When Rose walked back into the room, I pulled away. Her eyebrow went up and she pursed her lips.

I made an apologetic face and sat up. Ransom smiled at Rose and then looked at me. He lifted a hand to tuck a lock of my hair behind my ear.

Rose huffed and turned to walk out then paused and said, "The dinner Rosalind ordered is here. Come and eat. You said you were hungry." She stormed off to the dining room.

Ransom eased his legs over to the edge of the bed and rolled onto his side to gather some momentum, wincing painfully as he pulled himself to a standing position. I could feel his discomfort and wished I could take his pain away.

He saw the worried look on my face. "I'm fine," he said. "Just give me a few more days, and I'll be able to move around much easier."

Rosalind and Rose spread the meal along the length of the long teak dining table. The dining area was minimalist as was the rest of the house. I realized with some small pleasure how every time I saw the panoramic view of the mountains, I felt redeemed in a small but essential way. The sun was low in the sky and cast a golden glow over everything as it hovered just over the mountain tops, its rays making a ring of fire.

The five of us sat at the table with the splendor of nature on one side and greasy Chinese food on the other. Rosalind had gone a little overboard because the table was literally filled with numerous paper cartons of dishes I recognized, like Chow Mein, Sweet and Sour chicken, Guy Ding and mushroom fried rice, and other things I didn't know that she said were Soo Guy, Tay Dop Voy and some other stuff I didn't catch the names of.

Rosalind, Reinhardt and Rose began to fill their plates, and Ransom limped slowly to the table and followed their lead. He put loads of food on his plate, which made me almost snort up a noodle. He'd lost weight and looked enthusiastic enough to eat the whole table.

"Aah, no," called Rose hopping up to take his plate away. "You've just been through an awful lot and were living on IV fluid. Go easy."

"OK, OK," he laughed, sitting down. He gave her hand a grandmotherly pat and started eating.

"Norm and Alice sent a text," Reinhardt said. "They say that Felix has Amos and Hannah on a ship somewhere on the Atlantic. So far, they haven't been able to get a location on them."

"So, he got out of the country," Rosalind said, squishing up her face to think. "I wonder what he's up to now. Renegade has been tracing marine leases and booked passages. Especially private ones. But nothing is coming up under his name." She shrugged and sighed. "Not like that means much. He's remarkably well-connected."

"Or Felix has a yacht of his own but it's registered under someone else's name," I said. "But why would he flee the country by boat? Where would he be headed?"

"It actually makes perfect sense," said Ransom, his mouth full. "He's devised a whole new plan. Amos and Hannah are his insurance that he doesn't get blown out of the water if they're found, literally. Or maybe he's found out where we live and he's on his way to the Mediterranean."

Ransom said this last thing so easily, I almost didn't register what he'd said. "No, no, he couldn't possibly know where we live. We've never given anyone our name or address." I'd let myself forget about his usual bluntness in the last few days. He must have been feeling much more like himself, I figured ruefully.

"It's definitely possible. Hollinger knows you go by the alias, Ruby Draker," Ransom said. "Maybe one of Szabo's men overheard the conversation at the Jefferson. Or maybe threatened or tortured the information out of Amos or Hannah. But we don't have to get all hopped about it yet. That'd be the only way he'd know. As far I remember, Hollinger is the only person who knows the Draker name and he's on our side. Felix wouldn't have gotten any information from him."

"You don't suppose Hollinger is helping Szabo?" I asked, forming the words slowly. "I mean, there have been a few times when I wondered whether they were working together. Or if not, he could just be desperate enough to get his men back and sell us out. Do you think he'd have offered me to Felix in return for the release of his men?"

"Anything is a possibility," Rosalind said.

"Or Felix could have found out where were staying in Washington and had our hotel rooms bugged," Ransom said. "I already told you... all of you... he'll never give up trying to find us and kill us."

I couldn't understand why Ransom was talking like this. I was shivering even though the room was warm and bright. Then I did understand: this was his way of coping. Of preparing himself for the possibility that the worst thing could happen. "Then you think he already knows where our home base is?" I asked.

"As long as Felix is out there on the loose, it's safer for us to assume he knows our every move," Rosalind said.

"Then what do we do next?" Rose asked.

I thought about it. If Felix were on to us, again, we'd be running from him. We'd always be running. We would never be safe. "We fight him on our own turf," I blurted out. "Let him come to us. Enough of this cat and mouse game. I say we go home and prepare for an unwelcome guest. He might be surprised at how much we outnumber him. His desperation is his weakness, and we can work with that. This time, he'll regret coming after us." Saying this, I felt stronger and more convicted than I had ever felt since this whole thing started that we would fight him and win. At least now the authorities knew he was a criminal so the law was on our side. If he came after us again, we would defend ourselves and those we loved. He might be notorious, but I was determined to reclaim my life. To start it over.

"Ransom, you really need to slow down," Rose scolded him as she watched him inhale his dinner. "Your body isn't going to cope well with all that greasy stuff." Rose shook her head.

I had to smile. She was such a control freak. I wondered if he were eating like this in some way to spite her.

"Rose, how soon do you think I can travel again?" Ransom asked.

She shrugged and sipped her tea. "Ask me again in the morning." She put up an eyebrow.

I had to hand it to her. She was right. I could hear him heaving up his dinner all throughout the early part of the night. But worst of all, in the morning, he was weak and feverish.

Rose said we'd have to stay in Reykjavik a few more days, which was precious time inside of which Felix could close in on our home territory.

Ransom managed to whisper his regrets, but he was too sick to say much more than that.

Twenty-two

LATE IN THE MORNING, I went in alone to check on Ransom. He looked horrible: pale, weak, drenched in sweat. His breath was coming in little pants.

I ran to grab Rose who was brusque with him as she took his temperature. She scolded him as if he were a bad child for delaying our return home. But she was at least gentle when she changed his wound dressings, pausing at the bullet hole in his shoulder, her forehead wrinkled in concern. She read the digital thermometer she took from his ear and pursed her lips. "That temperature means you have an infection. Lucky for you, this has nothing to do with your binge last night—infections after incurring bullet wounds can go septic very quickly—but you're going to need an antibiotic. I'll call the clinic. I wonder if they do house calls." She left the room in a flurry to talk to Reinhardt and Rosalind about how to handle this complication.

"I was so stupid," Ransom said. "Rose knows what she's talking about. This is my fault and now Felix has more time to counterattack, to find Fairhaven." Ransom's words were slurred together, his body lethargic, his skin damp and glowing with moisture. "Renegade, Rowan, Rachel and Roscoe will be danger and we won't be there to help them." He shook his head in dismay and tried to get up as if that would make things better. But he didn't have the strength and fell back onto his pillow, disgusted with his weakness, his face and arms beading with perspiration, and his voice shaky and whispery.

"Don't beat yourself up," I said. "You weren't ready to be moved so soon. What did you expect after such a long plane flight and all the activity of getting you to this place? Most people are in hospital for a week at least. Rose knows what to do. She will handle this. She'll get you some medicine and you'll be better in a few days." I sat by his side, trying to sound reassuring and wiped his sweaty forehead and neck with a cool cloth.

He shivered with chills.

I tucked the blanket up to his shoulders to warm him and wished that Rose hadn't left the room because my nursing ability was clearly inadequate. My heart pounded. With each minute, Ransom was clearly deteriorating.

"I'm sorry," he said. "I hate being so weak and so much trouble. I should be protecting you not the other way around." His eyes were rolling around, and I wondered if he were nearing delirium. I feared the infection was becoming increasingly serious and septic shock was setting in. No wonder Rose had responded so urgently.

Reinhardt and Rosalind entered the room to see for themselves how bad the situation might be. Rose was already on the phone with the clinic.

"A doctor is on the way and will bring a strong antibiotic," Reinhardt said. He sat at Ransom's bedside on a chair and clapped his hand to Ransom's forearm, looking down at how sweaty and limp it was. "Don't worry, son, medical help is on the way. I know you're not feeling well, but hang in there."

Tears flowed quietly down my cheeks as I continued to wipe the moisture from his brow.

Now and then he would open his eyes and try to talk but now, no words came out. Soon, he closed his eyes and seemed to enter an unconsciousness state, still breathing shallow rapid breaths.

A loud knock at the front door startled us all. Shortly after, Rose escorted a man with a black doctor's kit and IV fluid bags into the room. "This is Doctor Jorgensen," Rose said to us.

He felt Ransom's forehead with the back of his hand before quickly helping her set up an IV drip.

"Doctor, this is my son," Reinhardt said. "He was wounded in an unfortunate encounter in Washington D.C. We thought he would be able to fly home, but as you can see, he's taken a turn."

"Please let me examine the patient," Doctor Jorgensen said. He politely touched Reinhardt's shoulder pointing him and the rest of us to the door.

"I'm a nurse and would like to stay with him," Rose said.

The doctor nodded but indicated the rest of us were to leave the room.

They were in with Ransom for a long time. Waiting was almost intolerable; I wanted desperately to be at his side. Reinhardt paced and Rosalind sat nervously shifting and changing positions on the sofa. I stood still, motionless, staring at the bedroom door. Minute after minute went by and we anguished over what that meant. Had the doctor and Rose acted quickly enough or… I didn't know what to think.

When the doctor and Rose emerged from Ransom's bedroom, Rosalind sprang to her feet.

"We've put him on a strong antibiotic and hooked up an IV drip," the doctor said. "I'll be back to re-examine him later this afternoon. If he hasn't improved, we'll have to move him to a hospital. If anything changes, you can call me immediately." He handed Rose a card and Reinhardt approached him with several bills of the local currency.

The doctor nodded at the money and looked up at Reinhardt. "I'll be completely at your service and only minutes away." He gave a little nod and let himself out.

"How is he?" I asked. "Is he going to be all right?"

"He's very weak but he's resting and his vitals are good," Rose said.

"I'll check on him often. We need to let him sleep. All we can do after that is wait."

"Let's check on news from Washington," Reinhardt said. He opened the laptop at the table.

"Reinhardt, did you get any more text messages from Norm or Hollinger?" I asked.

Reinhardt pulled out his phone. The light was blinking. He tapped the text icon and read the message. "Naval intelligence has spotted a vessel they think belongs to Felix in the mid-Atlantic. It appears to be heading for the Strait of Gibraltar. He'll keep us posted on its course."

"Felix is heading into the Mediterranean?" Rosalind asked, her voice shaky, her face sober. "We can't leave here yet. We have to notify Renegade to get ready with a defense plan. Felix is surely on his way to Fairhaven."

"Better yet," Reinhardt said, "I'm thinking that Rosalind and I should fly home to help on the home front and Rose and Ruby should stay with Ransom until he's well enough to join us."

"But he's critical," Rosalind said. "I don't want to leave him."

"The next twelve hours should tell us if the antibiotic is helping," Rose said. "It'll take Szabo at least a few more days to reach our location if he even knows where that is. We don't know what he knows."

"You're right, Rose," Reinhardt said, "but I will still tell Renegade to have a plane on standby." He punched in a message on his Blackberry and then returned to his pacing.

I nudged the door open a crack and peaked in on Ransom. His eyes were closed, and he seemed to be having a restless dream. His breathing was alternating between a soft snore and rapid excitement. The IV fluid bag was attached to a metal pole beside his bed, the clear tube snaking to his arm where the needle stabbed a vein, white surgical tape securing it to the skin of his inner elbow. Rose had forbidden us to bother him, so we took turns sneaking a peak through a narrow opening of his bedroom door. The hours passed slowly while he slept, sometimes restlessly and other times peacefully.

No one wanted to go out, so we tried to busy ourselves with household activities, making coffee, cleaning up dishes left from the night before, fluffing pillows on the sofa while we waited to see if Ransom would respond to the antibiotic. Reinhardt constantly checked his Blackberry even though it would ping if a message came in. Rosalind sat on the arm of the sofa and finally tuned in to an American television station, which we were able to get from the satellite dish on the roof of the house, and scanned every news station. Rose puttered in the kitchen and heated up leftover Chinese food for lunch even though no one was hungry. It sat on the counter by the microwave, leaving a heavy oily smell in the air.

Mid-afternoon, Doctor Jorgensen returned as he'd promised. Rose accompanied him as he entered Ransom's room. Moments later, the pair emerged from the room.

"His temperature isn't normal yet, but it is down considerably," the doctor said. "At minimum, we know the antibiotic is working and he's no longer critical. Rose can remove the IV as soon as his temperature is normal, but he should continue on oral antibiotics for a week, just to be safe. I brought the pills from the clinic pharmacy."

His mood and ours greatly lifted, Reinhardt smiled and handed him more bills for the medicine and for his services, and Dr. Jorgensen left again.

When I next peeked at Ransom, I saw that he was awake. He smiled as I walked over to his bed.

"Ruby, I'm sorry I made you worry. Are you mad at me?"

"I'm just relieved you're all right," I said. "But you did scare the hell out of me."

He held his hand out to me.

I took it and kissed it, then his forehead, and then his lips.

Rose came into the room. She seemed to have a radar for when Ransom and I were wanting a private moment. "You have to let him rest," Rose said. "He's too weak for this kind of excitement. His temperature isn't normal yet. Do you want him to relapse?" She stood with her hands planted firmly on her hips staring crossly at me, her head motioning for me to go to the door.

I looked at her for a long moment then leaned down and planted another kiss on him before pulling away from his grip that seemed faintly stronger now and assured me that he was getting better.

"I'll be back a little later," I said. "Rose is right. You have to rest."

He leaned back and closed his eyes, the smile fading slowly from his face as he fell asleep.

In the living room, I sat with Rosalind on the sofa, feeling dejected because I wanted to be at Ransom's side. I wanted him to be well. I wanted to not be hunted by a crazy person. I wanted a lot of things.

Rosalind looked at me sympathetically. "Rose won't let us see him either," she said, putting her arm around my shoulders.

I might have resented her tactics, but I also knew Rose was right. If Ransom knew I was in the room, he'd want to be awake and talk to me. I could feel smug about that. And I was hopeful that we would have lots of time later on to talk about things.

I leaned back on the sofa and crossed my legs. The afternoon was going to be long. "Can you tell me about the Cold War Days?" I asked. "What was it like spying on the Soviets? Was Felix always so notorious?"

"He was always a piece of work," Rosalind said, leaning back. "He had exacting standards and expected his agents to carry out the missions precisely the way he'd laid them out. He expected results. Information on missile silo locations, names of people in command, who they had spying on us, inventories of munitions… And we were expected to do whatever it took to get them. He also made no bones about our fates. If you were caught, you were on your own, a causality of war. We all had aliases so if we were killed in action, no one would even know. It made him look good in the eyes of the President.

"That's all that mattered to him." Rosalind's mouth twisted with disgust at the memory. "The power, the recognition, the glory, his name going down in history. He ranted about patriotism, how the commies were out to destroy the American way of life and how he was the only one who could keep the country out of enemy hands. But in Russia, they were afraid that we'd take them over, too, so both sides worked to get more nuclear warheads than the other."

"What a sad life. Felix was never a good guy?" I asked. "Didn't he care that his agents had families, maybe children of their own?" I was trying to understand him. I could see him doing this job for the good of America because that would protect his own family from a nuclear attack as well. "What happened to him in his life that turned him into the person he is now?"

"Felix always looked out for Felix," Reinhardt said. "He bragged about how loyal his agents were to him, that they'd put their country before everything else, even their lives. But it was all rhetoric, jargon, words that made him and the President look good in the media that reported him to be a hero. He just lapped it all up, savored the fame, let the whole thing go to his head and ego. I think he actually believed all the bullshit. He was an egotistical maniac even back then.

"In truth, his agents despised him. It was a blessing when the Cold War ended and the department was disbanded to get away from him. When all but a few of his agents agreed to the buyout package, it discredited him, and he's held a grudge ever since. One that grew into resentment so strong, his mind must have snapped. Amos and your father didn't trust him to the point where they petitioned for a special protection program, an identity change, sort of like the witness protection program. Only we were looking for protection from Felix. Even back then, everyone worried that he'd seek revenge. Anonymity was the only way to get him out of our lives. Adam, Amos and Hollinger took on the task. The government wouldn't buy the story that Felix might harm them, so they altered the story and made a strong case about protecting agents from Soviet retribution. Because the Russians may have still had spies on American soil, this story worked."

"He wasn't keen to retire because he considered his job unfinished," I said.

"You got that right. He thrived on mayhem and killing. If he'd retired and lived his life in peace and harmony, that life would have been a punishment for him. Staying with the government—any agency or department would've done—was all he cared about. But only so he could use his position for retribution, to get back at his agents who had 'betrayed' him."

Reinhardt shook his head. "In his mind he actually started to believe the story of us being double agents, agents who'd defected to the enemy. If he ever gets caught, that's the story he'll tell. And," he clapped his hands onto his thighs and leaned forward. "Rosalind and I were his first victims. Somehow he was able to access and steal our investments, our property, and even get access to our bank accounts. As he killed off more agents, slowly the estate thefts amounted to a fortune that he was able to use to hire hit men and clean-up crews to help him carry out his crimes. That money helped him go after even more people because who could argue with an accident or natural disaster? No one suspected him."

"But what about Hollinger," I asked. "You said he worked for Felix. Even went on missions with my mother and father. Why didn't Felix kill him first? Wouldn't he have been his most obvious first target?"

Reinhardt was shaking his head. "By the time the department was disbanded, Hollinger was already with the Defense Department. He didn't want anything to do with Felix, so he relegated him to an inconsequential and irrelevant department, which, it turns out, was fine with Szabo. With Hollinger off his back, he could do whatever he wanted. Hollinger figured that the disgrace of being demoted to such a lowly administrative position would force him into retirement. After all, for a man to go from having such a high public profile, and connections to people in high and powerful positions, to basically being ignored, should have irked the hell out Felix. Or maybe Hollinger figured that the demotion was punishment enough, that he would simply rot away in the underground levels of the Archives."

"That doesn't explain how Hollinger got the Defense Department position," I said.

Rosalind shot Reinhardt a look. "There was a lot more going on under the surface, things that Felix wasn't aware of. As spies, we always made alliances. With the Russians, with our own government officials, with outside members of criminal organizations who had money and influence to put their own kind into Congress, the Senate, and even the White House. And there were other reasons Hollinger had to leave the department..." Rosalind went silent and bit her nail. She looked apprehensively at Reinhardt, but he nodded and came to sit across from us and took my hands in his.

My stomach knotted as I waited to hear more of the story. Once my hands were in his, I had a bad feeling this was going to involve me.

"When your parents first came to work for External Affairs, they weren't married. Your mother, I'm sure you know this, was an extra-ordinarily beautiful woman. It was one of the reasons she got foreign soil missions. Soviet politicians had no problem making her their escort, and she was good. She played the part with great finesse. Both your father and Hollinger were stationed there to protect her. They both fiercely loved her. And... so did Felix. After their last mission went awry, after their arrest, after Felix sent in a special liberation team and brought them home, Felix and Hollinger came to blows when Felix..." Reinhardt paused and took a breath. "Ruby, Felix raped your mother. That's how she became pregnant with Christian. Hollinger almost murdered Felix. Your dad stopped him or else Hollinger might have had to spend the rest of his life in prison.

"Hollinger wanted to get away from Felix so much, he called a favor from a Congressman who had connections. These connections helped him get elected, but in turn, he owed them money. Hollinger traded some information that made the mafia lots of money and in return absolved that politician's debt. As a reward, the Congressman helped Hollinger get another job, and that's how he became head of the Defense Department. In the end, your mom married your dad, but I think Hollinger never stopped loving her."

Reinhardt shook his head. "She was the main reason he worked so hard to put the protection program together," he said. "He wanted to protect her from Felix, to let her have a normal life and be happy even if it meant living her life with a husband who had been his best friend."

I was shaking. Every time these people had a heart-to-heart with me, I found out deeper levels of crazy things about my parents. I knew so little about them. In hindsight, they were strangers and the lives we lived a lie. Which no longer even mattered, actually, because since I'd become Ruby Draker, our pasts had dissolved like sugar in water as if they never were. Worse yet, my present reality was in danger of the same fate. I lived under an alias with a contrived family whom I was actually starting to accept as my mother, father, aunts, uncles and brothers, all of us bonded over our mutual pain and desire to move on.

Part of me welcomed that feeling of being alone. Loss was a wound that never truly healed. The other part had been craving connection, familiarity. The comfort of others who seemed to genuinely care about me.

I looked at Rosalind. It was time for the rest of the truth. I deserved to know how we had become the family we were. "What about you and Reinhardt?" I asked. "What brought the two of you together? Did Felix destroy your pasts as well?"

She smiled sadly. "You deserve to know," she said, looking down at the floor. "I was stationed in Moscow, working as a secretary in the Kremlin. My job was to report names and events the CIA would be interested in. I didn't see much action, and my cover was never broken the same way your parents' cover had been."

She twisted her mouth. "One day the Russian diplomat I worked for became interested in another woman and decided, just like that, to make her his new secretary. So he fired me. When Felix found out, he simply made arrangements for me to be returned to the States. The Soviets never suspected a thing and my extrication was flawless. After Cold Force was disbanded, I happily took the retirement and relocation package. I decided to move to Canada—Quebec City actually—where I met and married a successful and rich businessman who ran a small local newspaper, *Le Québec Chronicle-Telegraph*. Albert was a good man, hardworking, kind and gentle. I loved him very much. We had a daughter, who was the love of our lives." Her voice threatened to break, but she cleared her throat and carried on. "One day, I took my daughter to pick him up at his office and go out for lunch. Albert was notorious for making us wait, so I let her go into the building to fetch him while I waited in the car to finish listening to a radio program on CBC. She ran in, and it got to be ridiculous how long they were taking.

"I was starting to get out of the car to collect them both when there was a huge explosion and the whole building was suddenly engulfed in flames. I tried to run toward the building to save my family but off to the side was Reinhardt. I knew as soon as I saw him that something was foul, and sure enough, within a minute, I understood that the fire had been Felix's work. I still wanted to go in after my husband and daughter, but the fire was instantaneously extensive and furious, and we knew they were dead. The next day, the newspapers reported that we had all perished. Our bodies were never recovered, cremated by the intense heat, and faulty wiring was blamed as the cause. It was, according to the report, tragic but explainable, requiring no further investigation.

"Reinhardt brought me to France, arranged for the surgery so my face couldn't be recognized, and since then, I have been living with him as my husband at Fairhaven."

Reinhardt came to her side, drew her close to him and kissed her gently on the cheek. Rosalind laid her head on his shoulder.

How complex their husband and wife relationship must be, I thought. They wore wedding rings, but that didn't mean much. I didn't know if they were ever legally married or simply acted as husband and wife. Right now, it wasn't really important.

"What was your name," I asked gently.

"Maxine Dumont."

"And your daughter's?" I asked, faltering slightly. I was afraid of the answer. I knew there were reasons Rosalind paid the kind of maternal attention she did, even if it was in her own peculiar way. She would have seasoned her own daughter as she did me, to protect herself and train her just as carefully.

She stared at me, her eyes filling. "Her name was Ruby—Ruby Dumont. She was the love of my life," Rosalind said. A tear slipped down her cheek but she took my hand and held it very tight.

She had named me after her dead daughter. I didn't know if that made me feel honored or just immensely sad. But I could deal with that later. Right now I needed to hear more about their pasts to start making sense of the present.

"But, Reinhardt, how did you know that Felix had targeted them so you could be there right at the right moment?" I asked.

"I'd seen a newspaper photo of the Dumont family the day before. It was some sort of charity event," Reinhardt said. "It was Felix's pattern to seek out a target after a public photo or footage appeared, and I figured... he'd arrange an accident, like he did with my family. That's how he worked, always an accident."

He lowered his eyes, staring at the floor and continued. "For me, after my retirement I chose to live in the south of France. I had been stationed there for a short while and fell in love with the climate and ambiance of the old villages. Like Rosalind, once I relocated, I met my spouse, a wonderful woman named Monique and we married, had two sons, and I got a job working in administration at a local winery. I was very happy. My life was easy and filled with love. The winery saw increased sales and we had a big promotion that was highly publicized throughout France that showed me holding a bottle of wine.

"That summer when my boys were five and seven, we decided to spend a few days holiday in Paris, like regular tourists, except that at the end, I would stay on a few extra hours to take some meetings for the winery. The promotion came out while we were there and people were calling to me on the street, asking me for my autograph. It was all very funny and my boys got an enormous kick out of their Papa, the celebrity."

He laughed, but then his face became sober just as quickly. "The next afternoon, when it came time for me to get to my first meeting, my wife and sons got on the TGV and our friend Marcel offered to pick them up at the train station and bring them home.

"I was so busy all afternoon in back- to-back meetings, I barely made it to my train and didn't have a chance to phone home first. When I arrived, the police were still at the car accident scene. I didn't let on who I was. When I asked what had happened, they told me that they had died in a motor accident not a few hours before. The police and Felix must have been convinced the man driving was me."

"What made you suspect that it wasn't an accident?" I asked.

"Because when I went to the accident scene, I saw him there, lurking in the darkness," Reinhardt said. "He was asking bystanders and people who had come to put flowers at the site, questions. The French people like to talk and freely give their opinion. I heard some of them tell Felix that the whole family had perished. I saw the smirk on his face, that evil grin that gave away his satisfaction.

"I had no other family that I knew of," Reinhardt continued. "I was so alone. While hiding out in Monte Carlo, I got drunk with some friends. They told me about a genetic test the French government was doing to identify family lines. I knew who my mother was. We were American, and though she never talked about my father, I could only assume he was American, too, so for me it seemed completely ridiculous, but my friends thought it was hilarious. We were drunk, loud and on a lark, the group of us went and got tested then went back to the bar.

I later learned that the test was really to search for members of the Rothschild line, one of the wealthiest and most powerful families in Europe. Beatrice Rothschild was the last of her family line. She and her husband had had no children, but Beatrice had been something of a flamboyant socialite," he said, winking, "if you know what I mean. When they both died, the State had to make sure there were no legitimate heirs—or illegitimate heirs for that matter—before they took over the estate and the fortunes the Rothschilds had amassed, which included a large villa in Saint-Jean-Cap-Ferrat.

"So the best part, the very strangest part, was that my DNA matched their line. You can imagine my shock when I opened the letter, being an American and believing that I didn't have a single blood tie to France. It turned out I was Beatrice's illegitimate son she'd given up for adoption. I found out that my mother was actually just a woman Beatrice hired to act as my mother. To keep us from being discovered, we moved to America where the woman, the mother I thought was mine, raised me as a single parent. I had no father or siblings. She died when I was still with Cold Force.

"Anyway," he continued, "to back up a bit, after the accident that took the lives of my family, I investigated and found that Felix Szabo was still a government employee but at the Archives Department, a branch that kept all the records from the Cold War. I didn't trust him when I worked for him, and I knew when I saw him at the accident scene in France that he was responsible. I believe I was his first victim.

"So years later, when I saw Maxine's photo, I strongly suspected she was in danger and wanted to warn her. I flew to Quebec City to tell Maxine everything, but I was too late for her family. I arrived at the scene only seconds before the explosion. We bonded through our grief and she agreed to come to France to live with me at Fairhaven until she could figure out what to do."

He looked at her, love evident in his gaze. "And we're still together, working side by side all these years to stop Felix. We've been able to save Renegade, Rowan, Rose, Rachel, Ransom and Roscoe—and of course you." His voice was soft and filled with emotion.

I reached for them and they pulled me into an embrace and we held onto each other, locked together in the pain of sorrow, in the memory of our lost loved ones, as silent tears streamed down our faces.

Rose came out of Ransom's room and rushed to the kitchen muttering to herself. "He's hungry," she said. "I think something soft and bland is a good idea." She pulled a container of mushroom soup from the refrigerator and put it into the microwave. A few minutes later, she was hurrying to return the food to Ransom's room when she noticed our faces. She stopped briefly, looking at us in confusion before she spoke, "You can stop the funeral. Ransom's fever has broken. His temperature is normal again."

Twenty-three

REINHARDT AND ROSALIND TALKED long into the night about the two of them leaving for Fairhaven. They were torn between the urgency of helping prepare a home defense and staying to help support the group and Ransom. He was better, but not out of the woods yet. In the end, they decided it would be best to keep the group together while Ransom recovered. They didn't say it aloud, but I know they were thinking: what difference did it make? We didn't feel safe anywhere. There was always that nagging, menacing fear in the back of our minds that things weren't as safe here in Reykjavik as we had hoped. It was hard to tell if the overriding urge was paranoia or if it was prudence that compelled us to be so cautious.

Too much had happened, my instincts twitched, acutely aware of everything around us. I was suspicious of everything; nothing felt secure. Although we had survived his attacks, Felix had won an important victory over us. He had infected us with fear.

We weren't completely sitting ducks; he had reason to be fearful as well. A federal warrant for attempted murder had been issued for him. How ironic that the government he so revered now considered him a high-level threat, a fugitive. I wondered how that might play on his sick mind—though if anyone were going to be fueled by such information, it'd be him. I was sure being wanted just made him more determined than ever to get us. His mental state was scary; we couldn't predict how he'd react. From what I knew of Felix, though, I suspected it was like cornering an animal. If pinned in, he'd strike out that much more ferociously.

Meanwhile, Rose hovered protectively around Ransom. She seemed to be using his slide backwards to keep him to herself. She restricted our access to him, telling us he was too weak and needed rest, that the excitement of stimulating him with our bedside visits, however brief, would impair his recovery. She insisted that he was still several days away from being able to travel. I ached to be with him, but I complied because in the end, I had to defer to her and didn't want to be responsible for doing anything that might worsen his condition. With each passing day, I watched her more intensely. It became clear to me that she had feelings of her own for Ransom. I tried to deny the idea and simply attributed her attention to dedication. Rose was one of us, and we couldn't allow ourselves to start doubting each other.

Reinhardt and Rosalind were uneasy as well. Rosalind's usually cheerful overconfidence became a sullen whispered silence. Reinhardt's fatherly confidence was replaced by suspicious stares out the window as he made phone calls and sent emails to Renegade. I had never seen them so tense. Perhaps he worried that he had made the wrong decision to stay, that he should be using this time to prepare for Felix's approaching attack at home. But we really had no givens, nothing we could count on. Felix would reveal himself on his own schedule and to his own advantage. He was a venomous reptile, a snake that could burrow into the darkness of the earth and then pop up at a time when you least expected. I think more than worrying about whether this was the time Felix would succeed, was the fear that no one felt he could second-guess Felix. It was a lawless feeling. I could see that Rosalind and Reinhardt felt helpless to protect us.

From years of experience, Reinhardt had become a cautious man.

He had learned the hard way that his family would always need protection, protection that he had failed to provide before, and which had cost his wife and two young sons their lives. He had vowed never to fail his family again. To that end, he ensured that Fairhaven was always armed. It was fenced like a fortress and patrolled by a security company at all times. But, with this new threat, he would need to double-down efforts to fortify the security of our home. His tension was palpable. I saw him on the opposite end of a duel: Reinhardt on one side obsessed with protection, and Felix on the other obsessed with destruction.

Reinhardt moved into action. He put Rowan in charge of securing extra weaponry while Renegade delved ever more deeply into the computer records, searching the Internet and social media for signs, anything that might give a clue as to where Felix was hiding, or where he might show himself. Neither prudence nor logic could anticipate the workings of his sick mind, so every option had to be considered. Felix, being the cocky bastard he was, might have even tried to taunt us into the open with a Twitter or Facebook posting. And so Reinhardt was now preparing for every contingency.

Even after several texts with Norm, there were still no coordinates on Felix's ship. That could only mean that he had established a land base, probably somewhere along the coast of the Mediterranean, and more probably, somewhere close to Fairhaven. We were relying on Hollinger to keep us posted on marine activity. I shuddered to think that Felix could attack by sea, taking over the water that surrounded the peninsula where Fairhaven stood. The majestic views of the Mediterranean could soon become scarred by battle and death.

Reinhardt's communication with Hollinger kept up this important alliance. Hollinger had military and naval connections that spanned the globe. He would also alert us if Felix's yacht were on the move again. After all, now that Felix was a wanted criminal, our involvement and intel was as important to Hollinger as his were to us. At the same time, Reinhardt was still reluctant to reveal our home location to him.

Norm and Alice were essential to us as well. They had been doing their own investigative work back in Washington, following every lead, inspecting harbors and shipping companies for departures both for commercial and leisure uses. They stopped at nothing to uncover information that might lead to a location on Amos and Hannah. Finding those two would lead us right to Felix.

Norm's text message told us that they had found some interesting facts. The problem was how to get that information to us in a secure way. Hollinger would have to be kept in the dark for now because if Felix discovered that Hollinger had inside information or maybe had sent agents or troops into the area where he was hiding, he would go even further underground. We couldn't risk that. An enemy we could see was at least an enemy we could deal with.

Reinhardt was sitting in a mid-century armchair in the corner, busy on his phone. "Looks like Norm and Alice have uncovered some important information," he said slowly. "They think they've found where Felix is holding Amos and Hannah. Hollinger is probably keeping them on a short leash so it would be good if we get them away from there. We have no idea what Felix will do if he intercepts their information. And let's face it, Hollinger's track record for successfully executing a mission hasn't been the greatest," he said regretfully. "And you know how Norm and Alice are. They'll try to save Amos and Hannah with or without us. For all of our sakes, it's better that we stick together on this rescue. It's time to move them out of Washington."

"Norm and Alice should meet us here in Reykjavik," Rosalind said. "Ransom still needs some time. We can make our rescue plans from here."

Rosalind sent a message to Renegade that read, "N, A to RD5."

Renegade would know that it meant to arrange a secret charter flight for Norm and Alice to where we were squirreled away at the base of the mountains of Iceland.

It didn't take Renegade long. A short time later, a message to Rosalind and copied to Norm read, "2AM W-P." He had arranged a charter out of Westport for the early hours of the morning.

Norm messaged back the emoticon of a thumbs-up.

Reinhardt arranged to meet them at the nearby airport in Keflavik at eight the next morning.

All we could do now was wait, something we weren't especially good at but which we'd had to do a lot of lately. We were waiting for messages from Hollinger; we were waiting for Ransom to heal and regain his strength; we were waiting for Norm and Alice to arrive.

That night I went to bed early, but the built-up anticipation for everything made it impossible to sleep.

My nerves felt frayed and tender, which made the minutes drag by over the night. We needed every one of those minutes, but the passage of each was torture.

Ransom's temperature was finally back to normal and Rose had removed the IV drip. He continued to take antibiotics under her strict supervision. She decided when and what he could eat, when he should sleep, how long he was allowed to be out of bed, and she monitored his vitals including whether or not his plumbing was working. He accepted his patient status mutely though I could see it was wearing on him being so smothered. As he gained his strength, I noticed he started locking the bathroom door when he went in to shower or dress. He then started arguing with Rose about how long he was allowed out of bed and how she restricted us from being with him. I could hear them bickering from behind his door, which she kept closed while she was inside. He still let her tend to him because he knew that any further misstep could cost us more time and the only reason we were stuck in this condo in Reykjavik was he wasn't able to travel, but I could see his nerves had also worn thin. Not a bad thing; it was a clear sign he was much better. Rose had to see it as well; she even begrudgingly let him join the group for dinner the night before.

"Are you going to let me have some real food, Rose?" Ransom said, encircling his wrist with his fingers to show how slim he'd gotten.

"Let's not push it," Rose said. She had prepared a casserole for him, nutritious, but with the vegetables and meat mashed as if for an invalid with no teeth. I felt so bad for him; Rosalind and I had cooked up a roast with potatoes and salad and our food beside his did seem unfair. Ransom looked longingly at what we ate, but he pressed his eyes closed and obediently choked down the soft food Rose had made. His night in the bathroom must have still been fresh in his mind.

I put my hand reassuringly on his shoulder and laughed at him.

"I'll eat this for you all," he said, "but don't blame me if I waste away."

We chuckled as he screwed up his face and took a tentative bite. Rose took a big breath, pushed herself away from the table and went into the kitchen.

"Oops," Ransom said, his eyes glinting.

"All right, darling," I said. "Eat your mush so you feel better by the time Norm and Alice arrive. I want you in good shape to help us make plans. Should be fun! Renegade has arranged another one of those 'disappear in the night' flights." I wiggled my fingers.

He looked at me strangely as did the others at the table.

I laughed. I realized I sounded almost exactly like Rosalind. When had that started? Rosalind sent an approving smirk in my direction.

"They have information about where Felix may have taken Amos and Hannah," Reinhardt said, "as long as Hollinger doesn't screw it up." He sneered.

Everyone laughed. Maybe we had all borrowed some of Rosalind's sarcasm.

"Good. Then we can go after him," Ransom said. "That's better than letting Felix attack us at home."

"We," Rose said, returning from the kitchen with some cloudy apple juice for Ransom, "doesn't include you. You might be able to have dinner with the rest of us, but you still have weeks of recovery ahead. Don't even think about it."

"Let's see what Norm and Alice have to report before we make any plans," Rosalind cut in. She knew Ransom would insist on being part of the rescue mission. He'd find a way to go even if it killed him.

Reinhardt suggested that Ransom use the laptop to find out some coordinates where a sizable yacht could disappear off the radar while sailing in the Mediterranean.

Ransom reluctantly finished his meager portion of mush and retrieved the laptop and started to type and scroll. "Let's assume that Felix knows about our home in Nice," he said. "We know he has Amos and Hannah on some kind of ship or yacht large enough and outfitted enough to sail on the high seas. So if you wanted to conceal yourself, where would you go?" He looked around the table as if waiting for an answer from us, but his eyes were glazed over in thought. He was starting to sound like his capable self, the Ransom who could always find the information we needed, information that might save our lives. He tapped the table with his finger. "Where would you make something of that size disappear?"

"More importantly," I asked. "How did he know to come to the Mediterranean?"

No one had any answers and that made us shift nervously in our chairs. None of us had ever given our names at any point when we were in Washington except me and our passports had always been kept in the locked safe in our room at the Hilton in Washington. My name couldn't be connected to a thing, but our passports could have easily done so.

I suddenly thought back to an incident I'd brushed off and forgotten about and grew instantly hot and sweaty all over.

One afternoon, we'd returned to our hotel room and I noticed that the closet door was open, which left the safe in view. When I'd put my passport away earlier, before we left for the restaurant, I'd set the lock to 1. But later, when I glanced over, it was closer to the 3. Maybe someone had brushed it, or the housekeeper had hit it with her hand when she was putting something away, but now I knew without a doubt that Felix had not only found out where we were staying, he'd gone into our room and had seen our passports. I didn't have the courage to say anything and excused myself to the bathroom.

Reinhardt left for the airport in Keflavik early and alone the next morning. He would blend in with the morning commotion of travelers and traffic. The charter would be landing within the next hour and it was imperative he hustle Norm and Alice away from the airport unnoticed. Some people felt night provided the best cover; Reinhardt felt that the more people there were, the more anonymous they'd be. Renegade had made arrangements for them to be cleared through customs quickly. I was learning that even airport security could be bought. Reinhardt would scoop them away to the rental car and they'd be at the guesthouse within twenty minutes.

Unlike me, Ransom clearly had a fine night's sleep and awoke in good spirits. He was looking almost back to his normal self, invigorated from having been helpful with his computer search the night before. He was showered and dressed before Rose even got up, and was already working on the laptop at the dining room table, trying to locate possible places where a yacht could be concealed. He marked the likely spots as favorites.

I stood behind him and rubbed his shoulders. He leaned in closer to the screen, so I came around and planted a soft kiss on his cheek. Men. When they got into something, almost nothing could distract them. I used to have a horrible time trying to get my dad to stop making calls and just read with me.

"Ms. Draker," Ransom teased, turning around and tickling me under the arms. "Are you trying to keep me from my very important work?" Of course, at that very moment, Radar Rose came into the room and he flipped back to the laptop.

I went over to join Rosalind at the window. It was 8:07 a.m., and she was watching for Reinhardt.

At 8:11 a.m., their car came up the drive.

"They're here," Rosalind said. She hurried to open the door.

Alice came through the front door first. "Such a long flight. I could use a coffee. I don't suppose you have any donuts?"

I started to laugh. Surely she was joking. Donuts? How did she keep such a sexy figure and eat like that? Or maybe she was so used to acting like a country bumpkin around us, she'd forgotten she didn't have to. Or maybe she just preferred that life; after all, being a spy and jetting all over the world with her life in danger probably got old after so many years.

A moment later, Norm and Reinhardt came in carrying suitcases much larger than I had expected to see, the size you'd pack for a long vacation, not like our little bags we packed with only the bare essentials. They'd clearly done more shopping in D.C. Were they expecting an extended stay or were they carrying concealed weapons?

"I'll make us some coffee," Rose said. "Come in and make your-selves at home."

"Hello, Alice, Norm," Rosalind said. "I trust you had a good flight?"

"Charter, all the way," Norm said. "It doesn't get much better than that." He looked at Reinhardt and then at the rest of us. He cocked his head as if he wanted to ask questions, probably like how we were able to afford all of the luxury, but he kept his mouth shut.

"Charters are flexible, and they don't ask too many questions," Reinhardt said, smiling warmly as if that were explanation enough. "As soon as Ransom is well enough, we'll take a charter to our home base. I can explain everything a little more fully once we're there."

"Do you have information on Felix's ship?" Ransom asked, going to the table and hunching over the laptop. "I've identified some possible locations, but tell us what you know. Maybe that will help point us to Felix's hiding spot."

We gathered in the dining room around the large teak table. It was a bright Icelandic summer's day. The sun shone cheerfully through the large expanse of glass that looked out onto the mountains and the North Bay. Alice and Norm were clearly smitten with the view and slow to focus on the computer.

I hung back and watched the day happen. The sun had risen at three-thirty in the morning and wouldn't set again until near midnight. I read that here at the northern-most part of the world, Iceland endured twenty-one hours of sunlight during the spring and summer months.

The glorious sunrises and sunsets behind rose and magenta-colored mountains were the reason this place was famously known as the land of the midnight sun. Right now, the mountains sparkled clear and blue in the crisp light of day, cargo ships sailed slowly in and out of the bay, a few seabirds glided and swooped from the dark blue water beyond and screeched loudly as they foraged for food that the tide had washed onto the shore. It was hard to imagine that in this pristine and tranquil setting our lives could be so troubled, so full of danger, so wrought with questions.

"Alice and I snooped around the harbors in D.C.," Norm said. "Felix must have boarded a vessel somewhere in Washington. There are several harbors along the Potomac that moor large ships. The problem was to find the one he used. We had almost given up when we found a registration document and a crew list bound for Europe, just at about the right time and right size of vessel. It had a crew of five and three passengers listed. The names must have been aliases. We notified Hollinger who said that while the Coast Guard didn't find it, a ship of that description was noted as it was on its way to Gibraltar. Then they lost it. There's always too much ocean traffic to spot one vessel once they're in the Mediterranean. But…" he broke into a smile, "then we got this."

Norm pulled out his cell phone. He opened a text message with a photo attached. The message read, "wish you were here." The photo was a picture of Amos and Hannah, the barrel of a gun clearly visible in the bottom right-hand corner of the photo, the ocean spread out behind them, and what looked like a ferry in the far-off background.

"Can you forward that to me?" Ransom asked.

Norm clicked it and in a few seconds, it came to Ransom.

Ransom enlarged it, and though it was grainy, we could make out the lettering on the side of the vessel: Corsica Ferries.

I didn't know if I felt relived or terrified. We had a location.

Ransom whistled. "And here we are. They're somewhere off the island of Corsica—or possibly Sardinia—a mere five-hour crossing to Nice."

That was too close for comfort.

Ransom looked up the ports where the ferry departed to Nice. It could only be Bastia. So that's where Felix was staying. The only reason he would have chosen this port was to get quick access to us, but did he actually know about Fairhaven? The rest of the family would have to be on the lookout for lingering vessels in our bay.

Reinhardt notified Hollinger immediately. We knew he would have his people dispatch local authorities in cooperation with United States naval forces to arrest Felix and hopefully free our friends. But could it really be that easy? Felix may have been crazy, but he wasn't ever careless or stupid. No, he was taunting us, luring us again into a trap.

Then it hit me: not only did he know about Fairhaven, but he knew we weren't there. This was his way of getting us back there.

Twenty-four

THE NEXT DAY, ROSE INTENSIFIED her hovering and fussing over Ransom. He was clearly feeling better yet she urged him over and over to take it easy, to rest, to let her take care of him. It was as if she were his warden keeping him in solitary confinement. She continued to caution the rest of us not to overtax his energy or to upset him by getting him involved in our survival plans. I saw an increasingly possessive nature in her that I hadn't seen before, and I sensed that Rosalind and Reinhardt saw the same. She had been instrumental in Ransom's quick recovery and I'm certain he was grateful to her and that's why he allowed her to go overboard, to re-dress his largely healed wounds or take his blood pressure or insist that he sleep or rest quietly in bed away from the rest of us.

But I had to admit that I was starting to resent her intrusion in *my* life, in *my* life with Ransom, and started to think she was trying to manipulate him into loving her, Stockholm Syndrome style, and lose his feelings for me.

I knew Reinhardt and Rosalind saw my bitterness, but they said nothing, just let the situation unfold, although they kept a careful watch on my reactions. I was the most junior Draker in residence, the newest

Draker, and I didn't feel I should stand up to Rose who had been around for a very long time and who had been pivotal to the Drakers' survival as well as Ransom's. I knew Rosalind could have intervened but chose not to. I started to suspect she was testing me again, waiting to see if I'd lose my temper and personally confront Rose about her possessiveness, but if I had learned anything from the events of the past several months, it was that strength did not come from wearing your emotions on your sleeve. Rosalind had become very in tune with me, the Ruby who had evolved over the time since the fire. I also felt she trusted my judgment so she didn't lecture or caution me. However, when our eyes met, I could see that she understood my turmoil. React only to real dangers, I could hear her say, that psychic bond between us as she telepathically sent messages of advice and compassion my way. Perceived danger presented only complications that exacerbated our already-volatile situation.

Two days passed and Ransom continued to recover. Norm and Alice, not accustomed to being confined to a small space with strangers, became restless and impatient, seeming to intellectually understand why we needed to wait, but nevertheless not wanting to, not while Amos and Hannah were still out there.

I overheard Norm complaining to Alice about the danger Felix posed, worrying that Felix's twisted and resentful motives might drive Norm to do the unthinkable. Alice also started dropping passive-aggressive hints that every minute we delayed diminished the chance of our being able to save them.

I wanted them safe as well, but rushing to Corsica and right into Felix's plan was exactly what Felix wanted. For all I knew, he could have deliberately set up the Corsican Ferry in the background of the photo to let us figure out his location—or just as likely, his fake location—and when we arrived, he'd have a nasty surprise waiting for us. We'd had it with playing to his game; this time it was vital that we outwit him, make him rethink his strategy, do something that would rankle and unsettle him, weaken his guile and give us the upper hand. It was when he was challenged that his sick mind was susceptible to mistakes. In that moment of weakness, Felix would falter. It was our only hope.

The clock on the dining room wall read 8 p.m., but though it was hanging low to the horizon, the Icelandic sun still diffused golden daylight into the condo and over the mountains, which turned from orange to fuchsia as the hours passed. It finally set around midnight, leaving the ocean dark.

Rose, perhaps feeling the tension among us, had confined Ransom to his room, and the rest of us, all five, paced or sat or fluffed pillows in the living room, occasionally turning on the television and then turning it off again.

"OK," said Alice, breaking the silence. "Seriously. What's Rose's problem?" She was about to explode; I could see it in the vein throbbing in her neck. "Ransom is perfectly able to leave this place. The only thing that's really keeping us here is our own indecision." She glanced scornfully at Ransom's bedroom door. "What are we doing to help Amos and Hannah? We've been here two days. What are we waiting for?"

I had never appreciated her bluntness more than now. Reinhardt and Rosalind were having a short walk outside, so I was the only one left. It would have been a delight to spend some quality time badmouthing Rose but I knew that wouldn't get us anywhere and would only come back to bite me. We had to be a united front. Or at least appear to be one. "Alice, Felix expects us to act quickly and carelessly," I said. "We're trying not to play into his game so easily. It seems clear he's not going to harm Amos and Hannah until he thinks he can get us all or he would've done it long ago. They're his bait!"

Alice glowered at me.

I tried to laugh, "What I mean is, without them he has no way of luring us to him. Anyway, he's probably already moved away from the port in Corsica. Let's give Hollinger a chance to grab him first. I only hope that if he was in touch with the Corsican police, they don't botch the whole thing."

"More probably," Rosalind said, coming in the front door and taking off her jacket, "Felix would have paid the Corsican police to help him come after us. He needs extra manpower resources. The police in Corsica are largely Mafia. Felix has been involved with them for decades. Even back in the Cold War days, they had reciprocal agreements." Her face turned sour.

"Mafia?" Norm asked, his voice getting squeaky. "You think he has Mafia helping him? What's in it for the Mafia?" His face looked more worried and agitated than ever.

Ransom peeked out of his room and, not seeing Rose, he came out into the living room. "It's always about money or power," Ransom said.

Rose came scuttling from the kitchen and tried to steer him back into his room by putting her arms affectionately around his waist and whispering in his ear, but he lifted his shoulder to shrug her off and ducked away from her arms. He came and sat with us as if it were any normal conversation between normal people.

He stared at me as he spoke, our eyes meeting one on one for the first time in what felt like a long time. "He might have promised them inside information from the Defense Department, some foreign threat to America. They have money and are always in need of weaponry. Inside information always enhances munitions sales, very lucrative for organized crime."

I didn't hear a word he said.

"So what do you suggest?" Norm asked. "Let's at least agree to do something. It's better than just sitting around here. I say we go after him as soon as tomorrow. Reinhardt, can you arrange that charter you talked about?"

"Just a few more days ought to do it," Rose hissed back at Norm through an artificial smile. She looked like a cobra ready to strike.

"Tomorrow is fine with me," Ransom said firmly. "Rose is being overly cautious. I'm fine. I'm ready to travel."

I breathed out.

Ransom stood and came over to me where I was standing at the window. He grinned widely and punched me playfully on the shoulder.

Well, I thought, a punch on the arm wasn't exactly the sign of affection I was hoping for, but at least he stood up against Rose.

Rose and I exchanged dagger glances, but Rosalind defused the tension and came to our rescue.

"Rose," Rosalind said. "I agree that he's not ready for an all-out battle, but surely you must agree that he's strong enough to fly home. He can continue his recovery at Fairhaven where he'll be much more comfortable and where we have the resources to further coax Felix out of hiding. We can get a lot more accomplished from there."

At this, Ransom looked tentatively at Rose, negating his earlier assertiveness as though he were asking Rose for permission to go.

"Oh, all right then," Rose said. "It's against my better judgment but don't blame me if he relapses."

I couldn't tell for sure, but in a way, she looked relieved too. It seemed that being here, trapped in the lap of the mountains, was wearing on us all.

It was raining when our charter landed at Cote d'Azur Airport in Nice. My luck, I thought, wondering why it always to seem to rain when our charter flights landed there. It was like it was an omen of gloom, bad things to come. But gray and soggy or not, at least the familiar sight made all the Drakers let their shoulders down a bit.

In spite of the rain, I was glad to be back at home, too. Strange, I thought; the last time I landed here, I had no idea what would happen to me. I was afraid for my life, terrified of what Rose and Reinhardt would do to me. Everything was so secret, so tense. This time, although I still felt that sense of lurking danger, at least the danger no longer came from the people who were with me. Now, I felt protected in their presence, a conflicting undertone that made me feel disloyal to my real family, whom I still mourned, but whose memory was slowly fading.

I knew what was in store for me and what we were up against this time, but I was still afraid, not of the Drakers, but of an enemy that meant to harm us, an enemy whose actions were unpredictable and irrational, an enemy who was singularly focused on erasing us from existence. Given our secret identities, killing us would conveniently satisfy Felix's rage. Like magic, we'd evaporate into thin air, our identities and aliases gone without a trace. But we didn't want to disappear. We had reasons to live. And we weren't giving up without a fight. It was our turn to lure him to us.

The ease with which we cleared through customs intrigued me now, an art that the Drakers had perfected and into which I had been inculcated. It seemed obvious now that a greased palm helped us slip around where we needed to go. It was always so easy, so smooth, never more than a few standard questions, and no searches or luggage inspection. When I smiled and calmly walked away from Customs down a hallway and out through the sliding doors that separated arriving passengers from people who came to meet them, I felt like I'd been doing this for years. And there, standing under giant black umbrellas outside in the rain, were Rowan and Renegade. When they saw us, they walked briskly to greet us.

It was a quick reunion before we went to the parking area. They'd brought two SUVs because between the seven of us, and Norm and Alice's giant suitcases—which still perplexed me—we wouldn't have fit into one.

"You brought guests," Renegade said, stepping up to them to shake hands. He glanced down at their bags and his eyes widened. Alice, in particular, was a petite woman, and he didn't yet know her strength. "Let me help you with that," he said to her, taking the suitcase from her hand. Alice initially resisted but then she let go and smiled tightly.

As we walked out, we all kept an eye out. It wasn't unreasonable to think that Felix had people watching us even now. Not seeing anyone following us, we still went quickly to the cars. We were soaked by the time we reached them, and climbed in for the long drive back to Fairhaven.

Thunder and lightning added to the rain, slowing our drive. Norm and Alice strained to see through the fogged-up windows. Under normal circumstances, they'd have been greeted with sparkling Cote d'Azur scenery, the beautiful gardens dripping with begonia, some palms and cypress, but most impressive of all, the panorama of turquoise waters below the tiered, mountainous road. Yet all any of us saw were a few feet of winding road and cliff, a charcoal sky, and sheets of rain pelting the car.

Maybe Alice and Norm would be sorry that their time in Nice was so ugly, but I was grateful for the inclement weather. I knew it'd be harder for anyone to follow us, and if anyone were there, he'd be the only one on the road besides us. Felix had eyes everywhere but for now we appeared to be alone.

Finally, we turned up the private road that led to the villa. Rachel, looking chic as usual in a slim black sheath, greeted us at the door and warmly embraced first Rosalind then me. I'd missed her light British accent. An exuberant Roscoe raced in from the side room where the glass silo staircase stood. He clutched me so tight around the waist, I could hardly breathe. Rune and Riemes yelped and jumped on us, bounding about, their nails clicking on the marble, happily sensing our joyful reunion. My heart pounded with excitement as we held each other.

"I'm so glad to see that everyone is in one piece," Rachel said, grinning. "Cook figured you'd be hungry so she set up food for you in the west dining lounge. Your rooms are ready, too. And how is Ransom?" she asked him and went to his side. "Have the bullet wounds healed? Will it hurt if I hug you?"

He reached for her hand and pulled her close into a sisterly hug. "Still a bit sore but OK, really."

Rachel embraced him gingerly, her smile fading to a frown of concern as she touched the sling that took the pressure off the healing bullet wound at his shoulder.

"You should probably rest for a while," Rose said. Her harsh tone momentarily broke the happy atmosphere. "I'll bring some food to your room."

Rachel looked at Rosalind questioningly. Rosalind discreetly shrugged her shoulders and shook her head gesturing to Rachel not to ask why Rose was so irritated. Rose hurried off to the dining room as everyone's homecoming smiles melted.

Ransom looked over to me, Roscoe still with his arms tightly around my waist. Rune and Riemes inched closer to assess Ransom. They sniffed him cautiously, their ears back, but not growling or baring their teeth as they usually did with the Draker men. Ever so slowly they lifted their heads to nuzzle his hands, whimpering softly.

I smiled. The dogs must have sensed his vulnerability as they had with me that first day when I arrived. Roscoe and I understood. The dogs knew their job: safeguard family members who needed protection.

Rowan reached down to grab Ransom's small bag. The dogs growled menacingly at him. Their keen instincts still interpreted him as a potential threat. It seemed the dogs' instincts bore only two distinctions: vulnerable or threatening, nothing in between.

"OK, then. I'll take your bag up to your room later." Rowan dropped Ransom's bag and raised his hands in surrender as he stepped back.

Rachel turned her attention to Norm and Alice, greeting them with her warm smile.

"Welcome to Fairhaven," Rachel said. She leaned forward to kiss them on each cheek. "We have a room ready for you. I'll show you where it is. Normally, because the staircase is off the side of the mansion in a glass silo, you'd be able to get a lovely view of the grounds and ocean. Today, not, I'm afraid."

Norm and Alice appeared rather overwhelmed by the grandeur of the house. They looked in amazement at the high ceilings painted with superb artwork, the crystal chandeliers, the marbled floors and the exquisite furniture and accessories. But they politely said nothing.

Reinhardt and Rosalind looked amused at their reaction.

Reinhardt tried to put them at ease. "Our home is completely at your disposal," he said. "Rachel is our resident… designer and art curator we'll call her, and she will show you around after you get settled in your rooms. The men will take up your bags."

The dogs gave no objection as Rowan took one heavy suitcase and Renegade the other.

In Ransom's room, Roscoe and I helped Ransom take off his jacket and then his shoes, and helped him into sweatpants and a fresh T-shirt.

I kept looking around for Rose, feeling like I was cheating on her, then felt annoyed with myself for feeling that way.

Ransom's shoulder where he'd been hit by the bullet was stiff and swollen from so many hours without rest. He looked pretty out of it now that he was comfortable and in bed. Maybe Rose was right. He still had lots of healing and recovery ahead of him.

I handed his jacket to Roscoe to hang in his closet and sat on the edge of his bed. He took my hand in his. I leaned over him and kissed him. So many days apart made the gesture feel different, not as intimate. Ransom kissed me back but he kept his eyes open. I sat up and saw Roscoe looking on curiously, his expression a little disconcerted.

Of course, just then, Rose came into the room with the food she'd gone to get. Her voice was thick and dark. "I certainly hope you didn't contaminate the wound dressings, *Ruby*. His wounds aren't completely healed yet so are still prone to infection. You're putting him at risk again. You should have let me do this." She yanked up his shirt to examine him.

"Ouch," Ransom complained. "Take it easy, Rose."

I stared at him. His words were admonishing, but his tone was almost... teasing. Or did I mishear?

"Go on downstairs," Rose said. "I'm sure he wants some privacy while I look after this." She stared at him. There was some kind of energy disturbance between Rose and Ransom that unsettled me.

I looked at Roscoe and nodded my head toward the door and the two of us left for the stairwell.

"Come on Rune, Riemes," Roscoe called. But the dogs remained stationary by Ransom's side.

"Go on," Rose said to the dogs.

They replied to her with a low, throaty growl.

She looked shocked at the dogs' reaction. They approached Ransom closer and lay protectively at his feet. They had never growled at a Draker woman before. Roscoe looked back in amazement but shrugged and followed me down the stairwell to the dining room.

"Why are they protecting him from Rose?" Roscoe asked, his voice uneasy.

I shrugged and took his hand. I could tell that he knew something had changed significantly, something he didn't fully understand. My heart ached for him. I didn't know if he had been aware of the danger we were in. Perhaps Rachel or the men had told him about Felix's plan to annihilate us. It was probably also weird to see me and Ransom expressing feelings for each other beyond that of brother and sister, and Rose so angry, and the dynamic between the three of us so off. I didn't even get it myself.

I looked at him, wondering whether he understood jealousy. I would have to talk to Rosalind and Reinhardt about managing Roscoe's inse-curities, making sure that what we told him, and how we explained it, could be processed by him, still barely an adolescent.

The warm glow of candles on the buffet and the dining table flick-ered and cast dancing shadows on the walls while the harsh swishing torrents of rain whipped against the windows. Reinhardt, Rosalind, Norm and Alice were seated at the dining room table, eating sandwiches and tomato soup. Rachel stood at the buffet, arranging several cups of espresso onto a tray.

"There you are, my boy," Reinhardt said. "Come and sit with your mother and me."

It felt odd to hear Reinhardt refer to himself and Rosalind as mother and father and immediately I flashed back to my first minutes with them, and the fear. But now that I knew better, I easily saw the love and care in Reinhardt.

He came to our side and laid a reassuring hand on Roscoe's shoulder.

"Let me get you some food, darling," Rosalind said. "You look hungry. It's late for you to have dinner." She got up and heaped a plate with sandwiches and sweets that she knew he loved. "I think you're old enough. Would you like a café au lait?" She nodded over to Rachel who quickly made him one and brought it over.

Positioned between Rosalind and Reinhardt, Roscoe sat with his head down, not touching the food, his adoptive parents' hands on each of his slender young shoulders trying to shield him from the harsh reality of what we would have to tell him.

"Rune and Riemes are acting funny," Roscoe said. "Different toward Ransom. And Rose. Something bad happened while you guys were away. I know it. Something you're not telling me."

I was glad he didn't know about what we'd been up to; it was too much for a young boy to process. They probably told him we'd run into complications but no one had elaborated beyond that. Still, he was an intuitive youngster. Life had dealt him experiences that children shouldn't have to deal with. I looked at Rachel. She shook her head, as did Rowan and Renegade in turn.

Roscoe saw them, too, and his face went pale. "He's after us again, isn't he?" he whispered. "He killed my parents and now he still wants me. He wants to kill all of us. Doesn't he?" He searched our faces again, looking for reassurance, but saw only our apprehension.

"Roscoe," Reinhardt said. "We are going to be upfront with you as much as we can be. The man's name is Felix Szabo. He was responsible for the death of your parents." Reinhardt was fidgeting in his chair and looked to Rosalind for help.

Rosalind pulled Roscoe into an embrace. Her face was full of emotion, her motherly instincts going into overdrive. "Please, Reinhardt," Rosalind said, her voice quavering. "He's just a boy. We can send him away. We can keep him safe."

"I'm almost fourteen," Roscoe said. "I'm an excellent marksman. And I might be scared but I'm not a coward. I'm staying to help you. I know you'll fight and I'd rather die with you than live with losing my family again. Now tell me what's going on and what we're going to do about it."

His bravery brought tears to my eyes, and I would've bet to the others' as well, but I couldn't look at them or risk breaking down, which would only alarm Roscoe more. He had so completely accepted us as his family, me as his sister replacing his biological sibling whom he missed so desperately. Telling us that he'd rather die than lose us confirmed how dearly he loved us.

I realized then that I loved him, too. A heartfelt memory of my little brother Johnny wanting to be with me everywhere I went pierced my soul. So, too, Roscoe couldn't bear to be away from us. I felt a fierce guttural arousal, a resolve to defeat that threat that loomed over us all. I would kill Felix personally if I had to, so strong was my determination to protect this boy, my brother. When I finally dared to look up, I saw that same resolve in the eyes of every other family member in the room. We struggled to talk, to try to lighten the moment.

Fortunately, Alice came to our rescue. "Well, Roscoe," Alice said, "it's like this. All us older family members were spies during something called the Cold War, when the Russians had nuclear bombs that threatened America. We worked for the CIA and Felix was our boss. When the government treaties ended the arms race, he went crazy. Something in his head snapped when his department was disbanded and his spies were given new lives and identities. Now he's hunting down every one of us because in his head, we've all turned on him and our country." Alice went on. "Oh, right. And Ruby has fallen in love with Ransom and Rose is jealous and trying to steal him away." She smiled calmly then looked around. "Speaking of the devils, where are they?"

I looked into my lap and cleared my throat. I knew where they were.

Roscoe processed the information for several moments, looked around the table, then started to laugh. "No wonder the dogs are so mixed up," he said. "They know more than you think. How soon do you think it will be before Felix attacks?"

"That's just it," Norm said. "No one knows. But the kicker is, we've kind of turned the tables on him. He's holding two friends of ours as hostages and expects us to go after him, to rescue Amos and Hannah. Instead, we're going to let him come after us here. It could get a little sticky. Are you really sure you want to stay?"

Before Roscoe could answer, a *ping* came from Norm's phone. He pulled it from his pocket and looked at the screen. "Well, speak of the other devil," he said.

Twenty-Five

As if we didn't trust our own ears to hear the message, everyone got up and gathered around Norm's chair.

The text said, Welcome home! and the attached photo was of all seven of us meeting Renegade and Rowan in the welcome area of the airport. For some reason, Renegade and Rowan were not in the photo. Felix would've recognized everyone except Rose and now she was a target as well.

Looked like our gut instincts weren't wrong after all. Felix did indeed have people watching the Nice Airport.

But why hadn't they followed us to Fairhaven? The storm may have discouraged a chase, but knowing his cunning, there was more to this omission. I could only assume that he wanted to set up the battle to his own advantage. He would have it orchestrated down to the last gory detail. I understood that Felix took failure personally. Failure enraged him. It drove the animal inside him to hunger for retaliation. He wanted to make us suffer for upsetting his previous attacks.

In my mind, I could see Felix's face, wild with frustration, rage and mania as his taunting failed to lure us into his trap. He wasn't the only person frustrated. I looked at the elder former spies whose faces were taut and intense. At home in Springfield, Norm and Alice were accustomed to doing things their own way. Here, Felix was proving to be more complicated than they liked. Felix kept changing locations, probably thanks to the help of the Mafia, though we couldn't prove it. Norm and Alice's strategy had always been to swoop in quickly, hit hard and accurately, find their friends, and whisk them away to safety.

I could see by their faces that before this whole thing finished, no matter how it would finish, they would leave their signature on Felix.

When the next day came, I could see that now that we were home at Fairhaven, behind fortified walls and situated high on a peninsula cliff—which made us seem safe from attack by land or sea—our tension decreased slightly. But it didn't disappear completely. The August sun, dappled gardens, and the warm winds that blew off a tranquil ocean were restorative, calmed the savage rush of adrenaline that had burned through my veins for so long, and already after my early morning run, had restored some of my humanity and reason.

Ransom seemed particularly relaxed now that we were home, and it showed in his body and attitude. Rose on the other hand, continued to push herself on him but at this point it was entirely unnecessary. Her behavior had shifted from caregiver to almost feral animal. If I so much as came close to him, she snarled and snapped at me, so rudely and dismissively, it was as if I'd wronged her at her core. Falling in love was supposed to be a beautiful thing, but it seemed she had as well, and this was how she protected her catch.

Ransom didn't seem to love her attention, but he also didn't stop her from lavishing it. Hours passed with the two of them in his room and as the days went by, I came to realize that their relationship had evolved much as mine and Ransom's had, for its short life span. I didn't know what to make of their circumstances, but it was best for me to simply stay away.

A few more days passed and life at Fairhaven seemed almost normal. The rain that had so aggressively welcomed our return cleared to blue skies billowing with cumulus clouds. The temperatures were sultry and the wind stirred up the scent of exotic flowers from the garden. We took advantage of the serenity, enjoying our meals on the outdoor marble terraces in the splendor of Fairhaven's man-made paradise. But while we were more at ease than we'd been in a very long time, no one was entirely relaxed. No one sat all the way back in his chair. We knew this tranquility could be shattered at any time.

Roscoe seemed to take it all in stride: the discord among us, Norm and Alice's nervous and blunt demeanor, Rose's claim to Ransom's heart, and the dogs' sudden acceptance and protection of Ransom. To cope with everything, Roscoe spent loads of time practicing his archery and marksmanship, working at his studies with his private tutor, and frolicking with the dogs who soon relaxed their protective guard against Rose, maybe because Ransom was now well enough to fend for himself. Roscoe would run through the garden paths and throw sticks and balls and the dogs would bounce and rebound in delight, the sound of happy barking and Roscoe's laughter filling the garden and casting a spell of normality over the estate.

Even Norm and Alice smiled as they watched the joyful play of a young boy and his dogs. It was weird—this bubble we were in—but we had no choice but to carry on as normally as we could. We couldn't surrender to fear and sit around our little Eden just waiting for the snake to slither in.

One morning, Cook and her assistant set up breakfast on the west veranda, a heavily trellised spot draped in bright magenta bougainvillea. The terrace overlooked the Bay of Villefranche where sailboats and smaller fishing vessels dotted the crystal blue waters that went hundreds of feet below, and who, even at this early hour, were already making their way to the indigo waters of the Mediterranean. The balmy morning air caressed my skin as I took a croissant from the buffet set up against the salmon, stuccoed wall of the villa and joined Rosalind and Reinhardt, who were sitting under the large umbrella table peacefully enjoying their morning café au lait.

"Good morning, Ruby," Rosalind said. "Did you sleep well? Have you seen Ransom? How is he doing?"

I stared at them. Either she was baiting me or she genuinely didn't know that I'd essentially been barred from seeing him, and he didn't seem to object.

"I don't know," I said. "Rose won't let me near him." I tried to laugh it off, but I could tell from the way Rosalind was staring at me that she hadn't known what was happening and that I was hurt.

I sipped slowly at my cappuccino. The wind blew my hair over my face and into the foam of my coffee. I tried to giggle at this but was actually seething. I tried to breathe in the sweet air to calm myself and smiled as I wiped my hair off with a napkin so they'd know I was all right, grounded and in control. And I was. The situation would just have to take care of itself. The last thing we needed was to fight among ourselves. I couldn't let anything disrupt our solidarity. We needed to be united in our goal.

"I know what you mean," Reinhardt said, trying to soothe my ego. "She's been quite vicious, actually. She won't let us too close, either."

Norm and Alice walked up the steps to join us on the veranda. I had seen them from my bedroom window earlier that morning, out walking in the garden. Or not walking, but more patrolling the perimeter, peering beyond the stone barricaded walls out to sea, checking from every jut out and overlook. Fairhaven was perched high on a cliff with a sheer drop, but they still remained watchful and ill at ease.

"Did you enjoy the gardens?" Rosalind asked. "Cook puts on a splendid breakfast. I hope you're hungry. Please help yourselves."

Alice went to the buffet. She'd be pleased, I thought. Cook always had cream puffs, her specialty, so Alice couldn't complain about not having donuts. I hoped coffee and donuts would soothe her tense and ruffled feathers. I was sure she wished they were all back in Springfield at the diner and that they had never met us.

"Quite the place you have here," Norm said. He did a slow turn, looking around the lavish landscape then stopped when his gaze met Reinhardt's. It was clear he was ready for the explanation Reinhardt had promised. "So are you going to tell me how you guys afford this on a government retirement pension?"

"It's a long story, Norm," Reinhardt said. "Grab some breakfast first."

Norm turned and trudged over to the tureens. He lifted them one by one causing the savory aromas to waft over our way. Eggs, spicy breakfast sausages specially prepared for our American guests, and sweet buttery pastries.

Norm and Alice filled their plates and balancing them and their coffees, settled in at the table and got ready for their feast and the long-awaited story.

"Here's the short of it," said Reinhardt. "After the department was disbanded, I decided to leave the States. I moved to Avignon in Southern France. I had been stationed here for a short while back in the '60s and the old world charm and easygoing lifestyle won me over. I vowed that some day I would return and retire there.

"When it came time to take the retirement package, I hopped a plane. The money bought me a house. And to live, I got a job managing a winery. Easy friendly stuff. More like visiting with friends every day than a job. I met a wonderful woman who worked at the vineyard. We fell in love, married and had two sons. I was a content and happy man. Life couldn't get any better."

Reinhardt stopped for a moment and examined the back of his hand for a few seconds. He looked out to the garden before returning to Norm. "I had no idea that Felix had a score to settle with me. I had no idea that he had a vendetta against all of us." Reinhardt shook his head from side to side as if trying to shake away the terrible memory of what he was going to tell Norm next.

"Remember, I told Hollinger and you how he killed my family and how our neighbor was mistaken for me. Felix thought he had killed me too. He was very sloppy back then, too arrogant to see his mistakes. When I realized what had happened and figured out why, I went into hiding under a new alias, Reinhardt Draker." He huffed in disgust.

"You'd think the name had meaning for me, but I picked it up from a tombstone where my wife is buried. I realized that if I wanted to stay alive, I had to become someone else again. The identity the CIA gave me, my pension and my job, these were gone. They buried who I was with the man they thought was me—and my family." Reinhardt's voice was strained with emotion and his eyes grew teary from the pain of remembering his wife and young sons.

He tried to continue past the lump that formed in his throat. "I moved to Monte Carlo and worked in the casino, administrative and security work mostly.

"One day while having had far too many drinks with my coworkers, we started talking about the Rothschild estate. Those of us who worked for a living resented the rich and snooty casino patrons and we talked about what it must be like to be that rich. The Rothschilds were an obscenely wealthy family involved in banking, gold and diamond mining, and just about anything else that made the aristocracy wealthy at that time.

"When the Rothschild's daughter, Beatrice, was nineteen, she married Maurice Ephrussi, another wealthy industrialist. He was much older than her, probably married her for her money even though he was insanely wealthy himself. He was never faithful to her. Maurice was a gambler and a womanizer, sleeping around with any woman he met or could buy. He contracted a venereal disease and gave Beatrice syphilis, which rendered her unable to have children, which meant she was never able to produce an heir to their estate.

"But, that said, before she married him, she had a secret of her own. As a teen, she'd been defiant, impetuous and promiscuous. While she was away at her prestigious boarding school, she got pregnant. She managed to keep it a secret by paying off her headmaster, and her parents never learned about her pregnancy. The school even arranged the adoption. I suppose she hoped she could put all that behind her when she married Maurice. But it was a loveless marriage and after several years of unhappiness, they divorced, and she built this villa. When she died, she left the estate to the Académie des beaux-arts, the one caveat being that they do an extensive search for the illegitimate child she had borne and given up for adoption. If the child were found, the estate would award ten million dollars to the Academy and the house and grounds along with the remaining fortune would go to the child.

"Extensive DNA tests were carried out on anyone who thought he might have a claim. Drunk, and for a lark, my coworkers convinced me to go with them. It seemed like a harmless activity to occupy an afternoon. They were giving out champagne and pastries to those who donated their blood." Reinhardt chuckled at the memory.

"Wait, so you were a positive match?" Norm said. "An American spy turned out to be the son of a wealthy French woman? Friggin' fairy tale ending, you lucky bastard!"

Alice, for once, was speechless. She huffed in disbelief, pushed back her chair and got up to get another coffee and refill her plate with cream puffs.

"Lucky?" Reinhardt said. "You could say that. To make a long story short, after all the testing and legalities, and after I was finally settled in the estate—all the while working diligently to ensure my real identity was never released, not a single photograph, nothing—two years later, I started doing some investigation of my own. The first person I decided to look up was Rosalind in Quebec, but by the time I arrived in Quebec City, Felix had already targeted her family. Having nothing left, she decided to return here with me where the two of us continued our work to rescue the others. We knew he had to be stopped, but his whole plot seemed so far fetched, we were sure no one would believe it. There was no record of who we were then or now. Felix looked after erasing our pasts and we used that as an opportunity to remain anonymous.

"But in helping our former colleagues stay alive, there were a lot of failures. Fortunately, though, while Felix was slippery, now and then he made mistakes, got cocky, careless, and let loose ends slide. Those loose ends are the people we have here today at Fairhaven, the name I gave to the Rothschild–Ephrussi villa. They're my family now."

"So you have an estate and so much money that you can buy just about anything," Norm said.

"Anything but our safety," Reinhardt replied. He cupped his face in his hands and leaned over as he said the words. All the money in the world couldn't keep safe what he valued the most.

Ransom appeared on the veranda, dressed in exercise shorts, jogging shoes and a T-shirt. He raised his face to the sun and breathed in deeply."Good morning, folks," he said.

"Going for a jog?" I asked, trying to sound casual. I looked around for Rose. "Where's the warden?" I asked. The others smiled and chuckled silently.

"I escaped," Ransom said. "I'll be finished with my run before she even realizes what I'm up to. I need to start getting back into shape. Anyone want to join me?" The question was open ended, but he was looking at me.

"Maybe another time," I said. I was wearing a white, lacy, sleeveless dress and sandals and wasn't sure, even with him boring a hole through my eyes, if he still had feelings for me. And if he did, he had a very strange way of showing it.

Just then Rose rushed onto the veranda. "Has anyone seen Ransom?"

Ransom turned as soon as he saw her and leaped off the steps. He headed to the path, first in a burst of energy, running to get away from her, and then slowing to a gentler pace as he disappeared among the shrubs and flowers.

"Why didn't any of you stop him?" Rose demanded. She glared at us in that accusing way she had developed, like we were responsible for his slide into debilitation, which was actually no longer an issue at all.

Then Renegade burst outside waving a printed copy of a photograph. "You have to see this," he yelped. He put it in the center of the breakfast table for all of us to see.

It was a photograph of yachts moored at the Port of Nice, with one in particular sticking out: a large dark vessel that looked about one hundred feet long with a helipad on the upper deck. Among the smaller, pastel yachts, this one looked like a big black shark. On the stern it read, *For Patricia* in red lettering. Two passengers, like tiny dolls, were visible on deck. My skin instantly bristled with goosebumps. My mother's name—though not the name I knew her by. Felix was casting his line again.

Above us, in the blue sky billowing with fluffy, white clouds came the whapping sound of a helicopter. The sound and air vibrated through my body.

Then we saw it. It flew over the estate, piercing our protective bubble. Shielding our eyes, we looked into the morning sun to try to see it, but it was too blinding, and then the helicopter was gone. We looked at each other in alarm. The timing was too perfect.

"Let's not jump to conclusions," Renegade said. "It's not as if this is the first helicopter to fly over here. We're the closest airport to Monaco so business types and royals use helicopters all the time."

I was shaking. "For Patricia," I murmured. "Can you enlarge the photo so we can see the people on the deck?"

"It won't be clear," Renegade said, nodding, "but let me try. Are you thinking it might be Norm and Alice's friends?"

"I'd bet money on it," Norm said.

Renegade gave us the thumbs-up and returned to the secret computer room below ground.

The whap of a helicopter filled the air again.

"So, Reinhardt," Norm said, leaning forward on an elbow. "How exactly do you intend to protect this place?

Twenty-Six

RENEGADE WAS RIGHT. It wasn't that helicopters weren't part of the normal skyscape. They came fairly often through the airspace above the estate, bringing the elite from Monaco over to nearby Nice or Cannes. But it was clearly one helicopter crisscrossing above us as if it were looking for something on the cliff-side grounds of Fairhaven.

Reinhardt cautioned us not to panic; it could easily be a tourist charter just trying to get a better look at the grandeur of the private estate. It was common for several helicopter charter companies to provide aerial views of the charming villages of the French Riviera, its coastline and the vastness of the azure Mediterranean. He said this in the low tones of someone who didn't believe his own story, but we went along with his caveat and kept calm.

Everyone was still clustered at the table, not speaking, nobody eating, when Ransom returned from his run, breathless, and mounted the veranda steps.

Roscoe and his dogs were close behind also wanting to find out what was going on.

Rose watched him with a scowl as he went past her without even looking her way.

"So what's with all the helicopter traffic?" Ransom asked.

Rose furrowed her brow. "It's far too soon for you to be—"

Ransom turned to her, his expression clearly annoyed, and curtly cut off her off. "Not now, Rose."

She closed her mouth and leaned back. She looked slightly shocked to be spoken to in such a way by her pet patient. Inside, I was gloating, though it didn't mean any kind of victory for me, or for us.

She turned her attention to the low-flying craft, its blades sending vibrations that shattered the serenity of the morning. She, like the rest of us, wasn't buying Reinhardt's tourist story. Clearly, Felix had found us. Not only was our safe house no longer secret, it looked like an attack was imminent.

"Felix is harbored at the port in Nice," I said to Ransom. "It's looking like he's inviting us aboard."

"Well," Norm said, jumping up and throwing back the dregs of his coffee, "let's take him up on his offer. We can't just sit around here."

"I'm in," said Alice. "Let's at least check it out. Anyway, I imagine there's lots to see in downtown Nice. Must be nice this time of year." She said the words ironically; this was no vacation, and she and Norm had had it with Felix's baiting. "Maybe we can get a better look. See if the people on the deck really are Amos and Hannah. And if they are…"

"Or maybe we first see how desperate Felix is?" I said. "It seems he's starting to crack a bit, showing us his hand. If we just give Renegade some more time to figure out what he's up to, we may have more to go on to mess his plans up."

Alice eyed me appreciatively.

Her acknowledgement made me feel warm, as though I'd arrived. As though I were an equal.

"I still think we should try to figure out what we're up against," she said. "It changes things if we're fighting off five or six versus a whole army."

She had a point. We had no idea how many people Felix had aboard his yacht or how many other forces he had at his disposal. I remembered what Ransom had said about Felix's involvement with organized crime. Did he have their support? Could he call on them at a moment's notice?

But still, it seemed important to hold Norm and Alice back for now. We'd been ignoring Felix's taunts for so long, I suspected he wasn't sure if or when we'd show up. That must have been why he was sending all the messages, dropping clues, and quite obviously, desperately using every possible means to get us to come to him. First, the welcome home message, then the yacht photo, and now the helicopter.

I snorted to myself. It was like a child needing his parents' attention and, when he didn't get it, resorting to destroying the house just to get anything out of them. Then again, if he was doing all this flying over Fairhaven, he might have just gotten too frustrated waiting for us and was going in for an attack.

"Will this help?" Roscoe asked, holding up his cell phone. "The helicopter was flying so low, I thought I could see whatever was written on it, but the sun was right in my eyes, so I took a video instead."

"Roscoe, you are so smart!" Rosalind exclaimed. She hurried over to him and embraced him tightly, kissing him on the forehead. I anticipated a sort of, "aw Mom, c'mon," objection while he pulled away from her—my little brother Johnny would have totally reacted that way—but Rosalind wasn't his mother.

He grinned, clearly enjoying the accolades of his surrogate parent.

Reinhardt also smiled proudly at him. "Let's see what Renegade can make of it," he said. "He's probably already got something on the yacht photo."

Everyone got up and followed Reinhardt, who let Roscoe lead, down to the control center, the dogs tagging protectively along, snuffling around our ankles. This would give us some answers, and then we'd be armed with enough knowledge to either enjoy the rest of the day, or start getting ready for the inevitable.

Roscoe looked proud that he was helping us against Felix. I felt afraid for him though, because his clever move might have been the leverage he would need against Rosalind's decision to send him away.

Norm and Alice followed watchfully. No longer having to maintain their country bumpkin act, it was obvious they'd been around long enough to see wealth of this magnitude, but it was also good that they could finally see the technology and the lengths to which the Drakers had gone in order to pursue Felix over the past several years. They would be impressed, I'm sure. They'd thought they were on top of Felix's two malicious assaults back in Springfield, but their actions were child's play in comparison. All that they'd feared their former boss was capable of was finally coming to fruition. Circumstances had tangled all of us together in our common goal of bringing him down. I was glad they were here. They were a handful, but they were trained in espionage and knew Felix well enough to consider his strategy.

I hoped, as we journeyed down the dark stairwell to the control room, that we'd get the answers we needed from the picture and video. I was worried about Amos and Hannah, but truthfully, I was worried for us all.

When we got to the room and spread out around Renegade's terminal, I felt calmer. He really knew computers, and though he was an odd man, and had loud taste in shirts, he truly seemed like a chess player: able to think ahead of his opponent—several steps ahead. This room was, in large part, his doing; something he built after he joined the Draker fold.

Ransom leaned over and the two of them began whispering tensely, pressing buttons and conferring. I nudged Norm and whispered, "These two know what they're doing. We'll be all right." Lucky for us, Ransom wasn't just technologically gifted, his experience at the CIA and knowledge of the inner workings of Felix's department at the Archives, helped him refine the computer programs Renegade had developed. That's when the facial recognition program, which monitored everything on the Internet, was customized and installed. He and Renegade also developed the grounds' monitoring system so nearly every square inch of the house and grounds could be seen at any time. They'd even positioned cameras to face out to sea so they could see the vessels in both the Bay of Villefranche to the west and the Bay of Beaulieu to the east.

Not to mention the room itself, which was seemingly impenetrable. Reinhardt was explaining a few of the safety precautions to the elder duo and gestured to a wall that I'd always thought was just a wall.

"We built a tunnel a few years ago that leads to an internal sea-level cavern. There, we keep a high-speed power boat large enough for all of us and six additional people." He smiled. "This villa is extremely well-protected, but on the off chance it did get breached, we'd always still be able to get out."

My mouth fell open. These people never ceased to surprise me.

Ransom gestured to Roscoe who came trotting over. "Our buddy here took a video of the helicopter," Ransom said, grinning.

Roscoe handed it to Renegade. A few clicks, and Renegade had the video transferred onto the computer and enlarged on the monitor.

He whistled. "And there we go," he said. The logo was AH with a gold circle around it. There was no other marking on the craft, not an ID number, not a name, nothing. That clearly didn't bother Renegade, who was happily clicking away. "OK, the chopper was leased from Azure Helicopter Tours in Nice. So now... A few little easy moves, and... Voila!" He leaned back with his hands behind his head.

Renegade had hacked into their computer system and had found the PDF of a contract. It had been signed by someone whose last name was Z-something, the signature illegible but for the firm Z that began the name. We had our proof: the chopper had been contracted by Monsieur Szabo, not exactly a surprise to us. But it had been too easy. We had him. We knew it was him, but was that exactly what he wanted us to do?

Norm was breathing impatiently and Alice seemed to be gathering herself together, getting ready to rush out and storm the yacht, drawn like a moth to a flame.

"I say we drive into Nice," Norm said. "Or I'll just go on my own, scout out the yacht, and get us more information."

Rosalind was shaking her head. "Too dangerous," she said. "Ruby's right. Let his mind marinate and when he's well pickled, he'll be much easier to take down."

I could almost feel Rose's hot breath as she fumed behind me. "What's the harm in looking around? I'll go with him. We'll just be a couple of tourists admiring the expensive boats in the harbor." She smiled winsomely and hooked her arm into Norm's.

"Hey, sister," Alice said. "You've already got your hooks into Ransom, leave my Norm alone. You ain't goin' nowhere without me." She not so gently removed Rose's arm from her husband's. Norm let the women handle him, looking mildly pleased.

Ransom's eyes flickered over me and settled on Rose. "Then I'll go too," he said. "So at least we're paired off. It's not as easy as just disguising ourselves. And Norm, you don't know the city and the harbor like I do. Anyway, a day of leisurely sightseeing should do me good. Right, Nurse?" He put his hand on Rose's shoulder and smiled down at her. Rose kissed it and smiled back.

My heart sank. Ransom had obviously made his choice. Or he hadn't, and this was just a friendly exchange between two close "family members," but I knew that if I believed that, someone should try to sell me some swamp land stat. But even if he didn't want me, I still had to live with the fact that my heart had opened itself to him, and it'd be a while before I could close it again. That said, I didn't like him going on this sleuthing mission, not so much because he was going with Rose, but because Felix was so unpredictable. I had a terrible knot in my stomach. I feared for them both.

"Be well-armed and keep your distance," Reinhardt said. "He'll have the harbor heavily patrolled with his own men."

"I'll change my clothes and get my Glock," Ransom said. "You don't mind if I drive, do you, Rose?"

The excited smile on Rose's face told him she had no objections. Maybe she considered it a date.

He pressed the fingerprint sensor pad by the door and the panel retracted into the wall. It opened and Rose followed him to the narrow stairs that led back up to the first floor level. A painful knot formed in my throat but I swallowed hard and tried to look neutral, at ease with a plan that felt wrong.

Norm and Alice hurried behind them. First they needed to go to their rooms to get their disguises and firearms. Alice was clearly delighted. "Always wanted to go to Nice," she said.

"I'll get the SUV and pull it into the driveway," Reinhardt said. Rosalind, Roscoe and I joined him as he left the computer room and waited in the foyer until the foursome returned from their rooms.

Ten minutes later, we were gathered together in the foyer. "Don't any of you worry," said Ransom, hoisting his bag onto his good shoulder. "We'll be careful, treat this like any reconnaissance mission and we'll be home in time for dinner." I couldn't understand why, but while he addressed all of us, he was looking right at me. I had no idea what game he was playing, like, what, he wanted me *and* Rose? I didn't work like that.

The four went out the door and got into the car. I waved with the others reluctantly as the car drove away from the house, watching it as the gates opened and the road beyond swallowed them, taking them out and away from Fairhaven's protection.

The iron gates banged closed and startled me from my thoughts. My heart jumped and I had to wait for it to calm down. I looked at my watch. He'd said they'd be home by dinner, but that was a long time from now.

Reinhardt paused before going back into the mansion and typed out a long text message. "Hollinger needs to know what's going on here," Reinhardt said when he saw me watching him. "We could use all the help he can give us. Plus, he has a vested interest. After all, Felix killed two of his men."

"You think he might come here to Saint-Jean-Cap-Ferrat?" I said. "We could probably use the reinforcements." My stomach knotted up again as I pictured the yacht. I imagined Amos and Hannah inviting all of us aboard and then and black, sickening feeling of disaster caused me to shake the image away. I was just oversensitive, I told myself. Everything would be fine.

Rosalind went off into the house and disappeared behind the heavy wooden door.

Reinhardt, however, just stood in the cobbled driveway, looking out at the side grounds. He pulled out his phone, typed out another message, put the phone back in his pocket, then took it out again.

Rowan and Rachel came around from the garden to talk with him, returned to the house, then came out again with items they then brought to various other parts of the property, and then went back to Reinhardt for further instructions.

They appeared to be busy with details—security details that I wasn't part of—so I left them to their work.

I was going around to the other side of the house when I heard barking. Roscoe was in the garden, practicing his moves with his Canne de combat, the instructor who also served as his tutor. The clicking and tapping of the poles and the man and the boy lunging and squatting in offense and defense, made Rune and Riemes hover close, their ears back, releasing a bark when the instructor gained an advantage that made Roscoe step back. Despite being admonished to "go lay down," they kept leaping to Roscoe's side, muscles tight and tensed. When his instructor delivered a particularly heavy blow to the stick that made Roscoe fall back, the dogs' lips retracted and they growled. But the instructor just laughed, helped Roscoe to his feet, demonstrated the proper technique and they went at it again.

It seemed that everyone was busy doing something but me. I felt adrift and irritable. I should have gone with them. Instead, I was wandering around in a haze, feeling useless and alone. I started down the garden path, not being able to make up my mind in what direction to go, what to look at. The helicopter had abandoned its fly over. All was still and normal, too still, too normal.

Down at the end of the estate, by the stone stairs and the temple, the ocean breezes blew softly, warmed by the sun that inched higher and higher into the sky. Rowan was there setting up a tripod. A triangular case lay a few feet away below the stairs, hidden partially out of view in the bushes that framed the base of the monument. I wanted to find out what he and Rachel were so preoccupied with. I approached and gestured toward the tripod. "What is that contraption for?"

"A little discouragement for those who don't respect barriers," Rowan said. He turned around and looked at me, squinting in the sunshine. "We're setting up extra armament around the estate. It will be concealed so as to not be obvious. If we were caught short-handed and off guard, there would always be a means of self-defense nearby. This one's an automatic with a swivel stand."

It looked like the one Felix had at the farm, the one he'd used to kill Robert and Myrtle. And Christian. The memories came flooding back. Now the situation was reversed. We would be the ones who would be spraying round after round of ammo at whoever dared to enter. That's what life as a Draker was about, something I was now more aware of than ever: defense and offense. It was incomprehensible that we had to live this way all because of one man with a vendetta.

I bent down to help Rowan, and for the next several hours, he took me around and showed me where he had set up protection points that he and Rachel had been working on, explaining in detail how each weapon operated. Considering the fire power stashed around the property, Fairhaven could be considered a war zone. Prudent perhaps, but the thought of the kind of destruction that could result from it saddened me. Guns in paradise. Such a travesty.

We were ready to return to the house when we heard a commotion over by the entry gate. The dogs ran barking and growling to the bars. Reinhardt and Rowan also ran toward the guard hut with their rifles pointed. I wondered where they'd been keeping their rifles so they could grab them so quickly.

"*Quel est le problème?*" Reinhardt asked the guard on duty.

"*Le député prétend qu'il a besoin de vous voir—de toute urgence,*" the guard answered.

"*Comment s'appelle-t-il?*" Rowan asked.

"*Monsieur Hollinger,*" the guard replied.

Reinhardt stepped backward to view the car idling by the gate. He nodded at the guard, "*C'est bon. Nous pouvons le laisser entrer.*"

The guard pressed the electronic release to open the iron gates and a single Citroen police vehicle rolled forward and stopped in front of Reinhardt and Rowan.

Hollinger stepped out. "I got your message," he said. "DND had already reported sightings, and I was here in Nice." He grimaced, and I wondered if it was just from the stress of continuing to hunt down Felix.

"Does that mean you have your people watching out for our group who have just gone into town?" Reinhardt asked.

Hollinger pulled off his sunglasses and squeezed his eyes shut, perhaps against the bright sun. He pressed the bridge of his nose. Rowan and Reinhardt looked at each other.

"Hollinger?" Reinhardt said again. "Tell me that you have your people looking after them. This is such a fragile situation, knowing your people are on it would reassure us tremendously."

"We've been watching your group," he said. He took a deep breath. "Szabo never fails to surprise us. He has a way of anticipating our every move."

Reinhardt's jaw tensed. "Tell me."

"Norm, Alice, Ransom and a pretty brunette I hadn't seen before were walking along the pier snapping pictures when a hoard of what looked like hooligans swarmed them."

Reinhardt's face tightened. "Where are they now?"

"They overpowered Ransom and pulled him onto a yacht," Hollinger said. "We managed to get to Norm and Alice. They're shaken but fine. They'll be here shortly. The local police are getting a statement from them." He paused, closing his mouth against the next thing he was going to say.

"Rose, the brunette. Where is she?" Reinhardt asked.

Hollinger's nostrils flared and he looked Reinhardt in the eye. "She was extremely brave. She fought well and hard, but there were just too many of them. It looked like an exuberant gathering, a bunch of people swarming together, so no one saw anything. Turns out one of them shot her, with a silencer. I didn't even realize she'd gone down until we got to Norm and Alice, and your friend was lying on the side of the pier. The paramedics worked on her a long time, but… It was just too late." He touched Reinhardt's arm. "I'm very sorry, Reinhardt."

Rosalind, Rachel, Renegade and I all stood in shock at the news. Rose was dead, Ransom had been taken, and Norm and Alice somehow had gotten away.

"But why didn't the authorities board the yacht and go get him, and maybe Amos and Hannah as well?" I asked. I blurted out the question, still trying to comprehend what had happened and why they had killed Rose. It hadn't sunk in yet. No, there must be some kind of mistake.

"By the time we got there, ascertained the situation, tended to Rose and spoke quickly to Norm and Alice, the yacht had pulled anchor and gone out to sea," Hollinger said. "Felix must be working with local forces because in that short time, he managed to evade us. You don't worry, though. Felix will show himself again. And this time, we will get him."

My emotions were numbed but my body took over; my muscles were trembling and tears escaped from the corners of my eyes. Rose had done nothing but fall in love, and now she was dead. No one deserved that. We were family, we had all had suffered personal losses, so our bond, however strained it might have been for silly reasons, was firm. We counted on each other for protection, for support, but most of all to replace the families that Felix had taken away from us. Now Felix was picking us off one by one, trying to get what was left of us. I felt then so scared, so frightened, I thought I would never feel safe again. He was going to kill us all.

Our black SUV came roaring up the private drive with Norm and Alice inside. The guard opened the gate, and they skidded to a stop behind the Citroen. The two got out and slowly approached, seeing in our solemn faces that we knew all about what had happened. They stormed over to Hollinger. "We didn't know it was a trap but you must have. Why was there nothing you could do?" yelled Alice. There was blood spattered over her white blouse and striped shorts.

"We should have looked like ordinary tourists," Norm said. "We were within a hundred feet of the black yacht. There were people on board but we couldn't get close enough to see them—especially since we tried not to look in the direction of the boat. As soon as we heard the engines engage, we knew something was happening. In seconds, we were surrounded by men, so many of them I couldn't count. Alice and I knifed a couple who grabbed us and we ran a ways down the pier, climbed up onto another yacht where the crew immediately offered to help and called the harbor police. We saw the whole thing, the attackers pulled their guns, and Rose—she was fierce—fighting off the whole crowd of them. But in the end, she got hit and we saw her go down. Next to her were four guys holding Ransom down. There was nothing he could do. He was overpowered. As soon as they saw the police approaching, they dragged him up onto the *Patricia*. It pulled away from the pier while we ran back to try to save Rose. Alice did CPR until the paramedics got there. But it was too late."

"Where is she now?" Rosalind asked. Her face was tear-stained and her expression was pure grief. "We have things to do, arrangements to make."

"The temple," Roscoe started to say. "We should spread her ashes here. My parents will welcome her and take care of her." He looked so sad, so lost. I knew how he felt about his temple, how he'd made it the place where he could always talk with his parents, where he felt a spiritual connection, where their voices always carried on the wind and their memories lived on in his heart. I remembered his words, "The temple is where I go to remember, and sometimes to cry."

A painful lump lodged in my throat. At the temple, at the precipice, where the Fairhaven gardens terminated and gave themselves up to the sea, is where that part of me that died lingered on and where the white rose that carried my former self to eternity would be her talisman and my pledge of love to her forever. "Kathleen too," I whispered.

"You were right," Alice said. "We should have let Felix come to us."

Hollinger was looking around, surveying the grounds. "What is this place?" he asked with incredulity. He looked back to Reinhardt for an explanation.

"This is my inheritance," Reinhardt said. "I named it Fairhaven. It's our home." Reinhardt pointed to the iron lettering on the gate, RD. "It's where the Drakers intend to take a stand. We've lost enough. Felix will have to put up one hell of fight to take this place down."

Twenty-Seven

IT SEEMED NO MATTER WHERE WE WENT, we couldn't hide from Felix's wrath. He took great pleasure wounding us physically and emotionally at every turn. I was suffering, hurting inside. Rose was a Draker and the Drakers were my only connection to something that resembled a family. I felt guilty for resenting her for loving Ransom. Ransom was a handsome, charming man, easy to become captivated with. I should have been more understanding. Now that she was gone, I felt a unique pain, like what I might have felt if I'd lost an older sister. I didn't know her well, or even like her, but there was love there based on our common need, the love and security of belonging to a unit that supported you unconditionally without question or reason, financially, physically and emotionally. I guessed that was what defined family. And what we had with each other was as close as any of us would ever come to: that real bond we'd lost with our own families. This was what we were about. We were Drakers, creating a new existence together, and in that effort, creating a family bond that depended on each person to function and stay strong, something Felix was exploiting so he could finally finish us off.

But I saw it now, clearer than ever. Our strategy was flawed. We kept forgetting that what would truly bring him down was to go on the offensive, to dig into Felix's insecurities where his soul was starved, and recognize and play into how that unfulfilled longing in him was what had tragically mutated into insanity.

The stronger the Drakers became, the angrier Felix got. His lifetime of loneliness was driving him to kill us off, all in the name of political betrayal. Wounded adults were no different than wounded children. I'd learned this in my first year of study, and this, what he was doing, was lashing out 101.

At some level, I wanted to feel sorry for him, have empathy for him as a fellow hurting human being, but he'd destroyed my life and the lives of everyone around me, blaming us for his own suffering, and even though I knew it would benefit our cause and probably help us bring him down more effectively, I just couldn't. It wasn't my fault that history had corrupted the present. It wasn't my fault that my parents had a secret and dangerous past. It wasn't my fault that the sins that robbed him of love and security drove him to incomprehensible actions.

But one thing was certain. I wasn't going to let Felix influence who I had become or corrupt me to become like him. Yes, Kathleen was gone forever, but underestimating Ruby Draker would be his downfall. My dream of being a psychologist wasn't dead yet; I was the body of my experiences. Suddenly, I had a new admiration for the Drakers' strength, and I knew I'd fight to hold on to it to the death.

No, I thought, as those around me murmured among them. I was wrong. I did have empathy for him. I felt sorry for him because he would never get what he wanted. Never. Felix thought that killing off those agents who had abandoned him like he felt his parents had done would somehow soothe those wounds of loss and anger, that his retributions could right all the wrongs done to him. But none satisfied him, so he needed more, then more. He killed like an addict needed drugs, the fix lasting only temporarily until he needed the next.

I had to better understand what drove Felix, from where he'd arrived at his need to try to satisfy his feelings of abandonment and resentment.

At dinner that evening, no one spoke much, but in my goal to get to know better what made Felix tick, I had to ask Norm or Hollinger, both of whom could reveal some of his past. Let the snake in, I told myself. I wasn't afraid of it anymore.

"What was Felix's life really like before he came to the CIA?" I asked.

Norm and Hollinger looked up, first at me in surprise, then at each other. Both shifted uncomfortably in their chairs. I knew that talking about the Cold War days stirred up old and unhappy memories, but this was the only way to get inside Felix's warped thoughts.

"Well, Madame Freud," Hollinger said playfully before thinking about something unpleasant and letting out a long disgusted huff of air. "Psychoanalyzing a bastard like him would take years."

I could see that this was going to be hard, but I was firm. We were sitting around the large dining room table in the glass-framed sun room, the sun hovering low over the water, its shadows causing eerie shapes to crawl along the walls. Reinhardt ran his fingers through his hair as he always did when things bothered him, Rosalind sat with her back straight and her face tight, and Renegade hung his head low. Rowan reached over to put a hand on Renegade's shoulder, and Rachel got up to get coffee for the table. Roscoe looked at Norm and Hollinger and waited eagerly for what Hollinger was about to say.

Norm made a fist and pounded it on the table, causing everyone to jump. "Tell her, Hollinger," Norm shouted. "All of us saw the signs and did nothing to stop him. We just tried to hide from it."

Hollinger closed his eyes, something I noticed he did when he had to keep going in an unpleasant moment. "Felix never married," Hollinger said, "not for lack of trying, but women just didn't like him. You could see it in his eyes, his desperation for companionship, for a pretty girl on his arm, but he never found anyone. So he forced himself on them. It was an obsession with him. He came into the employ of the CIA as a bachelor, no siblings, and as far as I know, only a father who'd spent most of Felix's life in jail for beating Felix's mother to death, leaving him alone at a very young age. Doesn't get much worse than that."

"What else do you know about him?" I asked.

"He was a hard man to understand," Norm said. "Not a likable person in any way. He was always distant and guarded. For us as agents, he expected us to follow orders and meet mission objectives. Said we had to be masters of our own destiny. We needed to get ourselves out of situations when they went sour. But the few times we got stuck and thought we were doomed to life in a Soviet prison or a firing squad, he'd come through at the last minute and bring us home. Then there was that one time you know about, Ruby. That was no gesture of goodwill. You know the price your mother had to pay for his 'help'."

"Is that what you think he wants us to do now?" I asked. "For us to come through at the last minute to save our own people?"

"Probably," Hollinger said. He paused, looking like he was starting to think about what Felix expected a rescue to look like, how we might go about it, and how he could counter our actions and kill us all.

"What are you thinking, Ruby?" Rosalind asked me. "You can't possibly think that Felix is going to let us board the yacht, punch down a few of his people, snatch his hostages and just leave."

"No," I said slowly, "but I'm wondering whether we could entice Felix to bring them here to us. Hollinger, I know you said that Felix's mother was murdered but was Felix's father released from prison? If yes, is he still alive? Because maybe, if he's reformed enough and could be reasonable, he could be enticed to share something with us about Felix's mother, some memory that Felix wants to cling to, to help us catch his son. And if Felix knew his father was here, and he hadn't seen him since he was a child, he might be compelled to see him, to get some closure about why his father beat his mother enough to kill her. That kind of confrontation would be valuable and would weaken Felix immeasurably."

"His father was sentenced to twenty-five years for domestic homicide, so unless he did something that got him locked up again, I suppose he's out now," Hollinger said. "I'll have my staff check it out."

"Never mind," Renegade said, waving his hand. "I'll get that information easily enough. But, Ruby, why do you think this is a good idea?"

"It's like this," I said, "Felix seems to have deep unresolved issues from his childhood, which would make sense given how he effectively lost both his parents when he was small. In a way, he's a bit like all of us," I said. "He had a family snatched away from him, too. So, at the CIA, as long as his agents gave him purpose and belonging, he was fine. But when they opted to leave, he felt betrayed and abandoned all over again. That kind of emotional pain never leaves a person and Felix exhibits the traits of someone who is affected by this pain every day of his life. Reuniting him with his father, no matter how much he might hate him for what he did, might just send him over the edge."

"That's all very cleverly deduced, Ruby, but how does that help us rescue Ransom, Amos and Hannah?" Reinhardt asked.

"Because on our turf," I said, "we make the rules. Isn't that what he's doing by trying to lure us to the yacht?"

"You think he'll just come here when we tell him that we have his father? So easily like that?" Alice said. "He must hate him for killing his mother. I'm not convinced that your strategy is sound. But then again, it's not like we have other options."

"There is a lot of supposition in this plan, Alice, I know. But you're right. We don't have a lot of options. I think, then, if he does want to come, in exchange for an opportunity to get back at his father, he has to pay a toll," I smiled. "His hostages for access to his father. And the only access is here at Fairhaven."

"OK, but how would we get his father here? The CIA would never allow a convicted felon to hold a passport," Norm said.

"They would if the Defense Department cleared it," Hollinger interrupted him. "I have the authority to allow it. Furthermore Szabo knows it."

"Well, this sounds just wonderful," Rosalind said, her voice thick with sarcasm. "Let's invite a convicted criminal who killed his wife in a drunken rage to join us in our home. We'll have tea!'"

"If it's the only way we can get Ransom released without getting killed ourselves," I said, "maybe we should try to make it happen. When the three of our guys are safe back here at Fairhaven and Felix is in custody, we can send his father home again. And this time we have Hollinger to make sure that nothing goes... amiss." I shot a warning look at Hollinger. He had let plans go bad before. If he let us down this time, we'd all be finished just like Felix wanted. I didn't really feel comfortable putting my trust into Hollinger, but short of our launching an open attack on the yacht, which was doomed to fail, I couldn't think of anything else to do.

Renegade retreated to the computer command center and before we finished our coffees, he was back with the full status of Demetri Szabo, Felix's father and convicted felon. It seemed that he had been paroled for many years and was living in a shabby apartment in Pittsburgh. "What I couldn't find is any evidence as to whether Felix has been in touch with him," Renegade said.

I figured whether he'd visited or not, Felix would have certainly known his father's location. I tried to imagine into Felix's life further: being raised in an orphanage hardened him against his humanity. To protect himself from further emotional pain, it seemed likely he would not have opened that particular wound by having a relationship with his father. I felt it was safe to assume they hadn't been in touch.

But then again, once his father was dangled in front of him, it could possibly ignite some kind of desire to reconnect with his only living parent if only to drill some answers out of him. This really could go either way. Understanding their relationship and presupposing Felix's reaction to it would help us determine his vulnerability. When we knew what buttons to push, we would have him at the disadvantage we needed.

No one actually said it, but I could tell that it had been decided: Demetri would be brought to Fairhaven, and it would be made clear to Felix that Demetri had some information about Felix's mother that had been haunting him all these years that he wanted to share with his son. This twist of events would hopefully elicit a reaction from Felix.

Hollinger excused himself and began making calls to arrange for Demetri to be flown to Nice. After he was conveniently installed at Fairhaven, the rules of the toxic game Felix was playing would change drastically. Hopefully, with a new player in the game, a player Felix never would have suspected could come onto the scene, he'd play right into our trap.

Still, looking around the room, I knew that as brave as the Drakers were, we were not enthusiastic at the thought of what might come next. Too much had happened. We knew enough to never take things for granted, that anything could go wrong and we'd have to take great care to be ready for the unexpected. Things had changed so dramatically in such a short span of time. Death of several members of our group was bad enough, but now we were facing the destruction of our home. I thought about all the guns Renegade had placed around the grounds and imagined shell casings and thick smoke, burned skin, death. I shivered and shook my head. He'd blacken the beautiful gardens and precious artifacts. He'd char the peninsula. That's what grief could do, I thought, destroy all that was beautiful in life trying to find a home for itself.

I tried to think calmly about our next steps as I quietly said my good nights and went to my room. By the morning, we'd have a house guest, the man who had spawned the evil that was Felix Szabo. As I brushed my hair, I looked around at the lavish details of the furniture in my room. I had come to accept it as my room now. It felt serene and comforting. It was my safe space.

I looked out the window. I thought about the splendid gardens designed by Beatrice, Reinhardt's birth mother whom he never knew, but whose attention to exotic living plants prevailed and remained, giving him a connection, a sense of what she valued. I then visualized the sanctuary that helped Roscoe when he was sad: the temple, the statue of Athena, the Goddess of Love, at its center. Felix could bring all of this to ruin.

The morning sun rose like the calm before the storm, gentle and sure, radiating warmth and goodness over the house and gardens. Rune and Riemes were particularly watchful as if they knew of the danger to come. As they roamed around the house, they kept stopping to sniff the air and look out to sea. Roscoe tried to engage them in a playful game of tag, but they romped only half-heartedly, their attention pulled elsewhere. I wondered if the dogs sensed our grief and tension or had caught a scent of a danger that lurked just beyond the walls.

"I wonder what they know," Roscoe said to me calmly, a new maturity emerging in his young voice. "Something bad is going to happen. I feel it, too." He had listened to our plan to bring Demetri to Fairhaven, participated in the conversation, and seemed to understand the danger involved. But now, the worried look on his face showed that the reality of what was to come was washing over him. I felt like he looked: that danger hung in the air like a smell, an assault on our senses that was strong and yet elusive as we waited, not knowing what, when, how, or even why about what was to come.

Hollinger and Rowan had left for the airport before breakfast to meet Demetri. Another hour and he'd be here among us. We sensed that soon after Demetri's arrival, Felix would make another move. But so far, no text messages had arrived. Waiting was hell. Maybe Felix was too busy gloating from having taken Ransom. With three hostages, he could be patient. But still, I figured he'd be keen to move things along.

No messages was unsettling. It was a war of nerves.

Shortly before eleven, the black SUV pulled up the driveway. Hollinger and Rowan got out. Rowan took some luggage from the vehicle and headed to the house. Hollinger waited by the back car door.

After a moment, an elderly man stepped out and paused, looking awestruck at the scenic view. Unlike Felix, he was quite tall. His thinning gray hair was cut short and his face was clean-shaven. He wore a tweed, wool jacket over a black T-shirt, much too warm for this climate, blue jeans and desert boots. He looked a little rumpled but distinguished, like a college professor, not all like what I'd imagined a hardened felon would look like.

"Come and meet the others," Hollinger said. He took Demetri by the arm as if he were escorting a criminal to detention. Demetri pulled away, and shot him a look. They walked together up to the house and came into the foyer where we were waiting to greet them.

"Mr. Szabo," Reinhardt said graciously, extending his hand. "Welcome to Fairhaven." Demetri looked at the extended hand but didn't offer his own. Instead, he walked into the receiving room and stared up and around as he twisted his head and body to take in the elegant space. I understood. The Drakers had a way of making an invited guest feel like a prisoner. I had done the same when I first arrived. But this was Felix's father, and a murderer at that, and I felt like we had invited a snake into the garden, one that would despoil everything it came in contact with. A cold shiver ran down my spine as I watched his movements, watched his gaze slither over the room.

Then he turned, clearly ready for an explanation. "Hollinger says that you want me to help you," Demetri said flatly. "He says that my son is a problem and is here somewhere in Nice."

"I'm sorry to say… and some of what I'm going to say may come as a shock to you, but Felix is holding our friends and my son hostage," Reinhardt said. "He killed a member of our household and several of Hollinger's men, and is wanted by the United States government."

"And what do you want me to do about that?" Demetri said. He was abrupt and defiant-looking. I thought that made sense: his son was a monster. This also didn't confirm, but felt like a strong hint, that Felix had not sought out his father since he'd come out of prison.

"We think he might want to meet up with his long lost father," Hollinger said.

Hollinger's sarcasm appeared to catch Demetri by surprise. He crossed his arms over his chest and an insolent smile formed on his face. The kind of smile Felix often used. Like father, like son, I thought. And this clinched it. Felix had not been in touch. Our gamble had paid off. "And why do you think I should help you?" Demetri asked.

"Because if you don't, I'll tell the parole board that you're aiding and abetting an enemy of the U.S. government, and that will land you back in prison," Hollinger said. "I'm sure you don't want that."

"What is it you want me to do?" Demetri asked. He tensed a bit. I couldn't imagine that going back to prison would be high on his bucket list, especially at this age.

"Nothing," Hollinger said, meeting Demetri's smile with his own. "Your being here is all we need. Rowan will show you to your room. And don't worry; you'll be very comfortable here... As long as you don't try to leave, of course. We do have very heavy security of our own. So relax and enjoy your... holiday."

Rowan led him away to the upper floor. We waited for him to be out of hearing range before anyone spoke. "I guess all we do now is wait," I said. The others nodded.

Roscoe and the dogs came bounding into the house, breathless and looking alarmed.

"There's a black yacht in the small harbor in Villefranche," Roscoe said. "I can see it from the west terrace. Rune and Riemes growl every time we pass by there. It's Felix, isn't it?"

Twenty-Eight

THE AFTERNOON SUN BURNED DOWN on our shoulders as we stood on the west terrace, the breeze fanning the heat away from our bodies, caressing and blowing our hair into our faces. The Bay of Villefranche lay peacefully in the sparkling waters far below, oblivious to any threat. There was a small sailing craft with its colorful canvas sails pointed into the wind, moving gracefully out to sea. A few smaller boats that belonged to local residents bobbed gently on adjacent docks. The bay seemed like a watercolor: calm, relaxed, and largely empty of the normal traffic. The morning fishermen had gone out to deeper waters to bring back the daily catch to the local restaurants. Only about half a dozen pleasure-crafters floated in the bay.

But there among the boats anchored in the deeper water off the docks, sat one big black vessel like a blight. The *Patricia* beckoned to us from the waters below, as if mesmerizing us into its trap. We stood high above with our binoculars poised for a better view. Felix stood on the deck also watching us with binoculars, his free hand waving back at us mockingly as if we were long lost friends, a wicked smile on his face.

A standoff!

We saw him and he us. It would be a dangerous dance to see who would lead from here on in.

Norm's phone buzzed. We turned to him and waited for him to read the text, the inevitable ultimatum: *Amos and Hannah say hello. They're disappointed you haven't come to get them.*

Then a second message pinged. Norm read it aloud as well, "*and Ransom, too.*"

"Give me the phone," Reinhardt said. "I'll do it." He typed for a few moments before reading the message to us and hitting send.

Say hi for us too. Tell them we apologize, but we've had a house guest and couldn't make it. Why don't all of you join us for dinner this evening? Demetri is looking forward to a reunion with his son. Bring Amos, Hannah and Ransom, and yourself, of course.

Reinhardt read on.

Demetri has an important message that your mother wanted you to know, something that's been bothering him for all these years. Six-ish OK?

We walked away from the terrace after he sent the message to Felix. This time, the Drakers had stipulated the terms of engagement. Hopefully Felix understood. We were not negotiating: either he could come to us or he could wait forever. Back at the house, the phone continued to buzz with text after text, each one a counter invitation to the yacht. Reinhardt deliberately avoided answering. After the tenth message, he wrote:

6 p.m. at Fairhaven. - RD.

The phone remained silent thereafter and Felix had to weigh his options. We prayed that we hadn't put the hostages' lives at risk with our unwavering demand.

All we had to do now was to wait: for Felix's arrival, or his attack, the latter being the most likely. Trusting that Felix's curiosity would get the better of him, we shifted into final preparation mode for the imminent attack.

Renegade retreated to the control room. Not only had he positioned firearms at every angle to blast any intruder from land, sea or air, but he'd also installed numerous additional cameras so every point of entry would be covered. He would monitor all movement or action around Fairhaven, and had wirelessly connected us to the control room through discreet earpieces and microphones. One word from him in the control room, and everyone would be aware of the situation. Further, he could guide us into our positions depending on where the property had been breached.

As for dinner, we hoped Felix would arrive the normal way, and the guards at the gate were on standby, but no one would have blinked if he came with ample backup.

Six o'clock came and went. Six-thirty. Six-forty. We discussed that maybe he was just one of those people who always arrived late to things, but that was nonsense. Everyone started feeling very tense. I had to pee. We paced and watched and waited, but nothing.

Then at five minutes to seven, the guardhouse announced that a banged up Ford carrying four people had arrived. The gates opened and the car proceeded to the mansion where Reinhardt and Rosalind stood at the front door to welcome the infamous guest and his hostages. Amos was driving, Hannah in the front seat beside him, Ransom in the back with Felix beside him holding a gun to his head. The car stopped and Felix got out, gun still in hand, gesturing with it that the others should hurry up and get out, too. My heart started to race when Ransom stepped out. He didn't look my way.

"You won't need your weapon," Reinhardt said, his voice peaceful as a monk's. "Let's just make this an amicable visit and everyone can get what he wants. We both have something to gain. Let's have a pleasant dinner, resolve a few issues and call it a day."

"Not a chance," Felix said. "I'll just hold onto this for… insurance." He grabbed Ransom and stuck his weapon hard into his ribs making Ransom grimace, his bullet wounds healed but still tender. I wanted to call out and tear into Felix, but I did nothing.

"Felix," Rosalind said, unable to contain her sarcasm. "How nice to see you again. Shall we have dinner? It's set up on the west terrace, so you can keep an eye on your... *Patricia*."

Felix scowled at her.

Rosalind always knew how to get under someone's skin. She led the way through the vestibule to the French doors that opened onto the sunny marble terrace.

The outdoor glass table had been set up with china and cutlery, a short distance away from the open French doors, its wide canvas umbrella open above it and the white tablecloth blowing gently in the ocean breeze. Rosalind would ring for Cook to serve the evening meal when, or if, we would actually eat.

Still in his firm grip, Felix pushed Ransom forward, his pistol wedged hard into Ransom's ribs, Felix looking fierce and somewhat demented like a diseased hyena surrounded by lions.

Demetri stood at the stone wall that edged the terrace from the treacherous cliff that tumbled to the bay far below. He would have had to hear us approaching, but he kept his back to us. He was leaning over the wall as if to get a better look. The late day sun reflected off his back as he looked pensively out to the golden, rippling water where the black yacht was anchored.

We stopped in the shade of the table's umbrella to evaluate Felix's reaction to seeing his father. The anger pulsating through his face was like a giant throbbing muscle. I worried he'd lunge forward and push his father over the wall, but as if she again could tell what I was thinking, Rosalind winked at me. Demetri was too valuable to Felix. His life was safe. For now.

"Felix," Rosalind said. "Your behavior is getting tiresome. Let poor Ransom sit and lower your gun for a moment. You might feel differently once you hear what your father has to tell you."

Felix could barely get the words out. "My father is a murderer," he said. "He killed the only person in this world who ever loved me. He can go to hell for all I care. He should have rotted in prison. I did just fine alone in the orphanage. He didn't care about me, and I didn't need him. So what does he think he has to tell me?"

The answer was for Rosalind, but he looked directly out to his father at the wall and spoke loudly enough for Demetri to hear.

Demetri took his time to turn and approach us. He walked slowly with his head down, his posture remorseful, and paused for a moment in front of Felix. He extended his hand. "Son," he said plainly.

Felix's face twitched and his eyes flamed. Felix spit into his father's outstretched hand with disdain.

Demetri calmly wiped his hand on his pants keeping his eyes fixed on his son. For a man whose story was one of violence and cruelty to his family, he seemed particularly gentle and sympathetic. Not getting any indication that Felix would be forgiving, he stepped backward a few paces and slumped into a chair under the wide umbrella.

"Sit down, Felix," Rosalind said. "You need to hear what your father has to say." Rosalind's voice was distinctly maternal then, fierce and powerful, and for some reason, Felix did, he sat.

Vibrating with emotion, he loosened his hold on Ransom, keeping his eyes trained on his father seated in front of him.

Rosalind grabbed Ransom and ushered him to another chair far away from Felix. She at least didn't try to make him go inside. I knew he'd have to be in a coma to do that.

Amos and Hannah followed him to put some distance between them and their captor, while Reinhardt stood firmly with his arms crossed over his chest.

Felix continued to aim the gun, but now it was at his father. His hand was trembling so hard, the gun was shaking all over. I'd done so many placements with mental health patients and tried to gauge what was going on between the dynamic of the two men, and Felix's body language, to determine what was going on. I couldn't do it; there was just too much happening in him. Was it rage and hatred, or was there some semblance of love for a parent he hadn't seen for decades, a parent he missed and wished he could have been close to? Was it so much more than that?

Demetri started to talk, his voice cracking with emotion as he spoke his son's name. "Felix, there are things you don't know, things that I should have tried to say to you, even while I was in prison. But I wanted you to have a better life. I thought the orphanage would have found adoptive parents for you and that you'd live a happy life and have a normal childhood. I was hoping you were young enough to forget."

"Every day, I still see you hitting my mother," Felix said. "Every night, I hear the sound of her head hitting the floor. I can still smell the blood, and I remember you standing over her doing nothing to help."

Demetri sighed and looked out at the water before returning his gaze to Felix. "I suppose a little boy is designed to have only unconditional love for his mother," he said. "I can understand how you'd shut out... certain memories. She wasn't the mother you created in your mind, son. She hit you, she let you cry when you were scared. There were many times when she just forgot to look after you and you ended up outside, a neighbor bringing you home, or didn't keep you clean, or feed you. Think hard, Felix. Try to remember. She wasn't the loving mother you think you knew."

Felix stood up abruptly and threw back his chair. It landed with a crash on the marble. He pointed his trembling pistol at Demetri, trying to steady it with both hands. His voice was strained, heavy with emotion. I glanced at Ransom, wishing I were in his arms. This man could easily lose control of what little grip he might have had left on the reality of the moment.

"She loved me," Felix said. "And... and you beat her, and you bashed in her head in a drunken rage, and she died because you hated us both."

"Yes, the day she died, I was drunk," Demetri said. "I'm not proud of that, and I've been sober for forty-nine years, every day regretting my actions. I never hated you, you or your mother. But I hated what her drug habit did to her and what she did to you. I hated that she loved booze and heroine more than she loved her own little boy." Tears were filling the older man's eyes. "I begged her to get help, but she couldn't see her dependence. She was in such denial and in those days there was little sympathy for addiction."

He wiped his face and cleared his throat. "She did have lucid moments," he said. "And I do remember how loving she could be, to both of us. I remember her rocking you in her arms and singing to you until you fell asleep." He paused and smiled gently to himself, a single tear trickling down his cheek. "You were a beautiful baby. My beautiful boy."

Demetri sniffed and wiped his face. "When the courts said it was a premeditated act," he said, "I was at such a loss for what I'd done, I didn't put up a defense. I felt too broken to fight. I loved her and you so much. So I gave up custody of you so you could have another family, one who would care for you, and love you."

"Well, guess what," Felix screamed, "your plan failed! No one wanted the son of a killer. I spent my entire childhood in that orphanage. I got nothing but the basics. No joy, no laughter, no love. No family. You failed even at that." His eyes grew yet bigger as he smiled. "But I survived, and I've made something of myself. Thanks to the bastards at the orphanage, I joined the military and then climbed the ladder to the CIA. I didn't need you or a family or anyone."

"Felix, you need to forgive," Rosalind said. "Forget what you think you know. It's all a lie. Listen to your father. Give yourself up." Rosalind wasted no time with words. Her message was always direct and blunt. This time, I was worried she was going too far. Tough love didn't work with this guy.

Felix turned and pointed his gun at her. "Rosalind, shut your mouth. You rejected me, too," he said, grinding his teeth. "You never accepted my compliments or signs of affection. You refused my dinner invitations and flowers and gifts. You knew I always desired you, but you didn't give a rat's ass."

"Oh, please," said Rosalind, rolling her eyes, "You've desired every woman you've ever come into contact with. And what about Patricia? You got her, didn't you? Look what happened to her."

Felix glared at Rosalind. His gun was now in firm control in his hand. He released the safety as he walked slowly in her direction. "Shut up, you bitch," Felix said. His teeth were clenched and his face was scarlet. He kept walking toward her. Sweat was beading up at his hairline. His teeth were in a grimace, yellow cast, with small gaps in between. "I'll bet my mother would have liked you," he said and looked around suddenly as if he wished he hadn't said that. I recognized that he'd entered a manic state. He was close to hyperventilating, his eyes too wild.

"Settle down, Felix," Demetri said. "Please," he put out his hands. "Put down the gun and let's just have a calm conversation. Rosalind has done nothing wrong. If you want to hurt someone, hurt me." He sounded sad when he said that.

"Oh, honestly, Felix," Rosalind said. "Even if I'd wanted to entertain you romantically, the fact was that you were my boss. It wouldn't have been appropriate, and," she said, barely concealing a dark smirk, "I'd had enough of pandering to men in power. Why would I want you? Especially after I'd just gotten back from the Kremlin where there were far richer and more powerful men to bed?"

I didn't know what Rosalind was doing, maybe trying to shock him into something, but I could see it wasn't working. I felt panic rising in my throat.

Felix stepped closer to Rosalind, his gun pointed at her heart, his mouth twisted into a sneer. "Another put down, another woman rejecting me," he said, "except this one wasn't worth two cents, the slut."

Rowan, Renegade and Reinhardt stepped closer.

But then it was too late.

Demetri lunged at his son who had gotten too close to Rosalind, the gun ready and him too unstable. The boom from it going off shattered the air. Everyone on the terrace looked on in horror. Rosalind grabbed her chest, blood filling her hands, then slowly she slumped to the hard marble surface of the terrace.

From Reinhardt came a tortured cry "Rosalind!" as he ran over to help her. It was over; this was it.

Ransom yanked his phone from his pocket and with shaking fingers dialed 112.

Reinhardt was pressing his fingers into the oozing wound, blood pouring from her torso onto the white marble beneath her. "Roz, Roz." He was half shouting, half weeping. Her head slumped onto his shoulder as he continued to shout and cry her name.

"Damn you, *Roz*. Damn all of you commie sympathizers," Felix shouted over and over again from where he stood, making no motion to run or save himself. Then as if he came into a new kind of consciousness, he backed up and began shooting wildly into the air. Another bullet found its way into Demetri, and he fell over motionless onto the terrace floor.

Felix laughed, "Good, because the bullet that killed Rosalind was actually meant for you, Daddy." While he stayed on the terrace, the rest of us fled through the French doors into the house. We hoped that would've been the worst of it, but seconds later, there was an explosion over by the guard house.

Renegade's message into our earpieces was so loud, we all winced, "The gates are breached! Six men are advancing to the house! Take cover! Take cover immediately!"

Felix's shot must have been the signal for his assault team to move in. After the initial six men came in, dozens more swarmed the grounds and a helicopter with men rappelling down ropes descended on the gardens.

We had expected that Felix would have assistance, but we hadn't expected this overwhelming show of strength. He'd clearly sold out the U.S. secrets to the right people because there were so many men, I lost count.

We retreated to the inner rooms of the mansion. Reinhardt carried Rosalind in his arms and laid her gently on a day bed in the sitting room. He sat behind her and held her body, rocking her, the room echoing with his sobs. I stayed with them, with him. Her hand, soaked in blood, had already gone cold. Silent tears ran down my cheeks, and I didn't think I'd be able to go on.

Men in black masks were trampling the garden, their shadows coursing by the windows.

She had always believed in my strength, from the first minute. "I'll show you the ropes," she had said, the memory playing back in my head. Rosalind had kept her word and had introduced me to myself, had helped me take on my new persona, my new life as Ruby Draker, her daughter and friend.

I knew I'd cared for her, but now I realized that I had indeed loved and needed her like a mother. A mother lost again to the savagery of Felix Szabo.

Outside, it was pandemonium. I heard Felix's frenzied voice shouting, "They've gone inside the mansion."

Ransom and Rowan locked and barricaded the doors but they knew this wouldn't keep the intruders out for long. We were terribly out-numbered and had to make a decision.

I considered suggesting that we escape to the tunnel where we could hop in the boat and get out of there, but I bit my tongue. Was I mad?

I knew I wasn't mad. Not in the least. I was suddenly as clear eyed as ever, maybe for the first time. I laid Rosalind's hand back down onto her bloodied chest and wiped my face. I wanted Felix. We weren't backing away from his attack, no matter how it ended up. This would end today.

"Roscoe is waiting in the speedboat," Rowan said. "I told him to go there and wait before Felix arrived this afternoon. We should go immediately."

I smiled gently at Rowan. "I'm not running anymore," I said. "Reinhardt? What do you want to do?"

He looked up at me, struggling to gain some composure. "Where's Hollinger?" he asked, speaking into the microphone at his collar.

Renegade was still in the computer control room and had been watching the drama unfold. "He's off grounds," Renegade said solemnly. "I've notified him to bring assistance. He's already reported gunfire to the local police. They're aware that a U.S. criminal has overtaken the Fairhaven property."

"How long?" I asked.

"Hollinger says no more than fifteen minutes."

My heart sank. For us, that would be an eternity. We needed to act now. We would have to fight back without his help. We couldn't wait.

"Can you see where Felix is now?" I asked, speaking into my earpiece's mic.

"He's gathered with his men at the east garden," Renegade said. "I've counted ten of them. If they move just a few inches closer, I can detonate the charge I planted near the east terrace door."

"Do you see more men?" I asked.

"They're everywhere," Renegade said. "His men are all around the house. They should be moving in on us any time."

He must have seen something new because he was suddenly shouting, "Get down to the control center. Now! There are too many of them. We can't fight them all."

Reinhardt was bent over Rosalind's body on the daybed. Tears ran down his face as he held her against his chest for one more moment, rocking her gently.

Ransom put his hand on Reinhardt's shoulder. "We have to go now," he said.

Reinhardt lovingly straightened her hair and kissed her lips. Reluctantly he turned, broken, and let Ransom guide him downstairs.

We thundered down the staircase and pressed the lever that opened the secret slider into the control room. We quickly entered, the slider closing behind us. We were safe.

Renegade was busy at the computer monitors that showed different parts of Fairhaven, the house, the guard house, the garden and several other pathways that looked out over the sea. Renegade monitored each for movement.

We gathered around the screens.

The house above us was now overrun with what looked like black ants, each carrying at least one gun, kicking down doors and toppling furniture. They went from room to room looking for us and found them all empty. Outside, Felix was standing on the terrace, looking like he was enjoying watching a show.

His men burst through the gate, surrounded the house and trudged recklessly through the gardens.

If we were to leave the control room, we wouldn't have a chance.

But then, on a clearing in front of the garden entrance, a different helicopter hovered low to the ground and men dressed in black riot gear jumped down from the still-hovering craft.

One after another, the armed riot team burst from the chopper.

Lastly, Hollinger, armed with an automatic rifle, jumped ably to the ground. He signaled to the pilot, who lifted the helicopter back into the sky.

Hollinger looked about and noticing Felix on the terrace, he took off in his direction.

There must have been a streak of cowardice in Felix because as soon as he noticed that Hollinger was coming toward him, Felix started for his car at the house entrance. He clearly hadn't expected other police vehicles to stream in through the blown-out gate and block his escape route. He turned and ran to the garden paths, disappearing into the dense bushes and shrubbery.

Hollinger followed with several other officers close behind.

We watched, incredulous, as reinforcements arrived and Felix's men left the mansion to join the fight outside.

I looked at the seniors, Rachel, and the men. "I have a job to finish," I said.

I picked up a rifle from the computer room munitions storage. The pistol Rosalind had personally selected for me was still tucked into my waistband.

"We all do," said Reinhardt, his voice hard and searing. "Let's get that bastard." Savage determination had etched itself into Reinhardt's face, a look on him I'd never seen before.

Ransom and Rowan picked up their own guns.

Just then, the tunnel entrance slider opened with a thud.

Roscoe entered the room, his eyes bulging and his voice strained with worry. "I heard the gunfire," he blurted out. "I came to help."

He looked around the control room searching and taking count of who was there, his gaze stopping at Reinhardt. "Where's Rosalind?"

"You have to stay here with Renegade," Reinhardt said. He looked wild, his eyes bulging back at Roscoe. His concern was not only with Roscoe's safety but with avenging Rosalind.

Roscoe recoiled at Reinhardt's belligerent tone, and he turned and joined Renegade at the monitors.

"You stay here," Reinhardt said. "Do you understand what I'm telling you? Renegade, evacuate to the boat if you have to. Get yourself and Roscoe away as fast and as far as possible."

Renegade nodded without turning around.

Roscoe stood at his side shaking and looking at us in horror.

I grabbed extra ammunition, checked the pistol in my waist band and firmly gripped the rifle in my hand. I went for the door.

Reinhardt grabbed me. "I'm right beside you. Felix is not getting away with this. This time, he's going down."

Ransom, Rowan and Rachel stood ready.

Norm and Alice looked at Amos and Hannah.

"Count us in," Amos said. "We're goin' huntin'."

I nodded to all of them, and we rushed to the steps leading back to the main floor of the mansion.

"Just like old times," Norm said. "Let's bring Felix to justice."

With Renegade watching the action on the control room monitors, we moved stealthily through the garden as if the manicured landscape were dense jungle where vicious animals lurked and could attack at any time. Felix was no different than a wild animal, mad with his delusions. The hunter had become the hunted.

We advanced with our senses on high alert, listening and watching every plant and bush for movement until we arrived at the fork in the path that opened to the circular marble stairs of the temple platform.

There at the top, in plain view, stood Felix staring at us. Was he surrendering? This wasn't the Felix we knew. What was he up to? I couldn't see it, but I felt his trap closing in around us.

"Such a beautiful place," Felix said. "I suppose you think you've got me." He threw his head back and laughed viciously and then manically changed his expression to one of menace and anger, gritting his teeth and crossing his arms across his chest. "Why don't you come up here and join me," Felix said. "Let's enjoy this beautiful day and beautiful view together." He stretched his right arm wide in a circling motion around the seascape.

He didn't seem to be holding a weapon, but he surely had one concealed. Still, even if he did pull it on us, he was only one man against the six of us. None of his ant men were around that I could tell. So while one of us might take a bullet, he had to realize that it'd mean he'd be taking the rest of ours.

We proceeded to the steps, three of us on each side, and met him at the top. He wasn't holding a gun but instead waved a blood-red rose in his hand, one he had picked from the rose garden below.

"Well, well," Felix said. "You people have certainly given me quite a challenge. And now here we are. The bunch of you all nicely armed, pointing your weapons against one man armed with nothing but a flower." He pointed the rose as if it were a gun, pricking his finger on a thorn and drawing blood.

"Oh, look," he said. "I'm bleeding." He laughed hysterically again and stopped short as his eyes grew wide and dark and his mouth grimaced with rage. "But wait," he said, "you might want to reconsider your situation." He pointed to the left and chortled.

Four men armed with automatic rifles stepped out into the open. "And just for some extra insurance," Felix said, pointing to the right with the rose still in his hand, a drip of blood dropping from his finger as he hooted in delight, at four more men who stopped, planted themselves, and took aim. The crunch of feet on the gravel at the base of the stairway made us turn to look behind us.

How had I thought he'd come here alone? I cursed myself for being so stupid.

More of Felix's men pointed their weapons upward at us. Felix had kept a posse in reserve and now we were trapped.

Reinhardt stepped forward so he was along the west side railing of the temple, standing tall without any trace of intimidation or fear. He lifted his arm and holding it steady, aimed his pistol at Felix. "You've taken everything from us," Reinhardt said. "This is for Rosalind." He squeezed the trigger of his pistol.

I shut my eyes, and heard the click then a bang. My eyes flew open and I crouched down.

One of Felix's snipers standing in the roses below had shot Reinhardt's hand. He fell to one knee, clutching his hand, the gun having spun across the terrace.

Then the rest of Felix's crew started moving up the stairs toward us. I guessed, from how they were taking their time, that Felix was going to kill us execution style, one at time, just for his own personal satisfaction and enjoyment.

My stomach dropped, and my lower half went numb.

But before his crew at the rear reached the steps, I heard a man with a commanding voice from the path further down shout, "Drop your weapons, now!"

Within seconds, Hollinger, followed by more police officers than I could count, scuffled onto the path and stood their ground.

Felix's men looked up at Felix for further instruction.

"Drop them now or we'll open fire," Hollinger screamed.

The men looked alarmed and dazed. One after the other lowered his weapon to the ground and held up his arms.

Hollinger and the French police moved in closer.

"No, you idiots! Open fire on them!" Felix shouted to the rest of his crew who remained on the ground and still held their weapons. They began to raise their automatics when there was a loud explosion that threw the men into the air.

Felix ran to the rail on right side of the temple platform where another group of his men waited in the shrubs. They raised their guns and in seconds, there was another blast, and the men were incinerated, gone to smoke.

Rowan! I thought gleefully. The charges he'd positioned strategically were paying off.

Hollinger waved and the police moved in, the last of Felix's thugs, now surrounded, dropped their weapons.

Within minutes, the police had gathered up the mobsters and led them off the property and into custody.

All except Felix.

He remained firmly at the top. The rose was lying at his feet, and the gun he held was pointed at me.

Reinhardt was still hunched over, his blood all over the marble platform. He looked up and saw what was going to happen; glancing at me, he tried to reach for his gun, but it was futile. It was about ten feet ahead of him.

Felix turned away from me and shot at him again, this time hitting him in the shoulder. Reinhardt fell back onto the marble.

A young male voice broke through the silent aftermath. "I'd rather die than lose my family again."

It was Roscoe.

He was standing down below the temple, tears raining freely down both his cheeks, but his body was straight and strong, and his face determined in the way of a man.

He drew the string on his bow and released it. The arrow sang slowly through the air to meet its target, and with a resounding thud, it lodged in the center of Felix's chest.

Felix's eyes went wide, and his mouth opened in surprise, blood trickling from his throat when he tried to speak.

Then like two demons from hell, Roscoe's pets came snarling

toward Felix and jumped into his chest. I didn't want to see how the dogs were shredding Felix's throat and face, but I had to look. The dogs were easily a hundred pounds of pure muscle each, and the force of them propelled him backward and over the railing. He fell, easily and gently, without a word, through the sea air, down over the cliff toward the dark and churning water below.

Roscoe's face was dark with pain and anger. He bent down and picked up the rose then smashed it in his fist, hurling it over after Felix's free-falling body.

"Now you can suffer forever in hell," Roscoe cursed, language I'd never heard him use, his voice of a whole new quality.

He paused only a moment to watch Felix's body hit the water before turning and rushing to Reinhardt. He dropped to his knees taking Reinhardt's good hand into his and pleaded to me, his sister, for help. "I can't lose my father, too."

Twenty-Nine

I RAN OVER TO THE RAIL and watched Felix's body disappear under the rolling indigo waves. It was an empty victory.

Roscoe's wail behind me brought me back to reality. "Dad," he yelled. I pushed myself off the wall and ran to help. Reinhardt had opened his eyes and was smiling weakly at Roscoe. He reached to him with his good hand. Roscoe crouched over Reinhardt, frantic with concern, and grabbed tight.

"Rosalind," Reinhardt said as his eyes filled with tears and his voice pained with loss as he spoke her name. It seemed like he was trying to tell Roscoe, but the boy put his face into Reinhardt's neck and wept.

"I know," Roscoe said. "I saw her. You can't die, too."

"Don't worry, my boy," Reinhardt said with a voice that seemed to have strength in it from a well deep within. "I'm not going anywhere."

I crouched beside Roscoe and put my arms around him, his young body convulsing with sobs. "No, you don't have to cry," I tried to say teasingly. "He's going to be all right." I cleared my throat. "Roscoe, this is very good. He was hit but he'll be fine." I heard the light yowl of ambulance sirens and almost wept with relief. "Reinhardt, hear that? Hang on. They'll be here in a minute."

The siren grew louder and louder until it was driving right through the garden, crushing plants and grass, and in that moment, I had never been happier to see something so beautiful be so ruined. It stopped on the gravel at the bottom of the temple steps, and within seconds, the paramedics had loaded Reinhardt onto a stretcher and had left for the hospital.

In the aftermath, with the birds cheeping and the *shush shush* of the surf below, Roscoe and I stood on the temple platform and watched the ambulance speed away.

Ransom soon joined us. His eyes were filled with tears and his face was tormented as he tried to speak but couldn't, so we just stood and held each other and let the horror and fear and grief flood out together until Hollinger came up what was left of the path and stood in front of us.

"We want to go to the hospital to be with Reinhardt," I said.

"I know, and you will, but the police have to ask you some questions first." Hollinger's voice was soft and understanding but firm. We didn't argue: as commander of an American agency, he was compelled to follow protocol. He needed statements. He needed to close this case he'd failed to open himself. He motioned down to Amos, Hannah, Norm and Alice and the rest of the Drakers, and led me, Ransom and Roscoe back to the house.

Police cars and unmarked cars and police officers filled the scene, overrunning the grounds, adding to the destruction already done. At least this time, it was the good guys trampling the place. With Reinhardt in good hands, we returned to the house to tell our complicated story, as unbelievable as it sounded. Luckily, Renegade had the surveillance video that would prove everything.

As the three of us mounted the steps of the east terrace, we stopped and looked back at the gardens that Beatrice had so lovingly designed for Fairhaven, the garden where Roscoe played, and where I spent countless hours in contemplation and healing. Felix had ransacked it. Much of the statuary and other ornamentation lay toppled and broken.

The flowers and plants had been crushed and trampled, the little red bridge at the Japanese garden was broken and splintered. The roses by the temple garden lay atop craters, bare rooted, the odd rose still clinging from a broken branch.

Oddly, the temple remained intact. My heart soared at seeing it. It was a symbol of perseverance, a symbol of hope, a symbol of renewal. We had lost so much, but we would take what was left and rebuild what had been destroyed today. The damage to our hearts could never be erased from our memories, but what was physical could be repaired.

After several hours' intensive questioning, they collected our finger-prints and evidence and then we were finally free to go to the hospital. We declined Hollinger's offer to drive us. Rowan drove up with our SUV and Rachel, Roscoe, Ransom and I pulled out through the blown-away metal gate. Renegade brought the second car and came with the seniors.

When we arrived at the hospital, Reinhardt was in surgery to remove the bullet that had lodged in his shoulder. But although he'd need to remain in hospital for a while, his injuries weren't life threatening and the doctor said he'd make a full recovery.

"Roscoe, he's going to be all right," I murmured, stroking his hair. He responded with a tentative smile. This would be a trauma that would take him a long time to come to grips with. He had endured so much loss and grief in his tender years. Like Felix did, I thought ruefully. But we were lucky; we had each other. The Drakers were family. Roscoe was not alone, and he would never be alone. We shared what he was going through and we would all help each other as we dealt with the terrible tragedies that had befallen the family today.

We sat close beside each other as we returned to our seats in the waiting room. Rachel sat stiffly, wringing her hands in her lap, Rowan with his arm around her shoulder sitting beside her, his lips moving in silent prayer. Roscoe sat clinging tightly to me, and Ransom on the other side, stroked his back. There weren't any more chairs on this wall, so Renegade pulled one from the other wall so he could sit close to us.

It was as if distance, however small, threatened to separate us, so we huddled together, as closely as we could.

Despite the assurances of the doctors and our best efforts to ease his fears, Roscoe hardly spoke. He mostly stared off into space, his eyes dark and questioning, and I feared that he was shutting himself off and retreating into a protected emotional world of his own. It was his arrow that had killed Felix. It was different from the practice and play that his combat instructors provided. Training him at defense and combat was indeed prudent in case he ever needed to defend himself, but today, when it came to putting those lessons into practice, the reality of killing another human being didn't seem to be what he'd imagined it would be. He had never taken a life before, and I could see that the responsibility of it weighed heavily on him. It didn't matter that it was in self-defense, or that he was saving our lives. I saw it in him, that fear that he'd broken some covenant that ought not be broken.

As for me, after all our efforts to bring down Felix, it seemed ironic that our villain was killed by a boy, sort of like David and Goliath. Was it seeing Rosalind's lifeless body that had propelled Roscoe to action? Grabbing his bow and arrow wasn't exactly an act of valor so much as one of vengeance. I saw his face when he let the arrow loose: he wasn't thinking about his own life.

Ransom wordlessly shared in Roscoe's melancholy, but he didn't share his feelings with me. That tender bond we'd had mere days before had been broken, first by his indecision, and later sealed by Rose's death. I left the two of them to sort themselves out. And whatever happened with Ransom, if anything, it would have to happen later, in its own time. We all needed time to sort out our feelings.

While we waited for Reinhardt to come out of surgery, we had a more-immediate task to deal with. Rose and Rosalind would need to be buried. No one wanted to bring it up, and it seemed like we needed to do one thing at a time, so we all tacitly didn't discuss any details until Reinhardt was out of surgery and we knew for sure that he would be fine. I didn't like the feeling of knowing that everything would now have to change. Without Rosalind, I felt adrift.

The doctor returned to the waiting room just after 9 p.m. Everyone stared at him anxiously. "Mr. Draker is out of surgery and in the recovery area," the doctor said. "Everything went well. You can see him in about an hour. The bullets didn't affect any vital organs. You'll be able to take him home tomorrow."

It seemed a funny time to get emotional. We had for the most part held it together throughout the day and this good news should have been a great reason to rejoice. Instead we hugged each other and that's when the tears started to flow. I was grateful for the release.

The following morning, Reinhardt was awake and ready to come home. Although he was weak, he was more than happy to get out of the clinical confines of the hospital and have a "proper breakfast." But as soon as he said it, his face crumpled. Without Rose to nurse him back to health and Rosalind to tell him to toughen up, it'd be a much longer road toward recovery. Like Roscoe, his old wounds had been torn open again. Those tended to heal much more slowly.

In the following days, Fairhaven bustled with repairmen and gardeners. Renegade and Rowan had wasted no time organizing the workers and creating a project schedule. But with everyone there working at once, it was a challenge to find peace in the dust and noise of tradespeople and equipment.

Fortunately, the west terrace was sheltered behind trellises heavily laden with bougainvillea and had not been damaged. We gathered there each day, enjoying the last of the summer's days, finding solace in the sun and the cool breeze coming off the sea. No one spoke much. Rune and Riemes nuzzled at our hands, comforting us, and giving support as only beloved pets could. I wondered what life would hold for us as fall descended, then winter.

Two days later, the dogs left us and darted off into the ruined garden, returning with a broken and dried-out red rose, probably from the destroyed rose garden at the temple, and dropped it at the center of the terrace on the crisp white marble. They looked up and whimpered.

"I suppose it's time," Reinhardt said. "We can't put this off any longer. We have to make a decision."

Everyone looked at each other. We knew what Reinhardt was talking about. Rowan and Rachel had arranged for both women to be cremated, and their remains were still waiting at the mortuary for us to bring them home.

"When I miss my sister and parents," Roscoe said. "I go to the temple and sit quietly for a while. Then I can hear them. They tell me that they're OK and that I will be too. Sometimes we talk about the wonderful times we had together and it makes me not miss them so much. Their spirits have found their way to me. I know that Rosalind and Rose's spirits will be at peace there, too."

He was pensive a moment. "Can we let their ashes go into the sky? Then the wind will carry them to join our other loved ones. They can all be together and when we need to talk to them, all we have to do is to go to the temple... Or anywhere."

Reinhardt went to Roscoe and embraced him the way Rosalind used to do. "That's a wonderful idea," he said, "and I think your mother would agree."

"And Rose, too," Ransom added.

We discussed a few details and decided that the temple rose gardens would be rebuilt with the garden to the left dedicated to Rose and the one to the right to Rosalind. The gardeners had nearly finished replanting, and many of the bushes already bore buds. For the ceremony, we would fill both gardens with large bouquets of red and white roses that would be placed around two white marble grottoes inside of which their urns would rest. They would forever be surrounded with flowers and with symbols of our love, which would never die.

**

The following morning, we walked slowly through the Fairhaven gardens, Reinhardt carrying Rosalind's urn and Ransom carrying Rose's. The sun and wind warmed everyone's melancholy as we made our way into the gardens that they had both loved so much.

We slowly climbed the temple stairs and stood at the railing's edge, Ransom and Reinhardt beside each other as they opened the vessels. Each held up his urn, letting the dust be picked up by the gentle and singing winds of the Mediterranean. The particles danced and swirled and were lifted high into the heavens.

Before I could barely make out any of the ash anymore, I swore I heard them, the voices of Rose and Rosalind and the rest of the families we'd lost. "We're all right now," they whispered in unison. "And all of you will be too."

***

Amos, Hannah, Norm and Alice stayed for another week. We begged them to stay longer, but they wanted to return home to Springfield, to their lives that were simple and slow and blessed with routine. They missed the diner and their infamous donuts. And, they explained, they'd come to truly love their Springfield selves, retired busybodies who knew the affairs of everyone in town. I felt especially saddened when they were packing to leave. They had helped and supported us so much. Soon, they too would be gone from our lives.

Reinhardt bought Robert's farm in Springfield, suggesting they might be more comfortable living there and could keep the old shack for guests, "should they ever need it," he said, winking.

They left in style just as they had come to Fairhaven: on a chartered flight. We all went with them to the airport and out onto the tarmac. It was weird to be in an airport and not feel afraid.

I hung back after the others had said their goodbyes.

"Ruby," Norm said, taking me by the shoulders, "take care of yourself and Roscoe. I know you've been through a lot, but you have a strength that you don't see often these days. It's a special gift."

"And don't worry about Ransom," Alice said. She winked playfully at me. I would miss her matter-of-fact ways, so similar to Rosalind's.

We said our last goodbyes and the four of them boarded their plane.

Minutes later, they were off the ground, heading back to resume their lives in America.

I felt empty. Then Alice's words hit me. She wasn't talking about regaining the romance Ransom and I had. She was talking about me. I would be all right whether Ransom and I ever re-claimed that feeling for each other. I would be all right with my place among the Drakers. I would be all right because even though I had lost myself as Kathleen, I hadn't lost my humanity. I'd never felt more human in my life. And, while part of me would forever remember Kathleen, I had become a new person whose name was Ruby Draker.

Acknowledgments

Writing a novel is a long and grueling task. This being my first literary work wasn't accomplished without assistance. Very special thanks go out to Jenna Kalinsky, my writing coach and editor. Jenna, you helped me accomplish a dream that I'd been harboring for most of my life. You also made me realize that writing is a passion for me. Thank you for holding my hand every step of the way.

I also want to thank my daughter Tiffany Eby Ferrie for beta reading several drafts. She caught all those errors that writers don't see. Thank you.

A special thank you to Sherrill Wark of Crowe Creations, my publisher, advisor, and trusted friend. You have made this publication everything it was meant to be. Thank you.

And never to be forgotten, I thank my late husband, Paul Stephen Scott, for the support and encouragement he gave me during the whole process. I hold him in my heart and miss him.

About the Author

IN ALL THE YEARS MARIANNE SCOTT WORKED IN BUSINESS, she never knew she had a flair for storytelling. Being tangled in the day-to-day challenges of meeting deadlines, dollar targets, and ever tighter delivery expectations left little time or energy for creativity. Yet at her core, she always felt something there. She didn't know how to name it, this yearning that grew inside her with every passing year.

At work, Marianne would jokingly threaten to write a "tell-all" about her colleagues, exposing the difficult personalities and the stressful foibles of the fast-paced manufacturing industry, but in fact, she found herself more interested in letting her imagination run with stories of conspiracy, forbidden affairs, corporate espionage and other sundry misdoings.

Once she left the corporate world, instead of penning non-fiction tales, she gave herself over to her imagined worlds. Her truest pleasure, amusement, and release soon came from turning the ordinary into the extraordinary. From this, *Finding Ruby Draker* was born.